BRENT WEEKS
SHADOW'S EDGE

orbit

orbitbooks.n

KT-163-432

ORBIT

First published in Great Britain in 2008 by Orbit
This paperback edition published in Great Britain in 2023 by Orbit

1 3 5 7 9 10 8 6 4 2

A CIP catalogue record for this book
is available from the British Library.

ISBN 978-0-356-52037-7

Printed and bound in Great Britain by Clays Ltd, Elcograf, S.p.A.

Papers used by Orbit are from well-managed forests
and other responsible sources.

MIX
Paper from
responsible sources
FSC® C104740

Orbit
An imprint of
Little, Brown Book Group
Carmelite House
50 Victoria Embankment
London EC4Y 0DZ

An Hachette UK Company
www.hachette.co.uk

www.orbitbooks.net

For Kristi, for never doubting—
not even when I did.
&
For Kevin, because it's a big brother's job to
make a little brother tough. What you taught me,
I've needed. (But I never have been right
since that dirt clod incident.)

MIDCYRU

YMMUR

The Steppes

FRIAKU

✛
X!Zassu

Broken Lands

Black Waters

The Ruins

Legion's Highway

✛ Skone
(Eastern Capital)

Ash Forest

Tover

The Deep

Gray Sea

Castle
Stormfast

Dragon's Teeth

Summer Isles

MAP BY TIM PAUL

1

"We've got a contract for you," Momma K said. As always, she sat like a queen, her back straight, sumptuous dress perfect, hair immaculately coifed if gray at the roots. This morning she had dark circles under her eyes. Kylar guessed that none of the Sa'kagé's surviving leaders had slept much since the Khalidoran invasion.

"Good morning to you, too," Kylar said, settling into the wing-backed chair in the study. Momma K didn't turn to face him, looking instead out her window. Last night's rain had quenched most of the fires in the city, but many still smoked, bathing the city in a crimson dawn. The waters of the Plith River that divided rich eastern Cenaria from the Warrens looked as red as blood. Kylar wasn't sure that was all because of the smoke-obscured sun, either. In the week since the coup, the Khalidoran invaders had massacred thousands.

Momma K said, "There's a wrinkle. The deader knows it's coming."

"How's he know?" The Sa'kagé wasn't usually so sloppy.

"We told him."

Kylar rubbed his temples. The Sa'kagé would only tell someone so that if the attempt failed, the Sa'kagé wouldn't be committed. That meant the deader could only be one man: Cenaria's conqueror, Khalidor's Godking, Garoth Ursuul.

"I just came to get my money," Kylar said. "All of Durzo's—my safe

houses burned down. I only need enough to bribe the gate guards."
He'd been giving her a cut of his wages to invest since he was a child.
She should have plenty for a few bribes.

Momma K flipped silently through sheets of rice paper on her desk
and handed one to Kylar. At first, he was stunned by the numbers. He
was involved in the illegal importation of riot weed and half a dozen
other addictive plants, owned a race horse, had a stake in a brewery
and several other businesses, part of a loan shark's portfolio, and
owned partial cargos of items like silks and gems that were legitimate
except for the fact the Sa'kagé paid 20 percent in bribes rather than 50
percent in tariffs. The sheer amount of information on the page was
mind-boggling. He didn't know what half of it meant.

"I own a house?" Kylar asked.

"Owned," Momma K said. "This column denotes merchandise lost
in the fires or looting." There were checks next to all but a silk expedition and one for riot weed. Almost everything he had owned was lost.
"Neither expedition will return for months, if at all. If the Godking
keeps seizing civilian vessels, they won't come back at all. Of course,
if he were dead—"

He could see where this was going. "This says my share is still
worth ten to fifteen thousand. I'll sell it to you for a thousand. That's
all I need."

She ignored him. "They need a third wetboy to make sure it works.
Fifty thousand gunders for one kill, Kylar. With that much, you can
take Elene and Uly anywhere. You'll have done the world a good turn,
and you'll never have to work again. It's just one last job."

He wavered only for a moment. "There's always one last job. I'm
finished."

"This is because of Elene, isn't it?" Momma K asked.

"Momma K, do you think a man can change?"

She looked at him with a profound sadness. "No. And he'll end up
hating anyone who asks him to."

Kylar got up and walked out the door. In the hallway, he ran into

Jarl. Jarl was grinning like he used to when they were growing up on the streets and he was up to no good. Jarl was wearing what must be the new fashion, a long tunic with exaggerated shoulders paired with slim trousers tucked into high boots. It looked vaguely Khalidoran. His hair was worked into elaborate microbraids capped with gold beads that set off his black skin.

"I've got the perfect job for you," Jarl said, his voice lowered, but unrepentant about eavesdropping.

"No killing?" Kylar asked.

"Not exactly."

"Your Holiness, the cowards stand ready to redeem themselves," Vürdmeister Neph Dada announced, his voice carrying over the crowd. He was an old man, veiny, liver-spotted, stooped, stinking of death held at bay with magic, his breath rattling from the exertion of climbing up the platform in Cenaria Castle's great yard. Twelve knotted cords hung over the shoulders of his black robes for the twelve shu'ras he'd mastered. Neph knelt with difficulty and offered a handful of straw to the Godking.

Godking Garoth Ursuul stood on the platform inspecting his troops. Front and center were nearly two hundred Graavar highlanders, tall, barrel-chested, blue-eyed savages who wore their black hair short and their mustaches long. On either side stood the other elite highland tribes that had captured the castle. Beyond them waited the rest of the regular army that had marched into Cenaria since the liberation.

Mists rose from the Plith River on either side of the castle and slid under the rusty teeth of the iron portcullises to chill the crowd. The Graavar had been broken into fifteen groups of thirteen each, and they alone had no weapons, armor, or tunics. They stood in their trousers, pale faces fixed, but sweating instead of shivering in the cool autumn morning.

There was never commotion when the Godking inspected his

troops, but today the silence ached despite the thousands gathered to watch. Garoth had gathered every soldier possible and allowed the Cenarian servants and nobles and smallfolk to watch as well. Meisters in their black-and-red half-cloaks stood shoulder to shoulder with robed Vürdmeisters, soldiers, crofters, coopers, nobles, field hands, maids, sailors, and Cenarian spies.

The Godking wore a broad white cloak edged with ermine thrown back to make his broad shoulders look huge. Beneath that was a sleeveless white tunic over wide white trousers. All the white made his pallid Khalidoran skin look ghostly, and drew sharp attention to the vir playing across his skin. Black tendrils of power rose to the surface of his arms. Great knots rose and fell, knots edged with thorns that moved not just back and forth but up and down in waves, pressing out from his skin. Claws raked his skin from beneath. Nor were his vir confined to his arms. They rose to frame his face. They rose to his bald scalp and pierced the skin, forming a thorny, quivering black crown. Blood trickled down the sides of his face.

For many Cenarians, it was their first glimpse of the Godking. Their jaws hung slack. They shivered as his gaze passed over them. It was exactly as he intended.

Finally, Garoth selected one of the pieces of straw from Neph Dada and broke it in half. He threw away one half and took twelve full-length pieces. "Thus shall Khali speak," he said, his voice robust with power.

He signaled the Graavar to climb the platform. During the liberation, they had been ordered to hold this yard to contain the Cenarian nobles for slaughter. Instead, the highlanders had been routed, and Terah Graesin and her nobles had escaped. That was unacceptable, inexplicable, uncharacteristic for the fierce Graavar. Garoth didn't understand what made men fight one day and flee the next.

What he did understand was shame. For the past week, the Graavar had been mucking stables, emptying chamber pots, and scrubbing floors. They had not been allowed to sleep, instead spending the nights polishing their betters' armor and weapons. Today, they would expiate their guilt, and for the next year, they would be eager to prove their heroism. As he approached the first group with Neph at his side, Garoth calmed the vir from his hands. When the men drew their straws, they must think it not the working of magic or the God-king's pleasure that spared one and condemned another. Rather, it was simple fate, the inexorable consequence of their own cowardice.

Garoth held up his hands, and together, all the Khalidorans prayed: "*Khali vas, Khalivos ras en me, Khali mevirtu rapt, recu virtum defite.*"

As the words faded, the first soldier approached. He was barely sixteen, the least fringe of a mustache on his lip. He looked on the verge of collapse as his eyes flitted from the Godking's icy face to the straws. His naked chest shone with sweat in the rising morning light, his muscles twitching. He drew a straw. It was long.

Half of the tension whooshed out of his body, but only half. The young man next to him, who looked so alike he must have been his older brother, licked his lips and grabbed a straw. It was short.

Queasy relief washed over the rest of the squad, and the thousands watching who couldn't possibly see the short straw knew that it had been drawn from their reactions. The man who'd drawn the short straw looked at his little brother. The younger man looked away. The condemned man turned disbelieving eyes on the Godking and handed him the short straw.

Garoth stepped back. "Khali has spoken," he announced. There was a collective intake of breath, and he nodded to the squad.

They closed on the young man, every one of them—even his brother—and began beating him.

It would have been faster if Garoth had let the squad wear gauntlets or use the butts of spears or the flat of blades, but he thought it was better this way. When the blood began flowing and spraying off flesh as it was pummeled, it shouldn't get on the squad's clothing. It should get on their skin. Let them feel the warmth of the young man's blood as he died. Let them know the cost of cowardice. Khalidorans did not flee.

The squad attacked with gusto. The circle closed and screams rose. There was something intimate about naked meat slapping naked meat. The young man disappeared and all that could be seen was elbows rising and disappearing with every punch and feet being drawn back for new kicks. And moments later, blood. With the short straw, the young man had become their weakness. It was Khali's decree. He was no longer brother or friend, he was all they had done wrong.

In two minutes, the young man was dead.

The squad reformed, blood-spattered and blowing hard from exertion and emotion. They didn't look at the corpse at their feet. Garoth regarded each in turn, meeting the eyes of every one, and lingering on the brother. Standing over the corpse, Garoth extended a hand. The vir poked out of his wrist and extended, clawlike, ragged, and gripped the corpse's head. Then the claws convulsed and the head popped with a wet sound that left dozens of Cenarians retching.

"Your sacrifice is accepted. Thus are you cleansed," he announced, and saluted them.

They returned his salute proudly and took their places back in the formation in the courtyard as the body was dragged away.

He motioned the next squad. The next fourteen iterations would be nothing but more of the same. Though tension still arced through every squad—even the squads who'd finished would lose friends and family in other squads—Garoth lost interest. "Neph, tell me what you've learned about this man, this *Night Angel* who killed my son."

Cenaria Castle wasn't high on Kylar's list of places to visit. He was disguised as a tanner, a temporary dye staining his hands and arms to the elbow, a spattered woolen tradesman's tunic, and a number of drops of a special perfume his dead master Durzo Blint had developed. He reeked only slightly less than a real tanner would. Durzo had always preferred disguises of tanners, pig farmers, beggars, and other types that respectable people did their best not to see because they couldn't help but smell them. The perfume was applied only to the outer garments so if need arose, they could be shed. Some of the stench would still cling, but every disguise had drawbacks. The art was matching the drawbacks to the job.

East Kingsbridge had burned during the coup, and though the meisters had repaired most of its length, it was still closed, so Kylar crossed West Kingsbridge. The Khalidoran guards barely glanced at him as he passed them. It seemed everyone's attention—even the meisters'— was riveted to a platform in the center of the castle yard and a group of highlanders standing bare-chested in the cold. Kylar ignored the squad on the platform as he scanned for threats. He still wasn't sure if meisters could see his Talent, though he suspected they couldn't as long as he wasn't using it. Their abilities seemed much more tied to smell than magi's—which was the main reason he'd come as a tanner. If a meister came close, Kylar could only hope that mundane smells interfered with magical ones.

Four guards stood on each side of the gate, six on each segment of the diamond-shaped castle wall, and perhaps a thousand in formation in the yard, in addition to the two hundred or so Graavar highlanders. In the crowd of several thousand, fifty meisters were placed at regular intervals. In the center of it all, on the temporary platform, were a number of Cenarian nobles, mutilated corpses, and Godking Garoth Ursuul himself, speaking with a Vürdmeister. It was ridiculous, but even with the number of soldiers and meisters here, this was probably the best chance a wetboy would have to kill the man.

But Kylar wasn't here to kill. He was here to study a man for the strangest job he'd ever accepted. He scanned the crowd for the man Jarl had told him about and found him quickly. Baron Kirof had been a vassal of the Gyres. With his lord dead and his lands close to the city, he'd been one of the first Cenarian nobles to bend the knee to Garoth Ursuul. He was a fat man with a red beard cut in the angular lowland Khalidoran style, a large crooked nose, weak chin, and great bushy eyebrows.

Kylar moved closer. Baron Kirof was sweating, wiping his palms on his tunic, speaking nervously to the Khalidoran nobles he stood with. Kylar was easing around a tall, stinking blacksmith when the man suddenly threw an elbow into Kylar's solar plexus.

The blow knocked the wind from Kylar, and even as he hunched over, the ka'kari pooled in his hand and formed a punch dagger.

"You want a better look, you get here early, like the rest of us did," the blacksmith said. He folded his arms, pushing up his sleeves to show off massive biceps.

With effort, Kylar willed the ka'kari back into his skin and apologized, eyes downcast. The blacksmith sneered and went back to watching the fun.

Kylar settled for a decent view of Baron Kirof. The Godking had worked his way through half of the squads, and Sa'kagé bookies were already taking bets on which number out of each group of thirteen would die. The Khalidoran soldiers noticed. Kylar wondered how many Cenarians would die for the bookies' callousness when the Khalidoran soldiers went roaming the city tonight, in grief for their dead and fury at how the Sa'kagé fouled everything it touched.

I've got to get out of this damned city.

The next squad had made it through ten men without one drawing the short straw. It was almost worth paying attention as the men got more and more desperate as each of their neighbors was spared and their own chances became grimmer. The eleventh man, fortyish and all sinew and gristle, pulled the short straw. He chewed on the end of his mustache as he handed the straw back to the Godking, but otherwise didn't betray any emotion.

Neph glanced to where Duchess Jadwin and her husband were seated on the platform. "I examined the throne room, and I felt something I've never encountered before. The entire castle smells of the magic that killed so many of our meisters. But some spots in the throne room simply...don't. It's like there was a fire in the house, but you walk into one room and it doesn't smell like smoke."

Blood was flying now, and Garoth was reasonably certain that the man must be dead, but the squad continued beating, beating, beating.

"That doesn't match what we know of the silver ka'kari," Garoth said.

"No, Your Holiness. I think there's a seventh ka'kari, a secret ka'kari. I think it negates magic, and I think this Night Angel has it."

Garoth thought about that as the ranks reformed, leaving a corpse before them. The man's face had been utterly destroyed. It was impressive work. The squad had either worked hard to prove their commitment or they hadn't liked the poor bastard. Garoth nodded, pleased. He extended the vir claw again and crushed the corpse's head. "Your sacrifice is accepted. Thus are you cleansed."

Two of his bodyguards moved the corpse to the side of the platform. They were stacked there in their gore so that even though the Cenarians couldn't see each man's death, they would see the aftermath.

When the next squad began, Garoth said, "A ka'kari hidden for seven hundred years? What mastery does it bestow? Hiding? What does that do for me?"

"Your Holiness, with such a ka'kari, you or your agent could walk into the heart of the Chantry and take every treasure they have. Unseen. It's possible your agent could enter Ezra's Wood itself and take seven centuries' worth of artifacts for you. There would then be no more need for armies or subtlety. At one stroke, you could take all Midcyru by the throat."

My agent. No doubt Neph would bravely volunteer to undertake the perilous task. Still, the mere thought of such a ka'kari occupied Garoth through the deaths of another teenager, two men in their prime, and a seasoned campaigner wearing one of the highest awards for merit that the Godking bestowed. That man alone had something akin to treason in his eyes.

"Look into it," Garoth said. He wondered if Khali knew of this seventh ka'kari. He wondered if Dorian knew of it. Dorian his first acknowledged son, Dorian who would have been his heir, Dorian the prophet, Dorian the Betrayer. Dorian had been here, Garoth was sure of it. Only Dorian could have brought Curoch, Jorsin Alkestes' mighty sword. Some magus had appeared with it for a single moment and obliterated fifty meisters and three Vürdmeisters, then disappeared. Neph was obviously waiting for Garoth to ask about it, but Garoth had given up on finding Curoch. Dorian was no fool. He wouldn't have brought Curoch so close if he thought he might lose it. How do you outmaneuver a man who can see the future?

The Godking squinted as he crushed another head. Every time he did that, he got blood on his own snow-white clothing. It was deliberate—but irritating all the same, and there was nothing dignified about having blood squirt in your eye. "Your sacrifice is accepted," he told the men. "Thus are you cleansed." He stood at the front of the platform as the squad took its place back on the parade ground. For the entire review, he hadn't turned to face the Cenarians who were sitting on the platform behind him. Now he did.

The vir flared to life as he turned. Black tendrils crawled up his face, swarmed over his arms, through his legs, and even out from his pupils. He allowed them a moment to suck in light, so that the Godking appeared to be an unnatural splotch of darkness in the rising morning light. Then he put an end to that. He wanted the nobles to see him.

There wasn't an eye that wasn't huge. It wasn't solely the vir or Garoth's inherent majesty that stunned them. It was the corpses stacked like cordwood to each side and behind him, framing him like a picture. It was the blood-and-brain-spattered white clothing he wore. He was awesome in his power, and terrible in his majesty. Perhaps, if she survived, he'd have Duchess Trudana Jadwin paint the scene.

The Godking regarded the nobles and the nobles on the platform regarded the Godking. He wondered if any of them had yet counted their own number: thirteen.

He extended his handful of straw toward his nobles. "Come," he told them. "Khali will cleanse you." This time, he had no intention of letting fate decide who would die.

Commander Gher looked at the Godking. "Your Holiness, there must be some—" he stopped. Godkings didn't make mistakes. Gher's face drained of color. He drew a long straw. It was several moments before it occurred to him not to appear too relieved.

Most of the rest were lesser nobles—the men and women who'd made the late King Aleine Gunder IX's government work. They had all been so easily subverted. Extortion could be so simple. But it gained Garoth nothing to kill these peons, even if they had failed him.

That brought him to a sweating Trudana Jadwin. She was the twelfth in the line, and her husband was last.

Garoth paused. He let them look at each other. They knew, everyone who was watching knew that one or the other of them would die, and it all depended on Trudana's draw. The duke was swallowing compulsively. Garoth said, "Out of all the nobles here, you, Duke Jadwin, are the only one who was never in my employ. So obviously you didn't fail me. Your wife, on the other hand, did."

"What?" the duke asked. He looked at Trudana.

"Didn't you know she was cheating on you with the prince? She murdered him on my orders," Garoth said.

There was something beautiful about standing in the middle of what should be an intensely private moment. The duke's fear-pale face went gray. He had clearly been even less perceptive than most cuckolds. Garoth could see realization pounding the poor man. Every dim suspicion he'd ever brushed aside, every poor excuse he'd ever heard was hammering him.

Intriguingly, Trudana Jadwin looked stricken. Her expression wasn't the self-righteousness Garoth expected. He'd thought she'd point the finger, tell her husband why it was his fault. Instead, her eyes spoke pure culpability. Garoth could only guess that the duke had been a decent husband and she knew it. She had cheated because she had wanted to, and now two decades of lies were collapsing.

"Trudana," the Godking said before either could speak, "you have served well, but you could have served better. So here is your reward and your punishment." He extended the straws toward her. "The short straw is on your left."

She looked into Garoth's vir-darkened eyes and at the straws and then into her husband's eyes. It was an immortal moment. Garoth knew that the plaintive look in the duke's eyes would haunt Trudana Jadwin for as long she lived. The Godking had no doubt what she would choose, but obviously Trudana thought herself capable of self-sacrifice.

Steeling herself, she reached for the short straw, then stopped. She looked at her husband, looked away, and pulled the long straw for herself.

The duke howled. It was lovely. The sound pierced every Cenarian heart in the courtyard. It seemed pitched perfectly to carry the Godking's message: this could be you.

As the nobles—including Trudana—surrounded the duke with death in their hearts, every one of them feeling damned for their participation but participating all the same, the duke turned to his wife. "I love you, Trudana," he said. "I've always loved you." Then he pulled his cloak up over his face and disappeared in the thudding of flesh.

The Godking could only smile.

As Trudana Jadwin hesitated over her choice, Kylar thought that if he had taken Momma K's job, now would be the perfect moment to strike. Every eye was on the platform.

Kylar had turned toward Baron Kirof, studying what shock and horror looked like on his face, when he noticed that only five guards stood on the wall beyond the baron. He recounted quickly: six, but one of them held a bow and a handful of arrows in his bow hand.

A harsh crack sounded from the center of the yard, and Kylar caught a glimpse of the back section of the temporary platform splitting off and falling. Something flashing scintillating colors flew up into the air. As everyone else turned toward it, Kylar turned away. The sparkle bomb exploded with a small concussion and an enormous flash of white light. As hundreds of civilians and soldiers alike cried out, blinded, Kylar saw the sixth soldier on the wall draw an arrow. It was Jonus Severing, a wetboy with fifty kills to his name. A gold-tipped arrow streaked toward the Godking.

The Godking's hands were clasped over his eyes, but shields like bubbles were already blooming around him. The arrow hit the outer-most shield, stuck, and burst into flame as the shield popped. Another arrow was already on the way, and it passed through the fraying outer shield and hit one closer in. The next popped and the next as Jonus Severing shot with amazing speed. He was using his Talent to hold his spare arrows in midair so that as soon as he released a shot, the next arrow was already coming to his fingertips. The shields were breaking faster than the Godking could reform them.

People were screaming, blinded. The fifty meisters around the yard were throwing shields up around themselves, knocking anyone nearby off their feet.

The wetboy who'd been hiding beneath the platform jumped onto the platform on the Godking's blind side. He hesitated as one last wavering shield bloomed inches from the Godking's skin, and Kylar saw that he wasn't a wetboy at all. It was a child of perhaps fourteen, Jonus Severing's apprentice. The boy was so focused on the God-king, he didn't keep low, didn't keep moving. Kylar heard the snap of a bowstring nearby and saw the boy go down even as the Godking's last shield popped.

People were charging toward the gates, trampling their neighbors. Several of the meisters, still blinded and panicked, were flinging green missiles indiscriminately into the crowd and the soldiers around them. One of the Godking's bodyguards tried to tackle the Godking to get him out of danger. Dazed, the Godking misinterpreted the move and a hammer of vir blasted the huge highlander through the nobles on the platform.

Kylar turned to find who'd killed the wetboy's apprentice. Not ten paces away stood Hu Gibbet, the butcher who had slaughtered Logan Gyre's entire family, the best wetboy in the city now that Durzo Blint was dead.

Jonus Severing was already fleeing, not sparing a moment of anguish for his dead apprentice. Hu released a second arrow and Kylar saw it streak into Jonus Severing's back. The wetboy pitched forward off the wall and out of view, but Kylar had no doubt he was dead.

Hu Gibbet had betrayed the Sa'kagé, and now he'd saved the God-king. The ka'kari was in Kylar's hand before he was even aware of it. *What, I wouldn't kill the architect of Cenaria's destruction, but now I'm going to kill a bodyguard?* Of course, calling Hu Gibbet a body-guard was like calling a bear a furry animal, but the point remained. Kylar pulled the ka'kari back into his skin.

Ducking so Hu wouldn't see his face, Kylar joined the streams of panicked Cenarians flooding out the castle gate.

2

The Jadwin estate had survived the fires that had reduced so much of the city to rubble. Kylar came to the heavily guarded front gate and the guards opened the sally port for him wordlessly. Kylar had only stopped to strip out of his tanner's disguise and scrub his body with alcohol to rid himself of the scent, and he was certain that he'd arrived before the duchess, but word of the duke's death had flown faster. The guards had black strips of cloth tied around their arms. "Is it true?" one of them asked.

Kylar nodded and made his way to the hut behind the manse where the Cromwylls lived. Elene had been the last orphan the Cromwylls took in, and all her siblings had moved on to other trades or to serve other houses. Only her foster mother still served the Jadwins. Since the coup, Kylar, Elene, and Uly had stayed here. With Kylar's safe houses burned or inaccessible, it was the only choice. Kylar was thought to be dead, so he didn't want to stay in any of the Sa'kagé safe houses where he might be recognized. In any case, every safe house was full to breaking. No one wanted to be out on the streets with the roving bands of Khalidorans.

No one was in the hut, so Kylar went to the manse's kitchen. Eleven-year-old Uly was standing on a stool, leaning over a tub of soapy water, scrubbing pans. Kylar swept in and picked her up under

one arm, spun her around as she squealed, and set her back down on
the stool. He gave her a fierce look. "You been keeping Elene out of
trouble like I told you?" he asked the little girl.

Uly sighed. "I've been trying, but I think this one's hopeless."

Kylar laughed, and she laughed too. Uly had been raised by servants in Cenaria Castle, believing for her own protection that she was
an orphan. The truth was that she was the daughter of Momma K and
Durzo Blint. Durzo had only found out about her in the last days of
his life, and Kylar had promised him that he would look after the girl.
After the initial awkwardness of explaining that he wasn't her father,
things had gone better than Kylar could have expected.

"Hopeless? I'll show you hopeless," a voice said. Elene carried a
huge cauldron with the grime of yesterday's stew baked onto the sides
and set it down next to Uly's stack of dishes.

Uly groaned and Elene chuckled evilly. Kylar marveled at how
she'd changed in a mere week, or perhaps the change was in how he
saw her. Elene still had the thick scars Rat had given her as a child:
an X across her full lips, one on her cheek, and a crescent looping
from her eyebrow to the corner of her mouth. But Kylar barely noticed
them. Now, he saw radiant skin, eyes bright with intelligence and
happiness, her grin lopsided not because of a scar but from planned
mischief. And how a woman could look so good in modest servant's
woolens and an apron was one of the great mysteries of the universe.

Elene grabbed an apron from a hook and looked at Kylar with a
predatory gleam in her eye. "Oh, no. Not me," Kylar said.

She looped the apron over his head and pulled him close slowly and
seductively. She was staring at his lips and he couldn't help but stare
at hers as she wet them with her tongue. "I think," she said, her voice
low, her hands gliding across his sides, "that..."

Uly coughed loudly, but neither of them acknowledged her.

Elene pulled him against her, her hands on the small of his back, her
mouth tilting up, her sweet scent filling his nostrils. "...that's much
better." She yanked the apron knot tight behind his back and released

him abruptly, stepping back out of range. "Now you can help me. Do you want to cut the potatoes or the onions?" She and Uly laughed at the outrage on his face.

Kylar leapt forward and Elene tried to dodge, but he used his Talent to grab her. He'd been practicing in the last week, and though so far he could only extend his reach a pace or so behind his own arms, this time it was enough. He pulled Elene in and kissed her. She barely pretended to put up a fight before kissing him back with equal fervor. For a moment, the world contracted to the softness of Elene's lips and the feel of her body tight against his.

Somewhere, Uly started retching loudly. Kylar reached out and swatted the dishwater toward the source of his irritation. The retching was abruptly replaced with a yelp. Elene disentangled herself and covered her mouth, trying not to laugh.

Kylar had managed to drench Uly's face completely. She raised her hand and swatted water back at him, and he let it hit him. He rubbed her wet hair in the way he knew she didn't like, and said, "All right, squirt, I deserved that. Truce now. Where are those potatoes?"

They settled smoothly into the easy routine of kitchen work. Elene asked him what he'd seen and learned, and though he checked constantly for eavesdroppers, he told her everything about studying the baron and helplessly watching the assassination attempt. Such sharing was, perhaps, the most boring thing a couple could do, but Kylar had been denied the boring luxuries of everyday love for his whole life. To share, simply to speak the truth to a person who cared, was unfathomably precious. A wetboy, Durzo had taught Kylar, must be able to walk away from everything at a moment's notice. A wetboy is always alone.

So this moment, this simple communion, was why Kylar was finished with the way of shadows. He'd spent more than half his life training tirelessly to become the perfect killer. He didn't want to kill anymore.

"They needed a third man for the job," Kylar said. "To be a lookout and backup knife man. We could have done it. Their timing was so good. One second different and they would have pulled it off with only the two of them. If I'd been there, Hu Gibbet and the Godking both would be dead. We'd have fifty thousand gunders." He paused at a black thought. " 'Gunders.' Guess they won't be calling them that anymore, now that all the Gunders are dead." He sighed.

"You want to know if you did the right thing," Elene said.

"Yes."

"Kylar, there are always going to be people so bad that we think they deserve to die. In the castle when Roth was...hurting you, I was this close to trying to kill him myself. If it had been only a little longer...I don't know. What I do know is what you've told me about what killing has done to your soul. No matter what good it seems to do for the world, it destroys you. I can't watch that, Kylar. I won't. I care about you too much."

It was the one precondition Elene had for leaving the city with Kylar: that he give up killing and violence. He was still so confused. He didn't know if Elene's way was right, but he'd seen enough to know that Durzo's and Momma K's wasn't. "You really believe that violence begets violence? That fewer innocent people will die in the end if I give up killing?"

"I really do," Elene said.

"All right," Kylar said. "Then there's a job I need to do tonight. We should be able to leave in the morning."

3

*H*ell's Asshole was no place for a king. Appropriately, the Hole was the lowest extremity of the gaol Cenarians called the Maw. The entrance to the Maw was a demonic visage carved from jagged black fireglass. Prisoners were marched straight into its open mouth, down a ramp often made slick by fear-loosened bladders. In the Hole itself, the stone carver's art had been eschewed for the sheer visceral fears evoked by tight spaces, the dark, heights, the eerie howling of the wind rising from the depths, and the knowledge that every prisoner with whom you shared the Hole had been deemed unworthy of a clean death. The Hole was unrelentingly hot and reeked of brimstone and human waste in its three forms: their shit, their dead, and their unwashed flesh. There was only a single torch, far overhead, on the other side of the grate that separated the human animals from the rest of the prisoners in the Maw.

Eleven men and one woman shared the Hole with Logan Gyre. They hated him for his knife and for his powerful body and for his cultured accent. Somehow, even in this nightmare menagerie of freaks and twists, he was different, isolated.

Logan sat with his back to the wall. There was only one wall because the Hole was a circle. In the middle was a hole five paces wide that opened into a chasm. The chasm's sides were perfectly vertical, perfectly sheer fireglass. There was no guessing how deep it was. When the prisoners kicked their waste into the hole, they heard no sound. The only thing that escaped the Hole was the deep stench of a sulphuric hell and the intermittent wailing made by the wind or the ghosts or the tortured souls of the dead or whatever it was that made that sanity-breaking sound.

At first, Logan had wondered why his fellows would defecate against the wall and only later—if ever—kick the feces down the hole. The first time he had to go, he knew: you'd have to be insane to squat near the Hole. You couldn't do anything down here that made you vulnerable. When one inmate had to move past another, he shuffled quickly and suspiciously, snarling and hissing and cursing in such strings that the words lost meaning. Pushing another inmate into the Hole was the easiest way to kill.

What made it worse was that the shelf of rock that circled the Hole was only three paces wide and the ground slanted down toward the Hole. That shelf was all the world to the Holers. It was the thin, slippery slope to death. Logan hadn't slept in the seven days since the coup. He blinked his eyes. Seven days. He was starting to get weak. Even Fin, who got most of the last meat, hadn't eaten in four days.

"You're bad luck, Thirteen," Fin said, glaring at him over the chasm. "They ain't fed us since you got here." Fin was the only one who called him Thirteen. The rest had accepted the name he'd given himself in a moment of madness: King.

"You mean since you *ate* the last guard?" Logan asked. "You think that might have something to do with it?"

That got chuckles from everyone except Gnasher the simpleton, who just smiled blankly through teeth filed to sharp points. Fin said nothing, just kept chewing and stretching the rope in his hands. The man already wore an entire coil of rope that was so thick it almost obscured a frame as sinewy as the ropes themselves. Fin was the most feared of the inmates. Logan wouldn't call him the leader because that would have implied that the inmates had a social order. The men were like beasts: shaggy, their skin so dirty he couldn't guess what color they had been before their imprisonment, eyes wild, ears alert to the slightest sound. Everyone slept light. They'd *eaten* two men the day he'd arrived.

Arrived? I jumped in. I could have had a nice clean death. Now I'm here forever, or at least until they eat me. Gods, they'll eat *me!*

He was distracted from his rising horror and despair by motion on the other side of the Hole. It was Lilly. She alone didn't cling to the wall. She was heedless of the hole, fearless. A man reached out and grabbed her dress. "Not now, Jake," she told the one-eyed man.

Jake held on for a moment more, but when she lifted an eyebrow at him, he dropped his hand and cursed. Lilly sat down next to Logan. She was a plain woman, her age indeterminate. She could have been fifty, but Logan guessed she was closer to twenty: she still had most of her teeth.

She didn't speak for a long time. Then, when the interest in why she had moved had subsided, she scratched at her crotch absently and said, "What you gonna do?" Her voice was young.

"I'm going to get out, and I'm going to take back my country," he said.

"You hold onto that King shit," she said. "Make 'em think you're crazy. I see you looking round like a little boy lost. You're living with animals. You want to keep living, you be a monster. You want to hold onto something, you bury it deep. Then do what you gotta." She patted his knee and went over to Jake.

In moments, Jake was rutting on top of her. The animals didn't care. They didn't even watch.

The madness was taking him. Dorian stayed in the saddle only from instinct. The external world seemed distant, unimportant, buried under mist while the visions were near, vital, vibrant. The game was on and the pieces were moving, and Dorian's vision was expanding as it never had before. The Night Angel would flee to Caernarvon and his powers were growing, but he wasn't using them.

What are you doing, boy? Dorian grabbed onto that life and followed it backward. He'd spoken with Kylar once, and had prophesied his death. Now he knew why he hadn't also foreseen that this Night Angel would die and wouldn't die. Durzo had confused him. Dorian had seen Durzo's life intersecting with other lives. He had seen but he hadn't understood.

He was tempted to try to follow Durzo's lives back to the first life, when Durzo had received the ka'kari that Kylar now bore. He was tempted to see if he could find Ezra the Mad's life—surely such a life would burn so brilliantly he couldn't miss it. Maybe there he could follow Ezra, learn what Ezra knew, learn how he had learned it. Ezra had made the ka'kari seven centuries ago, and the ka'kari had made Kylar immortal. It was only three steps to one of the most respected and reviled magi of history. Three steps! To find someone so famous who had been dead so long. It was tempting, but it would take time. Maybe months. But oh, the things he could learn!

The things I could learn about the past while the present falls apart. Focus, Dorian. Focus.

Clambering back onto Kylar's life, Dorian followed it from his youth in the Warrens, his friendship with Elene and Jarl, Jarl's rape, Elene's maiming, Kylar's first kill at eleven, Durzo's apprenticeship, Momma K's instruction, Count Drake's softening influence, Kylar's friendship with Logan, meeting again with Elene, stealing the ka'kari, the coup at the castle, killing his master, and finding Roth Ursuul—*My little brother*, Dorian thought—*and as much of a monster as I once was.*

Focus, Dorian. He thought he heard something, a yell, some motion in the mundane world, but he wouldn't let himself be distracted again. He was just starting to get somewhere. There! He watched as Kylar poisoned Momma K for justice, and gave her the antidote for mercy.

He could know what choices a man made, but without knowing

why, Dorian wouldn't be able to guess which way Kylar would turn in the future. Kylar had already taken less obvious routes, impossible routes. Given the choice of taking his lover's life or his mentor's, he'd chosen to give his own. The bull had offered each of its horns, and Kylar had vaulted over the bull's head. That was the Kylar that mattered. In that moment, Dorian saw Kylar's naked soul. *Now I have you, Kylar. Now I know you.*

There was a sudden pain in Dorian's arm, but now that he had a firm grip on Kylar, he wasn't letting go. Kylar ached to synthesize the cruel realities of the street with the pious impulses Count Drake had somehow infected him with. Infected? The word came from Kylar. So, like Durzo, he sometimes saw mercy as weakness.

You are going to be damnably difficult, aren't you? Dorian laughed as he watched Kylar dealing with Caernarvon's incompetent Sa'kagé, as Kylar picks herbs, as he pays taxes, as he will fight with Elene, as he tried to be a normal human being. But he isn't doing well, the pressure is building. Kylar takes out his wetboy grays, goes out on the roofs—*funny, he does that regardless of the choices he makes up to this point*—and then one night, there's a knock on the door and Jarl shows up to stretch Kylar on another crux between the woman he loves and the life he hates and the friend he loves and the life he ought to hate and one duty and another duty and honor and betrayal. Kylar is Shadow in Twilight, a growing colossus with one foot planted in the day and another in the night, but a shadow is an ephemeral beast and twilight must either darken into night or lighten into day. Kylar opens the door for Jarl, futures crashing—

"Dammit, Dorian!" Feir is slapping him. Dorian was suddenly aware that Feir must be about to do it several times, because his jaw had throbbed on both sides. Something will be seriously wrong with his left arm. He looks, confusions crashing in his head—trying to find the right speed of time.

There was an arrow sticking out of his arm. A black-bated Khalidoran highlander's arrow. Poisoned.

Feir slapped him again.

"Stop! Stop!" Dorian said, waving his hands around. It made his left arm blossom into pain. He groaned and squeezed his eyes shut, but he was back. This is sanity. "What's happened?" he asked.

"Raiders," Feir said.

"A bunch of idiots trying to take something home to brag about," Solon said. Something, of course, would have been Solon's, Feir's, and Dorian's ears. One of the four corpses already wore two ears dangling from a necklace. They looked fresh.

"They're all dead?" Dorian asked. It was time to do something about that arrow.

Solon nodded unhappily and Dorian read the story of the brief battle around their camp. The attack had come as Feir and Dorian were setting up camp. The sun was dipping into a notch in the Faltier Mountains and the raiding party had come from the mountain, thinking the sun would blind them. Two archers tried to cover their friends' approach, but the shot was steeply downhill and their first arrows had missed.

After that, the outcome had been a foregone conclusion. Solon was no mean hand with a sword, and Feir—mountainous, monstrously strong and quick Feir—was a second-echelon Blade Master. Solon had let Feir handle the swordsmen. He'd been too late to save Dorian taking an arrow, but he had killed both archers with magic. The whole thing had probably taken less than two minutes.

"The pity is, they're from the Churaq clan," Solon said, nudging one of the black-tattooed youths. "They'd have happily killed the Hraagl clan bastards guarding the Khalidoran baggage train we're following."

"I thought Screaming Winds was impregnable," Feir said. "How'd the raiders get on this side of the border?"

Solon shook his head. It drew Dorian's attention to his hair, which was a flat black except at the roots. Since Solon had killed fifty meisters by using Curoch—and nearly killed himself from the sheer amount of magic he'd used to do it—his hair was growing in white. Not old man salt-and-pepper white, but a snow-white that struck a sharp contrast against a face that showed a man in his prime, handsome, with olive Sethi-skin, and features chiseled from a military life. Solon had complained at first that his vision was either all in wild colors or black and white from using Curoch, but that seemed to have cleared. "Impregnable, yes," Solon said. "Impassable for an army, yes. But this late in the summer, these young men can climb the mountains. Lots of them die on the climb, or storms come up out of nowhere and wash them off the rock, but if they're lucky and strong, nothing stops them. You ready with that arrow yet, Dorian?"

Though all three men were magi, there was no question of them helping him, not with this. Dorian was a Hoth'salar, a Brother of Healing; his hopes to cure his own growing madness had driven him to the healers' highest ranks.

Water suddenly soaked Dorian's arm around the arrowhead.

"What was that?" Feir asked, looking green.

"All the moisture from the blood that's already poisoned. It should all stick to the arrow when you pull it out," Dorian said.

"Me?" Feir asked, the squeamish look on his face totally at odds with his huge frame.

"You're ridiculous," Solon said. He reached over and ripped out the arrow. Dorian gasped and Feir had to catch him. Solon stared at the arrow. The barbs had been bent down flat so they wouldn't tear flesh on their way out, but the shaft was covered in a black shell of blood and the poison coaxed into a crystalline structure. It had swelled the shaft to three times its original width.

Even as Dorian was heaving breaths in and out, flows of magic began dancing in the air like tiny fireflies, like a hundred spiders spinning glowing webs, tapestries of light. This was the part that impressed the other men. Theoretically, any magus could heal himself, but for some reason, it not only tended not to work well but was also intensely painful to heal more than the smallest wound. It was as if the patient had to feel every pain and discomfort and irritation and itching that a wound would have inflicted in the entire time it was healing. When a magus healed someone else, he could numb the patient. When he healed himself, numbing anything could lead to mistakes and death. Female mages, magae, on the other hand, had no such problems. They routinely healed themselves.

"You're incredible," Solon said. "How do you do that?"

"It's just focus," Dorian said. "I've had lots of practice." He smiled and shook himself as if casting off his weariness, and suddenly his face was animated and he was totally present with them in a way that was becoming rare.

Solon looked bereaved. Dorian's madness was irreversible. It would grow until he was a babbling idiot who slept outside or in barns. He would come to be totally disregarded and have only one or two moments of lucidity each year. Sometimes, those moments would come when no one was around for him to tell what he had learned.

"Stop it," Dorian told Solon. "I've just had a revelation." He said it with a little smirk to let them know it really had been a revelation. "We're going the wrong way. At least you are," Dorian said, pointing to Feir. "You need to follow Curoch south to Ceura."

"What do you mean?" Feir asked. "I thought we *were* following the sword. Anyway, my place is with you."

"Solon, you and I have to go north to Screaming Winds," Dorian said.

"Wait," Feir said.

But Dorian's eyes had glazed again. He was gone.

"Lovely," Feir said. "Just lovely. I swear he does that on purpose."

4

*I*t was past midnight when Jarl joined them in the Cromwylls' little hut. He was more than an hour late. Elene's foster mother was asleep in the bedroom they all shared, so Kylar and Elene and Uly were all sitting in the front room. Uly had fallen asleep against Kylar, but she jerked upright instantly, terrified, as Jarl came in.

What am I dragging this little girl into? Kylar thought. But he just squeezed her, and when she got her bearings, she calmed down, embarrassed.

"Sorry," Jarl said. "The palies are ... punishing the Warrens for the assassination attempt. I wanted to get back to check on some things, but they've sealed the bridges. No bribe's enough today." Kylar could tell Jarl was avoiding details because Uly was in the room, but considering how bad things were in the Warrens before the assassination attempt, Kylar could barely imagine how they must be tonight.

Kylar wondered how much worse it would have been if the God-king had actually been killed. Violence begets violence indeed. "Does this mean the job's canceled?" he asked, so Elene and Uly wouldn't ask more about the Warrens.

"It's on," Jarl said. He handed a purse to Elene. It looked suspiciously light. "I took the liberty of bribing the gate guards in advance. The price has already gone up, and I guarantee tomorrow it will go up again. You have the list of times when the guards we bribed are working this week?" Jarl opened a pack and took out a cream-colored tunic, trousers, and high black boots.

"Memorized," Kylar said.

"Look," Elene said, "I know Kylar's used to doing jobs where he doesn't know why he's doing what he's doing, but I need to understand this. Why is someone paying five hundred gunders for Kylar to pretend to die? That's a fortune!"

"Not to a Khalidoran duke. Here's the best I've been able to put it together," Jarl said. "The dukes in Khalidor aren't the same as our dukes because the nobility in Khalidor is always inferior to the meisters. But the meisters still need people to manage the peasants and so forth, so Duke Vargun is rich, but he's had to fight for every scrap of power he has. He came to Cenaria hoping to advance himself, but the position he thought he would get—leading Cenaria's royal guard—was given to Lieutenant Hurin Gher, now Commander Gher."

"To pay him off for leading Cenaria's nobles into an ambush during the coup, the traitor," Kylar said.

"Exactly. Commander Gher goes to the docks one morning a week with a few of his most trusted men to pick up Sa'kagé bribe money and pretend to be patrolling. This morning he's going to see his rival, Duke Vargun, commit the murder of a minor Cenarian noble, Baron Kirof. Commander Gher will happily arrest the duke. In a few days or weeks, the 'dead' Baron Kirof will show up. Commander Gher will be disgraced for arresting a duke for no reason, and most likely, Duke Vargun will take his job. A number of things could go wrong, which is why Kylar's only getting five hundred gunders."

"It sounds awfully complicated," Elene said.

"Trust me," Jarl replied, "when it comes to Khalidoran politics, this is simple."

"How's the Sa'kagé going to turn this to their advantage?" Kylar asked.

Jarl grinned. "We tried to get hold of Baron Kirof, but apparently the duke isn't too stupid. Kirof's already gone."

"The Sa'kagé would have kidnapped Baron Kirof? Why?" Elene asked.

Kylar said, "If the Sa'kagé grabbed Kirof, they could blackmail Commander Gher. Commander Gher would know the moment Kirof showed up, he'd be doomed, so the Sa'kagé would have owned him."

"You know," Elene said, "sometimes I try to imagine what this city would be like without the Sa'kagé, and I can't. I want to get out of here, Kylar. Can I come with you tonight?"

"There's not enough space for an adult," Jarl answered for him. "Anyway, they'll be back by dawn. Uly? Kylar? You ready?"

Kylar nodded, and, grim-faced, Uly copied him.

Two hours later, they were at the docks ready to split up. Uly would hide beneath the dock in a raft camouflaged to look like a clump of driftwood. When Kylar fell in the water, she would extend a pole for him to grab so that he could surface out of sight. There would barely be room enough in the little raft for Uly to crouch and Kylar's head to emerge. After he emerged, the "driftwood" would eventually drift downstream a few hundred paces to another dock where they would emerge.

"What if it all goes wrong? I mean, really wrong?" Uly asked. The night's cold had left Uly's cheeks red. It made her look even younger.

"Then tell Elene I'm sorry." Kylar brushed the front of his cream-colored tunic. His hands were trembling.

"Kylar, I'm scared."

"Uly," he said, looking into her big brown eyes, "I wanted to tell you...I mean I wish..." He looked away. "Uh, I wish you wouldn't call me by my real name when we're on a job." He patted her head. She hated that. "How do I look?"

"Just like Baron Kirof...if I squint real hard." That was for the head pat, he knew.

"Have I ever told you you're a pain in the ass?" he asked her.

She just grinned.

In a few hours, the docks would be swarming with longshoremen and sailors, preparing their cargoes for the rising sun. For the moment, though, it was quiet except for the lapping of waves. The dock's private night watch had been paid off, but the bigger fear was of the groups of Khalidoran soldiers who might wander by, looking for blood. Mercifully, it seemed most of them were in the Warrens tonight.

"Well then, see you on the other side," he said, smirking. It was the wrong thing to say. Uly's eyes filled with tears. "Go on," he said, more gently. "I'll be fine." She went, and when she was safely out of sight, his face began shimmering. Kylar's lean young face put on a second chin, a red beard sprouted in the Khalidoran fashion, his nose grew crooked, and his eyebrows became great, wide brushes. *Now* he was Baron Kirof.

He pulled out a hand mirror and checked himself. He scowled. The illusory nose shrank a little. He opened his mouth, smiled, scowled, and winked, seeing how the face moved. It wasn't good, but it would have to do. Uly would have helped him get the face right, but the less she knew about his little talents, the better. He started down the dock.

"Dear gods," Duke Tenser Vargun said as he approached. "Is that you?" The duke was sweaty and pasty pale even in the light of the torches on the end of the dock.

"Duke Vargun, I got your message," Kylar said loudly, extending his hand and clasping the duke's wrist. He lowered his voice. "You'll be fine. Just do everything like we planned."

"Baron Kirof, thank you," the duke said, a bit dramatically. He lowered his voice again. "So you're the player."

"Yes. Let's try not to put me out of work."

"I've never killed anyone before."

"Let's make sure tonight isn't your first," Kylar said. He looked at the jeweled dagger tucked into the duke's belt. It was an heirloom in the duke's family, and its inexplicable loss would be part of the evidence that the duke really had killed Baron Kirof. "If you do this, you'll be going to prison, and not a nice one. We can call it off." Kylar waved his hands around as he talked the way the real Baron Kirof did when he was nervous.

"No, no." The duke sounded like he was trying to convince himself. "Have you ever done this before?"

"Set up someone by pretending to be someone else? Sure. Pretended to get killed? Not so much."

"Don't worry," the duke said. "I—" Tenser's eyes flicked past Kylar and his voice went tight with fear. "They're here."

Kylar jerked away from the duke as if startled. "Is that a threat?" he barked. It was only a fair imitation of the baron's voice, but blood covers a multitude of acting sins.

The duke grabbed his arm. "You'll do as I tell you!"

"Or what? The Godking will hear about this." They definitely had the guards' attention now.

"You'll say nothing!"

Kylar shook his arm free. "You aren't smart enough to take the throne, Duke Vargun. You're a coward, and..." He dropped his voice. "One stab. The blood bladder is right over my heart. I'll do everything else." He contorted Baron Kirof's face into a sneer and turned away.

The duke grabbed Kylar's arm and yanked him back. With a savage motion, Vargun rammed the dagger—not into the sheep's bladder of blood, but into Kylar's stomach. He stabbed once, twice, then again and again. Staggering backward, Kylar looked down. His cream-colored silk tunic was dripping red-black blood. Tenser's hands were gory and flecks of red dotted the blue of his cloak.

"What are you doing?" Kylar choked out, barely hearing the whistle blowing at the far end of the dock. He swayed, grabbing at the end of the railing to hold himself up.

Sweating profusely, his black hair hanging in lank ropes, Tenser ignored him. Every trace of the hesitant, bumbling noble he'd been only a minute before had disappeared. He grabbed a fistful of Kylar's hair. For him, it was a lucky grab. An inch forward, and he would have destroyed the illusory face Kylar wore.

As footsteps began pounding down the dock, Duke Vargun let Kylar drop to his knees. Through eyes dimming with pain, Kylar saw Commander Gher charging down the dock with his sword drawn and two guards at his heels. Duke Vargun dragged the dagger across Kylar's throat, sending blood spurting. Then, with as much emotion as a woodcutter burying his ax in a stump for the next time he's going to split wood, Duke Vargun jammed his dagger into Kylar's shoulder.

"Stop! Stop now or die!" Commander Gher roared.

Duke Vargun propped a calfskin boot on Kylar's shoulder and smiled. With a shove, he propelled Kylar off the dock and into the river.

The water was so cold Kylar went numb—or maybe that was from the blood loss. He'd inhaled before he hit the water, but one lung wasn't cooperating. In moments air bubbled out of his mouth, and—disconcertingly—his throat.

Then there was agony as he breathed the thick, dirty water of the Plith. He thrashed weakly, but only for a moment. Then the calm descended. His aching body was only a distant pulse. Something jabbed his body and he tried to grab for it instinctively. He was supposed to grab. There was something he was supposed to remember about a catchpole.

But if his hand even moved, he couldn't tell. The world didn't go black, didn't fade into darkness. His vision went white, his brain starving as blood poured from his neck. Something jabbed him again. He wished it would go away. The water was warm, a perfect peaceful cloud.

Duke Tenser Vargun tore his eyes away from the hungry river and lifted his hands. He turned slowly and said, "I'm unarmed. I surrender." He smiled as if he couldn't help it. "And a good evening to you, *Commander.*"

5

Will this Godking flay me or fuck me?

Vi Sovari sat in the receiving chamber outside Cenaria Castle's throne room, straining to overhear the Godking while she toyed with the guard who couldn't help but stare at her. Anything she could learn about why she'd been summoned might save her life. Her master, Hu Gibbet, had just brought in Duke Tenser Vargun—one of the Khalidoran nobles who had come in to help assimilate Cenaria into the Khalidoran Empire. Apparently, the duke had murdered some Cenarian noble.

It had to pose an interesting problem for the king who styled himself a god. Tenser Vargun was a trusted vassal, but letting him off would have serious ramifications. The Cenarian nobles who'd bent the knee to serve Garoth and been allowed to keep at least portions of their lands might find their spines and rebel. The Cenarian nobles who were in hiding would have new evidence of Khalidoran brutality to rally more people to their banners.

But why is Master Gibbet here? Hu had exuded that air of clever self-satisfaction that Vi knew all too well.

She crossed her legs to recapture the guard's attention. In fighting terms, the terms Hu Gibbet had taught Vi, it was a feint. The motion of her legs got his attention, turning her head to the side gave him safety, and leaning forward gave him a view. She didn't dare invoke a glamour this close to the Godking, but that was fine. Cleavage had its own magic.

She wore a fitted cerulean dress, so light it was faintly translucent. She had made her intentions clear to Master Piccun, so the tailor kept the dress simple—hardly any embroidery, just a little in the old Khalidoran runic style around the hem and wrists, an inscription from an ancient erotic poem. No lace, no frills, just clean lines and curves. Master Piccun was an inveterate letch, and this was the only dress he'd declared fit for the Godking. "The man has dozens of wives," the tailor sniffed. "Let those cows speak with silk. You will sing the sweet tones of flesh."

If the guard was like most men, he would stare for two to four seconds, double-check that no one was noticing him stare, and then stare again. The trick was—*Now*.

Vi flicked her eyes up suddenly and caught the guard just as he was starting to stare again. She pinned him to the wall with her eyes. Guilt flashed across his features and before he could cover it with boldness or glance away, she stood and walked toward him.

He was Khalidoran, of course, so she adjusted accordingly. Khalidorans' sense of personal space didn't extend as far as Cenarians'. Pricking the bubble of his personal space, with all the attendant connotations, meant stepping so close that he could smell not just her perfume but her breath. She stepped in and held him with her eyes for one more second, until he was about to speak.

"Excuse me," she said, still looking him in the eye, her expression intense. "May I sit here?"

"I wasn't staring—I mean—"

She sat in his chair, a foot from the door, her shoulders forward, face turned up, angelic. She wore her blonde hair up so the elaborately woven plaits didn't obscure the view.

It was too tempting. The guard's eyes shifted the fraction of an inch from her eyes to her cleavage and then leapt back to her face.

"Please?" she said with a little smile that told him yes, she'd seen and no, she didn't mind.

He cleared his throat. "I, uh, don't think that would be a problem," he said.

Vi instantly forgot him and listened.

"...can't go directly to the Hole, that would defeat the purpose," a tenor voice said. That would be Duke Vargun. But he sounded confident.

What? How can he sound confident?

Vi heard her master reply, but couldn't tell what he said. Then the Godking spoke, but she caught nothing but "—common cells until the trial....Then the Hole..."

"Yes, Your Holiness," Duke Vargun said.

Vi's head spun. Whatever they were planning, the Khalidoran duke had nothing in his voice that suggested a prisoner begging for clemency. He sounded like an obedient vassal, accomplishing some high purpose with a reward waiting at the end of it.

She didn't have any time to try to put it together before the doors opened and her master led Duke Vargun out. Contradicting what she'd just heard, the duke looked beaten, both physically and mentally, his clothes disheveled and dirty, and his eyes stuck to the floor.

Hu Gibbet turned to her as they walked past. The wetboy had such delicate features that he couldn't be called handsome. With fine blond hair that reached his shoulders, large eyes, and a sculpted figure, he was still beautiful even in his mid-thirties. He smiled his serpent's smile at Vi and said, "The Godking will see you now."

Vi felt a chill, but she just stood and walked into the throne room. From this room, the late King Gunder had hired her to kill Kylar Stern. As she was apprenticed to Hu Gibbet, Kylar was apprenticed to the city's other great wetboy, Durzo Blint, who was more respected, equally feared, and less reviled than her own master. Killing Kylar was to have been Vi's master's piece, the last kill of her apprenticeship. It would have meant freedom, freedom from Hu.

She'd botched it, and later that very day in this very room, someone they called the Night Angel had killed thirty Khalidorans, five wytches, and the Godking's own son. Vi thought she might be the only person who suspected that Kylar *was* the Night Angel. *Nysos! Kylar stepped into legend the same day I had him under my knife. I could have aborted a legend.*

There was no sign of the battle now. The throne room had been cleaned of blood and fire and magic, and stood pristine. On each side, seven columns supported the arched ceiling, and thick Khalidoran tapestries draped the walls to fight the autumnal chill. The Godking sat on the throne, surrounded by guards, Vürdmeisters in their black-and-red robes, advisers, and servants.

Vi had expected her summons, but she had no idea of the reason for it. Did the Godking know Kylar was the Night Angel? Was she to be punished for letting the Godking's son die? Did the man with dozens of wives want to fuck another pretty girl? Or was he just curious to see the city's only female wetboy?

"You think you're clever, Viridiana Sovari?" the Godking asked. Garoth Ursuul was younger than she had expected, maybe fifty, and still vigorous. He was thick through the arms and body, bald as an egg, and his eyes fell on her like a millstone.

"Pardon me, Your Holiness," she started to make it a question, then changed her mind. "Yes. And it's Vi."

He beckoned her forward, and she climbed the fourteen steps to stand directly in front of his throne. He looked her up and down, not surreptitiously as men so often did, nor hot and boldly. Garoth Ursuul looked at her as if she were a pile of grain and he was trying to guess her weight.

"Take off your dress," he said.

The inflection of his voice gave her nothing to work with. It might have been a comment on the weather. Did he want her to seduce him? She didn't care if Garoth Ursuul banged her, but she planned to be lousy if he did. Becoming the Godking's lover was too dangerous. She'd been warming one monster's bed since puberty, and she didn't fancy trading up. Still, god or king or monster, Garoth Ursuul was one you didn't cross.

So Vi obeyed instantly. In two seconds, Master Piccun's dress slid to the floor. Vi hadn't worn undergarments, and she had worn perfume between her knees. It was the most punctilious obedience. He couldn't fault her for it, but at the same time, she knew sudden nudity wasn't nearly as enticing as slow disrobing or the tease of lace undergarments. Let Ursuul think her an ineffectual tease, let him think her a slut, let him think whatever he wanted, as long as he did it from a distance. Besides, she wouldn't give any man the satisfaction of seeing her back down. Vi felt the stares of every courtier, adviser, Vürdmeister, servant, and guard in the room. She didn't care. Her nudity was her armor. It blinded the drooling fools. They couldn't see anything else while they saw her body.

Garoth Ursuul looked her up and down again, his eyes not shifting in the least. "You wouldn't be any fun," the Godking said. "You're already a whore."

For some reason, from this terrible man, those words sank in with barbs. She stood naked before him, and he'd completely lost interest. It was what she'd wanted, but it still hurt.

"All women are whores," she said. "Whether they sell their bodies or their smiles and their charm or their childbearing years and submission to a man. The world makes a woman a whore, but a woman makes her terms. Your Holiness."

He seemed amused at her sudden fire, but his amusement passed. "Did you think I wouldn't see what you did with my guard? Did you think you could eavesdrop on *me?*"

"Of course I did," Vi said, but now her flippancy was a farce. *He saw me? Through the wall?* She knew she had to hold on to her bravado or she might dissolve right into the floor. With the Godking, if you wanted to win, you had to play as if you despised life. But she'd heard about gamblers who'd lost.

The Godking chuckled, and his courtiers followed his lead. "Of course you did," he said. "I like you, *moulina*. I won't kill you today. Not many women would get in a pissing match with a king, much less a god."

"I'm not like any woman you've ever met," Vi said before she could stop herself.

His smile withered. "You give yourself too much credit. For that, I will break you. But not today. Your Sa'kagé is giving us trouble. Go to your little underworld friends and find out who the real Shinga is. Not a figurehead. Find out, and kill him."

Vi felt naked for the first time. Her armor wavered. God or man, Garoth Ursuul had titanic confidence. He told her he would break her, and then exhibited not the slightest concern that she would disobey him. It wasn't a bluff. It wasn't arrogance. It was a simple exercise of the prerogatives of vast power. The courtiers eyed her now like the dogs under a king's table eyed a fine scrap of meat that might fall to the floor. Vi wondered if the Godking would give her to one of them—or all of them.

"Do you know," the Godking said, "that you're wytchborn? As you southrons say, Talented. So here's your incentive. If you kill this Shinga, we'll call it your master's piece, and not only will you be a master wetboy, but I'll train you myself. I'll give you power far beyond anything Hu Gibbet could even imagine. Power over him, if you wish. But if you fail me—well." He smiled a thin-lipped smile. "Don't fail. Now begone."

She went, her heart thumping. Success meant betraying her world. Betraying the Cenarian Sa'kagé, the most feared underworld in Midcyru! It meant killing their leader for a reward she wasn't sure she wanted. Train to become a wytch with the Godking himself? Even as he spoke, she imagined his words were webs, binding her tighter and tighter to him. It was almost tangible, a spell draping over her like a net, daring her to struggle. She felt sick. Obedience was the only possibility. However bad success was, failure wasn't an option. She'd heard the stories.

"Vi!" the Godking called. She stopped, halfway to the door, feeling a shiver at that horror using her name. But the Godking was smiling. Now his eyes touched her naked body the way a man's eyes might. Something flashed like a shadow toward her and she snatched the wad of cloth out of the air on reflex. "Take your dress," he said.

6

I feel like I've been breathing sawdust for a week," Kylar said.

"River water. Five minutes," Uly answered. Terse. Snotty.

Kylar struggled to open his eyes, but when he did, he still saw nothing. "So you did pull me out. Where are we, Uly?"

"Take a whiff." She was acting tough, which meant he'd really scared the hell out of her. *Is this what little girls do?*

He got half a breath in before coughing on the stench. They were in Momma K's boathouse on the Plith.

"Nothing like warm sewage on a cool night, huh?" Uly said.

Kylar rolled over. "I thought that was your breath."

"Which smells as good as you look," she said.

"You ought to be respectful."

"You ought to be dead. Go to sleep."

"Do you think domineering is cute?"

"You need to sleep. I don't know what dumb earrings have to do with it."

Kylar laughed. It hurt.

"See?" Uly said.

"Did you get the dagger?"

"What dagger?"

Kylar grabbed her by the front of her tunic.

"Oh, the one I had to use a prybar to get out of your shoulder?" she asked. No wonder his shoulder hurt. He'd never seen Uly quite so snotty and glib. If he didn't watch it, she'd burst into tears. It was one thing to feel like an ass. It was another to feel like a helpless ass.

"How long have I been . . . out?"

"A day and a night."

He cursed quietly. It was the second time Uly had seen him murdered, his body mutilated. If she had an ironclad conviction that Kylar was coming back, he was glad. He had promised her that he would, but he'd never known. All he knew was that he'd come back once. The Wolf, the strange yellow-eyed man he'd met in the place between life and death, hadn't made any guarantees. Indeed, this time Kylar hadn't met him at all. Kylar had been hoping to ask him a few questions, like how many lives he got. What if it had only been two?

"And Elene?" he asked.

"She went to get the wagon. The guards Jarl bribed are only on duty for another hour."

Elene had gone alone to get the wagon? Kylar was so tired. He could tell Uly was right on the verge of tears again. What kind of a man put a little girl through this? He wasn't much of a substitute father, but he used to think that he was better than nothing.

"You should sleep," she said, doing her best to be gruff again.

"Make sure . . ." He was so sore he couldn't complete the thought, much less the sentence.

"I'll take care of you, don't worry," Uly said.

"Uly?"

"Yes?"

"You did good work. Great work. I owe you. Thanks. I'm sorry." Kylar could almost feel the air around the girl go all warm and gooey. He groaned. He wanted to say something witty and mean like Durzo would have, but before he could find the words, he was asleep.

7

When Kaldrosa Wyn joined the queue behind the Lightskirt Tavern at noon, there were already two hundred women standing behind the brothel. Two hours later, when the line started moving, it was three times that. The women were as diverse a group as could be found in the Warrens, from guild rats as young as ten who knew that Momma K wouldn't hire them but were so desperate they came anyway to women who had lived on the rich east side just a month ago but had lost their homes in the fires and then been herded into the Warrens. Some of those were weeping. Others just wore vacant expressions, clutching shawls tight around them. And some were long-time Rabbits, laughing and joking with their friends.

Working for Momma K was the safest gig a rent girl could get. They traded stories how the Mistress of Pleasures dealt with their new Khalidoran clientele. They claimed that when the twists hurt you, they had to pay you enough silvers to cover the bruise. Another claimed it was enough crowns to cover it, but no one believed her.

When Duchess Terah Graesin—the old duke her father had been killed in the coup—led the resistance out of the city, her followers had all put their shops and homes to the torch. The fires, of course, didn't stop after devouring the properties of those who left. Thousands who'd stayed had been made homeless. It was even worse in the

Warrens, where the poor were packed like cattle. Countless hundreds had died. The fires had burned for days.

The Khalidorans wanted the east side to get productive as quickly as possible. Those who were homeless were seen as an encumbrance, so soldiers forced them into the Warrens. The dispossessed nobles and artisans had become desperate, but desperation changed nothing. Being forced into the Warrens was a death sentence.

For the past month, the Godking had allowed his soldiers to do whatever they wished in the Warrens. The men would descend in packs to sate whatever lusts motivated them. Chanting that gods-damned prayer to Khali, they raped, they killed, they stole the Rabbits' meager possessions merely to throw them in the river and laugh. It seemed it couldn't get worse, but after the assassination attempt, it had.

The Khalidorans had moved through the Warrens in an organized fashion, block by twisting block. They made mothers choose which of their children would live and put the others to the sword. Women were raped in front of their families. Wytches played sick games blasting off body parts. When anyone offered resistance, they rounded up and publicly executed dozens.

There were rumors of safe hideouts deeper in the Warrens, underground, but only people well-connected in the Sa'kagé could get into those. Everyone had places to hide, but the soldiers came every night and sometimes during the day. It was only a matter of time before they caught you. Beauty had become a curse. Many of the women who had lovers or husbands or even protective brothers had lost them. Resistance meant death.

So women came to Momma K's brothels because they were the only safe places in the Warrens. If you were going to get raped, many figured, you might as well get paid for it. Apparently the brothels still did good business, too. Some Khalidorans didn't like the risks of going into the Warrens. Others just liked being assured of bedding a clean and beautiful woman.

Already though, the brothels didn't have many openings—and no one wanted to speculate why they had any at all.

Kaldrosa had held off as long as she could. It wasn't supposed to be like this. That Vürdmeister, Neph Dada, had recruited her specifically because she was a former Sethi pirate who'd been marooned in the Warrens years ago. She hadn't sailed in ten years—and had never been a captain, despite what she told the Vürdmeister. But she was Sethi, and she had promised she could navigate a Khalidoran ship through the Smugglers' Archipelago up the Plith River to the castle. In return, she would get to keep the ship.

It had sounded like a fine price for an unsavory bit of work. Kaldrosa Wyn had no loyalty to Cenaria, but working for the Khalidorans was enough to make anyone's skin crawl.

Maybe they even would have kept their part of the deal—giving her that sea cow of a barge that wasn't worth the nails holding it together. Maybe she could have cobbled together a crew to join her, too—except that some bastard had sunk her ship during the invasion.

She'd been able to swim to shore, which was more than she could say for the two hundred armored clansmen she'd been ferrying, who were now feeding fish. Four rapes and two times of Tomman being beaten half to death later, here she was.

"Name?" the girl at the door asked, holding a quill and paper. She had to be eighteen, a good decade younger than Kaldrosa, and she was stunning: hair perfect, teeth perfect, long legs, tiny waist, full lips, and a musky-sweet scent that made Kaldrosa aware of how foul she herself must smell. She despaired.

"Kaldrosa Wyn."

"Occupation or special talents?"

"I was a pirate."

The girl perked up. "Sethi?"

Kaldrosa nodded, and the girl sent her upstairs. In another half an hour, Kaldrosa Wyn stepped into one of the small bedrooms.

The woman here was young and beautiful, too. Blonde, petite but curvy, with big eyes and amazing clothes.

"I'm Daydra. You ever worked the sheets?"

"I assume you don't mean sails."

Daydra chuckled, and even that was pretty. "A real pirate, huh?"

Kaldrosa touched her clan rings, four small hoops in a crescent framing her left cheekbone. "Tetsu clan off Hokkai Island." She gestured to the captain's chain she wore—which she put on herself as soon as she got the job for Khalidor. She opted for the finest silver herringbone chain she could afford. It looped from her left earlobe to the lowest of her clan rings. It was a merchant captain's chain, a merchant captain of humble birth. Military captains and the bolder pirate captains wore chains looped from earlobe to earlobe behind their heads so there was less chance they'd get ripped off in battle. "A pirate captain," she said, "but never caught. If you're caught, you're either hanged or they rip out your rings and exile you. There's some disagreement about which is worse."

"Why'd you quit?"

"I tangled with a royal Sethi pirate hunter a few hours before a storm. We gave almost as good as we got, but the storm drove us onto the rocks of the Smugglers' Archipelago. Since then, I've just done whatever." Kaldrosa didn't mention that "whatever" included getting married and working for Khalidor.

"Show me your tits."

Kaldrosa untied her laces and wriggled out of her top.

"I'll be damned," Daydra said. "Very good. I think you'll do fine."

"But you're all so beautiful," Kaldrosa said. Stupid as it was to protest, she couldn't believe her luck was turning.

Daydra smiled. "Beautiful we've got. Every one of Momma K's girls has to be pretty, and you are. What you've got is exotic. Look at you. Clan rings. Olive skin. Even your tits are tanned!"

Kaldrosa was suddenly thankful that she'd been so stubborn on her ship that she'd gone topless to make the Khalidoran soldiers stare. It had given her a fierce sunburn, but her skin had darkened and the color hadn't faded yet.

"I don't know how you've managed a tan," Daydra said, "but you'll have to keep it up, and talk like a pirate. If you want to work for Momma K, you're going to be the Sethi pirate girl. You have a husband or a lover?"

Kaldrosa hesitated. "Husband," she admitted. "The last beating nearly killed him."

"If you do this, you'll never get him back. A man can forgive a woman who leaves whoring for him, but he'll never forgive one who goes whoring for him."

"It's worth it," Kaldrosa said. "To save his life, it's worth it."

"One more thing. 'Cause sooner or later you'll ask. We don't know why the palies do it. Every country's got twists who like hurting rent girls, but this is different. Some will take their pleasure first and only hurt you afterward, like they're embarrassed. Some won't hurt you at all, but they'll brag afterward that they did and pay Momma K's fines without complaining. But they'll always say those same words. You've heard them?"

Kaldrosa nodded. "*Khali vas,* something or other?"

"It's Old Khalidoran, a spell or a prayer or something. Don't think about it. Don't make excuses for them. They're animals. We'll protect you as well as we can and the money's good, but you'll have to face them every day. Can you do that?"

Words stuck in Kaldrosa's throat, so she nodded again.

"Then go to Master Piccun and tell him you want three pirate girl costumes. Make him finish taking your measurements before he bangs you."

Kaldrosa's eyebrows shot up.

"Unless you have a problem with that."

"You don't think we'll have any trouble, do you?" Elene asked. They were lying down in the wagon, spending one last night under the stars after three weeks on the road. Tomorrow they would enter Caernarvon and their new life.

"I left all my troubles in Cenaria. Well, except for the two that tagged along with me," Kylar said.

"Hey!" Uly said. Despite being as scary-smart as her real mother, Momma K, she was still eleven and easily baited.

"Tagged along?" Elene asked, propping herself up on an elbow. "As I recall, this is my wagon." That much was true. Jarl had given them the wagon, and Momma K had loaded it with herbs Kylar could use to start an herbiary. Perhaps in a nod to Elene's sensibilities, most of them were even legal. "If anyone tagged along, it was you."

"Me?" Kylar asked.

"You were making such a pathetic spectacle that I was embarrassed for you. I just wanted to stop your begging."

"Well, here I thought you were a helpless—" Kylar said.

"And now you know better," Elene said, self-satisfied, settling back into her blankets.

"Ain't that the truth. You've got so many defenses, a man would be lucky to get lucky with you once in a thousand years," Kylar said with a sigh.

Elene gasped and sat up. "Kylar Thaddeus Stern!"

Kylar giggled. "Thaddeus? That's a good one. I knew a Thaddeus once."

"So did I. He was a blind idiot."

"Really?" Kylar said, his eyes dancing. "The one I knew was famous for his gigantic—"

"Kylar!" Elene interrupted, motioning toward Uly.

"His gigantic what?" Uly asked.

"Now you did it," Elene said. "His gigantic what, Kylar?"

"Feet. And you know what they say about big feet." He winked lasciviously at Elene.

"What?" Uly asked.

"Big shoes," Kylar said. He settled back down in his own blankets, as smug as Elene had been moments before.

"I don't get it," Uly said. "What's it mean, Elene?"

Kylar chuckled evilly.

"I'll tell you when you're older," Elene said.

"I don't want to know when I'm older. I want to know now," Uly said.

Elene didn't answer her. Instead, she punched Kylar in the arm. He grunted.

"Are you going to wrestle now?" Uly asked. She had climbed out of her blankets and was sitting between them. "Because you always end up kissing. It's gross." She scrunched up her face and made wet kissing noises.

"Our little contraceptive," Kylar said. Much as he loved Uly, Kylar was convinced that she was the only reason that after three wonderful weeks on the trail with the woman he loved, he was still a virgin.

"Will you do that again?" Elene asked Uly, laughing and wisely heading off the what's-a-contraceptive question.

Uly scrunched her face and made the kissing sounds again, and soon the three of them dissolved in laughter that devolved into a tickle fight.

Afterwards, sides aching from laughing so hard, Kylar listened to the sounds of the girls breathing. Elene had a gift for falling asleep as soon as her head touched a pillow, and Uly wasn't far behind. Tonight, Kylar's wakefulness was no curse. He felt his very skin was glowing with love. Elene rolled over and nuzzled on his chest. He inhaled the fresh scent of her hair. He couldn't remember having felt so good, so accepted, in his entire life. She would drool on him, he knew, but it didn't matter. Drool was somehow cute when Elene did it.

No wonder Uly got disgusted. He *was* pathetic. But for the first time in his life, Kylar felt like a good man. He'd always been good at things, good at lock picking, climbing, hiding, fighting, poisoning, disguising himself, and killing. But he'd never felt *good* until Elene.

When she looked at him, the Kylar he saw reflected in her eyes wasn't repulsive. He wasn't a murderer; he was the substitute father who had tickle fights with an eleven-year-old; he was the love who told Elene she was beautiful and made her believe it for the first time in her life; he was a man with something to give.

That was the man Elene saw when she looked at him. She believed so many good things about him that Kylar alternated between believing it himself and thinking she was absolutely crazy. But being persuaded felt great.

Tomorrow, they'd reach Caernarvon, and for a time, they would stay with Elene's Aunt Mea. With her help—she was a midwife who knew herbs—Kylar would set up a little herbiary. Then he would overcome Elene's fading objections to fornication, and the way of shadows would be behind him forever.

8

After maybe twelve days, maybe fifteen, maybe it only felt like so many, Logan finally surrendered to sleep. In his dream, he heard voices. They were whispering, but in the stone environs of the Hole, every whisper carried.

"He's got a knife."

"If we all take him, it doesn't matter. Look how much meat there is on him!"

"Quiet," someone said. Logan knew he should move, should check the knife, should wake up, but he was so tired. He couldn't stay awake forever. It was too hard.

He thought he heard a woman's voice, screaming through a hand covering her mouth. There was a slap and the scream stopped. Then there was another slap and another and another.

"Easy, Fin. You kill Lilly, we'll fuckin' gut you. She's the only slit we got."

Fin cursed Sniffles, then said, "You scream again, bitch, and I'll rip out your hair and your fingernails. You don't need those to fuck. Got it?"

Then the voice faded, and the heat faded, and the howling faded, and the stink faded, and Logan was truly dreaming. He was dreaming of his wedding night. He was married to a girl he barely knew, but as he talked in their bedchamber, as nervous as the beautiful fifteen-year-old girl across from him, he felt sudden hope blossom in his heart. This girl was a woman he could love, and inexplicably, she was his. Jenine would be his wife and one day, his queen, and he knew he could love her.

Jenine's dead. Stop this.

He saw in her big eyes that she could love him, too, that their marriage bed would not be a place of duty, but one of joy. Her cheeks colored as he stared at her as his wife. His eyes claimed her—not arrogantly, but confidently, gently, accepting her and rejoicing in her beauty—and when he pulled her close, she folded into him. Her lips were hot.

Then, it seemed like only a second later, they were still kissing, still taking off each other's clothes, and feet were pounding up the stairs toward their room. Logan was pulling back from her and the door burst open and Khalidoran soldiers poured into the room—

Logan's eyes snapped open and his fists flew as bodies landed on top of him.

As far as fights went, it was pathetic. Logan hadn't eaten in two weeks, so he was as weak as a puppy. But the other inmates, aside from the meat they'd gorged on a few weeks ago, had been subsisting on bread and water for months or years. They were gaunt, hollow shadows of the men they had once been, so the fight proceeded slowly and clumsily.

Logan heaved one man off and punched another across the jaw, but two more were there instantly, their flesh made slick and muddy by their filth and their sweat. Fin landed on Logan's hip while Jake tore at Logan's face with long nails. Shaking another man off, Logan fought his way to his feet and flung Jake off.

The man fell into the Hole and disappeared.

Just like that, the fight was over.

"What'd you do that for?" Sniffles asked. "We could have used that meat. You fucker, you threw away meat."

For a moment, their fury crested and Logan thought they would attack him again. He reached to his hip to pull out the knife. It was gone.

On the other side of the Hole, Fin looked at him. He picked his bloody, scurvied gums with the point of the knife. Time was on his side, now.

Logan had thought the Holers had no society, but he'd been wrong. There were camps down here, too. The Holers were split into the animals and the monsters, the weak and the strong. Fin led the animals, who ranked mostly according to their crimes: murderers then rapists then slavers then pedophiles. The monsters were Yimbo, a big-boned red-haired Ceuran whose tongue had been cut out; Tatts, a pale Lodricari covered in tattoos who could speak but never did; and Gnasher, a misshapen simpleton with massive shoulders and a twisted spine and teeth filed to sharp points. The monsters survived only through the others' fear of them, and their willingness to fight.

Now, as they all starved, the tenuous society was breaking down. Logan had no friends, no knife, no place. Among the animals, he was now a wolf without a pack. Among the monsters, he was a dog without his steel tooth.

He had tried to see the inmates as men. Men debased and humiliated and reviled and evil, but men. He tried to see in them something good, some image within them of the gods or the God who had made them. But in the shadows of the Hole, he saw only animals and monsters.

Logan went and sat by Gnasher. The man gave him a simpleton's smile made horrible by his filed teeth.

Then there was a sound that made everyone freeze. Footsteps resounded through the corridor above the Asshole. Logan slipped into the one narrow overhang that would hide him from view as a torch-illumined face appeared over them. "I'll be," the guard said. He was black-haired, pale, and hulking, with a smashed nose, plainly Khalidoran.

The guard opened the grate but kept a close eye on the inmates fifteen feet below him. Fin didn't even unlimber his ropes.

"Figured a few of you would have died by now," the guard said. "Thought you'd be real hungry." He reached into a sack and pulled out a large loaf of bread. Every inmate looked at him with such longing that he laughed. "Well, then, here you go." The guard tossed them the loaf, but it sailed into the Hole.

The prisoners cried out, thinking it was a mistake. The guard produced another loaf and tossed it into the Hole too. The prisoners crowded around the Hole, even Fin and Lilly. The next loaf bounced off of Sniffles's fingertips and he almost fell in after it.

The guard laughed. He locked the grate and walked away, whistling a cheery tune. Several of the inmates wept.

He didn't come back. The days passed in agony. Logan had never known such debilitating weakness.

Four nights later—if the term wasn't meaningless, Logan thought of it as night because most of the Hole's inhabitants were asleep and the howling winds shrieked loudest at what the Holers called noon—Fin cut one of his pedophiles' throats. In moments, everyone was awake and fighting over the body. When Sniffles started beating on Gnasher to try to get the man to let go of some bloody scrap Logan preferred not to identify, Gnasher dropped the scrap and attacked him. Sniffles tried to fight him off, but Gnasher handled him like he was a child. Yanking Sniffles's arms out of the way, Gnasher sank his filed teeth into the man's neck.

In the ensuing fight over the body, an entire leg was thrown clear and landed next to Logan. When Scab came after it, Logan snatched it up. To his own horror, he stared Scab down until the man turned and left.

Logan took the leg back to the wall and wept, because no matter how hard he looked at it, he saw only meat.

9

Compared to Cenaria, Caernarvon was paradise. There were no Warrens here, no stark division of have and have-not, no occupying army, no stench of ash and death, no vacant stares of despair. The capital of Waeddryn had flourished under an unbroken line of twenty-two queens.

Twenty-two queens. The thought was strange to Kylar, until he realized that Momma K had ruled the Sa'kagé and the streets of Cenaria for more than twenty years.

"State your business," the gate guard said, eyeing their wagon. The people here were taller than Cenarians, and Kylar had never seen so many with blue eyes or with such bright hair—every color from almost white to fiery red.

"I buy and sell medicinal herbs. We've come here to start an apothecary," Kylar said.

"Where from?"

"Cenaria."

The guard looked pensive. "Heard things are real bad there. If you're setting up shop on the south side, be careful. There's some tough neighborhoods down..." he trailed off as he caught sight of the scars on Elene's face.

Faster than he would have thought possible, Kylar was furious.

Elene's scars were all that marred otherwise perfect beauty. A brilliant smile, deep brown eyes that defied the boring plainness of the word brown, eyes that only a poet could adequately describe and only a legion of bards adequately praise, skin that begged to be touched and curves that demanded it. *With all that, how can he only see scars?* But saying anything would only cause a scene. The guard blinked. "Uh, go on," he said.

"Thanks." Kylar wasn't worried about Caernarvon's Sa'kagé. They were strictly small time: mugging, picking pockets, street prostitution, and gambling on the dog fights and bull baiting. Some brothels and gambling dens actually stayed in business without being affiliated with them. Kylar's childhood street gang was more organized than the crime here.

They drove through the city, gawking at the people and the sights like bumpkins. Caernarvon sat at the confluence of the Wy, the Red, and the Blackberry rivers, and its streets were bursting with commerce and the multiplicity of people who flowed with the money. They passed olive-skinned, strong-featured Sethi wearing short loose trousers and white tunics, red-haired Ceurans with their two swords and their odd fashion of braiding multicolored locks of hair into their own, a few Ladeshians, and even an almond-eyed Ymmuri. They made a game of it, surreptitiously pointing and trying to guess who was from where.

"How about him?" Uly asked, pointing at a nondescript man in plain woolens. Kylar scowled.

"Yes, let's hear it, hotshot," Elene said, wearing an impish grin. "And don't point, Uly." The man had no distinguishing characteristics. No tattoos, standard tunic and trousers for Caernarvon, brown hair cut short, no Modaini patrician nose, nothing distinctive; even his fairly tan skin could have come from half a dozen countries. "Ah," Kylar said. "Alitaeran."

"Prove it," Elene said.

"Only Alitaerans look that smug."

"I don't believe it."

"Ask him," Kylar said.

Elene shook her head, sinking back, suddenly shy.

"Hey, master!" Uly shouted as their wagon rolled past him. "Where ya from?"

"Uly!" Elene said, mortified.

The man turned and drew himself to his full height. "I hail from Alitaera, by the grace of the God the greatest nation in all Midcyru."

"The gods, you mean," the Waeddryner he was bargaining with said.

"No, unlike you Waeddryner dogs, Alitaerans say what they mean," the merchant said, and in a moment they were arguing about religion and politics and Uly was forgotten.

"I am pretty amazing," Kylar said.

Elene groaned. "You're probably Alitaeran yourself."

Kylar laughed, but that "probably" soured in his mouth. *Probably*, because he was a guild rat, an orphan, maybe slaveborn. Like that Alitaeran, he couldn't even guess where his parents had been from. He couldn't guess why they'd abandoned him. Were they dead? Alive? Important somehow, like every orphan dreams? While Jarl had been busy saving pennies to get out of the guild, Kylar had been dreaming of why his noble parents might have been forced to abandon him. It was useless, foolish, and he thought he'd given it up long ago.

The closest thing he'd had to a father was Durzo—and Kylar had become what all men curse: a patricide. Now here he was, a loose string, tied to nothing before or behind.

No, that wasn't true. He had Elene and Uly. And he had the freedom to love. That freedom cost something, but it was worth the price.

"Are you all right?" Elene asked him, her brown eyes concerned.

"No," Kylar said. "As long as we're together, I'm great."

In a few minutes, they had left the northern markets and were getting deeper into the shipping district. Even here almost all the buildings were stone—a big change from Cenaria, where stone was so expensive that most of the houses were wood and rice paper. Local punks lounged in the stoops of houses and warehouses and mills, sullenly watching them go past with the universal expression of adolescents with something to prove.

"Are you sure this is the right road?" Kylar asked.

Elene winced. "No?"

Kylar kept the wagon moving, but it didn't matter. Six of the teens stood and followed a black-toothed man with a mop of greasy black hair toward them. The youths reached under steps or beneath piles of trash to find weapons. They were street weapons, clubs and knives and a length of heavy chain. The man leading them stood in front of the wagon and grabbed the near horse's bridle.

"Well, honey," Kylar said, "time to meet our friendly neighborhood Sa'kagé."

"Kylar, remember what you promised," Elene said, taking his arm.

"You don't really expect me to..." He let the question die as he saw the look in her eyes.

"Afternoon," their leader said, slapping a club into his palm. He smiled broadly, showing off two black front teeth.

"Honey," Kylar said, ignoring him. "This is different. You have to see that."

"Other people get through this sort of thing without anybody dying."

"Nobody will die if we do this my way," Kylar said.

The black-toothed man cleared his throat. Dirt looked permanently tattooed into his visage and two protruding, crooked, and blackened front teeth dominated his face. "Excuse me, lovers. I don't mean to interrupt—"

"You can wait," Kylar said in a tone that brooked no argument. He turned back to Elene. "Honey."

"Either do what you promised or do what you've always done," Elene said.

"That's not permission."

"No. It's not."

"Excuse me," the man said again. "This—"

"Let me guess," Kylar said, mimicking the man's swagger and accent. "This here's a toll road, and we need to pay a toll."

"Uh. That's right," the man allowed.

"How'd I guess?"

"I was gonna ask that—hey, you shut your mouth. I'm Tom Gray and this here—"

"Is your road. Sure. How much?" Kylar asked.

Tom Gray scowled. "Thirteen silvers," he said.

Kylar counted the seven men aloud. "Wait, doesn't that screw your bashers? They get one silver each and you get six?" Kylar asked. Tom Gray blanched. The boys looked at him angrily. Kylar was right, of course. Small-time thugs. "I'll give you seven," Kylar said.

He pulled out his small coin purse and started tossing silvers to each of the young men. "You get that much with no effort. Why risk a fight? That's as much as Tom was going to give you anyway."

"Hold on," Tom said. "If he gave us that much that easy he's got to have more. Let's take him."

But the young men weren't buying it. They shrugged, shook their heads, and shuffled back to their stoops.

"What are you doing?" Tom demanded. "Hey!"

Kylar flicked the reins and the horses started forward. Tom had to jump aside to avoid being crushed. He twisted his ankle as he landed. Kylar pulled his front lips back to make himself look as buck-toothed as Tom and raised his hands helplessly. The young men and Uly laughed.

10

They spent the night at an inn, and Aunt Mea found them early in the morning and guided them through a tangle of alleys to her house. She was in her forties, looked a decade older, and had been widowed for almost twenty years, since soon after her son, Braen, was born. Her husband had been a successful rug merchant, so her house was large, and she assured Kylar and Elene that they could stay as long as they liked. Aunt Mea was a midwife and healer with plain features, twinkling eyes, and shoulders like a longshoreman.

"So," Aunt Mea said, after a breakfast of eggs and ham, "how long have you two been married?"

"About a year," Kylar said. He figured that if he initiated the lies, Elene might be able to keep them going. Elene was a terrible liar. He looked at her, and sure enough, she was blushing.

Aunt Mea took it to be embarrassment and laughed. "Well, I did figure you were a little young to be this young lady's natural mother. How'd you find your new mother and father, Uly?"

Kylar sat back, stifling the urge to supply the answer himself. If he answered for everyone, not only would he look like an ass, he'd look suspicious. Sometimes you just had to let the bones roll where they may.

"The war," Uly said. She swallowed, looked down at her plate, and said nothing more. It wasn't even a lie, and the emotion on Uly's face

was plainly real. Uly's nurse had been killed in the fighting. Uly still
cried about it sometimes.

"She was at the castle during the coup," Elene said.

Aunt Mea set down her knife and spoon—they didn't use forks in
Caernarvon, much to Kylar's irritation. "I tell you what, Uly. We're
going to take good care of you. You'll be safe and you'll even have
your own room."

"And toys?" Uly asked.

Something about the open, hopeful expression on Uly's face made
Kylar ache. Little girls should be playing with dolls—why hadn't he
ever given Uly a doll?—not fishing bodies out of rivers.

Aunt Mea laughed. "And toys," she said.

"Aunt Mea," Elene said. "We're already putting you out enough.
We have money for toys, and Uly can stay with us. You've already—"

"I won't hear of it," Aunt Mea said. "Besides, you two are still new-
lyweds. You need all the privacy you can get, although heaven knows,
Gavin and I managed to plow the row quite a few times when we
shared a one-room shack with his parents." Elene blushed crimson,
but Aunt Mea kept talking. "But I'd guess an eleven-year-old isn't
quite as good about ignoring noises in the night. Am I right?"

Now Kylar blushed. Aunt Mea looked at him, and then looked at
Uly, who looked puzzled.

"Are you telling me you haven't since you left Cenaria?" Aunt Mea
said. "Surely you'd slip away sometimes in the morning when Uly
was still asleep? No? That trip has to be what, three weeks? That's an
eternity for you youngsters. Well. This afternoon, Uly and I will go
for a good long walk. The bed in your room creaks some, but if you
worry too much about that sort of thing, Uly will never have a little
brother, eh?"

"Please," Kylar begged, shaking his head. Elene was mortified.

"Hmmph," Aunt Mea said, looking at Elene. "Well. If you're finished with your breakfast, why don't we go meet my son?"

Braen Smith worked in a shop attached to the house. He had

his mother's broad, plain features and wide shoulders. As they approached, he threw a barrel hoop he was shaping onto a stack of similar ones and removed his gloves. "Morning," he said.

His eyes immediately went to Elene. A quick glance at her scarred face and then a too-appreciative weighing of her assets. It wasn't the quick up-and-down that men instinctively gave every woman. Kylar wouldn't have minded that. But this wasn't a look. It was a linger, and right to Elene's face. Or rather, right to her breasts.

"Niceta meetcha," Braen said, sticking his hand out to Kylar. He looked at Kylar, weighing, evaluating. Predictably enough, he tried to crush Kylar's hand.

A trickle of Talent took care of that. Without a whisper of tension in his face or his forearm, Kylar clamped down on the monstrous paw in his grip and took it right to the edge of breaking. A little more and every bone in the man's hand would shatter. After a moment, he backed off and merely matched the man, rough hand to rough hand, muscle to muscle, and eye to eye—even if he did have to look up and Braen outweighed him by a third. The panic cleared from Braen's eyes and Kylar could see him wondering if he'd imagined the initial force of Kylar's grip.

"Kylar," Elene muttered through clenched teeth as if he were making a spectacle of himself. But Kylar didn't break eye contact. There was something being settled here, and if it was primal and barbaric and petty and stupid, it was still important.

Elene didn't like being ignored. "I suppose next you'll compare the size of your—" she broke off, embarrassed.

"Good idea," Kylar said as the man finally released his hand. "What do you say, Braen?" Kylar loosened his belt.

Mercifully, Braen laughed. The rest of them followed, but Kylar still didn't like him. Braen still didn't like him, either. Kylar could tell.

"Well, niceta meetcha," Braen said again. "I got a big order to finish." He bobbed his head and picked up a hammer, flexing his pained fingers surreptitiously.

For the rest of the morning and afternoon, Aunt Mea showed them around Caernarvon. Though it was larger than Cenaria, the city didn't have the chaotic feel of Kylar's home. Most streets were paved and wide enough for two wagons and numerous pedestrians to pass at the same time. Vendors who set up shop infringing on that space were so quickly punished that few tried it. Sudden crushes pushed the crowds together whenever two wagons did pass, but there were accepted standards here and had been long enough that the wagons all traveled in six-inch-deep ruts in the paving stones. Even the sewers in the streets passed through pipes, with grates at intervals for the collection of new sewage. It made the city almost not smell like a city.

Castle Caernarvon dominated the north side. It was sometimes called the Blue Giant for its bluish granite. The blue walls were seamless, as flat and smooth as glass except for the numerous arrow slits and murder holes at the gates. Two hundred years ago, Aunt Mea said, eighteen men had held the castle for six days against five thousand.

Around the castle, of course, were the great houses. The city got dirtier and more crowded the closer it came to the docks. As in most places, the rich and noble liked to live away from everyone else and everyone else liked to live as close to the rich as they could. Here though, that was one line that was not regulated—unlike Cenaria's poor, who were legally bound to the west side of the Plith. Those who made the money to move could do so here. The possibility for advancement seemed to energize the entire city.

Caernarvon was the gold and glittering fools' gold of hope. Its vice was greed. In his own imagination, every merchant here was the emperor of the next trading empire. Cenaria was the smothering, stinking blanket of despair. Its vice was envy. No one built empires there. They just wanted a piece of someone else's.

"You're awfully quiet," Elene said.

"It's different here," Kylar said. "Even before Khalidor came, Cenaria was sick. This is better. I think we can make a home here."

Gods, he was about to become one of those merchants he'd been despising. Not that he had great ambitions. Being an herbalist and apothecary was really the only thing he could do besides kill. It wasn't anything he would ever dream about. What would he dream? About opening a second shop? Dominating the city's herb trade? He'd once held a country's future in his hands—he could have changed everything with one betrayal, killing a man he'd ended up killing anyway.

If I had, Logan would be alive...

As Aunt Mea led them home, he tried to force his mind into a merchant rut. He had a small amount of gold hidden in the wagon, and a fortune in herbs. Had they been robbed on the way here, the bandits wouldn't even have known what to steal.

"Well, the house is just down this street," Aunt Mea said. "Braen's out buying supplies. Uly and I are going to a little sweetmeats shop to give you two some time to get reacquainted." She winked at Kylar while Elene blushed, but then Aunt Mea's face darkened. "What's that?" she asked.

Kylar looked toward the house. Wisps of smoke were rising and thickening rapidly.

He joined the crowd running toward Aunt Mea's house—in the city, a fire was such a threat that everyone grabbed buckets and ran to help—but by the time he got there, the barn was entirely consumed with flame. It was too late to save anything. The crowds threw water on the nearby buildings while Kylar held Elene and Uly mutely.

The barn was a total loss. Their two horses and Aunt Mea's old nag were left as smoking, stinking mounds of meat. There was almost nothing left of the wagon. The arsonist had found the hidden chest with its gold. The fortune in herbs had gone up in smoke.

The only thing left was a long, thin box bound to the wagon's bent axle. The lock was intact. Kylar opened it and there were his wetboy grays and his sword Retribution, untouched, not even smelling of smoke, mocking his impotence.

11

"Bad news, Your Holiness," Neph Dada said as he came into the God-king's bedchamber. A young Cenarian noblewoman named Magdalyn Drake was tied to the bed and whimpering into her gag, but both she and the Godking were still dressed.

Garoth was sitting on the bed beside her. He caressed a knife up her bare calf. "Oh, what is it?"

"One of your spies in the Chantry, Jessie al'Gwaydin, is dead. She was last seen in the village of Torras Bend."

"The Dark Hunter killed her?"

"I assume so. Our man said that Jessie was planning to study the creature," Neph said.

"So she went into the wood and never came back."

"Yes, Your Holiness," Neph said. He rubbed his stooped back as if in pain. It wasn't only to remind the Godking of his age, but also of the burdens Neph bore in serving.

With a savage motion, the Godking stabbed the mattress so high between Magdalyn's legs that Neph thought he'd stabbed the girl. She squealed through the gag and bucked, trying to get away. Heedless, Garoth cut toward her feet, shearing her dress to the hem and sending feathers into the air.

Abruptly, he was calm once more. He left the knife sticking out of the mattress, folded the cut dress back and put his hand gently on the girl's naked thigh. She trembled uncontrollably.

"It is *so* hard to get spies in the Chantry. Why do they insist on throwing their lives away, Neph?"

"For the same reason they join us in the first place, Your Holiness: ambition."

Garoth looked at the Vürdmeister wearily. "That was a rhetorical question."

"I have some good news as well," Neph said. He straightened a little, forgetting his back. "We've captured a Ladeshian bard named Aristarchos. I think you'll want to interrogate him personally."

"Why?"

"Because I Viewed him, and what he's seen is remarkable."

Garoth narrowed his eyes. "Out with it."

"He believes he has seen the bearer of a ka'kari. A black ka'kari."

"Stop looking at me!" Stephan said. He was a fat cloth merchant, some former lover with a grudge who swore that he could tell Vi who the Shinga was. Either the Shinga was a woman, or Stephan had little preference which field he plowed, because this had been his price.

Vi lay under him. She moved with the dexterity of an athlete and the skill of a courtesan trained by Momma K herself, but her eyes were utterly dispassionate. She wasn't moaning, wasn't making faces. She wouldn't pretend pleasure and it was giving Stephan problems. Like most men, he was three-quarters talk and one-quarter cock. A little less than a quarter, at the moment.

He pulled back and cursed his limpness. He was sweaty and he stank under the smell of his fine oils. Vi couldn't help but give him a condescending smile. "I thought you were gonna give it to me good," she said.

His face flushed, and she wondered why she was sabotaging him. He was no more or less than any man, and she still needed to learn what he had to tell her. Taunting him was only going to make this take longer.

"Let your hair down," he said.

"Forget my hair." Nysos, couldn't they leave one damned thing alone? She rolled over and shimmied her hips, reaching out with her Talent to grab him. Then she did things to help him forget.

When she was fifteen and Master Gibbet had taken her to Momma K, the courtesan had watched the wetboy bang her, then said, "Child, you fuck like you don't even feel it. Do you?"

There was no lying to Momma K, so Vi had admitted it. Her sex was totally numb. "Well," Momma K had said, "you'll never be the best, but it's nothing we can't overcome. The oldest magic is sex magic. With your tits and all the Talent you've got, I can still make you into something special." So Vi used her skills now, cursing the effete asshole in a whisper—the words didn't have to match her intent, but like all Talented women, she had to speak to use her powers.

Stephan moaned like a dumb animal and in moments he was finished. While he was still in a stupor, as a little fuck-you, she wiped herself clean on his fine cloak and sat cross-legged on the bed in the armor of her nudity.

"Tell me, fat man," she said, looking at his pale rolls with such distaste that he covered himself in shame. He turned away.

"By all the gods, do you have to—"

"Tell me."

Stephan covered his eyes. "He used to get runners. They knew to come to my house. I sometimes overheard bits and pieces, but he was always so careful. He burned the few letters he got, always went outside to talk with the runners. But the night of the invas—the liberation—he got a runner, and he wrote a note here." Stephan grabbed a robe and pulled it around himself before walking over to his desk. He pulled out a sheet of Ceuran rice paper and handed it to her. It was blank.

"Hold it up to the light," he said.

Vi held the paper up in front of a lantern and could see faint impressions on it. "Save Logan Gyre," it read, in a neat, tiny script, "and the girl and the scarred woman if you can. I will reward you beyond your wildest dreams." Instead of a name, it was signed with two symbols: a heavy-lidded eye circumscribing a star, drawn without lifting pen from paper, and beside it a nine-pointed star. The first was the glyph of the Sa'kagé; the second the symbol of the Shinga. The two together meant every resource the Sa'kagé had was at the recipient's disposal.

"He left after that," Stephan said. "And never came back. I told him I loved him and he won't even see me."

"His name, fat man. Tell me his name."

"Jarl," he said. "Gods forgive me, the Shinga is Jarl."

In one of her poorest safe houses, all darkness and rats and roaches like everywhere in the Warrens, Jarl and Momma K were meeting with a dead man. He smiled as he pulled himself into the room. His right leg was bound with splints so he couldn't bend his knee, and his right arm was in a sling. Blood had seeped through the bandages around his elbow. He had a crutch, but instead of tucking it under his arm, he had to hold it in his right hand. The injury to his elbow kept him from using the crutch on the side his knee demanded, so he more hopped than limped. He had short-cropped gray hair, was muscular in a stringy-tough-old-man way, and though his face was drawn and gray, he smiled.

"Gwinvere," he said. "It's good to see that the years have respected you at least."

She smiled, and rather than commenting on his appearance—he looked like he'd been sleeping in gutters, his fine garments were soiled, and he stank—she said, "It's good to see you've not lost your silver tongue."

Brant Agon hopped to a chair and sat. "Reports of my demise and all that."

"Brant, this is Jarl, the new Shinga. Jarl, this is Baronet Brant Agon, formerly Lord General of Cenaria."

"What can I do for you, Lord General?" Jarl asked.

"You're too kind. I come here as little more than what you see: I look like a beggar, and I've come to beg. But I am more than a beggar. I've fought on every border this country has. I've fought in duels. I've led squads of two men, and I've led campaigns with five thousand. You're facing a fight. Khalidor has scattered our armies, but the power in Cenaria is the Sa'kagé, and the Godking knows it. He'll destroy you unless you destroy him first. You need warriors, and I am one. Wetboys have their place, but they can't do everything—as you saw a few weeks ago, they might only make things worse. I, on the other hand, can make your men more efficient, more disciplined, and better at killing. Just give me a place and put me in charge of men."

Jarl rocked back in his chair and tented his fingers. He stared at Brant Agon for a long time. Momma K schooled herself to silence. She'd been Shinga for so long, it was hard to risk letting Jarl make missteps, but she'd made her decision. Let Jarl take the life and the power and the gray hairs. She would help until he didn't need her help anymore.

"Why are you here, Lord Agon?" Jarl asked. "Why me? Terah Graesin has an army. If you'd had your way, the Sa'kagé would have been wiped out years ago."

Momma K said, "We heard you were killed in an ambush."

"Roth Ursuul spared me," Brant said bitterly. "As a reward for my stupidity. It was my idea that Logan Gyre marry Jenine Gunder. I thought that if the king's line were assured, it would prevent a coup. Instead, it just got Logan and Jenine killed, too."

"Khalidor would never have let them live," Momma K said. "In fact, it's a mercy for Jenine. She could've been taken for Ursuul's entertainment, and the stories I've heard—"

"Anyway," Agon interrupted, unwilling to hear any absolution. "I crawled away. When I got home, my wife had been taken. I don't know if she's dead or if she's one of the 'entertainments.'"

"Oh, Brant, I'm so sorry," Momma K said.

He continued without looking at her, his face rigid. "I decided to live and make myself useful, Shinga. The noble houses want to fight a regular war. Duchess Graesin will try to wink and flatter her way to a throne. They don't have the will to win. I do, and I think you do too. I want to win. Failing that, I want to kill as many Khalidorans as I can."

"Are you proposing to serve me or be my partner?" Jarl asked.

"I don't give a rat's ass," Brant said. He paused. "And I know a lot more about rats' asses now than I ever thought I would."

"And what happens if we win?" Jarl asked. "You go back to trying to eliminate us?"

"If we win, you'll probably decide I'm too dangerous and have me killed." Brant smiled thinly. "At the moment, that doesn't bother me much."

"So I see." Jarl ran his hands over his dark microbraids, thinking. "I'll have no divided loyalty, Brant. You'll serve me, and only me. Do you have a problem with that?"

"Everyone I've sworn anything to is dead," Brant said. He shrugged. "Except maybe my wife. But I have some questions. If you're the new Shinga, who's the old one? Is he still alive? How many fronts is this war going to have?"

Jarl was silent.

"I'm the old Shinga," Momma K said. "I'm retiring, and not because Jarl is forcing me to. I've been grooming him for this for years, but now events have forced our hand. The Warrens are our center of power, Brant, and they're dying. Starvation is already a problem, but pestilence comes next. The Godking doesn't care what happens here. He hasn't set up any power structure at all. If we want to survive— and by we, I mean the Sa'kagé, but I also mean Cenaria and every wretched soul in the Warrens—things have to change. We can still get wagons and boats in; the soldiers check the cargoes for weapons, and they demand bribes, but we can survive that. What we can't survive is what happens once every wagon that comes in loaded with food gets plundered. People are starving and there are no guards to stop the theft, and if one wagon is plundered, every wagon thereafter will be. If that happens, the merchants will stop sending anything in. Then everyone will die. We aren't there yet, but we're close."

"So what are you going to do?" Brant asked.

"We're going to set up a quiet government. Everyone knows me," Momma K said. "I can hire bashers to guard wagons; I can adjudicate disputes; I can direct the building of shelters."

"That makes you a target," Brant said.

"I'm a target no matter what," Momma K said. "We've lost some of the wetboys, and I don't mean they're dead. The wetboys swear a magically binding oath of obedience to the Shinga. The Godking has broken that bonding. I've learned that Hu Gibbet told the Godking who I was. Garoth doesn't believe a woman could be the Shinga, so now he's searching for the real one. But he might change his mind any day, whether I act publicly or whether I stay in the shadows. I can't control that, so I might as well do what needs to be done."

Momma K was as calm as any veteran warrior going into battle. She could tell that Brant Agon was astounded.

"Tell me my part," Brant said.

Jarl said, "You take your pick of my men and make them wytch hunters. After that, I want you to make defenses we can use if the army comes to the Warrens in force. The Khalidorans have wytches, soldiers, and some of our best people on their side. The only reason I'm still alive is that they don't know who I am. But welcome aboard."

"My pleasure." Brant Agon bowed awkwardly because of his injuries and followed a big bodyguard out the door.

When he was gone, Jarl turned to Momma K. "You didn't tell me you knew each other."

"I don't think I do know this Brant Agon," she said.

"Answer the question."

A slight smile touched her lips, amused and a little proud that Jarl was taking command. "Thirty years ago Brant fell in love with me. I was naive. I thought I loved him, too, and I ruined him."

"Did you love him?" Jarl asked, rather than ask what happened. The question was proof to Momma K that she'd chosen the right man to succeed her. Jarl could find cracks. But it was one thing to admire his ability, and another to experience it.

She smiled a smile that didn't reach her eyes. It wouldn't fool Jarl for a second, but after all these years, the mask was pure reflex. "I don't know. I don't remember. What does it matter?"

12

$\mathcal{G}$aelan Starfire is said to have thrown the blue ka'kari into the sea, creating the Tlaxini Maelstrom," Neph said. "If so, it may well be there still, but I have no idea how we would recover it. The white has been lost for six centuries. We once believed it to be at the Chantry, but your grandmother disproved that. The green was taken to Ladesh by Hrothan Steelbender and lost. I verified that Hrothan arrived in Ladesh some two hundred and twenty years ago, but could find nothing more. The silver was lost during the Hundred Years' War, and could be anywhere from Alitaera to Ceura, unless Garric Shadowbane somehow destroyed it. The red was cast into the heart of Ashwind Mountain—what is now Mount Tenji in Ceura—by Ferric Fireheart. The brown is rumored to be at the Makers' school in Ossein, but I doubt it."

"Why?" Garoth Ursuul asked.

"I don't think they could resist using it. With the mastery of earth, those petty Makers would become a hundred times more skilled in a heartbeat. Something they Made would appear sooner or later, and it would be clear that someone was Making at the level they did of old. That hasn't happened. Either the men of that school are less ambitious than I believe possible, or it isn't there. The other rumor was that it was bound into Caernarvon's Blue Giant—the castle. I take that to be nothing more than a semi-educated boast. It's not a particularly clever place to hide a ka'kari."

"But we have a solid lead on the red?"

"When Vürdmeister Quintus passed through Ceura, he said that the explosions of Mount Tenji are at least partly magical. The problem with that, and with the blue, is that—even if we could get at it—there's some doubt about whether even a ka'kari would be intact after having been exposed to so much elemental power for so long."

"You don't give me much, Neph."

"It's not exactly collecting seashells." His voice sounded greasy. He hated that.

"A deep insight." Garoth sighed. "And the black?"

"Not so much as a whisper. Not even in the oldest books. If what I Viewed was real, and the Ladeshian isn't simply delusional, it's the best kept secret I've ever heard of."

"That is the point of a secret, isn't it?" Garoth asked.

"Huh?"

"Fetch our Ladeshian songbird. I'll be needing some Dust."

Elene wanted him to sell the sword. For the past ten nights, they'd played their parts as if they were wooden puppets. Except that once in a while even puppets got to play different roles.

"You don't even look at it, Kylar. It just stays in that chest under the bed." Her dark eyebrows pushed together, forming the little worry wrinkles that he was getting to know so well.

He sat on the bed, rubbing his temples. He was so tired of this. So tired of everything. Did she really expect him to answer? Of course she did. It was all words and wasted air. Why did women always believe that talking about a problem would fix it? Some issues were corpses. Hot air made them fester and rot and spread their disease to everything else. Better to bury it and move on.

Like Durzo. Worm food.

"It was my master's sword. He gave it to me," Kylar said, only a little late for his cue.

"Your master gave you a lot of things, beatings not least among them. He was an evil man."

That one stirred some rage. "You don't know anything about Durzo Blint. He was a great man. He died to give me a chance—"

"Fine, fine! Let's talk about what I do know," Elene said. She was on the verge of tears again, damn her. She was just as frustrated as he was. What made it worse was that she wasn't trying to manipulate him with those tears. "We're destitute. We lost everything, and we made Aunt Mea and Braen lose a lot, too. We have the means to make it right, and they deserve it. It's our fault those hoodlums torched the barn."

"You mean my fault," Kylar said. He could hear Uly crying in her room. She could hear them shouting through the wall.

If he'd dealt with Tom Gray his way, the man would have been too frightened to come within five blocks of Aunt Mea's. Kylar knew the music of the streets. He spoke the language of meat, played the subtle chords of intimidation, sang fear into the hearts of men. He knew and loved that music. But the notes of the songs Durzo taught weren't syllogisms. There was no thesis, counterpointed with antithesis, harmonized into synthesis. It wasn't that kind of music. The music of logic was too patrician for the streets, too subtle, the nuances all wrong.

The wetboy's leitmotif, whenever he played, was suffering, because everyone understands pain. It was brutal—but not without nuances. Without betraying his Talent, Kylar could have dealt with all six street toughs and Tom Gray. The young men would have left with bruises and astonishment. Tom, Kylar would have hurt. How much would have been Tom's choice. But even if she had had let him, could he have shown Elene that? What if she had seen his joy?

He looked at her face and she was so beautiful he found himself blinking back tears.

What the hell was that about?

Kylar said, "Why don't we skip all the horseshit where I say the sword is priceless and you say that means we'd have enough to start our shop and I say I just can't do it but I can't explain why so you say that I really do want to be a wetboy and you're just holding me back— and then you start crying. So why don't you just start crying, and then I'll hold you, and then we'll kiss for an hour, and then you'll stop me from going further, and then you'll fall asleep easily while I lie awake with my balls aching? Can we hop right to the kissing part? Because the only part of our whole fucking lives that I enjoy is when I think you're enjoying yourself as much as I am and I think maybe tonight we'll finally fuck. What do you say?"

Elene just took it. He could see her eyes welling, but she didn't cry.

"I say I love you, Kylar," Elene said quietly. Her face calmed and the worry wrinkle disappeared. "I believe in you, and I'm with you, no matter what. I love you. Do you hear me? I love you. I can't understand why you won't sell the sword..." she breathed. "But I can accept it. All right? I won't bring it up again."

So now he was really the bastard. He was sitting on a fortune instead of using it to support his wife and his daughter and pay back people who'd suffered for him. But she was going to accept him. How noble. The worst of it was he knew—dammit, he knew because he could always see through her—that she wasn't grabbing the moral high ground to be a bitch. She was trying to do the right thing. It just made the contrast between them that much more pronounced.

She doesn't know me. She thinks she knows me, but she doesn't. She accepted me thinking Kylar was just an older, slightly dirtied version of Azoth. I'm not dirty, I am filth. I kill people because I like it.

"Come to bed, honey," Elene said. She was undressing, and the swell of her breasts through her shift and the curves of her hips and her long legs roused the same fire in him it always did. Her skin glowed in the candlelight and his eyes fixed on the point of one nipple as she blew out the candle. He was already in his undergarments, and he wanted her. He wanted her so fiercely it shook him.

He lay down, but he didn't touch her. The ka'kari had cursed him with perfect vision despite any darkness. Cursed, because he could still see her. He could see the pain on her face. His lust was a chain and he felt a slave to it and it disgusted him, so when she turned toward him and touched him, he didn't move. He rolled onto his back and stared at the ceiling.

Looks like I skipped everything to the balls aching part.

I shouldn't be here. What am I doing? Happiness isn't for murderers. I can't change. I'm worthless. I'm nothing. An herbalist without herbs, a father who's not a father, a husband who's not a husband, a killer who doesn't kill.

That sword is me. That's why I can't get rid of it. It's what I am. A sheathed sword worth a fortune sitting in the bottom of a trunk. Worse than useless. A waste.

He sat up in the bed, then stood. He reached underneath the bed and pulled out the narrow chest.

Elene sat up as he started pulling on his wetboy grays. "Honey?" she said.

He dressed in moments—Blint had made him practice even this—strapping knives to his arms and legs, securing a set of picks to a wrist and a folding grapnel to the small of his back, adjusting the gray folds of cloth so they'd dampen all sound, strapping Retribution to his back, and pulling on a black silk mask.

"Honey," Elene said, her voice tight. "What are you doing?"

He didn't go out the door and walk down the stairs. No, not tonight. Instead, he opened the window. The air smelled good. Free. He sucked a great breath deep into his lungs and held it as if he could trap that freedom within him. At the irony of the thought, he let it out all at once and looked at her.

"Just what I always do, love," Kylar said. "I'm fucking it up." With a surge of his Talent, he leapt out into the night.

*   *   *

Ferl Khalius had been given the shit duty again. After his unit had been slaughtered during the invasion, he'd been picked for every bad assignment: throwing bodies off that rickety half-burnt bridge; helping the cooks move supplies into the castle; helping the meisters build the Godking's new wall around the city; double and triple guard duties—and never a choice assignment like on the Vanden Bridge where the guards took a week's pay home in bribes every shift just for letting a few crooks across. Now this.

He looked at his prisoner with disgust. The man was fat, with the soft hands of a southron noble, though he wore his red beard in the Khalidoran fashion. His nose was crooked and his eyebrows looked like brushes. He stared at Ferl with obvious anxiety.

Ferl wasn't supposed to talk to him. Ferl wasn't supposed to know who he was. But from the first, he'd had a bad feeling about this, ever since a captain had told him the Vürdmeisters wanted to see him. They'd requested him by name. He was to report immediately.

That was something no Khalidoran wanted to hear. Ferl thought it was about his little souvenir, the dragon-hilted sword he'd taken from the bridge. But that hadn't been why they'd wanted him, though he'd nearly wet himself when he saw he was speaking with the Lodricari Vürdmeister Neph Dada himself. No Vürdmeister was normal, but Neph was spooky even for a Vürdmeister. Ferl had stared at the twelve knotted cords representing the shu'ras Neph had mastered for the entire time Neph spoke. It was too scary to look at his face.

Neph had given Ferl and Ferl alone this assignment. He was forbidden to speak about it with other soldiers, forbidden to even associate with them for the duration of the assignment. He and the noble were confined to some tradesman's house on the east side. Meisters had hastily made part of the house a prison. *Meisters* had done the work. There was only one reason for that: this was so important it had to be done instantly and without anyone's knowledge. Then they'd left him with enough food for several months and forbidden him to leave.

That left everything feeling wrong. Ferl Khalius hadn't become second—now first—in his warband by being stupid. He'd spoken with the noble and learned his name was Baron Kirof. The baron claimed not to know why he had been imprisoned. He protested his innocence and loyalty to Khalidor—and the fact he wasted his breath telling a mere soldier told Ferl that Baron Kirof wasn't very bright.

Disobeying his orders, Ferl snuck away and found out that Baron Kirof had supposedly been murdered. The good Khalidoran duke, Tenser Vargun, was now rotting in the Maw for having killed a Cenarian noble who wasn't dead.

That's when Ferl knew he was screwed. His imagination couldn't paint any picture in which things turned out well for Ferl Khalius. Why would you assign a man without a unit to this? Because you could kill him and no one would notice. When the time came, Baron Kirof would be released or killed—the only reason to keep him alive when he was supposed to be dead had to be so they could produce him at some point. But Ferl? Ferl would just be evidence that the Vürdmeisters were lying.

I should have gone back to Khalidor. He'd been offered a job tending the oxen of the baggage train. He'd almost taken it. If he had, he might be on his way back to his clan by now. But everyone who escorted the treasure to Khalidor was thoroughly searched before they were released, and that would mean losing his precious sword. So he'd stayed, sure he could pick up a small fortune while they sacked the city. Right.

"I should kill you," Ferl said. "I should kill you just to spite them."

The fat man turned a paler shade. He could tell that Ferl meant it.

"Tell me, fatty," Ferl said. "If the Vürdmeisters told you that you could live if you lied about who kidnapped you, would you do it?"

"What kind of stupid question is that?" Baron Kirof asked.

So they'd known Kirof would play along. "You're a brave man, aren't you, fatty?"

"What?" Baron Kirof asked. "I can't understand your accent. Why do you keep calling me forty?"

"Fatty. Fatty!"

"I'm not forty. I'm thirty-six."

Ferl's hand darted through the bars and he grabbed a handful of the baron's blubber and squeezed it as hard as he could. Baron Kirof's eyes widened and he squealed and tried to pull away, but Ferl held him against the bars by his fat. "Fatty! Fatty!" he said. He grabbed the baron's cheek and squeezed it with his other hand. The man flailed, trying to knock Ferl's hands away, but he was too weak. He wailed. "Fatty!" Ferl yelled in his face. Then he released him.

The baron dropped back in his cell onto his bed and rubbed his cheek and his love handle, his eyes misty with tears. "Fatty?" he asked, wounded.

Ferl was lucky he didn't have a spear on hand. "Get your fat ass moving," he said. "We're leaving."

13

Just moving, leaping from roof to roof, flying over the world below, filled Kylar's heart with joy. Cenaria's buildings had been a mix of Ceuran-style rice fiber and bamboo houses with steep clay-shingled roofs and red brick and wood homes with thatch. It was rarely possible to move from roof to roof. Here, hundreds of miles from the nearest rice paddy and without the threat of snow, all the roofs were flat and solid clay, supported with good wood. For a man of Kylar's talents, they made a highway in the air.

Kylar reveled in it. He reveled in the strength of his muscles, reveled in the way the night air tasted and the secret power of moving through the night as a shadow. Everything was right. Nothing fit like his wetboy grays. Designed by Cenaria's best tailor, Master Piccun, they moved with him. The mottled colors broke up his silhouette and would have made even a man without Talent difficult to see.

He paused at the edge of a building, rolling his neck, and limbering up his back as he scooted back. The gap to the warehouse roof was a good twenty feet wide. He blew out a breath, and ran. His steps made scritching noises as he sprinted toward the edge. He leapt and his legs kept pumping as if he were running on air as he flew over the alley. He cleared the warehouse roof easily, landing six feet in.

He hurtled straight at a wall where part of the roof rose to a smaller third story. It was too high for him to jump and grab the edge. Instead, he ran up the wall as far as he could and then vaulted off it. He reached for the roof beams that extended out of the building, but he missed. His fingers were half a foot below the bottom of the beam.

Phantom hands whooshed out from his hands, extending his reach, and pulled the beam into his grasp. Kylar flipped up and landed on the top of the three-inch-wide beam. He wobbled for a moment, then steadied himself and stepped onto the roof.

He pumped his arm and whooped. It had only taken him three tries. Not bad. Not bad at all. Next time he'd try it while invisible. He was beginning to understand what his master had told him once about how much he would have to learn once he could use his Talent. Just shifting from using his Talent to leap to using it to extend the phantom hands was almost more than he could manage. Doing that while invisible and running full speed—well, he had nothing but time to train, did he?

For what? Time to train for what?

The thought soured the night air blowing in off the rivers. The freedom he'd felt blew away like fog. He was training for nothing. He was training because he couldn't stand to lie next to Elene with his thoughts and emotions and lust warring in him. He alternated between wanting to tear her clothes off and take her roughly and wanting to shake her and scream at her. He feared the intensity of those emotions, feared how they overlapped. That wasn't making love. That he even thought of it made him sick.

He leapt across another huge gap and a couple strolling arm in arm and he heard their surprised questions to each other—did something just fly over us?—he laughed aloud, and all his thoughts dissolved in the poppy liquor of action, movement, freedom.

As he slid past a small gang waiting to ambush whatever drunk might stumble down their alley, Kylar was fully alive. He didn't even need his powers. He was just there, every sense attuned, every fiber of his being poised to act—if one of the hoodlums discovered him, he'd have to use his powers, flee, attack, jump, duck, hide—something. As he slid past a hood holding a knife in one hand and a wineskin in the other, he could smell the man. Kylar had to regulate his breathing in time with the hood's so he wouldn't be heard, had to test every footstep, had to watch the changing light as the moon slid in and out of the clouds, had to watch the faces of all four young men as they joked and talked and passed a pipe of riot weed around.

"Hey, shut up!" the man nearest Kylar said. "We'll never get anyone if you idiots keep talking."

The men quieted. The hood's eyes passed straight over Kylar. Kylar had to keep himself from gasping aloud—there was something in the man's eyes. Something dark. It itched at something in the back of Kylar's mind.

Down the alley, a man stumbled out of an inn. He braced himself against a wall and then turned to walk toward the ambush.

What am I doing? Kylar realized that he didn't even have a plan. *I'm mad. I have to get out of here.* He hadn't broken his word to Elene. Not yet. After all, he'd never promised not to go out at night. He'd sworn not to kill.

He had to go. Now. If they started beating the drunk, he didn't know what he'd do. Or maybe he knew exactly what he'd do, and he couldn't do that.

The ka'kari oozed out of his pores like a sheen of iridescent black oil. It covered his skin and his clothes in an instant—covered him, shimmered for the briefest instant, and disappeared.

One of the hoodlums on the other side of the alley frowned and opened his mouth, but changed his mind and shook his head, sure that he'd imagined whatever-it-was he thought he saw.

Kylar leapt five feet in the air and grabbed the edge of the roof. He pulled himself up and started running away. When he heard a shout—and was that the thud of a cudgel hitting flesh?—he didn't stop. He didn't look.

He was only four blocks away, still fleeing, heading toward Aunt

Mea's house when he saw a girl being followed by three more hoodlums.

What the hell was she doing out this late? Anyone in this part of town had to know how stupid it was for a girl—a pretty golden-haired girl, of course—to travel alone.

It was none of his business. Golden Hair looked over her shoulder and Kylar could see her tear-streaked face. Wonderful. Some stupid emotional girl being emotional and stupid.

He stopped. *Dammit. You can't save the world, Kylar. You're not really the Night Angel. You're only a shadow and shadows can't touch anything.*

Now he swore again, loudly. In the street below, all four characters in the little melodrama looked up to the rooftop, but of course they didn't see him. They didn't see him drop into the street and start following them.

If they caught her, he'd have to kill them. He'd have to hurt them to get them off her, and then what was he going to do? Beat them up as an invisible man? Let them spread those stories? Someone would connect him to the Night Angel, sooner or later, and then everything would go to hell. No, if they caught her, and he had to break his promise to Elene, then he'd go all the way. So there was only one thing to do: make sure they didn't catch her.

Golden Hair did the first sensible thing she'd done all night—she started running. The hoodlums split up and started after her. Kylar drew Retribution off his back, but in its scabbard. He ran behind one of the running hoodlums, timed the man's steps, and with the sheathed sword he knocked one foot behind the other in the middle of the man's stride. The hoodlum went down hard, and his partner barely had time to look over his shoulder before he too encountered the ground in a far more intimate fashion than he would have liked.

Both men cursed, but they weren't too bright. They jumped up and started running after the girl again, once more closing ground rapidly. This time, Kylar tripped one into the other one. The men went down in a tangle of limbs and began cursing and hitting each other. By the time they got up, the girl was gone.

Kylar lost sight of the girl and the last hoodlum. He leapt up to a roof and sprinted after the girl. As he ran, he dropped his invisibility so he could use all of his Talent for speed. After flying across several more rooftops, he caught sight of Golden Hair again. She was a block away from the only house in a dim alley that had a lantern burning in the window. Doubtless it was her home.

Then Kylar saw the last hoodlum, coming down an intersecting alley Golden Hair would have to pass. The man caught sight of her and sank back into the shadows.

There was no time. Kylar was still more than a block behind them. He sprinted to the edge of a building and leapt unseen over Golden Hair, drawing Retribution before he landed in the little alley, right in front of the hoodlum.

The man had drawn a knife and in an instant Kylar saw from the pools of darkness in his eyes a deep, unreasoning hatred spawned from some perceived slight. The man had murdered before, and he planned to murder Golden Hair tonight. Kylar didn't know how he knew, but he knew. And seeing that darkness that demanded death, it came to him that he'd seen it before. He'd seen it in Prince Ursuul's eyes. Only afterward had he decided he must have been imagining things.

There was a moment of stunned silence as hoodlum and Night Angel stared at each other.

"Mother? Father?" the girl called out as she passed the alley.

The hoodlum attacked and Retribution darted out, punching through the hoodlum's solar plexus, driving the air from his lungs and pinning him to the wall.

Around the corner, a door was flung open and Golden Hair was ushered inside in a storm of blubbered apologies and forgiveness and tears. Kylar gathered that she'd fought with her parents about something none of them remembered and had stormed off.

The hoodlum twitched. He was straining to breathe, but he couldn't because Retribution had crushed his ribs and pushed them hard against his diaphragm. His legs were completely limp. Kylar must have at least partially cut his spine, because the only thing keeping him standing was the sword pinning him to the wall.

The man was already dead, he just hadn't figured it out yet.

Damn me, what have I done? Kylar pulled Retribution back and the hoodlum fell. Dispassionately, Kylar stabbed the sword into his heart. He was committed now. He couldn't leave the body here. It was unprofessional, and its discovery would certainly wreck the tenuous happiness he could hear through the open windows. There was a little blood on the wall, so Kylar blotted it up with the hoodlum's cloak, and then scrubbed dirt over it.

Inside, it was all joy and reconciliation. Mother served a kettle of ootai and clucked about how worried they had been. The girl was telling her story of how she'd been followed and run away and been so terrified and somehow the men kept falling.

Kylar felt a surge of pride, followed by disgust at how sweetly domestic it was.

But that was a lie. He wasn't disgusted. He was moved. Moved and profoundly lonely. He was left outside, in the streets with the dead, alone. He kicked dirt over the blood on the ground, and stuffed rags into the corpse's wounds.

"Praise the God," mother said. "Your father and I have been praying for you the whole time."

That's me, Kylar thought as he hefted the body over his shoulder, *the answer to everyone's prayers. Except Elene's.*

"Why would anyone destroy a ka'kari, Neph?" The Godking was pacing in one of his state rooms.

"The southrons are frequently illogical, Your Holiness."

"But surely these heroes who supposedly destroyed the ka'kari—Garric Shadowbane, Gaelan Starfire, Ferric Fireheart—surely they must have been wytchborn. Not trained as meisters, of course, but Talented. Such warriors could have bonded the ka'kari themselves. And they didn't? We're saying that at least three warriors chose to destroy artifacts that could have made them ten times more powerful than they already were? Great men are not so selfless."

"Your Holiness," Neph said, "you're attempting to duplicate the thought processes of a people who embrace the virtues of weakness. These are people who tout compassion over justice, mercy over strength. Theirs is a diseased philosophy, a species of madness. Of course they do the inexplicable. Look at how eagerly Terah Graesin rushes to her doom."

The Godking waved that away. "Terah Graesin is a fool, but not all southrons are. If they were, my forefathers would have overrun them centuries ago."

"Surely they would have," Neph Dada said, "if not for the incursions from the Freeze."

Garoth dismissed that. The average meister had always been stronger than the average mage, often had more companions in his craft, and he and his fellows weren't split into bickering schools spread halfway across Midcyru. The Khalidoran armies were as good as most and better than many. Despite those advantages, the Godkings' ambitions had been foiled time and again.

"I feel…opposed," Garoth said.

"Opposed, Your Holiness?" Neph asked. He coughed and wheezed.

"Maybe these southrons really believe what they claim to about mercy and protecting the weak, though our experience here tells me they don't. But the call of power is not easily ignored, Neph. Perhaps one saint of their faiths might destroy a ka'kari that he could use. But how could all six ka'kari disappear and stay hidden for so long? You're talking generations of saints—each new guardian as virtuous as the one before. It doesn't make sense. One of them would fail."

"The ka'kari *have* surfaced from time to time."

"Yes, but ever more rarely as the centuries have passed. The last time was fifty years ago," Garoth said. "Someone has been trying to destroy or at least hide the ka'kari. That's the only thing that makes sense."

"So *someone* out there has been squirreling away ka'kari for seven centuries?" Neph asked, deadpan.

"Of course not some*one*," Garoth said. "But some...group. I find a small conspiracy much easier to swallow than a conspiracy of every southron saint who ever lived." He paused, following the idea. "Think about their very names—Shadowbane, Fireheart, Starfire?—those aren't surnames. They're assumed names. If I'm right, it may be that Garric Shadowbane, Ferric Fireheart, and Gaelan Starfire were the champions of this group, their avatars, as it were."

"And their avatar today...?" Neph asked.

Garoth smiled. "Now has a name. This morning, my Ladeshian bard sang. The man who walked these halls with a ka'kari, who killed my son, was either the legendary Durzo Blint or his apprentice Kylar Stern. Durzo Blint is dead. So if Kylar Stern is this avatar..." Garoth stopped dead. "It would explain why those heroes were willing to destroy a ka'kari. Because they couldn't use another. Because they'd already bonded one. They were the bearers of the black ka'kari."

"Your Holiness, is it not possible that rather than destroy those ka'kari they kept them?"

Garoth considered it. "It's possible. And Kylar might not be allied with them at all."

"In which case they might be trying to add the black to their collection," Neph said.

"We can't know that. We can't know anything until we get Kylar Stern. My songbird will make the perfect assassin. In the meantime, Neph, contact every meister and agent we have in the southlands and tell them to keep an eye out. I don't care if it costs me this entire kingdom, get me Kylar Stern. Alive, dead, whichever, just bring me that damned ka'kari."

14

The first weeks in Hell's Asshole had been the darkest, before Logan had become a monster. He'd made his bargains with the devil and with his own body. He'd eaten the meat that came to him that awful day, and when Fin had killed Scab, Logan had eaten flesh again. Logan had to kill Long Tom for that meat, and that killing had made him a monster. Being a monster made him safe. But he wasn't content to be safe. He wasn't content to merely survive. Logan lived with the feral, primal side of himself, but he wouldn't let that be all he was.

He shared his meat. He'd given some to Lilly, not for sex as the other Holers did, but for decency. She'd given him the advice that kept him human. He also shared with the other monsters: Tatts and Yimbo and Gnasher. He kept the choicest parts for himself—at least the choicest parts he could bear to eat. Arms and legs were one thing, but eating a man's heart, his brains, his eyes, cracking his bones to suck the marrow, that Logan wouldn't do. It was a thin line, and one he knew he would cross if things got much worse, but for now, he'd sunk deep enough, so he shared for squeamishness and he shared for nobility.

It was his first step to reclaiming his humanity. Fin would kill him the first chance he had. The monsters didn't care, so it was still possible to get them on his side. It wouldn't be loyalty, but anything might make all the difference.

Gnasher was a different story. Logan stayed close to Gnasher. He figured that the simpleton was the least likely to betray him, although he'd learned early on why Gnasher had been given his name. Every night, Gnasher ground his teeth. It was so loud that Logan was surprised the man had molars left.

The third week in, Logan woke to the sudden silence of Gnasher's teeth and listened in the darkness. Gnasher was listening, and his ears must have been better than Logan's, because a moment later, Logan heard footsteps.

Two Khalidoran guards appeared above their grate and looked down with distaste. The first was the one they hated. He opened the grate as he always did, and tossed their bread down the hole as he always did. It didn't matter that they knew he was going to do it, the monsters and the animals alike, even Logan, got up and stood around the Hole, hoping to get lucky with a bad throw. It only happened once or twice, but that was enough to keep their hope alive.

"Watch this," the guard said. He tore open the last loaf and pissed all over it, soaking it in urine. Then he tossed it in.

Logan, being the tallest, got most of it. He devoured it instantly, ignoring the stench, ignoring the warm wetness dripping down his chin, ignoring the debasement.

The Khalidoran roared with laughter. The second guard laughed uncertainly.

The next day the second guard came back, alone. He had bread, and it was clean, and he threw it to them, one loaf for each prisoner. With a thick accent and not looking any of them in the eye, he promised that he would bring bread every time he had a shift that he didn't share with Gorkhy.

That gave them all strength and hope and a name for the man they hated above all others.

Slowly, society returned. That first night, everyone had been so overwhelmed just to have bread that they hadn't even tried to steal loaves from each other. As they gained strength, they did fight. Within a few days, the mute Yimbo tangled with Fin and got killed. Logan watched, hoping for an opportunity to get Fin, but the fight was over too quickly. Fin's knife was too much of an advantage.

When the bread came, Logan made sure he got more than most—not only for the status, but to stay strong. He'd already lost every ounce of fat he'd ever had, and now he was losing his muscle. He was all sinews and lean hard muscles, but he was still big and he needed his strength. Still, he shared what he could with Lilly and Gnasher and Tatts.

More than two months in he made a breakthrough. He'd been feeling nervous, getting more and more on edge about Fin, with his damn sinew ropes that kept getting longer. Logan slept and woke to the sound of the demons that he now sometimes imagined made the howling noise—it wasn't wind, he was sure of that. It was either demons or the spirits of all the poor bastards who'd been thrown into the Hole over the centuries. His head throbbed in time with the howling. His jaw ached. He'd been grinding his teeth all night.

Then he found his humanity.

"Gnash," he said. "Gnasher, come here."

The big man looked at him blankly.

Logan scooted over and very slowly put his hands on Gnasher's jaw. He was afraid that Gnasher might snap at him—and if Gnasher bit him, down here an infection and death were more likely than not—but he reached up anyway. Gnasher looked puzzled, but he let Logan slowly massage his jaw. In moments, the look on the simple man's face changed. The tension in his face that Logan had assumed was part of his deformity relaxed.

When Logan stopped, the man roared and grabbed Logan. Logan thought that he was going to die, but Gnasher just hugged him. When Gnasher released him, Logan knew he had a friend for life, no matter this Hole life was nasty, brutish, and short. He would have wept—but he had no capacity for tears.

*   *   *

She had to kill Jarl.

Vi stood outside of Hu Gibbet's safe house and leaned her head against the doorframe. She needed to go inside, face Hu, get ready, and go kill Jarl. As simple as that, and her apprenticeship would be done and she'd never have to face Hu again. The Godking had even promised she could kill Hu if she wanted.

During the year Vi had spent learning the trade at Momma K's, Jarl had been her only friend. He had gone out of his way to help, especially in her first weeks when she'd been such a disaster. Because of his handsome, exotic Ladeshian features, quick tongue, intelligence, and warmth, everyone had liked Jarl, and not just the men and women who lined up for his services. (Lined up only figuratively, of course. Momma K would never tolerate anything so crass as a queue in the Blue Boar.) But Vi had always felt a kind of special bond between them.

Vi stopped thinking. She had a job to do. She checked the door again for traps. There were none. Hu got careless when he had company. She opened the door slowly, standing to one side and holding her open hands in the gap. Sometimes when Hu was blasted on mushrooms, he attacked first and didn't ask questions. When no attack came, Vi walked in.

Hu sat bare-chested in the corner of the cluttered front room in a rocking chair, but the chair was still and his eyes were closed. He wasn't asleep, though. Vi was intimately attuned to her master's every nuance; she knew how he breathed when he really slept. He held crochet hooks in his hands and a tiny, nearly completed white wool cap. A baby's bonnet this time, the sick fuck.

Pretending to believe he was asleep, Vi glanced in the bedroom. Two women were lying in the bed. Vi ignored them and started gathering her gear.

Finding Jarl would be no problem. She had only to put out word that she wanted to meet with him, and he'd welcome her. His guards would make sure she had no weapons, but after a time alone with him, they'd relax or Jarl would dismiss the guards and she could kill him with her bare hands. The problem was how not to kill Jarl.

She wasn't going to do it. Fuck the Godking. But the only way the Godking would excuse her disobedience in this was if she could do something else that pleased him even more.

Vi unlocked a wide cabinet and slid a drawer out. It held her collection of wigs, the best money could buy. Vi had become an expert at taking care of them, styling them, putting them on, and affixing them firmly enough for the rigors of her trade at a moment's notice. There was something comforting about the tug on her scalp of a firm ponytail, sometimes drawn so tight under her wig that it gave her a headache. At Momma K's, Vi had been introduced to a Talented courtesan who told Vi she could teach her to change the color or style of her own hair with the Talent, but Vi wasn't interested. She might share her body, or Hu might take her body, but her hair was her own, and it was precious to her. She didn't even like men to touch the wigs, but she could tolerate it. When she whored, she wore a wig for the slight margin of disguise it gave her—flaming redheads weren't that common outside Ceura. When she was working as a wetboy, she wore her hair in that same tight ponytail. It was sensible, controlled, and efficient, just like her. The only time her hair hung loose was in the few minutes before bedtime, and then only when she was alone and safe.

After selecting a fine, straight chin-length black wig and a long, wavy brunette, Vi grabbed the creams she needed to dye her eyebrows and makeup to darken her complexion, then packed her weapons.

She was tying her saddlebags closed when a hand grabbed her breast and squeezed viciously. Vi gasped, flinching in pain and surprise, and hating herself a moment afterward. Hu chuckled low in her ear, pressing his body against her back. "Hello, gorgeous, where've you been?" he asked, trailing his hands down to her hips.

"Working. Remember?" she said, turning with difficulty. When he let her turn, she knew he was still blasted.

He wrapped himself around her, and the revulsion and hatred warred for one moment with the familiar passivity before losing. She let him push her head to one side so he could nuzzle her neck. He kissed her gently, then stopped. "You're not wearing that perfume I like," he said, still mellow, but with a note of surprise in his voice that she could be so stupid. Vi knew him well enough to know he was a hairsbreadth from violence.

"I've been working. For the Godking." Vi didn't let the smallest iota of fear sneak into her voice. Showing fear to Hu was like throwing bloody meat to a pack of wild dogs.

"Oooh," Hu said, abruptly mellow once more. His eyes were widely dilated. "I've been having a little party. Celebrating." He waved toward the bedroom. "I got a countess and a...damn, can't remember, but the other one's a wildcat. You wanna join us?"

"What are you celebrating?" Vi asked.

"Durzo!" Hu said. He released Vi abruptly and danced in a little circle, grabbing another mushroom off a table and popping it in his mouth, and trying to grab one more, but missing. "Durzo Blint is dead!" He laughed.

Vi scooped up the mushroom he'd missed. "Really? I heard that rumor, but you're sure?" Hu had always hated Durzo Blint. The two were mentioned in the same breath as the city's best wetboys, but usually Durzo's name came first. Hu had killed men for saying that, but he'd never gone after Durzo. If he'd thought he could kill Durzo, she knew, he would have.

"Momma K was friends with him, and she didn't believe he was dead, so she took some men to where he was buried—and sure enough! Dead dead dead." Hu laughed again. He grabbed the mushroom from Vi, then stopped dancing. "Unlike his apprentice, the job you fucked up." He took a flask of poppy spirits and drank. "I was going to go kill him, you know, just to piss off Blint's ghost. A hundred crowns I wasted in bribes, and turns out he left the city. Whoa," he rocked on his feet. "That one was potent. Help me sit down."

Vi's chest tightened. That was her answer. Kylar Stern was the Night Angel. He'd killed the Godking's son. Killing Kylar was the only thing that might please the Godking enough for him to forgive her for not killing Jarl. She grabbed Hu's arm and guided him to his chair, making sure he avoided the razor-lined baby bonnet. "Where is he, master? Where did he go?"

"You know, you don't come around enough. After all I've done for you, you bitch." His face turned ugly and he pulled her roughly into his lap. The minutes before Hu passed out were dangerous: he might fumble weakly as a drunk, and then use the crushing strength of his Talent to compensate and hurt or kill her accidentally. So she fell into his arms, quiescent, making herself numb. Hu was distracted by her body. He tried to caress her, but fumbled his hand across the folds of her tunic instead.

"Where is Blint's apprentice, master?" Vi asked. "Where did he go?"

"He moved to Caernarvon, gave up the way of shadows. Who's the best now, huh?"

"You're the best," Vi said, easing off his lap. "You've always been the best."

"Viridiana," Hu said. She froze. He never called her by her full name. She turned warily, wondering if the mushrooms had been harmless, the poppy wine just water. It wouldn't be the first time he'd pretended intoxication to test her loyalty. But Hu's eyes were half-lidded, his figure totally relaxed in his chair. "I love you," Hu said. "These bitches got nothing..." his words trailed off and his breath took on the cadence of sleep.

Vi suddenly wanted to bathe. She grabbed her saddlebags and her sword. Then stopped.

Hu was unconscious. She was sure of it. She could draw her blade and bury it in his heart in less than a second. He deserved it a hundred times over. He deserved a hundred times worse. She took the hilt in her hand and drew the blade slowly, silently. She turned and looked at her master, thinking of a thousand humiliations he'd inflicted on her. A thousand defilements until he'd broken her. It was hard to breathe.

Vi turned on her heel, sheathed the sword, and flung the saddlebags over her shoulder. She got as far as the door, then paused. She walked back to the bedroom. The women were awake now, one blasted with a glassy-eyed stare, the other one buck-toothed and busty.

"Hu gets bored," Vi said. "I give you a coin flip chance of living through every day you spend with him. If you want to leave, he's asleep now."

"You're just jealous," the buck-toothed one said. "You just want him for yourself."

"Your funeral," Vi said, and left.

15

"Is the Sa'kagé at war, or not?" Brant asked.

Jarl shifted in his seat. Momma K said nothing. She was letting him lead, if he could.

The safe house had taken on the appearance of a war room, that was sure. Brant had brought maps. He was gathering data on Khalidoran troop strength, noting where each unit was stationed, where food and supplies were distributed, and constructing a chart of the Khalidoran military hierarchy, cross-referenced with where the Sa'kagé had informants, along with ratings of the informants' reliability and access.

"That's a more difficult question to answer than—" Jarl said.

"No," Brant said. "It's not."

"I feel that we're in a kind of war—"

"You feel? Are you a leader or a poet, sissy boy?"

"Sissy boy?" Jarl demanded. "What's that mean?"

Momma K stood up.

"Sit down," both men said.

They looked at each other, scowling. Momma K sniffed, and sat. After a moment, Jarl said, "I'm waiting for an answer."

"Do you have a dick or do you just suck them?" Brant asked.

"Are you hoping to get lucky?" Jarl asked.

"Wrong answer," Brant said, shaking his head. "A good leader is never snide—"

Jarl punched him in the face. The general collapsed. Jarl stood over him, and drew a sword. "That's how I lead, Brant. My enemies underestimate me, and I hit them when they aren't expecting it. I listen to you, but you serve me. The next time you make a dick comment, I'll have yours fed to you." His face was cool. He brought the sword up between Brant's legs. "That's not an idle threat."

Brant found his crutch, stood with Jarl's help and brushed off his new clothes. "Well, we've just had a teachable moment. I'm touched. I think I'll write a poem. Your answer is...?"

The poem comment almost set Jarl off. He was about to say something when he saw Momma K's mouth twitch. It was a joke. *So this is military humor.* Jarl shook his head. This was going to be a challenge.

Good gods, the man was a bulldog. "We're at war," Jarl said, not liking the feeling of giving in.

"How good is your grip on the Sa'kagé?" Brant asked. "Because I've got serious problems here. Or rather, you do."

"Not great," Jarl said. "The Khalidorans have had a galvanizing influence, but revenue is way down, and command is breaking down: people not reporting to superiors, that sort of thing. A lot of people think the occupation is bound to get easier now. They want business as usual."

"Sounds smart of them. What's your master plan to oppose them?"

Jarl frowned. There was no master plan, and Brant made that seem incredibly stupid. "We—I—had planned to see what they did. I wanted to learn more about them and then oppose them however I needed to."

"Does it strike you as a good idea to let your enemy launch fully formed stratagems on you and then be forced to react from a position of weakness?" Brant asked.

"That's more a rhetorical bludgeon than a question, general," Jarl said.

"Thank you," the general said. Momma K suppressed a smile.

"What do you propose?" Jarl asked.

"Gwinvere ruled the Sa'kagé in total secrecy, with puppet Shingas, right?"

Jarl nodded.

"So who's been the puppet Shinga since Khalidor invaded?"

Jarl winced. "I, uh, haven't exactly installed one."

"Not exactly?" Brant arched a bushy gray eyebrow.

"Brant," Momma K said. "A little gentler."

Brant adjusted his arm in its sling, wincing. "Look at it from the street, Jarl. For more than a month, they've had no leader. Not just a bad leader. None. Gwinvere's little government has been helping everyone and so far it's going well, but your Sa'kagé thugs—sorry, *people*—have been in the same boat as everyone else. So why keep paying dues? Gwinvere was able to be a shadow Shinga, because there was never a threat like this. This is a war. You need an army. Armies need a leader. You need to be that leader, and you can't do that from the shadows."

"If I announce who I am, they'll kill me."

"They'll try," Brant said. "And they'll succeed unless you can collect a core of competent people who are absolutely loyal to you. People willing to kill and to die for you."

"These aren't soldiers from good families who've been brought up on loyalty and duty and courage," Jarl said. "We're talking about thieves and prostitutes and pickpockets, people who only think about themselves and their own survival."

"And that's what they'll say," Momma K said so quietly Jarl barely heard her, "unless you see what they may be, and make them see it."

"When I was a general, my best soldiers came from the Warrens," Brant said. "They became the best because they had everything to gain."

"So what exactly do you propose?" Jarl asked.

"I propose you work yourself out of a job," Brant said. "Give your crooks a dream of a better life, a better way for their children, and a chance to see themselves as heroes, and you'll have yourself an army."

He paused to let it sink in, and soon Jarl's heart was pounding, his mind racing. It was audacious. It was big. It was a chance to use power for more than just keeping power. He could see the outlines of a plan starting to fit together. His mind was already tapping what people he would place in which positions. Fragments of speeches were glomming together. Oh, it was seductive. Brant wasn't just telling Jarl to give the crooks a dream; Brant was giving Jarl a dream. He could be a different type of Shinga. He could be noble. Revered. If he were successful, he could probably even become legitimate, be given real titles by whichever noble family he put back in power. Gods, it was seductive!

But it meant revealing himself. Committing himself. Right now, he was a secret. Everyone thought he was just a retired rent boy. Less than a dozen people knew he was the Shinga. If he wanted to, he could just stop communicating with them. If he didn't try, he couldn't fail.

"Jarl," Momma K said, her voice gentle. "Just because it's a dream doesn't mean it's a lie."

He looked from one to the other of them, wondering how deeply they read him. Momma K probably read him to the core. It was scary. He should have suspected something just by her silence, but he couldn't be angry with her. She'd had more patience with him than he deserved.

Work myself out of a job. Elene had said she couldn't imagine Cenaria without the Sa'kagé polluting everything, but Jarl could. It would be a city where birth on the west side didn't mean hopelessness, exploitation, time in the guilds, poverty, and death. He'd been lucky to get a job working for Momma K. The Warrens offered almost no honest jobs, certainly not for orphans. The Sa'kagé was fed directly from a self-renewing underclass of whores and thieves who abandoned their children as they themselves had been abandoned before. But it could be different, couldn't it?

Just because it's a dream doesn't mean it's a lie. They were suggesting he inject hope into the Warrens. "Fine," Jarl said. "On one condition, Brant: if they kill me—whichever they it happens to be—I want you to write a poem for my funeral."

"Agreed," the general said, grinning, "and I'll make it real emotional."

16

Kylar sat on the bed in the darkness looking at Elene's sleeping form. She was the kind of girl who just couldn't stay up late, no matter how she tried. The sight of her filled him with such tenderness and wretchedness he could hardly bear it. Since she'd promised not to ask him to sell Retribution, she'd been true to her word. No surprise there, but she hadn't even hinted.

He loved her. He wasn't good enough for her.

He'd always believed that you became like those you spent your time with. Maybe that was part of it. He loved all the things about her that he wasn't. Openness, purity, compassion. She was smiles and sunshine, and he belonged to the night. He wanted to be a good man, ached for it, but maybe some people were just born better than others.

After that first night, he'd sworn to himself that he wouldn't kill again. He would go out and train, but he wouldn't kill. So he trained for nothing and honed abilities he'd sworn not to use. Training was a pale imitation of battle, but he would be satisfied with it.

His resolution held for six days, then he was down at the docks and found a pirate savagely beating a cabin boy. Kylar had only intended to separate them, but the pirate's eyes demanded death. Retribution delivered it. On the seventh night, he'd been practicing simply hiding outside a midtown tavern, trying to avoid places that were likely to bring him across pimps or thieves or rapists or murderers. A man had passed by who ran a circle of child pickpockets—a tyrant who kept the children in line through sheer brutality. Retribution found the man's heart before Kylar could stop himself. On the eighth night, he'd been in the nobles' district, hoping to find less violence there, when he heard a nobleman beating his mistress. The Night Angel came in invisibly and broke both the man's arms.

Kylar held Retribution in his lap, looking at Elene. Every day, he promised himself he wouldn't kill, not ever again, and he hadn't killed for six nights. But part of him knew that was because he'd been lucky. The worst part of it was that he didn't feel guilty for the murders. He'd felt awful every time he'd killed for Durzo. These kills did nothing. He felt guilty only for lying.

Maybe he was becoming a Hu Gibbet. Maybe he needed killing now. Maybe he was becoming a monster.

Each day he worked with Aunt Mea. Durzo had rarely praised Kylar, so he'd never realized how much he had learned from the old wetboy, but as Kylar spent hours with Aunt Mea, cataloguing her herbs, repackaging some of them so they would keep longer, throwing out those that had lost their potency, labeling the rest with dates and notes on their origins, he began to see how much he did know. He was nowhere near Durzo's level of proficiency, but the man had had a few centuries on him.

He had to be careful, though. Aunt Mea used many herbs medicinally that he had used for poison. She had once set aside the roots of a silverleaf, saying they were too dangerous and that she could only use the leaves. Without thinking, he'd drawn up a chart of the lethal doses of the plant's leaves, roots, and seeds by their various preparations, whether in a tincture, a powder, a paste, or a tea, cross-referenced by body weight, sex, and age of the—he almost wrote of the "deader," and only changed it to "patient" at the last second. When he looked up, Aunt Mea was staring at him.

"I've never seen such a detailed chart," she said. "This is…very impressive, Kylar."

He tried to be more careful after that, but they consistently ran into the same problems. Over his career, Durzo had experimented thousands of times with all kinds of herbs. When he'd had a deader that he could kill without a deadline, he'd tried five or six different herbs. Kylar was beginning to appreciate that Durzo had probably known more about herbs than anyone alive—though he had usually been hired to kill healthy people, so sometimes what Kylar knew was useless.

One day, a man came to Aunt Mea's shop desperate for help. His master was dying and four other physickers had been unable to help him. Aunt Mea sometimes did more than midwifing so the servant had come to her as a last resort. But Aunt Mea had been gone. Kylar had felt too awkward to go to the sick man's house, but after quizzing the servant, he'd made a potion. He heard later that the man recovered. It was strangely warming. He'd saved a life, just like that.

Still, he felt guilty living on Aunt Mea's charity. He'd spent several weeks putting her shop in order, because despite her gift for working with people, her organization skills were abominable. But he hadn't done anything valuable for her. He wasn't making her any money. Elene had gotten a job as a maid, but the pay was barely enough to cover their food. Braen was getting more and more surly, muttering about freeloaders, and Kylar couldn't blame him.

Kylar brushed his fingertips over Retribution. Every time he strapped the blade on, he acted as judge and executioner. The blade had become the emblem of his oath-breaking.

Not tonight. Kylar put it back in its box and, gathering his Talent, leapt out the window. He crossed the roofs to find Golden Hair's house and put everything else out of his mind. He had to worry all day long; he wasn't going to ruin his nights too.

The whole family was there, asleep in their little one-room shack. Kylar turned to go but something stopped him. The girl and her father were asleep. The mother's lips were moving. At first, Kylar thought she was dreaming, but then her eyes opened and she got out of bed.

She didn't light any candles. She briefly looked out the narrow

window, where Kylar stood invisible. She looked afraid, so much so
that he double-checked his invisibility. But her eyes weren't fixed on
him. He looked behind himself, but there was nobody in the street.
Golden Hair's mother shivered and knelt by the bed.

Praying! Sonuvabitch. Kylar was at once embarrassed and angry to
witness something so personal. He wasn't sure why. He cursed silently
and turned to go.

Three armed men were coming down the street. Kylar recognized
two of them as the guys who'd chased Golden Hair the other night.

"She's a wytch, I'm telling you," one of the thugs said to the man
Kylar didn't recognize.

"It's true, Shinga, I swear," the other said.

You're joking. Caernarvon's Shinga himself was checking out
some thugs' story about a wytch? A wytch! As if a wytch would have
tripped the men rather than killing them.

Kylar heard something and looked back inside. The woman had
woken her husband and both were praying now. It was odd, because
from their bed, there was no way they could have seen the Sa'kagé
thugs. Maybe the woman had some Talent.

Praying for protection. Kylar sneered, and the small mean part of
him wanted to leave. Let their God solve his own problems. Kylar got
as far as turning his back, but he couldn't do it.

"Barush," one of the thugs whispered to the Shinga. "What do
we do?"

The Shinga slapped the man.

"Sorry! Sorry!" the man whined. "I mean, Shinga Sniggle, what do
we do?"

"We kill them."

Good gods. It was stunning. The Sa'kagé here was such a bad par-
ody of a Sa'kagé that Kylar wanted to laugh. Except it wasn't funny.
The Shinga *slapped* men to get their respect? In Cenaria, when Pon
Dradin had looked at men with less than full approval, they wilted.
And he hadn't even been the real Shinga.

Kylar almost left from sheer disgust. The ineptitude!

Still, one didn't need much to kill. A wetboy knew that.

Oh, it made a lovely quandary, didn't it? Here he was, maybe one of the most skilled killers in the world. He could kill all three men before they could make a sound. And yet he couldn't even hurt them. In front of him were the dregs of the underworld, and they would kill while he couldn't. Lovely.

They were only twenty paces away. "What if...what if she uses wytchery again, Shinga?" Of course they didn't bother to formulate their plan before they got to the target. That would be a bit professional.

Barush Sniggle snorted, approaching the door. "I ain't afraid of that shit."

As Kylar saw the man's eyes, his hand went to his back—but Retribution was gone. His momentary surprise was enough to break him free of the killing impulse. He'd sworn. Damn him, he'd sworn. There had to be another way. Tonight, there would be another way.

So Kylar materialized in front of the Shinga. Or rather, parts of him did. He let some light shine through the ka'kari that covered him so that he appeared with a smoky translucence. The curve of an oily-iridescent black bicep shimmered in and out of visibility, then the curve of broad shoulders, the V of his torso, the lines of his chest muscles—all of them exaggerated so they seemed larger than they were. They faded in and out of sight like a ghost.

Barush Sniggle froze, and then Kylar topped it with his masterstroke. The ka'kari became solid over his eyes, making them gleam like metallic black jewels in midair. Then the rest of his face appeared, covered in a mask of black shimmering metal molded to his skin. It was menacing. It was more than menacing. It was the very face of Judgment, of Retribution made flesh, and at what Kylar saw within the Shinga's eyes—hatredenvygreedmurderbetrayal—the mask became fierce. Kylar had to dig his fingernails into his palms to keep from ending him.

The Shinga dropped his cudgel, nerveless. Kylar wasn't surprised;

he knew what the man was seeing—because, well, because he'd practiced it in the mirror.

"This family," Kylar said in a voice as silky soft as a stalking cat, "is under my protection."

He brought his left hand up and flexed it. With a hiss, the ka'kari slid out into a long, smoking punch dagger. Low blue fire sprang up in his eyes. It was totally gratuitous—it spoiled his night vision, not to mention feeling unpleasant, but the effect was worth it.

The Shinga shook, petrified, his mouth slack, and Kylar saw a stain spreading on the man's trousers and a puddle collecting around his feet.

"Run," Kylar said, showing a glimpse of blue fire in his mouth. *I'm not going to taste anything for a week.*

The thugs broke and ran, dropping their weapons, but Kylar felt no satisfaction. Just when he thought he couldn't paint himself any further into a corner, he'd done so brilliantly. What had Durzo Blint told him more than a decade ago? "A threat's a promise, boy. On the street, you can lie about everything except your threats. An empty threat is surrender."

Feeling sick, Kylar looked into the house. The woman and her husband were still kneeling by their bed, holding hands. They hadn't seen or heard anything. As Kylar looked in, though, the woman squeezed her husband's hand.

"We're going to be all right," she finally said aloud. "I can tell. I feel better now."

I'm glad one of us does.

"Not that long ago, you in this room were wives, mothers, a potter, a brewer, a seamstress, a ship captain, a glass blower, an importer, a moneychanger," Jarl said.

This was Jarl's sixth time preaching and it hadn't gotten easier. As he looked around at the rent girls and bashers of the Craven Dragon gathered before their shift, he saw awkwardness. They were whores now—and not by choice. Most didn't like to acknowledge that they had ever been anything else. It was too hard.

"Not that long ago," Jarl said. "I was a bender."

That lifted eyebrows, though Jarl bet they already knew he'd been a rent boy. He'd chosen the slur on purpose, to show it had no power over him. Even among whores, rent boys were second-class. They might be adored by the girls, but the clientele treated male prostitutes like dirt. A whore—though a whore—was still a woman, but a bender was something less than a man. That the new Shinga used to be one wasn't the kind of thing one would expect him to admit, much less announce.

"Not that long ago, the Sa'kagé was primarily smuggling riot weed and tobacco and whiskey," he said.

Together, Jarl and Momma K had set up a lot of new brothels since the invasion. Most of them barely broke even, but that wasn't the point. They'd done it to protect as many women and men as they could. The Craven Dragon, however, was one of the lucrative ones because it catered to the exotic. There was a girl named Daydra who could have been Elene Cromwyll's twin, without the scars. Virginal was her gig. Her suitemate, Kaldrosa Wyn, played a Sethi pirate. There were silk-clad Ladeshians and heavily kohled Modainis and bell-wearing Ymmuri dancing girls.

"Now," Jarl said, and paused, "you're whores, I'm the Shinga, and the Sa'kagé still smuggles the same damned things. Like nothing's changed. But I'll tell you something: I've changed. I got out. I'm different. I took my second chance and did something with it, and you can, too." It was the only part of the sermon Jarl thought might be a lie.

He'd asked Momma K about it. "Why don't people argue about whether the earth is flat?" she asked.

Jarl shrugged. "It's general knowledge."

"Exactly," she said. "The things that evoke passion are the things we can't know for certain."

"Ah, like the gods," Jarl said.

"It doesn't matter whether you're sure everything you say is true. It matters that you passionately want to believe they're true—because then you'll be compelling. And in the end, what matters is not whether the girls believe your arguments. What matters is that they believe in you."

It was the kind of thing the old Momma K would have said. Jarl was vaguely disappointed. She had seemed different after the coup, after Kylar had poisoned her and given her the antidote. Perhaps the pressure of looking in the face of unrelenting evil was destroying her hope. But her pragmatism had the ring of truth, so Jarl preached on.

Jarl hadn't banged since he'd become Shinga. He hadn't slept with a man since he left Stephan's house the night of the invasion, but he hadn't slept with a woman, either. He'd survived all his life by doing what he had to, always building his web of friends and influence, always looking to the future when he wouldn't have to whore.

That future had arrived so suddenly he didn't know what to do with it. Freedom lay useless in his hands. He didn't know how to feel. It reminded him of Harani iron bulls. He'd never seen one, of course, but it was said they captured the young calves and bound them to a stake with thick chains. By the time the iron bulls were full grown—more than fifteen feet high at their mighty shoulders—they could snap the chains, but they didn't. Their handlers staked them out with thin rope. The iron bulls were so sure they couldn't get free, they never tried.

Jarl had been chained to sex and pleasing his clientele for so long that now he felt sexless. He'd never had a choice before. Most of his clients were men, but there had been women too, from the entire range of levels of attractiveness. Now that he had a choice, he couldn't make it. He couldn't have said with any certainty whether he would have preferred men or women if the life of a rent boy hadn't been forced on him.

The girls at the brothels treated him differently now. They looked at him differently. They flirted.

It was terrifying. Flirtation carried demands. There were appropriate and inappropriate responses to learn and he didn't know the rules of sex outside a brothel. His regulars had always spoken of it as being unsatisfying—but then their experiences couldn't exactly be representative or everyone would be regulars at a brothel, wouldn't they?

He was losing his focus. He couldn't think about this now. Hope had to be sold as a whole package.

"Of all the women in the Warrens," Jarl said, "you're the luckiest. You were lucky enough to become whores here." He shook his head. "Lucky enough to become whores. Six months ago, most of you would have crossed the street rather than pass a whore. Now you are whores, and I'm the Shinga, and the Sa'kagé is still doing the same damn things.

"King Ursuul thinks you're finished. He plans to let the winter kill off most everyone in the Warrens. He figures that by the time the food riots get going, everyone will be so weak his soldiers will have no trouble with us. He figures that the Sa'kagé is too passive and too greedy to stop him. He plans to split us apart by offering us scraps off his table to destroy each other. The funny thing is," Jarl said, "he's right. We've learned that in the spring he's bringing down another army and a few thousand colonists, all of them men. He plans to kill everyone in the Warrens except you. Again, you'll be the lucky ones. You'll be married off to whichever Khalidoran buys you.

"Now maybe the Khalidorans will change and they'll stop with the beatings and the bedroom humiliations once you're their wives. Ursuul expects that you are such cowards you'll hold onto that diseased hope. He expects that sick hope to paralyze you until it's too late, until your men are dead, your friends are scattered, and the Sa'kagé's strength is broken. In a year, you'll start bearing sons for your new Khalidoran husbands and have the joy of watching them turn into monsters who treat their wives as their fathers treat you. It'll be normal. You'll bear daughters who will think it's normal to be kicked and spit on and forced to—well, you know all the things they'll be forced to do. Your daughters won't resist. They'll look to your cowardice and believe that such is a woman's lot. It'll be normal. That's what the king expects will happen, and he's been right about everything so far."

Jarl had them now. He could see the horror in their eyes. Most rent girls thought only of today. They weren't stupid. They knew they couldn't work the sheets forever, but because they didn't see any good options for the future, they decided not to think about the future at all. It was too crushing.

These women were in survival mode. Raising the specter of bearing their own daughters into the same life forced them to think beyond themselves, beyond today. And Jarl hadn't been lying. These women would be the best off. If he could sell the women who had the most to lose, half the battle would be won.

"Things have changed in the last few months for each of us, for each of you and for me. Now I say it's time for things to change for all of us together. I say it's time for the Sa'kagé to change. We've been at war and we've been losing. Do you know why? Because we haven't been fighting. The Khalidorans want us to quietly die? Fuck 'em. We'll fight in ways they've never seen. The Khalidorans are going to starve us? Fuck 'em. If we can smuggle riot weed, we can smuggle grain. They want to kill your men? We'll hide 'em. They want to conduct raids? We'll know where they're going before they do. They want to gamble? We'll cheat. They want to drink? We'll piss in their beer."

"What can we do?" one of the girls asked. It was a planted question.

He smiled. "Right now? I want you to dream. I want you to think—not about going back to what we had before Khalidor came—I want you to dream of something better. I want you to dream of a day when being born in the Warrens doesn't guarantee dying in the Warrens. I want you to dream of getting a second chance and what could happen for this city and this country if everyone got a second chance. Dream of raising your children in a city where they don't have to be afraid all the time. A city without corrupt judges or Sa'kagé extortion. A city with a dozen bridges over the Plith, and not a guard on one of them. A city where things are different—because of us.

"I know you're scared right now. Your shift starts in a few minutes, and you have to go face those fuckers again. I know. It's fine to be frightened, but I'm telling you, be brave inside. The time is coming when you will be needed. If the nobles want to win this war and take this country back, they're going to need us, and our help is going to come at a price. Our price is a city that's different, and you and I get to decide how. You and I have that power. So for now, we can go on with things as usual, or we can dream and get ready. Out of everyone in the Warrens, you ladies have the most to lose." He walked over to the pirate girl Kaldrosa Wyn and touched her cheek beneath one blackened eye.

"But tell me, is this what you gave up your husband for? A crown for a black eye, one more when they hurt you so bad you can't work the next day? Is this what you deserve?"

Tears leaked from Kaldrosa's eyes.

"I say hell no. You came here because it was the best you could do. You get a crown for a black eye because it's the best Momma K could negotiate. As your Shinga, I'm here to tell you that the best isn't good enough. We've been thinking too small. We've been trying to survive, and I for one am sick of surviving. The next time I hear a scream of pain, I want it to come from a Khalidoran throat."

"Hell yes," one of the girls whispered.

He could see passion burning in their eyes now. Gods, they looked fierce!

Jarl raised a hand. "For now, just watch, just wait. Be ready. Be brave. Because when our chance to roll the bones comes, we're gonna cheat and we're gonna roll three sixes."

"Honey," Elene said, shaking Kylar gently. "Honey, get up."

"Ass," he said.

"What?"

"AAASSSS."

Elene laughed. "You do look like someone sat on you," she said, hugging him. She sniffed and grimaced. "And you do stink..."

"Ass," he said, wounded.

"Honey. We've got to go shopping today, remember?"

He grabbed a pillow and pulled it over his head. Elene leaned over to grab the pillow, but Kylar wouldn't let go of it. So she sang the good morning song. It consisted of the words *good* and *morning,* repeated thirty-seven times. It was one of Kylar's favorites. "GOOD morn-ing, good MORN-ing, good morning, GOOD morning..."

"ASS assing, ass ASSing, ass assing," Kylar harmonized into the pillow.

She pulled on the pillow and Kylar grabbed her and flipped her onto the bed next to him. He was so strong and so quick there was no resisting. He pulled the pillow away, rolled on top of her, and kissed her.

"Uhn uhn!" she said. Oh, his lips felt good.

"What?" he asked thirty seconds later.

"Morning mouth," she said, grimacing. It was a lie, of course. With the way his lips felt, she wouldn't have cared if he did have bad breath. But he didn't. His breath never smelled. Not just never smelled bad; he could chew mint leaves or moldy cheese and his breath wouldn't smell at all. It was the same with the rest of his body. Put perfume on him, and it just disappeared. Probably something to do with the ka'kari, he'd guessed.

So now he smiled his mock-predatory smile. "I'll show you morning mouth," he said. He pushed through her flailing hands and kissed her neck, and then lower on her neck, and then he was pulling down the neckline of her dressing gown and her hands weren't flailing anymore and his lips—

"Ah! Shopping!" she rolled out of his arms. He let her go.

Kylar flopped back on the bed and she pretended to straighten her dress while she admired the muscles of his bare torso. Aunt Mea had taken Uly out for the day. The house was empty. Kylar was so cute when his hair was squashed from sleep, and he was gorgeous, and his lips were the most amazing things in the world. Not to mention his hands. She wanted to feel his skin against hers. She wanted to put her hands on his chest. And vice versa.

Sometimes in the morning they cuddled while he was barely

conscious, and it had become her favorite time of day. Once or twice her shift had ridden up during the night and she had found herself spooned against him, skin to skin. Well, maybe her shift didn't ride up all by itself, and she wouldn't have dared it if she didn't know he'd been out for hours the night before and wouldn't possibly wake up.

It made her warm just thinking about it. Why not? part of her asked. So there were the religious reasons. Can an ox and a wolf be yoked together? She didn't even know if Kylar believed in the God. He always got uncomfortable when she talked about it. Her foster mother had told her to make her decisions before she got her heart involved, but that was water under the bridge and down the river and around the bend. Uly needed her. Kylar needed her, and she had never been needed like that before. Kylar made her feel beautiful and good. He made her feel like a lady. He made her feel like a princess. He loved her.

He practically was her husband. They said they were married, they lived together, slept in the same bed, acted as father and mother to Uly. Probably the only reason she hadn't already made love with Kylar was that by the time he actually touched her most nights, she was so tired she could barely move. If he tried in the morning what he did at night, she'd have surrendered her maidenhead in about five seconds. She could almost feel his breath in her ear. She imagined doing some of the things Aunt Mea had talked about so blithely—things that had set her face burning, but sounded ever so wonderful. She was feeling so brazen that she even knew which one she'd try first.

Didn't the scriptures say "let your yes be yes and your no be no"? She'd said she was Kylar's wife. He'd said he was her husband. She'd take him past the ringery Aunt Mea had told her about and they could formalize things in the Waeddryner way later. Afterward.

Kylar sat up in bed and she leaned close behind him, her hands moving to the ties of her dressing gown. She opened it.

"Gods," Kylar said, giving her a quick peck on the cheek without turning around far enough to see the rest of her, "I've got to piss like a warhorse."

He stood and started pulling on clothes. For a moment, Elene was frozen. Her dressing gown hung open, her body exposed.

"What are we shopping for?" Kylar asked, pulling his tunic over his head.

She had barely laced up her dress when his head poked out of his tunic.

"Well?" he asked.

"What?" She felt like someone had just dumped cold water over her head.

"Oh, Uly's birthday, right? We getting her a doll or something?"

"Yes, that's it," she said. What had she been thinking?

17

Tenser performed his job capably enough, Vürdmeister Neph Dada thought. At one point, he even managed to cough up blood. For the time being, his performance would be remembered as cold-blooded defiance. Once he was exonerated, it would be reinterpreted as brave defiance.

The man Tenser was alleged to have murdered, the Cenarian Baron Kirof, had never been found. But on the troth of the Cenarian captain of the guard who said he'd seen Tenser do the deed, Tenser was quickly found guilty. The announcement of his punishment from the Godking's own mouth had garnered gasps. The Cenarian nobility had expected a fine, perhaps imprisonment with credit for time already served, maybe deportation to Khalidor. That he would be thrown into the Hole was viewed as worse than a death penalty. Of course, that was the point.

Tenser couldn't very well infiltrate the Sa'kagé if he were dead or deported. By doing time in the worst gaol in the country, he would earn unrivalled credibility with the Sa'kagé. When Baron Kirof was produced—alive—Tenser would be exonerated and he would again have all the access of a Khalidoran duke—but, more important, he would pretend to hold an abiding hatred for the Godking for his false imprisonment. Duke Tenser Vargun would offer the Sa'kagé whatever they wanted. And then he would destroy them from within.

The Godking, as always, had more than one plan. By punishing a Khalidoran duke so severely, he showed that he was a just ruler. The Cenarians who were wavering would have one more excuse to submit. They would go back to their lives and the noose would only tighten on the rebels as their friends abandoned them.

At the same time, the news of Tenser's imprisonment would overshadow anything else, so today he was releasing dozens of criminals from the Maw and incarcerating hundreds of suspected rebels. With the shocking news about Tenser, people would barely notice.

After the sentence was announced, Neph escorted Tenser and the guards to the Hole.

Tenser looked at him suspiciously. A lot of Khalidorans didn't think much of their long-vanquished Lodricari neighbors, but with Tenser, the antipathy seemed both general and personal. "What do you want?"

"Just to share some news that might be helpful," Neph said. He couldn't hide his pleasure. "Baron Kirof has disappeared. Someone kidnapped him, apparently."

The blood drained from Tenser's face. If the baron was lost, he would never leave the Hole.

"We'll find him," Neph said. "Of course, if we find him dead…" Neph chuckled. If Kirof was dead, Vargun was useless. If useless, a failure. If a failure, dead. With magic, Neph opened the iron gate that separated the castle's tunnels from the Maw's. "My lord? Your cell awaits."

Jarl rubbed his temples. They'd been interviewing prisoners released from the Maw all day. The prisoners had only learned of the coup after the fact, when wytches appeared, searching for something. The wytches left empty-handed, so it didn't seem important.

What was important was that a former brothel manager called Whitey had been awake when two guards had led a prisoner toward the Hole. He'd been awake and he'd stayed awake. He swore that neither the two guards nor their prisoner, a big blond naked man, had left.

Furthermore, Whitey recognized one of the guards, a foul man who'd been on Jarl's payroll, whom Jarl had sent to the castle with a very specific task. The wytches coming after them had gone as far as the Maw, but there had been no sounds of fighting, no indications that they had seen anyone. It was impossible, and Whitey couldn't make any sense of it.

Jarl dismissed Whitey. "Is it possible?" he asked Momma K.

"What do you think," she said, stating the question.

"What are you talking about?" Brant Agon asked.

"It proves he was alive later than we thought," Jarl said.

"And we know that the head they put up wasn't his," Momma K said. "That's suggestive."

"Gods," Jarl said.

"What?" Brant asked. "What?"

"Logan Gyre," Jarl said.

"What? He was killed in the north tower," Brant said.

"What would you do if you had just killed a guard deep in the Maw and were changing into his clothes when you saw six wytches were coming your way? There's only one way out, and that way was blocked by the wytches," Jarl said.

Brant was thunderstruck. "You're not saying Logan jumped into the Hole," Brant said. He'd been down to the Hole once.

"I'm saying Logan Gyre might still be alive," Jarl said.

"Hold on," Momma K said. She got up and started looking through a stack of papers. "If I recall correctly...ah, here. Remind me that we need to give this girl a bonus. She has a regular who likes to brag. 'Gorkhy throws their bread down the Hole and watches them try to grab it without falling in. He says at least three of the prisoners have been...'" Momma K cleared her throat, but when she continued her voice was level. "'Three of the prisoners have been eaten by the others in the time Gorkhy's been starving them.' She describes 'a giant of a man almost seven feet tall. Several times he's been able to reach bread that Gorkhy tried to throw down the Hole. Gorkhy has special hatred for the man, the one they call King.'" Momma K looked up. "This report is only three days old."

Quietly, Brant said, "No one like that has been thrown in the Hole in the last ten years."

All three of them sat back.

"If this Gorkhy tells his superiors about a giant of a man named King..." Momma K said.

"Logan will die that day," Jarl said.

"We have to save him," Brant said.

Jarl and Momma K shared a look.

"We need to think where this fits in with our strategy," Momma K said.

"You're not thinking of leaving him there," Brant said.

Momma K examined her blood-red nails.

"Because that isn't an option," Brant said. "He's the only man we could possibly rally the country behind. Jarl, if you really want to do what you've said, this is your chance. If you rescue Logan, he'll give you lands and titles and a pardon. So don't tell me that you're even thinking of leaving our king in that hell."

"Are you done?" Momma K asked. He said nothing, but his jaw tensed. "We are thinking of it. We're thinking of it because we think of everything. That's why we win. I'm even thinking how we could save him if we want to. Have you started thinking about that yet, or are you still blustering about how noble and good you'll be?"

"Dammit, I'm still blustering," he said, but a smile escaped. Momma K shook her head and smiled despite herself.

"How are your men coming, Brant?" Jarl asked.

"I'll make good soldiers of them, given a decade or two."

"How many do you have?" Jarl asked.

"No, no," Momma K said.

"A hundred," Agon said. "Maybe thirty would be of some use in a fight. Ten might be formidable. A few great archers. One who might make a third-rate wetboy. All of them undisciplined. They don't trust each other yet. They fight as individuals."

"We haven't even talked through this yet," Momma K said.

Jarl said, "Consider it talked through. We're doing it."

Momma K opened her mouth. Jarl held her gaze until she looked down. "As you will, Shinga," she said.

"I'll assume that our source wouldn't be able to get Gorkhy to help us?"

Momma K looked at the paper, but she wasn't even reading it. "Not for this."

As Brant and Momma K debated different ways of getting into the Maw, Jarl was thinking. He'd announced himself two weeks ago, and he was preaching to an eager audience. The people of the Warrens—the Rabbits, as they were derisively called for their numbers, their fears, and their maze of alleys—wanted hope. His message was water for parched tongues. Rebellion sounded great to people who had nothing to lose. But in speaking, he'd necessarily spoken to the Godking's spies.

He'd already avoided one assassination attempt. There were bound to be more. Unless Jarl got some wetboys to protect him, they'd get him sooner or later.

"I'm going to Caernarvon," Jarl said.

"You're running away?" Brant asked.

"If I travel light, I can be back in a month."

"Granted, but what does that give you?"

"Another month of life?" Jarl said with a smile.

Momma K said, "You think he'll come back?"

Brant looked confused.

"For Logan? In a heartbeat," Jarl said.

"If anyone can get Logan out, he can," Momma K said.

"Who?" Brant asked.

"And once Hu Gibbet and the other wetboys hear he's protecting you, I wouldn't be surprised if they back off," Momma K said.

"Who? Who?"

"Since Durzo Blint died, probably the best wetboy in the city," Jarl said.

"Except he's not in the city anymore," Momma K said.

"Fine, the best in the business."

"Except he's not in the business anymore."

"That's about to change," Jarl said.

"Will you take anyone?" Momma K said.

"You're just trying to spite me, aren't you?" Brant asked.

"No," Jarl said, ignoring him and answering Momma K. "It'll be less conspicuous to smuggle one out." Jarl turned to Brant, "Brant, I have a task for you while I'm gone."

"You're talking about Kylar Stern, aren't you?"

Jarl smiled. "Yes. Are you an honest man, General?"

The general sighed. "Everywhere except on the battlefield."

Jarl clapped him on the shoulder. "Then I want you to figure out how Logan Gyre's army is going to destroy the Godking's."

"Logan doesn't have an army," Brant said.

"That's Momma K's problem," Jarl said.

"Pardon me?" she asked.

"Terah Graesin does. I want you to figure out how it's going to become Logan's."

"What?" Momma K asked.

"Now if you'll excuse me," Jarl said, "I've got a date in Caernarvon."

18

"Did I die and not notice?" Kylar asked. He was moving through the death fog again, the familiar moving-without-moving feeling against his skin. A cloaked figure stood beyond the edge of the fog, as ethereal as the fog itself, and Kylar was sure it was the Wolf, but he hadn't died. Had he? Had someone killed him in his sleep? He'd just lain down—

"What is this? A dream?" Kylar asked.

The cloaked man turned, and Kylar's tension melted. It wasn't the Wolf. It was Dorian Ursuul.

"A dream?" Dorian asked. He squinted at Kylar through the fog. "I suppose so, if a peculiar variety thereof." He smiled. He was a handsome man, if intense. His black hair was disheveled, his blue eyes intelligent, his features balanced. "Why is it, my shadow-striding friend, that we don't fear dreams? We lose consciousness, lose control, things happen with no apparent logic and abiding by no apparent rules. Friends appear and morph into strangers. Environments shift abruptly, and we rarely question it. We don't fear dreams, but we do fear madness, and death terrifies us."

"What the hell is going on?" Kylar asked.

Dorian smirked. He looked Kylar up and down. "Amazing. You look exactly the same, but you're totally different, aren't you?"

Gods, had it only been a couple of months since he'd met Dorian?

"You've become formidable, Kylar. You have gravitas now. You're a force to be reckoned with, but your mind hasn't caught up with your power, has it? Reforming your identity is taking you time. That's understandable. Not many people have to kill a father figure and become an immortal on the same day."

"Get to the point." Dorian always knew too much. It was unnerving.

"This is a dream, as you said. And yes, I did summon you. It's a nice bit of magic I just discovered. I hope I remember it when I wake. If I wake. I'm not sure I'm asleep. I'm in one of my little reveries. I have been for a long time now. My body's at Screaming Winds. Khali is coming. The garrison will fall. I'll survive, but worse days are to come for me. I've been watching my own future, Kylar, something very dangerous to do. I've found a few things that have made me lose heart and stop looking. So while I've been marshaling my courage, I've been following you. I saw that you needed someone you could be honest with. Count Drake or Durzo would have been better, but they clearly can't be here, so here I am. Even killers need friends."

"I'm not a killer anymore. I've given that up."

"In my visions," Dorian said as if Kylar hadn't spoken, "I see myself coming to a place where my happiness is one lie away. I will look into the eyes of the woman I love who also loves me and know that whether I lie or tell the truth, she'll be devastated. In this, we are brothers, Kylar. The God gives simpler problems to lesser men. I'm here because you need me."

Kylar's pique unraveled. He looked into the fog. The entire place seemed a fit metaphor for his life—stuck in twilight with nothing definite, nothing solid, no simple path.

"I'm trying to change," Kylar said, "but I'm not making it. I thought I could just break with my past and move and be done with it. I walk into a room and I case it. I look for exits, see how high the ceilings are, check potential threats, how good the traction on the floor is. If a man stares at me from an alley, I figure out how I'll kill him—and it feels good. I feel in control."

"Until?" Dorian asked.

Kylar hesitated. "Until I remember. I have to make myself think that my instincts are wrong. And then I hate what I've become."

"And what have you become?" Dorian asked.

"A murderer."

"You're a liar and killer, but you're no murderer, Kylar."

"Well, thanks."

"What's the Night Angel, Kylar?"

"I don't know. Durzo never told me."

"Horseshit. Why don't you trust yourself? Why don't you ask Elene to trust you? Why don't you trust her with the truth?"

"She'd never understand."

"How do you know?"

What if she did? What if, once she knew him all the way down to the depths, then she rejected him? What would that do to him?

"You two are so young you don't know your asses from your elbows," Dorian said. "But *you* are starting to figure yourself out. Elene's accepted a tiny box as her faith, and you're way outside of what she knows about the God. She's got the arrogance of youth that tells her that what she knows about the God is all there is to know about Him. She loves you, so she wants you to stay in that box with her. And that box is too small for you. You can't understand a God who's all mercy and no justice. That cute, fuzzy God wouldn't last two minutes in the Warrens, would he? Well, I hate to tell you this, but Elene's eighteen. All she knows about the God isn't all that much.

"Kylar, I don't think the God finds you abhorrent. The horror is having profound power in one hand and a strong moral sense in the other and absolutely no foundation to stand on. For the last couple of months, you've tried to accept Elene's moral conclusions while rejecting her premises. And you say she's not logical? Where do you stand, Shadow in Twilight?

"You've got choices to make, but here's another hard truth: you *can't* be whatever you want to be. The list of things you'll never be is a long one—even if you do live forever. Do you want to know what's at the top? Mild-mannered herbalist. You're as meek as a wolf, Kylar— and that's what Elene loves about you and it's what she fears about you. You can't keep telling her it's all right, that this disguise is who you really are. It's not. Why don't you trust Elene enough to ask her to love the man you really are?"

"Because I hate him!" Kylar roared. "Because he loves killing! Because she doesn't understand evil and he does. Because he never feels so alive as when I'm bathed in blood. Because he is a virtuoso with the sword and I love what he can do. Because he is the Night Angel and the angel is in the night and the night is in me! Because he is the Shadow That Walks. Because he believes some people cannot be saved, only stopped. Because when he kills an evil man, I feel not just the pleasure of mastery, I feel the whole world's pleasure at the retribution—an evil man is an affront and I erase the blot. I balance the imbalance. He loves that—and Elene would have to lose the innocence I love about her for her to understand that man."

"This man," Dorian said, poking Kylar's chest, "and this one—" he poked Kylar's forehead—"are on their way to madness. Take it from one who knows."

"I can change," Kylar said, but his voice was hopeless.

"A wolf might become a wolfhound, son, but it will never be a lap dog."

"We are at war," Speaker Istariel Wyant said. Her voice was nasal, the accent High Alitaeran. She liked making pronouncements.

Ariel had wedged her bulk into a too-small chair in the Speaker's office, high within the Alabaster Seraph. She was puffing from the climb up the stairs. *One meal a day until I can manage the climb without wheezing. One.*

Sometimes Ariel hated flesh, hated being chained to something so weak and needy. It took such care, such slavish devotion, and wanted such pampering. It was a perpetual distraction from things more important, like what the Speaker wanted of her.

Istariel Wyant was a tall, imperious woman with a patrician nose and brows plucked down to thin lines. She had knobby joints that made her look lanky rather than willowy, and despite her pinched middle-aged face, she had the most beautiful long blonde hair of any woman Ariel knew. Istariel adored her hair. Not a few of the Sisters whispered that she must have rediscovered some lost weave to make it so thick and glossy. It wasn't true, of course, Istariel's mother had had the same hair. It was one reason their father had married her after Ariel's mother died. Besides, Istariel wasn't that Talented.

"This war is not just over what it means to be a maja, but what it means to be a woman."

Seeing the undisguisedly ironical look on Ariel's face, Istariel changed tack. "How have you been, sister?"

Of course, every full maja was addressed as "Sister," but Istariel warmed the word. Used for Ariel, "sister" hearkened back to the supposedly halcyon days of their youth together, some fifty years ago. Istariel definitely wanted something.

"Fine," Ariel said.

Istariel tried again, valiantly. "And how are your studies progressing?"

"The last two years of my life have probably been a complete waste," Ariel said.

"Still the same old Ariel." Istariel tried to say it lightly, as if amused, but she didn't quite put in the effort to make it convincing. She probably thought that because Ariel didn't use any finely nuanced social snubs, she wasn't aware of them.

When they had been younger and Ariel had cared more about what her aristocratic little sister thought of her, it had been a bitter irony for her. Ariel had always fallen squarely in Istariel's blind spot. The near-genius with which Istariel instantly understood the men and women around her had never extended to Ariel, with whom she spent so much time. When Istariel looked at her, she saw Ariel's broad peasant face and thick peasant limbs, her lack of social graces and lack of concern for the important things—privilege, power, and position—and she saw a peasant. Istariel thought she understood Ariel, so she stopped thinking about her at all. Now she even allowed her eyes to flick down.

"Yes, I've gotten fat," Ariel said.

Istariel blushed. *How she must hate how I can still make her feel like a child.* "Well," Istariel said, "I, I suppose you have put on a little..."

"And how are you, Speaker?" Ariel asked. Why was it she could master the eighty-four variations of the Symbeline weave with perfect timing, structure, and intonation, but not make conversation? Surely small talk should be reducible to perhaps a few hundred typical questions, delineated into conversation trees according to the conversant's responses, how well one knew the conversant, what the current events were, and one's position relative to the conversant.

Timing of the questions and the length of one's responses would have to be studied as well, but many weaves required exact timing, too, and Ariel's rhythm was perfect. One might have to take into account the physical setting: one would speak differently in the Speaker's office than in a tavern. Topics of study could include how to deal with distractions, appropriate degrees of eye contact or physical touch, taking into account cultural variations, and of course the differences in speaking with men and women, subdivided by whether one were oneself a man or a woman. Ariel supposed she might have to include children in the study as well, and it would be important to include how to speak with those toward whom you had varying degrees of friendship or interest, romantic or otherwise. Or should it? Should one make small talk differently with a woman whom you thought you might like to befriend than with a woman you had no interest in? Were there socially appropriate ways to curtail dull conversations?

That made Ariel smile. In her book, curtailing dull conversations would be a huge plus.

Still, the project as a whole had little to do with magic. Perhaps nothing. Indeed, she decided that the study, while worthy, would be a poor use of her own gifts.

"But you're really not listening, are you?" Istariel said.

Ariel realized that her sister had been speaking for some time. It had all been meaningless, but Ariel had forgotten to pretend to be paying attention. "Sorry," she said.

Istariel waved it away, and Ariel realized that Istariel was almost relieved that Ariel was back to acting the way she expected—Ariel, the distracted, oblivious genius, big brain and bigger Talent and nothing else. It allowed Istariel to feel superior. "I got you thinking, didn't I?" Istariel asked.

Ariel nodded.

"About what?"

She shook her head, but Istariel cocked an eyebrow at her. It was an I'm-the-Speaker look. Ariel grimaced.

"I was thinking about how bad I am at small talk, and wondering why," Ariel said.

Istariel grinned—they might have been teenagers again. "And formulating a course of study on it?"

She frowned deeply. "I decided I'm the wrong person for the task."

Istariel laughed out loud. It was irritating. Istariel was a snorter. "What were you saying?" Ariel asked. She tried to look interested. Istariel, though pompous and a snorter, was the Speaker.

"Oh, Ariel, you don't care, and you're not very good at pretending you do."

"No, I don't. But you do, so I can listen politely."

Istariel shook her head as though she couldn't believe Ariel, but she settled down and—mercifully—stopped snorting. "Forget it. The war I was talking about? Some of the younger sisters want to form a new order."

"Another bunch who want to disavow the Alitaeran Accord and become war magae?" What a waste. They spent their time trying to change the rules rather than ignoring them and making them moot.

"Nothing so simple. These ladies propose to call themselves the Chattel."

"Oh my."

Tyros were not allowed to marry, but many Sisters eventually decided to. Of those, most went back to wherever they had come from or where their husbands lived. Some stayed on at the Chantry, but few rose to high levels. Often, that was simply a matter of choice: the women decided that with children, husbands, and homes, they'd rather be with their families full time.

Sometimes, though, ambitious Sisters wanted it all. They wanted to be married to the Chantry and to a man. Those never rose as high as they believed they deserved, because after a certain level, the other Sisters wanted leaders for whom the Chantry was their whole family. The women who sacrificed family for the Seraph saw it as their right to be promoted beyond those who worked half-jobs, no matter how brilliantly. The attitude even extended to married Sisters who didn't have children, because Sisters assumed that they would eventually throw away everything worthwhile to tend a man and his brats, like any peasant woman. The Sisters quietly called them chattel, voluntary housekeepers and broodmares to men, and they said the chattel wasted the Chantry's time and money and—worst—their own talents.

Usually, the comments went unchallenged because the vast majority of the Sisters at the Chantry were single. Either they were instructors or they were students. It was considered rude to call a married Sister a chattel to her face, but it happened.

If the married Sisters formed an order—and Ariel couldn't see how they could be denied—they would have tremendous power. Their numbers included more than half of all the Sisters. If they became a bloc, things would change radically.

"It's a ploy, of course," the Speaker said. "Most of the…married Sisters aren't militant enough to rally behind such a name. It's just a shot over the bow to let us know they're serious."

"What do they want?" Ariel asked.

Istariel's eye twitched, and she rubbed it. "Many things, but one of the primary demands is that we start a new school of magic here. A school that breaks with our traditions."

"How much of a break?"

"A men's school, Ariel."

That was more than a break from tradition. It was a seismic upheaval.

"We believe some of them have married magi already."

"What do you want me to do?" Ariel asked immediately.

"About this?" Istariel said. "Nothing. Heavens no. Forgive me, sister, but you're the last person to help with this. It requires a lighter touch. I have something else for you. The leader of the married sisters is Eris Buel. I can't oppose her directly. I need someone ambitious, respected, and young to carry our standard."

Which of course excluded Ariel. "You describe perhaps a third of our sisters, or would, if you added unscrupulous."

Istariel's eyes went hot and then cold. Ariel knew she had overstepped the bounds, but Istariel wouldn't do anything about it. She needed her. Besides, Ariel had said it not so much because it was true as for the quarter of a second when Istariel would either look guilty or not.

She had.

"Ari, not even you may speak that way to me."

"What do you want?" Ariel asked.

"I want you to bring Jessie al'Gwaydin back to the Chantry."

Ariel thought about it. Jessie al'Gwaydin would be an ideal rock to crush Eris Buel against. She was everything the Chantry loved: well-spoken, good-looking, intelligent, nobly born, and willing to pay her dues to climb to the top. She wasn't terribly Talented, but she might be a good leader one day, if she had some sense knocked into her.

"She's studying the Dark Hunter in Torras Bend," Istariel said. "I know it's dangerous, but I gave her sufficient warning that I'm sure she won't do anything precipitous." Istariel chuckled. "In fact, I threatened to send you after her if she wasn't good. I'm sure it will please her enormously to see you."

"And if she's dead?" Ariel asked.

Istariel's grin faded. "Find me someone the Chattel can't ignore. Someone who will do what needs to be done."

There was a terrible latitude in that ambiguity. But latitude could be used both ways, and the fact was, Ariel would rather be included. *Oh, sister, you play with a terrible fire. Why would you use me for this?* "Done," Ariel said.

Istariel signaled that she was dismissed, and Ariel walked to the door. "Oh," Istariel said, as if it had slipped her mind, "whomever you bring, make sure she's married."

19

$\mathcal{K}$ylar was outside the shop closing up when he sensed he was being watched. He curved his fingers unconsciously to check the knives strapped to his forearms, but there were no knives there. He closed the big shutters over the counter where they displayed their wares and fitted the lock on it, feeling suddenly vulnerable.

It wasn't being weaponless that made him feel vulnerable. A wetboy was a weapon. He felt vulnerable because of his oath. No killing, no violence. What did that leave him with?

Whoever it was, they were standing in the shadows of the alley beside the shop. Kylar had no doubt they were waiting for him to walk to the front door, which was only steps away from the alley. With his Talent, he could get into the door and lock it—and give away his abilities. Or he could run away—and leave Uly unprotected.

Seriously. Before there had been a woman in his life, things had been so simple.

Kylar walked toward the door. The man was disheveled and wearing rags, with the bloodshot eyes and missing teeth of a riot weed addict. The knives the Ladeshian held seemed serviceable enough, though. He leapt out of the alley. Kylar expected the man to demand money, but he didn't.

Instead, he attacked instantly, screaming insanity. It sounded like he was saying, "Don't kill me! Don't kill me!" Kylar simply moved and the addict went sprawling. Kylar leaned against the wall, puzzled. The man picked himself up and charged. Kylar waited. Waited. Then he moved abruptly. The addict smashed into the wall.

After kicking away the bleeding man's daggers, Kylar rolled him over with a foot.

"Don't kill me yet," the man said, spluttering through the blood streaming from his nose. "Please, immortal. Don't kill me yet."

"I brought you a present," Gwinvere said.

Agon looked up from the paper he was writing. It was a list of the strengths and weaknesses of their tactical situation in the Warrens. So far, it was a depressing list. He got up from the table and followed Gwinvere into the next room of her house, trying not to think about how good she smelled. It made his heart ache.

Her dining room table was covered with a cloth that had ten lumps beneath it.

"Aren't you going to open it?" Gwinvere asked.

Agon raised an eyebrow at her; she laughed. He pulled the cover cloth off and gasped.

On the table were ten unstrung short bows. They were adorned with simple, almost crude scrimshaw of men and animals, mostly horses.

"Gwinvere, you shouldn't have."

"That's what my accountants tell me."

He picked one up and tried to bend it.

"Careful," she said. "The man who...procured these bows said you need to warm them by a fire for half an hour before you string them. Otherwise they'll break."

"They really are Ymmuri bows," Agon said. "I've never even seen one before." The bows were one of the marvels of the world. No one but the Ymmuri knew the secret of their construction, though Agon could plainly see that somehow they used not only wood but also horn and glue from melted horse hooves. They could punch an arrow through heavy armor at two hundred paces, a feat only Alitaeran longbows could match. And these bows were short enough to be used from horseback. Agon had heard stories of the lightly armored horse lords riding circles around heavily armored companies, outside the range of traditional archers, shooting the entire company to pieces. Every time lancers charged, the light Ymmuri on their little ponies fled, shooting arrows the whole way. No one had yet figured out how to counter such an attack. Thank the gods no one had ever united the Ymmuri, or they would overrun all of Midcyru.

The bows would be perfect for Agon's wytch hunters. He caressed the one in his hand.

"You know the way to a man's heart, Gwinvere," he said, delighted as a child with a new toy.

She smiled and for a golden moment he smiled too. Gwinvere was beautiful, so smart, so capable, so formidable, and now as she looked in his eyes, somehow fragile, rocked by the death of Durzo, the man she'd loved for fifteen years. Gwinvere was deep and mysterious, and though he'd thought himself too old to be stirred by such things, he was stirred by her beauty. Her smell—gods, was that the same perfume she'd worn all those years ago? It shook him to his core. But there, at his core, he saw his wife. Whether she was dead or alive, he might never know. He could never mourn, never move on, never give up hope without giving up on her and somehow betraying her.

His smile dropped a notch, and Gwinvere saw it. She touched his arm. "I'm glad you like them." She walked to the door, then turned. "Just tell your men that each of those bows cost more than they'll make in their lives." And she smiled. It was a smile to give them a ramp back up to levity. A smile that told him she saw, she knew, and though she didn't reciprocate his interest, she wouldn't use it against him.

Agon barked a laugh, accepting her lead. "I'll take it out of their hides."

*   *   *

More shocking than the mugger's words was his face. He was the same man whom Kylar had sworn he'd seen briefly from Count Drake's window the day Vi tried to kill him.

Kylar dosed the man with poppy wine, and took him to a home for the treatment of addicts. Addicts from wealthy families, of course. The treatment itself was simple: mostly, time. The attendants administered teas and other herbs of doubtful usefulness, restrained the addict, cleaned up the diarrhea and vomit, and waited. The walls were thick, the cells separate and private. Kylar had no trouble with the guards, who took one look, saw an addict, and let them in.

"Please restrain me," the Ladeshian said as they entered a tiny cell. There was a writing desk, a chair, a basin and pitcher, and a bed, but the walls were blank brick. It was deliberately spartan. The fewer things in the room, the less likely a suicide attempt would be successful.

"I don't think you'll get out of control for a few hours at the least," Kylar said.

"Don't be so sure."

So Kylar bound him to the bed with the thick leather straps and the man looked relieved. He smiled his gap-toothed addict's smile. It turned Kylar's stomach. Hadn't this man once had a brilliant smile?

"Who are you?" Kylar asked. "And what is it you think you know about me?"

"I know that you have a ka'kari, Kylar Stern. I knew Durzo Blint and I know you were his apprentice and I know this is your second incarnation. You used to be called Azoth."

Kylar's stomach flipped. "Who are you?"

The man smiled again, a huge smile, as if he had gotten so used to smiling to show his perfect white teeth that he hadn't yet adjusted to his addict's grin. Oddly, now that he was bound, he seemed arrogant. "I am Aristarchos ban Ebron, shalakroi of Benyurien in the Silk province of Ladesh."

"Is shalakroi the Ladeshian name for a riot weed addict?"

The hauteur fell from the man's face like a load of bricks. "No. I'm sorry. And I'm sorry for the attempt on your life. I wasn't in control of myself."

"I could tell."

"I don't think you understand," Aristarchos said.

"I've seen addicts before."

"I'm not just an addict, Kylar." He smiled a wry, lopsided smile that showed more of his rotten teeth. "Same thing every addict would say, huh? I tried to get out of Cenaria when the city fell, but my Ladeshian skin betrayed me. The Khalidorans stopped me and interrogated me about the silk trade. They hate the silk monopoly as much as the rest of you Midcyri. That interrogation would have been fine, but a Vürdmeister named Neph Dada saw me. He has the Viewing. I don't know what he saw, but they began torturing me." His eyes grew distant. "That was bad. What was worse was that they force-fed me some seeds after every time. They took the pain away. They made everything better. I didn't even recognize what they were. The Khalidorans didn't let me sleep. They'd just torture me, feed me seeds, torture me. They didn't even ask questions until he came."

"He?" Kylar felt sick to his stomach.

"I...fear to speak his name," Aristarchos said, ashamed of his fear and yet frightened to silence nonetheless. He began drumming his fingers.

"The Godking?"

He nodded. "The cycle just kept going until they didn't have to force the seeds on me anymore. I begged for them. The second time he came, he used magic on me....He's fascinated with compulsion. Magical, chemical, and blends of the two, he said. I was just another experiment. After a while, I...I gave them your name, Kylar. He laid a compulsion on me to kill you. I had a box with my seeds in it that would only open once I obeyed." A tremor passed through him. "You see? I tried riot weed to get me by. I tried poppy wine. Nothing works.

I thought if I could get here fast enough, I could warn you. I did hold some things back. They don't know you come back from death. They don't know about the Society or your incarnations."

It was all going too fast for Kylar. The implications were exploding in a hundred different directions. "What society?" Kylar said.

Aristarchos looked incredulous, his fingers even stopped their drumming. "Durzo never told you?"

"Not a word."

" 'The Society of the Second Dawn.' "

"Never heard of it."

" 'The Society of the Second Dawn is devoted to the study of reputed immortals, the delineations of their abilities, and the confinement of said powers to those who would not abuse them.' We're a secret society, spread over all the world. It's how I was able to find you. We were founded centuries ago. Back then we thought there were dozens of immortals. Over the years, we concluded that there were at most seven, and maybe just one. The man you knew as Durzo Blint was also Ferric Fireheart, Vin Craysin, Tal Drakkan, Yric the Black, Hrothan Steelbender, Zak Eurthkin, Rebus Nimble, Qos Delanoesh, X!rutic Ur, Mir Graggor, Pips McClawski, Garric Shadowbane, Dav Slinker, and probably a dozen others we don't know."

"That's half the stories of Midcryu."

Aristarchos was starting to shiver and sweat, but he continued in a level voice, "He successfully masqueraded as a native of at least a dozen different cultures, probably twice that. He spoke more languages than I've even heard of—at least thirty, not counting dialects—and all of them so fluently natives couldn't detect an accent. There were times when he would disappear for twenty or even fifty years—we don't know if he lived in solitude or married and settled down in remote regions. But he appeared in every major conflict for six centuries, and not always on the side you would expect. Two hundred years ago, as Hrothan Steelbender, he fought with the Alitaeran expansion campaigns for the first thirty years of the Hundred Years' War, and then 'died' and fought with the Ceurans against them as the sword-saint Oturo Kenji."

Now it was Kylar who was shivering. He remembered when his guild had tried to mug Durzo. When they saw who he was, they shrank back from the legendary wetboy. Legendary wetboy! How little they knew. How little Kylar had known. He felt an unreasoning stab of resentment.

How could Durzo not tell him? He'd been like a son to the man. He'd been closer to him than anyone—and he hadn't told Kylar anything. Kylar had only seen a bitter, superstitious shell of a man, and thought himself somehow superior to him.

Kylar hadn't known Durzo Blint at all. And now the hero out of legends—dozens of legends—was dead. Dead at Kylar's hands. Kylar had destroyed something without knowing its worth. He hadn't known the man he'd called his master and now he never would. It felt like a hole in his stomach. He felt numb and distant and angry and near tears all at once. Durzo was dead, and Kylar missed him more than he could have imagined.

The beads of sweat were sticking out on Aristarchos's face now. He had wadded the bed sheets in his fists. "If you have any questions you need to ask me about his incarnations or yours or anything at all, please ask quickly. I'm not... feeling well."

"Why do you keep saying incarnations like I'm some kind of god?" It wasn't a great question, but the real questions were so big that Kylar didn't even know how ask them.

"You are worshipped in a few remote areas where your master wasn't very careful about showing the full extent of his powers."

"What?!"

"The Society says incarnations because 'lives' is too confusing, and we aren't sure if you have as many lives as you want, or a finite number, or just one life that never ends. None of us have ever actually seen you die. 'Incarnations' has its critics, too, but that's mainly among the Modaini separatists who believe in reincarnation. Let me tell you, your existence really throws them for a theological loop." Aristarchos's legs were twitching, almost convulsing. "I'm sorry," he said, "there's so much I wish I could tell you. So much I wish I could ask."

Suddenly, among all the big questions about Durzo, about Kylar's powers, about the Godking and what he knew or thought he knew, Kylar just saw a man sweating on a table, a man who'd lost his teeth and his good looks for Kylar, a man who'd been tortured and made an addict, who'd been compelled to try to kill Kylar and had fought against it with everything he had. He'd done all that for a man he didn't even know.

So Kylar didn't ask about the Society, or magic, or what Aristarchos could do for him. That could come later, if they both lived until later. "Aristarchos," he said, "what is a shalakroi?"

The man was taken off guard. "I—it's a little below a Midcyri duke, but it's not an inherited position. I scored better than ten thousand other students on the Civil Service examinations. Only a hundred scored higher in all Ladesh. I ruled an area roughly the size of Cenaria."

"The city?"

Aristarchos smiled through his sweat and clenched muscles. "The country."

"It's an honor to meet you, Aristarchos ban Ebron, shalakroi of Benyurien."

"The honor is mine, Kylar ban Durzo. Please, will you kill me?"

Kylar turned his back on the man.

Pride and hope whooshed out of Aristarchos with his breath. He slumped in the bed, suddenly small. "This is no kindness, my lord." He convulsed again, and strained against the leather bonds. His veins bulged on his forehead and his emaciated arms. "Please!" he said as the convulsion passed. "Please, if you won't kill me, will you give me my box? Just one seed? Please?"

Kylar left. He took the box and burned it. Aside from a poisoned-needle trap, it was empty.

20

"Your Holiness, our assassin is dead," Neph Dada said as he stepped onto the Godking's balcony. "I apologize to report this failure, though I do wish to point out that I recommended—"

"He didn't fail," Garoth Ursuul said, not turning from his view of the city.

Neph opened his mouth, remembered to whom he was speaking, and closed it. He hunched a little lower.

"I gave him a task he could thwart so that he might accomplish the one I desired," the Godking said. Still staring over the city, he massaged his temples. "He found Kylar Stern. Our ka'karifer is in Caernarvon."

He picked a note from his pocket. "Transmit this message to our agent there to give to Vi Sovari. She should be arriving any day."

Neph blinked convulsively. He'd thought he knew everything the Godking was doing. He'd thought that his own mastery of the vir was within a hairsbreadth of the Godking's, and now, blithely, the man had given him this. It set Neph's ambitions back months. Months! How he hated the man. Garoth could track exact locations magically? Neph had never heard of such a thing. What did it mean? Did Garoth know about the camp at Black Barrow? Neph's meisters had been abducting villagers for his experiments, but it was so far away, Neph had been so careful. No, it couldn't be that.

But the Godking was giving him notice. He was telling Neph that he had his eye on him, that he had his eye on everything, that he would always know more than he told even Neph, that his powers would always be beyond what Neph expected. As the Godking's warnings went, it was gentle.

"Is there something else?" the Godking asked.

"No, Your Holiness," Neph said. He managed to keep his voice perfectly calm.

"Then begone."

Despite all the reasons he had to be grumpy, when Elene was in a good mood, it was hard not to be happy. After a quick breakfast and a cup of ootai to stave off weariness, Kylar found himself wandering the streets with her, hand in hand. She was wearing a cream-colored dress with a brown taffeta bodice the color of her eyes. It looked fabulous in its simplicity. Of course, Kylar had never seen Elene wear anything that he thought looked less than great, but when she was happy she was twice as beautiful as usual.

"This is cute, isn't it?" he asked, picking up a doll from a merchant's table. Why was Elene happy? He couldn't remember having done anything good.

Ever since he'd started going out at night, he'd expected to have The Talk. Instead, one night she'd grabbed his hand—he'd almost jumped out of his skin, so much for being the imperturbable wetboy—and she said, "Kylar, I love you, and I trust you."

She hadn't said anything since then. He sure hadn't. What was he supposed to say? "Um, actually, I have killed some people, but it was an accident every time, and they were all bad"?

"I don't think we can really afford much," Elene said. "I just wanted to spend the day with you." She smiled. Maybe it was just a mood swing. Mood swings had to have an up side, right?

"Oh," he said. He only felt a little awkward holding hands with her.

At first, he'd felt like everyone was staring at them. Now, though, he saw that only a few people looked at them twice, and of those, most seemed to be approving.

"Aha!" a round little man bellowed at them. "Perfect. Perfect. Absolutely lovely. Marvelous, you are. Yes, yes, come right in."

Kylar was so startled he barely stopped himself from quickly rearranging the man's face. Elene laughed and poked the tense muscles of Kylar's arm. "Come on, brawny," she said. "This is shopping. It's fun."

"Fun?" he asked as she pulled him into the little well-lit shop.

The fat little man quickly handed them off to a pretty girl of maybe seventeen who smiled brightly at them. She was petite, with a slender figure, dazzling blue eyes, and a large mouth that made her smile huge. It was Golden Hair. Kylar goggled as his daylight and shadow worlds crossed.

"Hello," Golden Hair said. She glanced down at the wedding bands on their hands. "I'm Capricia. Have you ever been to a ringery before?"

After Kylar didn't say anything for a long moment, Elene gently dug an elbow into his ribs. "No," she said.

Kylar blinked. Elene was shaking her head at him, obviously thinking he was ogling Capricia, but she didn't look mad, just bemused. He shook his head, *No, it's not like that.*

She cocked an eyebrow at him. *Right.*

"Well, let's start at the beginning then," Capricia said, pulling out a wide drawer lined with black velvet and putting it on a counter. It was filled with tiny, paired rings of gold and silver and bronze, some decorated with rubies or garnets or amethyst or diamonds or opals, some plain, some textured. "You've seen people wearing these all over the city, right?"

Elene nodded. Kylar looked at her blankly. He looked at Capricia. She wasn't wearing one, not that he could see. Were they toe-rings? He stood on his tiptoes to see over the counter to see Capricia's feet.

Capricia caught him looking and laughed. She had the kind of laugh that made you want to join in, even when she was laughing at you. "No, no," she said. "I don't wear one! I'm not married. Why are you looking at my feet?"

Elene slapped her forehead. "Men!"

"Oh," Kylar said. "They're earrings!"

Capricia laughed again.

"What?" he asked. "Women wear matching earrings where we come from. These are all different sizes."

The girls laughed louder and it dawned on him. The earrings weren't for women; they were for couples. One for the man; one for the woman. "Oh," he said.

That would explain all the men he'd seen wearing earrings. He scowled. He could have said which men were concealing weapons in their clothing and known their likely degrees of proficiency with them; what did he care about what they wore in their ears?

"Wow. Look at those," Elene said, pointing out a pair of silvery-gold sparkling rings that looked suspiciously expensive. "Aren't they beautiful?" She turned to Capricia. "Will you tell us all about the rings? We're, ahem, a little unfamiliar with the tradition." Conspicuously, they didn't look at Kylar.

"Here in Waeddryn, when a man wishes to marry a woman, he buys a set of rings and gives them to her. Of course, there is a public ceremony, but the wedding itself is performed in private. You two are married already, right?"

"Right," Kylar said. "We're just new to the city."

"Well, if you're looking to get married in the Waeddryner way, but maybe don't have the money or the inclination for a big ceremony, it's very simple. You don't have to worry about the ceremony at all. The marriage is recognized as long as you've been nailed."

"Nailed?" Kylar asked, his eyes widening.

Capricia flushed. "I mean, as long as you've affixed the seal of your love, or been ringed. But, well, most people just call it getting nailed."

"I'm guessing that's not part of the usual pitch," Kylar said.

"Kylar," Elene said, elbowing him as Capricia flushed again. "Can we see the wedding knives?" she asked sweetly.

Capricia pulled out another drawer lined with black velvet. It was full of ornate daggers with tiny tips.

Kylar recoiled.

Capricia and Elene giggled. "It gets scarier," Capricia said. She smiled her huge smile. "Generally right before...ah, right before the marriage is consummated," she was trying to sound professional, but her ears were bright pink. "Sorry, I've never actually had to explain this. I—Master Bourary usually—never mind. When a man and woman marry, the woman has to give up a lot of her freedom."

"The woman does?" Kylar asked. The look Elene gave him this time was less amused. He swallowed his laughter.

"So the nailing—the ringing or affixing of the seal—"

"Just call it nailing," Kylar said.

"I slipped up, I'm really supposed to call it—" she saw the look on Kylar's face "—right. When the bride and groom retire to their bedchamber, the man gives the rings and the wedding knife to the bride. The man must submit to her. Often, she will..." Capricia blinked and her ears went pink again. She cleared her throat. "Often, she will entice the groom for some time. Then she pierces her own left ear wherever she desires and places her ring there. Then she sits astride her husband on the marriage bed and pierces his left ear."

Kylar's mouth dropped open.

"It's not that bad. It just depends on where your wife decides to—" Capricia looked up as Master Bourary walked into the shop, "affix the seal. Through the ear lobe isn't that bad, but some women will pierce, well, like Master Bourary's wife."

Kylar looked at the round, grinning little man. He wore a glittering gold earring sparkling with rubies. It was through the top of his ear. "Hurt like hell," Master Bourary said. "They call it breaking the maidenhead."

A little moue of pain escaped Kylar's lips. "What?"

Elene was blushing, but her eyes were dancing. For a second he could swear that she was imagining nailing him.

"Well, it's only fair, isn't it?" Master Bourary said. "If a woman has to deal with pain and blood on her wedding night, why shouldn't a man? I tell you what, it makes you gentler. Especially if she twists your ear to remind you!" He guffawed. "That's what you get after twenty generations of queens." He laughed ruefully, but he didn't seem displeased by it.

These people, Kylar realized, were totally mad.

"But that's not the magical part," Capricia said, realizing Kylar was fast losing interest. "When the wife places the ring on her husband's ear, she has to focus all of her love and devotion and desire to be married on the ring, and only then will it seal. If the woman doesn't truly want to be married, it won't even seal."

"But once sealed," Master Bourary said, "neither heaven nor hell can open the ring again. Look," he said. He reached over and slipped the wedding ring off of Kylar's left hand. "Barely a difference in the tan under your ring, huh? Haven't been hitched long?"

"You could make some good ring mail with that trick," Kylar said, trying to circumvent the pitch.

"Oh, honey, stop it, I'm swooning," Elene said, tugging at the bodice of her dress as if she were getting overheated. "You're so romantic."

"Well, actually," Master Bourary said, "the first practitioners of our art were armorers. But look," he said, turning his attention to Elene, obviously seeing her as a more friendly target for his pitch. "With this ring, he can slip it off, it could fall off by itself, who knows? He goes to a tavern and bumps into some tart, and how's she to know that she's poaching on another woman's land? Not that you would ever do that, of course, sir. But with our rings, a married man is always known to be married. Really it's a protection even for women who would flirt with a man without realizing he was married.

"And...if a man or woman wants a divorce—well, you've got to rip that damn ring right out of your ear. Cuts down on divorces, I promise you. But affixing the seal isn't done out of fear, to keep a man or a woman from cuckolding their spouse. It's deeper than that. When a man and woman are sealed, they activate an ancient magic in these rings, a magic that grows as their love grows. It's a magic that helps you feel what your spouse is feeling, a magic that deepens your love and understanding for each other, that helps you communicate more clearly, that—"

"And let me guess," Kylar said. "The more expensive rings have more magic."

Elene's elbow was anything but gentle this time. "Kylar," she said through her teeth.

Master Bourary blinked. "Let me assure you, young master, every ring I make is imbued with magic, even the simplest and cheapest copper band of mine won't break. But yes, I absolutely do spend more time and energy on the gold and mistarille rings. Not only because the people who buy those rings pay more, but also because those materials hold a spell far better than copper or bronze or silver ever could."

"Right," Kylar said. "Well, thanks for your time." He pulled Elene out of the store.

She was not pleased. She stopped in the street. "Kylar, you are a complete ass."

"Honey, didn't you hear what he just said? Some armorer a long time ago had a Talent that would seal metal rings together. Good Talent for an armorer, he can bang out ring mail in days rather than months. Then he gets smart and figures that he can make a lot more money by selling each ring for hundreds of gold than for selling a full set of ring mail for maybe fifty. And lo and behold, an industry's born. It's all horseshit. All that 'growing to understand each other better' stuff? That's what happens to everyone who gets married. And oh, the gold ones have more magic...how obvious is that? Did you see how many of their rings were gold? They probably get nine tenths of the poor idiots in this city to save up for a gold ring they can't afford because what woman is going to be happy if she gets a copper ring that 'barely holds the spell'?"

"I would," she said quietly.

It took the wind out of him.

She covered her face. "I thought if you ever wanted to get married for real, that, you know. It would be a way we could make it official. If we ever wanted to. I mean, I know we're not ready for that. I'm not suggesting that we do that right away or anything."

Why am I always the asshole?

Because she's too good for you.

"So you knew what that place was?" he asked, more gently, although he was still pissed off, though he couldn't have said whether it was at her or at himself.

"Aunt Mea told me about it."

"Is that why you've been nibbling on my ears at night?"

"Kylar!" she said.

"Is it?"

"Aunt Mea said it works wonders." Elene couldn't meet his gaze; she was totally mortified.

"Well maybe for these twists!"

"Kylar!" Elene raised her eyebrows, as if to say, *We are in the middle of a crowded market, would you shut up?*

He looked around. He'd never seen so many earrings in his life. How hadn't he noticed it before? And he was right, almost every one of them was gold and everyone wore their hair in ways that left their ears exposed.

"I've seen that girl before," Kylar said.

"Capricia?"

"I was out the other night and some hoodlums were coming to hurt her. Before, I would have killed them. Instead, I scared them."

She looked uncertain why he was telling her this now. "Well, that's great. You see? Violence doesn't solve—"

"Honey, one of them was the Shinga. I made a vengeful man *wet* himself in front of his subordinates. Violence was the only solution. That girl's in deeper trouble now than before I helped her." He swore under his breath. "Why'd you even take me in there? We don't even have enough to buy Uly a birthday present. How would we afford those?"

"I'm sorry, all right?" Elene said. "I just wanted to see what it was like."

"It's the sword, isn't it? You still want me to sell the sword."

"Quit it! I haven't said anything about the sword. I'm sorry. I thought you might be interested. I'm not asking you to buy me anything." She wasn't looking at him now, and she certainly wasn't holding his hand. Well, that was better than tears. Wasn't it?

He walked beside her for a while as she pretended to browse through the open air shops, picking up produce, examining cloth, looking at dolls they couldn't afford.

"So," he said finally. "Since we're already fighting..."

She turned and looked up at him, not laughing. "I don't want to talk about sex, Kylar."

He raised his hands in mock surrender. Still trying to be funny. Still failing.

"Kylar, do you remember how it feels to kill?"

He didn't have to think back that far. It was triumphant, the terrible pleasure of mastery, followed by desolation, a sick hollowness in his chest, knowing that even a hardened criminal might have changed and now would never have that chance. Did she understand part of him loved it?

"Honey, we all only have so much time and so many gifts. You have more gifts than most, and I know you want to do good. I know you're passionate about that, and I love that about you. But look what happens when you try to save the world with a sword. Your master tried, and look what a bitter, sad old man he became. I don't want to see that happen to you. I know that after the wealth you had and the things you did that being an apothecary seems like a small ambition. It's not small, Kylar. It's huge. You can do so much more good for the world by being a good father, and a good husband, and a healer, than you ever could by being a killer. Do you think it's a mistake the God has given you an ability to heal? That's the divine economy. He is willing to cover over what we've destroyed with new and beautiful things.

"Like us. Who'd have imagined that you and I could get safely off the streets and find each other again? Who would have imagined we could adopt Uly? She's got a chance now—after being born to an assassin and a madam. Only the God could do that, Kylar. I know you don't believe in him yet, but his hand is at work here. He's given us this chance, and I want to hold onto it. Stay with me. Leave that life. You weren't happy there. Why would you want to go back?"

"I don't," he said. But it was only half true. Elene came into his arms, but even as he held her, he knew he was false.

21

In the early afternoon heat, Kylar paused outside a shop in the nobles' district. He stepped into an alley and thirty seconds later thought that he was wearing a fair facsimile of Baron Kirof's face. He wished he'd thought to change into a nicer tunic. Of course, after the fire, he only had one other tunic, and it was worse than this one. It was probably possible to wear illusory clothes like his illusory face, but that was too much for Kylar to juggle—he imagined trying to make an illusory robe flap realistically as he moved and quickly decided his own clothes would do. He tucked the box under his arm and headed inside.

Grand Master Haylin's shop was a huge, squat square. The inside was well-lit and more richly appointed than any smithy Kylar had ever seen. Row on row of armor lined the walls, and rack on rack of weapons sat before them. It was clean, too, and hardly smoky—Grand Master Haylin must have figured out a clever flue system, because the sales area and the work area weren't separated. Kylar saw one of the under-armorers helping a noble pick out the ore that would become his sword. Another noble watched as apprentices hammered on steel that would become his cuirass. The customers were funneled through the work area, confined to special blue rugs so they didn't get in the way of the apprentices and journeymen. It was a good gimmick, and doubtless worth its weight in gold. Though whether the nobles were paying for great weapons and armor or just an experience, Kylar wasn't sure.

The racks of weapons and armor here by the door were nothing special, doubtless the work of the under-armorers and journeymen. But that wasn't what he was looking for. Kylar looked to the back and finally saw the man himself.

Grand Master Haylin was mostly bald, with a fringe of gray hair around a knobby pate. He was lean and stooped and appeared to be near-sighted, though of course he had the muscular shoulders and arms of a much younger man. His leather apron was pitted and stained from work, and he was guiding an apprentice's hand, showing the boy the correct angle to strike the metal. Kylar headed toward him.

"Excuse me? Hello, my lord, how may I help you?" a smiling young man said, intercepting him. He was a little too smiley.

"I need to speak with the Grand Master," Kylar said, the sinking feeling in his stomach telling him that Haylin was going to prove to be much farther away than just across the shop.

"I'm afraid he's working, but I'd be happy to help you with whatever you require." Smiley's brief glance down at Kylar's clothes told him he didn't expect this to be important. Just what Kylar needed: some bureaucratic *lut*.

Kylar looked over Smiley's shoulder and gaped. It was an expression he'd never tried with Baron Kirof's face, but it must have been acceptable, because Smiley turned to see what was wrong.

Kylar went invisible. He felt like a bad child when Smiley turned around and saw no one there.

"What the...?" Smiley said. He rubbed his eyes. "Hey," he said to a coworker behind the counter, "did you just see me talking to a fat red-bearded guy?"

The man behind the counter shook his head. "You seein' things again, Wood?"

Smiley shook his head and walked back toward the counter, cursing under his breath.

Kylar walked through the shop, invisible. Dodging scurrying apprentices, he came to stand by Grand Master Haylin's elbow. The man was inspecting a dozen of his under-armorer's swords that were laid out on a table for his approval.

"The third one wasn't properly fired," Kylar said, appearing behind the smith. "There's a weakness right just above the hilt. And the next one's poorly tempered."

Grand Master Haylin turned and looked at Kylar's feet—two paces outside the blue carpet, then he looked at the weak sword. He tossed it into an empty red crate. "Werner," Haylin said to a young man who was swearing at an apprentice. "That's the third reject this month. One more and you're done."

Werner blanched. He immediately left off cursing the apprentice.

"As for this," Grand Master Haylin said to Kylar, gesturing to the poorly tempered sword. "You know what happens when you scatter diamonds in front of chickens?"

"Tough poultry?"

"Valuable gizzards. It's a waste, son. This is for an army order. For two hundred fifty queens for a hundred swords, some peasant sword swinger can spend more time with a whetstone. You know your swords, but I'm a busy man. What do you want?"

"Five minutes. Privately. It'll be worth your time."

The Grand Master raised an eyebrow but acquiesced. He led Kylar up the stairs to a special room. As they passed Smiley, the young man said, "You can't—you can't—"

Grand Master Haylin cocked an eyebrow at the young man. Smiley's greasy smile withered. "Don't mind that," Haylin said. "That's my fifth son. Bit of a throw-off, huh?"

Kylar didn't know what that meant, but he nodded. "I'd toss him in the reject crate."

Haylin laughed. "Wish I could do the same with his mother. My third wife is the answer to all the first two's prayers."

The special room was obviously used as infrequently as possible.

A fine walnut table with several chairs occupied the center, but most of the room was given to display cases. Fine swords and expensive suits of armor filled the room like an elite guard. Kylar looked at them closely. Several were the Grand Master's work: master pieces to demonstrate what he was capable of, but others were old, in a variety of styles and periods of armament, show pieces. Perfect.

"You're down to three minutes," Haylin said, squinting at Kylar.

"I'm a man of special talents," Kylar said, sitting across from the man.

The Grand Master arched an eyebrow again. He did have terrifically expressive eyebrows.

Kylar ran his fingers through his red hair and changed it to dirty blond. He passed his hand over his face and his nose grew sharper, longer. He scrubbed his face as if washing it, and the beard disappeared to reveal lightly pockmarked cheeks and sharp eyes. Of course, it was all show. He didn't have to touch his face—but this man seemed to appreciate demonstrations.

Grand Master Haylin's face went dead white and his jaw dropped. He blinked rapidly and his voice came out as a croak. He cleared his throat. "Master Starfire? Gaelan Starfire?"

"You know me?" Kylar asked, stunned. Gaelan Starfire was the hero of a dozen bard's tales. But the face Kylar was wearing was Durzo Blint's.

"I was—I was just a boy when you came to my grandfather's shop. You said—you said you might come back long after we'd given up on you. Oh, sir! My grandfather said it might be in my father's time or mine, but we never believed him."

Disoriented, Kylar tried to think. Durzo was Gaelan Starfire? Kylar knew that Durzo hadn't been known by the same name for seven hundred years, of course. But *Gaelan Starfire?* That name hadn't even been mentioned among all the others that Aristarchos had claimed for his master.

It sent a pang of grief through Kylar. He hadn't known, and some smith in Caernarvon had. How little he knew the man who'd raised him, the man who'd died for him. Durzo had turned bitter by the time Kylar had known him. Who had he been when he'd been Gaelan Starfire, fifty years ago? Kylar suspected that he could have been friends with that man.

"We've kept it secret, I swear," Grand Master Haylin said. Kylar was still disoriented. This man, who was old enough to be his grandfather, who was at the height of his fame, was treating Kylar like— like he was an immortal, nearly a god. "What can I do for you, my lord?"

"I don't, I don't..." Kylar said. "Please, don't treat me differently because of your grandfather. I just wanted you to take me seriously; I didn't think you'd remember that. I didn't even remember you. You've changed quite a bit." He smirked to seal the lie.

"And you haven't changed at all," Haylin said, stunned. "Um, all right," he said, his eyebrows waggling up and down in quick succession as he tried to pull himself together. "Um. Well. What are you looking for?"

"I'm looking to sell a sword." Kylar drew Retribution off his back and laid it on the table.

Haylin picked up the big sword appreciatively in his thick, callused hands, then immediately set it down. He stared at the hilt, blinking. He ran his fingers over it, his eyes wide. "You never drop this sword, do you?" he said.

Kylar shrugged. Of course he didn't.

Still looking like he wasn't sure he was awake, the Grand Master spit on his palm and grabbed the sword again.

"What'd you—"

A drop of moisture wicked off the hilt onto the table. Grand Master Haylin released the sword and opened his palm. It was completely dry. He gave a little cry, but he couldn't take his eyes off the sword. He leaned closer and closer until his nose was almost against it. He turned the blade to look at it on edge.

"By the gods," he said. "It's true."

"What?" Kylar said.

"The coal matrices. They're perfect. I'd bet my right arm every last one has four links, don't they? The blade's a perfect diamond, my lord. So thin you can barely see it, but unbreakable. Most diamonds can be sheared with another diamond, because they're never perfect, but if there are no flaws anywhere—this blade is indestructible, and not just the blade, the hilt, too. But my lord, if this is...I thought your sword was black."

Kylar touched the blade and let the ka'kari whoosh out of his skin to cover it. The word MERCY inscribed in the blade was covered with JUSTICE in ka'kari black.

Grand Master Haylin looked pained. "Oh my lord....My grandfather told us....I never understood. I feel blind, yet I'm almost happy for my blindness."

"What are you talking about?"

"I don't have the Talent, Lord Starfire. I can't begin to see how amazing this blade is. My grandfather could, and he said it haunted him all his days. He knew what Talent had gone into this blade, he could see it, but he could never equal it. He said it made the work of his own hands look cheap and tawdry—and he was famous for his work. But I never thought to see Retribution with my own eyes. My lord, you can't sell this."

"Well, it doesn't come in black," Kylar said lightly, sucking the ka'kari back into his hand. "If that knocks a bit off the price."

"My lord, you don't understand. Even if I could give you what this is worth—even if I could somehow fix a price on it—I could never— it's worth more than I'll make in my whole life. Even if I could buy it, I could never sell it; it's too valuable. Maybe one or two collectors in the world have the wealth and the appreciation to buy such a sword. Even then, my lord, this isn't a sword that belongs on display, it belongs in the hand of a hero. It belongs in your hand. Look, a hilt that won't slip from your hand even if it's bloody or wet. The moisture slides right off. It's not just brilliant, it's practical. That's not a showpiece. It's art. It's killing art. Like you." He threw his hands up and slumped in his chair, as if exhausted just by the sight of Retribution. "Though my grandfather did say the inscription was in Hyrillic—oh my."

The MERCY on the blade shifted before their eyes, into a language Kylar couldn't read. He was stunned. It had never done that before.

A snake wriggled in his stomach and strangled his guts, a snake of losing something whose value he couldn't even calculate. It was the same feeling he felt as he thought of his dead master, a man whose worth he had barely known.

"Nonetheless," he said, his throat tight. "I must sell it." If he kept it, he would kill again. He had no doubt of it. In his hand, it was pitiless justice. He had to sell it, if he was to stay true to Elene. As long as he held onto the sword, he held onto his old life.

"My lord, do you need money? I'll give you whatever you want."

The small, mean part of Kylar considered it. Surely this man could spare more than enough money for what Kylar needed. "No, I, I need to sell it. It's... it has to do with a woman."

"You're selling an artifact worth a kingdom so you can be with a woman? You're immortal! Even the longest marriage will end in a tiny fraction of your life!"

Kylar grimaced. "That's right."

"You're not just selling this sword, are you? You're giving it up. You're giving up the way of the sword."

Looking at the tabletop, Kylar nodded.

"She must be some woman."

"She is," Kylar said. "What can you give me for it?"

"It depends on how soon you need it."

Kylar didn't know if he could keep his courage up. He knew what he was about to say would probably cost him thousands, but losing Elene would cost more. He'd never really cared about being rich anyway. "Just whatever you can get me before I leave."

"Before you leave the city?"

"Before I leave the shop." Kylar swallowed, but that damn lump wouldn't disappear.

The Grand Master opened his mouth to protest, but he could see Kylar's mind was made up. "Thirty-one thousand queens," he said. "Maybe a few hundred more, depending on what sales we've done today. Six thousand in gold, the rest in promissory notes redeemable at most money changers, though for that sum, you'd have to hit half the money changers in the city. You'll have to go to the Blue Giant directly if you want to change it all."

Kylar goggled at the sum. It would be enough to buy a house, repay Aunt Mea, start a shop with a huge inventory, buy an entire wardrobe for Elene, and still put some away, in addition to buying a pair of the finest wedding rings money could buy. And the man was protesting it wasn't nearly enough?

~A good price for your birthright, huh?~

The thought almost took the wind out of Kylar. He stood abruptly. "Done," he said. He walked to the door and grabbed it.

"Um...my lord," Grand Master Haylin said. He gestured to his own face.

"Oh." Kylar concentrated and his features fattened and his hair reddened again.

Within five minutes, a still-stunned Smiley had helped load a chest of sovereigns—worth twenty queens each—and watched as his father put a thick wad of promissory notes on top of that. It totaled 31,400 queens. The chest wasn't large, but it weighed as much as two large men. The Grand Master called for a horse, but Kylar asked if they would put two broad leather straps on it instead. Journeymen and apprentices stopped to watch, but Kylar didn't care. Smirking, Haylin attached them himself.

"My lord," Haylin said, finishing with the straps. "If you ever want it back, it's here."

"Perhaps. In your grandsons' time."

Grandmaster Haylin smiled broadly.

Kylar knew he shouldn't have said it so loudly. He shouldn't have waved off the horse. He didn't care. Somehow, it just felt so good to be speaking with a man who knew something of what he was and wasn't afraid or disgusted—even if the man did think he was his master. But then, Kylar was probably more like Gaelan Starfire than Durzo Blint had been anyway. It felt so good to be known and accepted, he didn't care that he was being reckless.

With a surge of his Talent, Kylar hoisted the chest onto his back. Open gasps filled the smithy. The truth was, it was almost too heavy to carry even with the Talent. Kylar nodded to Grand Master Haylin and walked out.

"Who the hell was that?" Kylar heard Smiley ask.

"Someday, when you're ready, I might tell you," the Grand Master said.

22

"Hello," Kylar said to Capricia when he returned to the ringery.

"Hello," she said, surprised. She was alone, closing up the shop.

"The ass is back." He grimaced. "Sorry about...before."

"What?" she said. "No, you were fine. I understand that it all seems strange if you're not from here. Men never like it—though the women have to pierce their ears, too, and they never complain." She shrugged.

"Right, well..." Kylar said, then he realized he had nothing to say. What was it about jewelry that made him feel inadequate? "Right," he finished lamely.

"Honestly," she said, "most men barely notice the pain. I mean, their brides make sure they're distracted. Technically, you consummate the marriage only after the nailing, but most cases, it's pretty much only technically."

Kylar coughed. He'd been thinking about that. "Uh, do you remember which ones she was pointing to?" Kylar asked.

"Of course," Capricia said. She laughed. "I'm afraid they're the ones that really hold the spells." Her eyes twinkled and he blushed.

"I have the misfortune of having a wife with excellent taste."

"It reflects well on her other choices," Capricia said, smiling her big smile at him. Whatever the fallout with the Shinga was going to be, Kylar was glad he'd saved her. She pulled out the drawer and set it in front of him. As she set it down, she scowled and grabbed a pair of rings out of the drawer. "Just a second," she said, and knelt behind the counter, tucking them away, then she stood back up. "I think it was one of these," she said, pointing to several along the top row of woven gold and mistarille entwined.

"How much are these?" he asked.

"Twenty-four hundred, twenty-eight hundred, and thirty-two hundred."

He whistled in spite of himself.

"We do have similar styles in white and yellow gold that are more affordable," Capricia said. "The mistarille makes them pretty ridiculous."

Jorsin Alkestes' sword had been mistarille with a core of hardened gold, Durzo said. It took a special forge to melt mistarille because it wouldn't melt until it was three times hotter than steel. Once it attained its working heat, it retained it for hours, unlike other metals that had to be reheated over and over. Smiths found it a pure joy and a pure terror to work with, because after that first heating and the first hours they had to work with, it wouldn't melt again. They only got one chance to get it right. Only a smith with substantial Talent could attempt any large-scale work with mistarille.

"Does anyone wear pure mistarille rings?" he asked as he scanned the rings. He could have sworn Elene's eyes had lit up when she saw one of these sets. Which one was it?

She shook her head. "Even if you could afford it, you wouldn't want it, Master Bourary says. He says that some of the simpler spells actually hold better in gold. Even the oldest rings combine the two metals. He has a pair that his great-great-great-something grandfather made that look like pure mistarille, but they contain a core of yellow gold and diamond. It's pretty amazing. He lined the mistarille with tiny holes so you can see the gold and diamonds sparkling through it if the light is right."

Kylar was almost starting to believe the talk about spells. Either Master Bourary was the real thing, or he'd been very careful to learn how to speak about magic from people who were.

It still felt like madness, to be looking at rings that cost two or three thousand gold. He should have asked Grand Master Haylin about the rings this afternoon. The Grand Master would have known if they were legitimate. But Kylar's heart was light. He'd already sold his birthright. He was committed. Now it was just a matter of finding the perfect ring to please the woman he loved, the woman who was saving him from becoming the bitter wreck Durzo Blint had become.

Really, the magic in the rings didn't matter. What mattered was letting Elene know what she was worth to him.

"There was one set, I swear it was in this box," Kylar told Capricia. "What were those ones you put away?"

"Those were just a display set—well, not actually a display set. The queen got furious with a gem merchant who wouldn't sell her some jewels a decade ago and she outlawed display sets. So it's not technically a display set, but it's not really for sale. We have other drawers; it might have been in one of those."

"Just show me the ones I asked about," Kylar said. He was suddenly skeptical. Was this a sales ploy? He'd seen it done before—a pretty girl tells a guy, "Here, this is very nice," as she sets aside something ridiculously expensive and pulls out something cheap, and the man instantly says, "What about those?" to prove his manhood.

But Capricia didn't come across like that. She seemed genuine. She pulled out the rings and set them in front of him. Just looking at them, Kylar could see the size of his shop's inventory shrinking.

"Those are the ones," he said. The design was seductively simple and elegant, a bare half-twist of silvery metal that somehow sparkled gold in the light when he picked up the larger one.

Capricia gasped and raised a hand as if he were going to break it. He gazed into one of the shop's mirrors and held up the earring by his left earlobe. It looked kind of effete, but then, apparently none of the thousands of men he'd seen around the city worried about looking effete.

"Hmm," he said. He moved the earring up higher on his ear. That looked a little more masculine. "What's the most painful place a woman can nail a guy?"

"Right about," she leaned forward and pointed, but he couldn't see it in the mirror. He moved and her finger touched his ear. "Oh!" she said. "I'm so sorry. I didn't mean to touch—"

"What?" he said. Then he remembered. "Oh, no, it's my fault. Seriously, where I come from, ears are no big deal. Did you say right here? So it goes over the top?" He checked the mirror. Yes, definitely more masculine, and it would hurt like hell. For some reason, that made him feel better.

He picked up the smaller earring and—being careful not to touch her—held it up to Capricia's ear. It was beautiful.

"I'll take them," he said.

"I'm really sorry," she said. "We don't have anything exactly like that for sale, but Master Bourary could make something that looks almost identical."

"You said there were no display items," Kylar said.

"Not technically. After the queen proclaimed the law—well, everything's for sale. They just put ridiculous prices on what they don't want to sell."

"And these are one of those?" Kylar asked. Now the house was getting smaller.

"These are actually the rings I was telling you about earlier. The ones Master Bourary's great-great-great grandfather made, mistarille over gold with diamonds?" She smiled weakly. "I'm sorry. I'm not trying to embarrass you. They weren't even supposed to be in this case."

"How ridiculous a price are we talking?" Kylar asked.

"Ridiculous," she said.

"How ridiculous?"

"Totally ridiculous." She winced.

Kylar sighed. "Just tell me."

"Thirty-one thousand four hundred queens. Sorry."

It hit Kylar in the stomach. It was a coincidence, of course, but...

Elene would call it the divine economy. He'd sold Retribution for exactly what it would cost to marry her.

With nothing left over? *Elene, if this is your God's economy, you serve a niggardly God. I don't even have enough left to buy a wedding knife.*

"On the bright side," Capricia said, forcing a chuckle, "we'd throw in a wedding knife free."

A block of ice dropped into Kylar's stomach.

"I'm sorry," she said, mistaking the stricken expression on his face. "We do have some lovely—"

"You get paid a commission on your sales?" he asked.

"One-tenth of anything over a thousand in sales a day," she said.

"So, if you sold these, what would you do with—what?—more than three thousand queens?"

"I don't know—why are you—"

"What would you do?"

She shrugged and started to answer, stopped, and finally said, "I'd move my family. We live in a pretty rough neighborhood and we keep having trouble with—oh, what does it matter? Believe me, I've dreamed about it ever since I started working here. I thought about selling those rings and how it would change everything for us. I used to pray about it every day, but my mother says we're safe enough. Anyway, the God doesn't answer greedy prayers like that."

Kylar's heart went cold. They'd move away from that vengeful, arrogant little Shinga. Kylar wouldn't have to commit murder to keep them safe.

"No," Kylar said, pocketing the mistarille earrings and grabbing a wedding knife. "He answers them like this." He heaved the chest onto the counter and opened it. Capricia gaped. Her hands shook as she unfolded note after note. She looked up at Kylar, tears filling her eyes.

"Tell your parents your guardian angel said to move. Not next week. Not tomorrow. Tonight. When I saved you, I embarrassed the Shinga. He's sworn revenge."

Her eyes stayed huge, but she nodded imperceptibly. Her hand popped up like an automaton's. "Gift box?" she asked in a strangled voice. "Free."

He took the jewelry box from her hand and walked out the door, locking it behind him. He tucked the earrings in the decorative box, and dropped it all in a pocket, suddenly as poor as a pauper. He'd sold his birthright. He'd given away one of the last things he had to remember Durzo by. He'd traded a magical sword for two metal circles. And now he didn't have a copper to his name. Thirty-one thousand four hundred queens and he didn't even have enough left over to buy Uly a birthday present.

We're finished, God. From now on, you answer your own fucking prayers.

23

"Are you and Elene going to be all right?" Uly asked. They were working together that evening, Uly fetching ingredients while Kylar brewed a draught that reduced fevers.

"Of course we are. Why?"

"Aunt Mea says it's fine you fight so much. She says that if I'm scared I just have to listen and if I hear the bed creaking after you fight, I'll know things will be all right. She says that means that you've made up. But I never hear the bed creaking."

Blood rushed to Kylar's cheeks. "I, well, I think ... You know, that's a question you should ask Elene."

"She said to ask you, and she got all embarrassed too."

"I'm not embarrassed!" Kylar said. "Hand me the mayberry."

"Aunt Mea says it's wrong to lie. I've seen horses mating at the castle, but Aunt Mea says it's not scary like that."

"No," Kylar said quietly, mashing the mayberry with a pestle, "it's scary in its own way."

"What?" Uly asked.

"Uly, you are way too young for us to have this conversation. Yarrow root."

"Aunt Mea said you might say that. She said she'd talk to me about it if you were too embarrassed. She just made me promise to ask you first." Uly handed him the knotted brown root.

"Aunt Mea," Kylar said, "thinks about sex too much."

"Ahem," a voice said behind Kylar. He flinched.

"I'm going out to check on Mistress Vatsen," Aunt Mea said. "Do you need anything?"

"Um, uh, no," he said. Surely she couldn't have that bland look on her face if she'd heard what he just said.

"Kylar, are you all right?" she asked. She touched his hot cheek. "You look strangely flushed." She rummaged through the newly organized shelves—it seemed to take her longer than when they had been a mess—and tucked a few things in her basket. When she walked past Kylar, who was bent over the potion as if it took all of his concentration, she pinched his butt.

He practically hit the ceiling, though he strangled back a shout. Uly looked at him quizzically.

"You're right," Aunt Mea said at the door. "But don't you get any ideas. I'm too old for you."

Kylar flushed brighter and she laughed. He could hear her continuing to laugh heartily even as she walked down the street.

"Crazy old coot," he said. "Noranton seed."

Uly handed him the vial of flat, purplish seeds, and screwed her mouth into a tight line. "Kylar, if things don't work out with Elene, will you marry me?"

He dropped the entire vial into the mixture.

"WHAT?"

"I asked Elene how old you were and she said twenty. And Aunt Mea said her husband was nine years older than her and that's even further apart than you and me. And I love you and you love me and you and Elene fight all the time but you and me never fight..."

Kylar was confused at first. He and Elene hadn't fought for more than a week. Then he realized that Uly had been spending her nights over at one of her new friends' houses—probably because Kylar and Elene's fighting had upset her so much. Now Uly had an eager, scared look on her face that told him how he answered her could break her heart. Specifically, the first thought that popped into his head—*I don't love you like that*—was not going to be a good choice.

How did I get into this? I've got to be the first father in Midcyru to ever have to explain sex to his daughter while still a virgin myself.

What was he supposed to say? "I'm not actually married to Elene yet, so when we fight we can't make up the way I'd like. In fact, if we could make up the way I'd like, we probably wouldn't fight in the first place"? Kylar couldn't wait until he actually married Elene. All their conflicts about sex would finally be behind them. What a relief!

In the meantime, Uly was staring at him, waiting, big eyes wide, uncertain. Oh no, that looked like a lip quiver.

The opening door saved him. A well-dressed man stepped inside, a house crest embroidered in the chest of his tunic. He was tall and spare, but his face was pinched, making him look like a rodent.

"Is this Aunt Mea's?" he asked.

"Yes, it is," Kylar said. "But I'm afraid Aunt Mea just stepped out for a while."

"Oh that's fine," the man said. "You're her assistant, Kyle?"

"Kylar."

"Ah, yes. You're younger than I expected. I've come here for your help."

"Mine?"

"You're the man who saved Lord Aevan, aren't you? He's been telling everyone who will listen that you did with one potion what a dozen physickers couldn't with months of treatment. I am the head steward of High Lord Garazul. My lord has gout."

Kylar rubbed his jaw. He stared at the bottles lining the walls.

"I can return later if you wish," the steward said.

"No, it won't take a minute," Kylar said. He started grabbing bottles and giving orders to Uly. She was the perfect helper, quick and silent. He soon had four bowls mixing simultaneously, two over heat, two cold. In another two minutes, he was done. The steward looked utterly fascinated by the whole process. It made Kylar think that Grand Master Haylin was onto something in showing off the creation process. He knew in that moment that if he ever had a big shop, he'd set it up in exactly the same way—give people a show along with their potions. It was an oddly satisfying little dream.

"Here's what you need to do," Kylar said. "Give him two spoonfuls of this every four hours. I'm guessing your master is fat, hardly ever gets out? Loves his drink?"

The steward said, "He's got a little extra... well, yes, fat as a leviathan, in fact. Drinks like one, too."

"That potion will take care of the pain in his feet and joints. It will help the gout a little, but as long as he's fat and drinks a lot of wine, he'll never get better. He'll need to buy this same potion every time his gout flares up for the rest of his life. You tell him if he wants the gout gone, he needs to stop drinking. If he won't, which I'm betting will be the case, start putting two drops of this—" Kylar handed the man the second vial, "in every glass of his wine. It will give him a terrific headache. Make sure you do it every time he takes wine. While you're at it, you can give him this each morning and night for his bad stomach. And feed him less. Give a little of this last one with each meal, it should help him feel full sooner."

"How'd you know he had a bad stomach?"

Kylar smiled mysteriously. "And take him off everything else the physickers have ordered, especially the bloodletting and the leeches. He should be a new man in six weeks, if you make him lose weight."

"How much?" the steward asked.

"Depends on how fat he is," Kylar said.

The steward laughed. "No, how much do I owe you?"

Kylar thought about it. He did some math of what the ingredients had cost and doubled it. He told the steward.

The mousy man looked at him, astonished. "A bit of advice, young man. You should get a shop on the north side, because if this works, there's a lot of noble business that's going to be coming your way. And another thing: if this even helps a little, you should charge twice that. If it actually does what you said, you should charge ten times that—otherwise the nobles won't believe it's real."

Kylar smiled, warmed just to hear someone speak to him as if he knew what he was doing—which he did. "Well then, you owe me ten times what I said before."

The steward laughed. "If Lord Garazul gets better, I'll do better than that. Here's all I've got on me in the meantime." He tossed Kylar two new silver coins. "Good day, young master."

Watching the man go, Kylar was surprised how good it felt. Maybe it was better to heal than to kill. Or maybe it was just good to feel appreciated. How had Durzo done it? He'd been a dozen different heroes over the ages—maybe scores of different heroes. Hadn't he ever wanted to just announce himself? Tell everyone who he was, and have them show the proper awe? *Here I am, adore me.*

But Durzo had never come across like that. Kylar had grown up with him and had never had a clue that his master was the Night Angel, much less any of the other identities he'd had. Why not? Durzo had seemed arrogant in certain parts of his life. He'd certainly shown a huge disdain for most wetboys and most of the Sa'kagé, but he'd never equated himself with the great heroes of history.

The pang of loss cut Kylar again. Gods, Durzo had been dead three months—and despite the passage of time, it wasn't getting any better.

Kylar felt the little box in his pocket. *He died so I could have Elene.* Kylar tried to push Durzo from his mind with that thought. *Let's just get through Uly's birthday, and then I can ask Elene to marry me. Then Uly can hear more creaking than she's ever imagined.*

"Kylar," Uly said, jerking him out of his reverie. "Are you going to answer my question?"

Ah, shit. "Uly," he said gently. "I know you don't feel like it, and

you're certainly as smart as someone a lot older, but you're still a..."
He furrowed his brow, knowing the next part wasn't going to go over
well. "You're still a child." It was true, dammit.

"No I'm not."

"Yes, you are."

"I just had my first moon blood this week. Aunt Mea says that
means I'm a woman now. It really hurt and it scared me at first. My
stomach got real sore and my back and then—"

"Ah!" Kylar waved his hands, trying to make her stop.

"What? Aunt Mea said it was nothing to be embarrassed about."

"Aunt Mea's not your father!"

"Who is?" Uly asked, quick as a whip.

Kylar said nothing.

"And who's my mother? You know, don't you? My nurses always
treated me different from the other children. The last one always got
scared whenever I got hurt. When I got a cut on my face once, she was
so afraid it would be a scar that she didn't sleep for weeks. Sometimes
a lady would watch us play in the gardens, but she always wore a cloak
and hood. Was she my mother?"

Mute, Kylar nodded. It was exactly what Momma K would have
done. She had doubtless stayed away for Uly's safety as much as she
could bear, but every once in a while, the defenses would have broken
down.

"She's important?" Uly asked. Every orphan's wish. Kylar knew.

Kylar nodded again.

"Why'd she leave me?"

Kylar blew out a breath. "You deserve the answer to that, Uly, but I
can't tell you. It's one of the secrets I know that don't belong to me. I
promise I'll tell you when I can."

"Are you going to leave me? If we got married, I could go with
you."

If anyone thought children couldn't suffer pain as deeply as adults,
Kylar wished they could see Uly's eyes now. For all he loved her, he'd

been treating her as a child rather than as a human being. Uly's brief life was a history of abandonment: her father, her mother, one nurse after another. She just wanted something solid in her life.

Kylar hugged her. "I won't abandon you," he swore. "Not ever. Not. Ever."

24

Vi rode into Caernarvon as the sun set. In her weeks on the trail, she'd decided her strategy. Surely Kylar would be known to the Sa'kagé here. If he was at all like Hu Gibbet, he wouldn't like to go long without killing. If he had taken any jobs, the Shinga would know him. Such a skilled wetboy wouldn't pass without notice.

On the other hand, if Kylar hadn't taken any work, chances were still good that the Sa'kagé's eyes and ears would know he had come to Caernarvon. Vi had heard precious little praise for Caernarvon's Sa'kagé, and if Kylar were truly committed to hiding himself, Vi would never find him, but it had been three months. Criminals always went back to their crimes, even if they had plenty of money, if only because they didn't know what else to do with themselves. What was a wetboy without killing?

The shops were all closed. The decent families were home for the night, and the inns and brothels were just starting to roar as Vi passed deeper into the southern section of the city. She was wearing white fawn-skin riding pants and a loose men's tunic of cotton. Her red hair was pulled back in a simple tight ponytail. In Cenaria, the rainy season was starting, but here the summer lingered on and Vi believed in being comfortable as she traveled, fashion be damned. She only worried about fashion when she needed something from it. Still, after two hard weeks in the saddle, she wouldn't mind a bath.

She rode down the fourth bad street in a row, wondering why she hadn't been mugged yet. She'd concealed all her weapons to make herself look totally vulnerable. What was wrong with these people?

Twenty minutes later, someone finally stepped out of the shadows.

"Nice night we're having, innit?" the man said. He was scruffy, dirty, inebriated. Perfect. He held a cudgel in one hand and a wineskin in the other.

"Are you robbing me?" Vi asked.

Half a dozen teenagers came out of the shadows and surrounded her.

"Well, I—" the man grinned, displaying two black front teeth. "This here's a toll road and you're going to have—"

"If you're not robbing me, get the hell out of my way. Or are you a complete idiot?"

The smile disappeared. "Well, I am," he said, finally. "Robbing you, that is. Tom Gray don't get outta no bitch's way." Then he almost brained himself as he tried to drink from his cudgel instead of the wineskin. The boys laughed, but one of them took her black mare's reins.

"I need to see the Shinga," she said. "Can you take me to him, or do I need to find someone else to mug me?"

"You're not going anywhere until you give me thirteen—"

One of the boys coughed.

"—err, fourteen silvers." His eyes traced over her breasts, and he added, "And maybe a little somethin' somethin' besides."

"How about you take me to the Shinga, and I'll leave your pathetic manhood intact?" Vi said.

Tom's face darkened. He threw the wineskin to one of the boys and stepped toward Vi, raising his cudgel. He grabbed her sleeve and yanked her out of the saddle.

Using the momentum of his pull, Vi flipped off the saddle and kicked him in the face, landing lightly on her feet as Tom Gray went sprawling.

"Can any of the rest of you take me to the Shinga?" she asked, ignoring Tom.

They all looked confused at how Tom had ended up on the other side of the street with a bloody nose, but after a moment, a scrawny young man with a big nose said, "Shinga Sniggle don't let us just come up to him any old time. But Tom's friends with him."

"Sniggle?" Vi asked, smirking. "That's not really his name, is it?"

Tom picked himself up off the ground. He roared and charged Vi.

Not even looking at him, she waited until he was two steps away and poked her foot into his hip in mid-stride. When his foot didn't come forward to take the next step as he'd expected, he went skidding across the cobblestones at Vi's feet. She didn't break eye contact with the boy.

"I, uh, yes, Barush Sniggle," the boy said, looking at Tom. He didn't seem to find anything comical about it. "Who are you?" he asked.

She contorted her fingers into the thieves' sign.

"That's a little different than ours," the young man said. "Where you from?"

"Cenaria," she said.

All of them took a step back. "No shit?" he said. "Cenarian Sa'kagé?"

"Now you," Vi said, grabbing Tom Gray by his greasy hair. "Are you going to take me to the Shinga? Or do I have to break something?"

He swore at her.

She broke his nose.

He sputtered blood and swore again.

"Slow learner, huh?" She hit him in his broken nose, and then grabbed his head. Jamming her fingers deep into the pain points behind his ears, she lifted him to his feet. He screamed with surprising vigor. It was unfortunate she'd broken his nose first, because he sprayed blood all over her. Vi didn't mind, though. Nysos was the god of the potent liquids: blood, wine, and semen. It had been weeks since she'd given him an offering. Perhaps this would appease him until she found Kylar.

She held her fingers deep in those pain points, letting Tom Gray scream, letting him spray blood over her shirt and face. The boys cowered back, about to break and run.

"Enough!" a voice called from the darkness.

Vi released Tom and he fell.

A short, squat figure walked forward. "I am the Shinga," he said.

"Barush Sniggle?" she asked. Shinga Barush Sniggle had a potbelly, small eyes under lank blond hair, and a cruel mouth. He walked with a swagger despite his small size. Perhaps the hulking bodyguard by his side helped with that.

"What do you want, wench?" the Shinga demanded.

"I'm hunting. My deader's name is Lord Kylar Stern. He's about my height, light blue eyes, dark hair, athletic, about twenty years old."

"A deader?" Sniggle asked. "Like you're a wetboy? A wet girl?"

"Wasn't Kylar the name of that guy who busted Tom's chops a couple weeks ago?" the big-nosed young man asked one of the other teenagers.

"Sounds like him," another young man said. "Think he's still staying with Aunt Mea. But he ain't no lord."

"Shut up," Barush Sniggle said. "You don't say another damn word, you got me? Tom, get your ass off the ground and bring that bitch here."

Amazing. Kylar had made it so simple. He thought he was far enough away, was confident that everyone thought he was dead. She had all she needed now. It would be a simple matter to find him, and it would be an easy matter to kill him, too. She tingled with excitement. She still had a two-inch scar on her shoulder from him, despite having let one of those foul wytches heal her.

"I think I might just have to take you back to my place," Barush Sniggle said. "We'll find out how much of a wet girl you are."

"Never heard that one before," she said. The bodyguard had one of her arms, and a triumphant Tom Gray had the other.

"She's one hot bitch, ain't she?" Tom Gray said, grabbing a breast.

She ignored him. "Don't make me do something you'll regret," she told the Shinga.

"Can I have her after you're done?" Tom asked. He squeezed her breast again and then he petted her hair.

"DON'T TOUCH MY HAIR!" she yelled.

Both the bodyguard and Tom flinched at her sudden fury. Barush Sniggle forced a laugh a moment later.

"You little guttershite, you sewer froth, you touch my hair and I swear I'll rip you apart," Vi said, trembling.

He swore at her and ripped out the leather thong that bound her hair back. Her hair fell loose around her shoulders for the first time in years. She stood exposed, naked, and the men were laughing.

She went out of her mind. She was swearing, the Talent arching through her so powerfully it hurt. Her arms blasted through the men's hold on them and her fists cracked Tom Gray's and the bodyguard's ribs simultaneously. Before Tom could double up, she grabbed his hair in one hand. She stabbed fingers at the corners of his eyes, deep into the sockets, and tore his eyes out. She spun and men were screaming and running and in her confusion and fury she didn't even know which one to chase.

Vi didn't know how much time passed while she vented her shame and fury on the two men.

When she came to herself, her hair covered with a blood-soaked rag, she was sitting on a stoop. The Shinga and the boys had fled. There was no one on the street except for her imperturbable horse, standing still until she called it as she trained it, and two man-shaped lumps lying in the street.

Walking unsteadily toward the horse, she passed right by what had been Tom Gray and the bodyguard. The corpses were a ruin. She'd— Nysos—she'd never even drawn a weapon, and she'd done this. Her stomach lurched and she vomited in the street.

It's just a simple job. The Godking will forgive me for not killing

Jarl. I'll be a master. I'll never have to serve Hu Gibbet in the bed or anywhere else, not ever again. I kill Kylar, and then I'm free. It's close, Vi. So close. You can make it.

Sister Jessie al'Gwaydin was dead. Ariel was sure of it. The villagers hadn't seen her for two months and her horse was still in the innkeeper's stable. It wasn't like Jessie, but taking risks was. Stupid girl.

Sister Ariel knelt as she entered the oak grove, not to pray, but to extend her senses. This grove was as far toward the Iaosian Forest as the locals were willing to go. The villagers of Torras Bend prided themselves on their practicality. They saw nothing superstitious or foolish about giving the Hunter the same wide berth their ancestors had. The tales they had told her weren't wild-eyed ravings. Indeed, they were believable because of their lack of detail.

Those who entered the forest didn't leave. Simple as that.

So the villagers fished in the meandering Red River and collected wood right up to the edge of the grove, but there they stopped. The effect was jarring. Centuries-old oaks abutted directly on bare fields. In some places, younger oaks had been cut down, but once the trees reached a certain age, the villagers wouldn't touch them. The oak grove had been slowly expanding for centuries.

She felt nothing here, nothing beyond the cool of a forest, smelled nothing except clean damp air. When she rose and walked slowly through the low undergrowth, she kept her senses attuned, pausing frequently, stopping when she imagined she felt the slightest trembling in the air. It made for slow progress, but Ariel Wyant Sa'fastae was noted for her patience, even among the Sisters. Besides, it was recklessness that had gotten Jessie al'Gwaydin killed. Probably.

Though it was only a mile wide, it took her a long time to traverse the oak grove. Each afternoon, after marking her progress, she returned to the inn and slept and took her only meal of the day—the

weight was coming off, blast it, if slowly. Each night she returned to
the forest, on the chance that whatever magics had been placed on the
forest were affected by the time of day.

On the third day, Ariel came within sight of the forest itself, and the
line between the oak grove and the forest proper was stark—obviously
magical. Still, she didn't hurry her progress. Instead, she moved even
more slowly, more carefully. On the fifth day, her patience paid off.

Ariel was thirty paces from the line between oak grove and forest
when she felt the ward. She stopped so abruptly she almost fell down.
She sat, heedless of the dirt, and crossed her legs. The next hour she
spent simply touching the ward, trying to get a feel for its texture and
strength, without using magic of her own.

Then she began to chant softly. Though she worked long into the
night checking and double-checking and triple-checking that she was
right and that she hadn't missed anything, the weaves were simple.
One simply registered whether a human had crossed the boundary.
The second, slightly more complicated, marked the intruder. It was a
weak weave that clung to clothing or skin and dissipated after only a
few hours. Cleverly, Ezra—Ariel was making an assumption, but she
thought it was good one—had put the weave so low to the earth that
it might mark the intruder's shoes, so low that it would be covered by
the undergrowth.

The real cunning of it, though, was the placement. How many magi
had seen the obvious line thirty paces beyond this and walked right
through the trap before they raised their defenses?

It would be easy to circumvent the trap now that she saw it, but
Sister Ariel didn't. Instead, she wrote her findings in her journal,
and returned to Torras Bend. If she'd made any mistakes, she would
die before she got back to the inn. It made for a tense walk. Her soul
soared at the thought of dismantling Ezra's ancient magic, but she
didn't give in to the temptations of arrogance.

The Speaker's letters were getting shriller, demanding that Ariel
find Jessie, that Ariel do something to help her avert the rising crisis

with the Chattel. Ariel kept her eyes open, hoping to find a woman who might serve her sister's purposes, but the villagers of Torras Bend were careful to send away every child who showed the least Talent. Ariel wouldn't find what Istariel needed here.

So she ignored the letters. There was a time and a place for haste. It wasn't here and it wasn't now.

25

"*V*iridiana Sovari?"

Hearing her name made Vi skid to a stop in the crowded market. A dirty little man bobbed his head nervously. He extended a note toward her, but she didn't take it. He was being careful not to stand close to her and he wasn't ogling her, so she guessed that he had an inkling of what she was. He smiled obsequiously, shot a look at her breasts, then stared stubbornly at his feet.

"Who are you?" she asked.

"No one important, miss. Just a servant of our...mutual master," he said, eyeing the crowd around them. Her heart turned to ice. No. It couldn't be. He extended the note again, and as soon as she took it, he disappeared into the crowd.

"*Moulina,*" the note read. "We are curious indeed how you knew Jarl was going to Caernarvon, but that you did know tells us that you are indeed the best. We also desire that you deal with Kylar Stern. We prefer him alive. If this is not possible, we require his body and all belongings, no matter how trivial. Bring them immediately."

Vi closed the note. It was impossible that the Godking knew where she was. Impossible that a note from him had beat her here. Impossible that Jarl could be here—Jarl, whose identity was supposed to be secret. Jarl, whom she'd been fleeing! Impossible to do what the

Godking asked. But the greatest impossibility was the only impossibility now: it was impossible to escape. Vi was the Godking's slave. There was no way out.

Somehow Kylar had been roped into making the dinner for Uly's birthday. Aunt Mea had said no man should be intimidated by a kitchen, and Elene had said that compared to the potions he made, a dinner and dessert should be easy, and Uly just giggled as they put him in a frilly lace apron and dabbed his nose with flour.

So Kylar found himself with his sleeves rolled up, trying to figure out arcane cooking terms like blanching and roux and proofing. From Uly's giggles, he suspected they'd stuck him with the hardest recipe they could find, but he played along.

"What do I do after the jelly, uh, weeps?" he asked.

Uly and Elene giggled. Kylar struck a pose with the spatula, and they laughed out loud.

The door to the smithy opened and Braen walked in, dirty and smelly. He gave Kylar a flat look that made him lower the spatula, deflated, but he refused to wipe the flour from his nose. Braen turned his eyes to Elene and looked her up and down.

"When's dinner?" he asked her.

"We'll bring it out to your cave when it's ready," Kylar said.

Braen grunted and told Elene, "You ought to find yourself a real man."

"You know," Kylar said as Braen shuffled back toward the smithy, "I know a wetboy who'd like to pay that cretin a visit."

"Kylar," Elene said.

"I don't like the way he looks at you," Kylar said. "Has he tried anything with you?"

"Kylar, not tonight, all right?" Elene said, nodding toward Uly.

He was suddenly aware of the ring box in his pocket. He nodded. Putting a serious look on his face, he attacked Uly, who squealed, and flipped her upside down and draped her over his shoulder. He pretended not to realize she was there as he went back to cooking.

Uly yelped, kicking her legs and holding onto the back of his tunic with a death grip.

Aunt Mea came into the kitchen, clucking. "I can't believe it, we're all out of flour and honey."

"Oh, no," Kylar said. "How am I going to make the fifth mother sauce?" He set down his spatula and hunched over, extending his hands through his legs. On cue, Uly slid headfirst down his back and grabbed his hands in time for him to pull her through his legs. She landed on her feet, breathless and laughing.

"Isn't it someone's birthday?" Kylar asked.

"Mine! Mine!" Uly said.

He pulled silver out of each of Uly's ears while she giggled. Two silvers—it was a bonus the noble had given him. It left him and Elene with nothing again, but Uly was worth it. When he put them in Uly's hands, her eyes got big. "For me?" she asked like she couldn't believe it.

He winked. "Elene will help you find something good, all right?"

"Can we go right now?" Uly asked.

Kylar looked at Elene, who shrugged. "We can go with Aunt Mea," she said.

"I've got to peel the peas anyway," Kylar said. They snickered. He smiled at Elene and marveled again at how beautiful she was. He was so in love he thought his chest would burst.

Uly pranced to the door and showed Aunt Mea her coins. Elene touched Kylar's arm. "Are we going to be all right?" she asked.

"After tonight we are," he said.

"What do you mean?"

"You'll see." He didn't smile. He didn't want to give it away. If he smiled, he'd grin like a fool. He couldn't wait to see the look on her face. He couldn't wait for other things as well. He shook his head and went back to cooking. Contrary to what he'd said, the meal wasn't hard to prepare. It was just messy. He slipped off his ring and put it on the counter before he picked up the raw meat—there wasn't much romantic about smelling like dead cow.

Elene and Uly and Aunt Mea had only been gone for about thirty seconds when there was a knock on the door. Kylar put down the spatula again and walked to the door. "What'd you forget this time, Uly?" he said as he grabbed a hand towel and opened the door.

It was Jarl.

Kylar felt like the wind had been knocked out of him. He couldn't believe his eyes. But there he was, lean, athletic, impeccably dressed, as beautiful a man as you'd ever see, his dazzling white teeth showing an uncertain smile. "Hey-ho, Azo," he said.

Why that greeting? Was Jarl just being cute, or was he also throwing in an appeal to their history together? Definitely the latter. For a long moment, they just stood there, looking at one another. Jarl wasn't here for a visit. Jarl didn't visit. For the God's sake, the man was the Shinga. A true Shinga, the leader of the most feared Sa'kagé in Midcyru.

"How in the nine hells did you find me, Jarl?" Kylar said, being cute too. It was what Jarl had expected Kylar to say the last time Jarl had shown up unexpectedly.

"Aren't you going to invite me in?"

"Please," Kylar said. He put some ootai on and sat across from Jarl, who helped himself to a seat by the window. Silence.

"There's this job—" Jarl began.

"Not interested."

Jarl took that in stride. He pursed his lips and looked around the humble room quizzically. "So, uh … what is it about this that you like again?"

"Didn't Momma K teach tact?"

"I'm serious," Jarl said.

"So am I. You show up after I tell you I'm out of the business, and the first thing you do is insult the place I live?"

"Logan's alive. He's in the Hole."

Kylar just stared at him, uncomprehending. The words collided with each other and shattered on the floor, shards sparkling with the light of truth, but the whole nothing more than splinters and points too sharp to touch.

"All the wetboys are working for Khalidor. The resisting nobles have retreated to the Gyre estates. Several of the frontier garrisons are still manned, but we have no leader who can unite us. There's some trouble up in the Freeze that the Godking is worried about, so he hasn't done anything to consolidate his power yet. He thinks that the noble families will tear each other apart. And if we don't have Logan, he's right."

"Logan's alive?" Kylar asked stupidly.

"The Godking has our former wetboys looking for me. It's part of why I came here. I had to get out of Cenaria until we could get word out that Kagé himself is protecting me."

"No," Kylar said.

"Every day, the chances that Logan will be discovered get worse. Apparently none of the prisoners in the Hole has recognized him, but they've started throwing a lot of people down there. It might please you to know that Duke Vargun is one of them. Look at it as a little bonus. When you rescue Logan, you can kill that twist, too."

"What?" Kylar said. Wheels were turning too fast for him to catch up. "Jarl," he said. "Tenser isn't Tenser Vargun. Don't you see? He got himself thrown in the Hole so he can do the hardest time there is. Then they produce the real baron—alive—and Tenser is released. He comes to the Sa'kagé a month later with a grudge for his false imprisonment and all the access of a duke and what happens?"

"We take him in," Jarl said quietly. "How could we resist?"

"And he destroys you, because he's not Tenser Vargun," Kylar said. "He's Tenser Ursuul."

Jarl sat back, stunned. After a minute, he said, "You see, Kylar? This is why I need you. Not just for your skills, for your mind. If

Tenser's there right now, he's only going to wait long enough that his stay in the Hole is credible, and then he'll tell his father that Logan's in there. We have to go now. Now!"

The ring box was burning against Kylar's leg. He looked through the open window as Jarl spoke, seeing the city he'd hoped would be his home for the rest of his life. He loved this city, loved the hope here, loved healing and helping, loved the simple pleasure of being praised for his potions. He loved Elene. She proved to him that he could do more good by healing than by killing. It all made sense...and yet... and yet....

"I can't," Kylar said. "I'm sorry. Elene would never understand."

Jarl rocked back on two legs of the chair. "Don't get me wrong, Azo, because I grew up with Elene too, and I love the girl. But why do you give a shit what she thinks?"

"Fuck, Jarl."

"Hey, I'm just asking." Then he let the question sit, his eyes never leaving Kylar's face.

The bastard, he really had been studying under Momma K for all those years.

"I love her."

"Sure, that's part of it."

Again, that I'm-waiting stare.

"She's good, Jarl. I mean, like people aren't good where we came from. Not good because it will get her something. Not good because people are watching. Just good. At first I thought she was just made that way, you know, like your skin is black and I'm devastatingly handsome."

Jarl raised an eyebrow. He didn't laugh.

"But now I've seen that she has to work at it. She does work at it, and she's been working at it for as long as I've been working at learning to kill people."

"So she's a saint. Doesn't answer my question," Jarl said.

Kylar was silent for a full minute. He rubbed the grain of the wood table with a fingernail. "Momma K used to say that we become the masks we wear. What's under the mask for us, Jarl? Elene knows me in a way no one else does. I've changed my name, changed my identity, left everything and everyone I've ever known. I'm all lies, Jarl, but as long as Elene knows me, maybe there is a real me. Do you know what I mean?"

"You know," Jarl said. "I was wrong about you. When you got yourself killed saving Elene and Uly, I thought you were a hero. You're no hero. You just fucking hate yourself."

"Excuse me?"

"You're a coward. So you've done bad stuff. Join the club. You know what? I'm glad you did; it made you something better than a saint."

"A killer's better than the saint? What sort of fucked-up Sa'kagé thinking is—"

"It made you *useful*. Do you know what it's like in Cenaria right now? You wouldn't believe me. I didn't come here to find a killer. I came to find The Killer, the Night Angel, the man who's more than just a wetboy because the problems we have now are bigger than any wetboy could handle. There's only one man who can help us, Kylar, and that's you. Believe me, you weren't my first choice." He stopped abruptly.

"What's that supposed to mean?"

Jarl wouldn't meet his eye. "I didn't mean—"

"What were you about to say?" Kylar said in a dangerous tone.

"We had to be sure, Kylar. We were very respectful, I want you to know that. It was Momma K's idea. He used to be immortal, we had to make sure…"

"You dug up my master's corpse?" Kylar demanded.

"We put it—him—back just how you'd buried him." Jarl winced. "It was maybe a week after the invasion—"

"You dug him up while I was still in the city?"

"We couldn't tell you beforehand, and afterward there was no reason to. Momma K said the body would be there, that Durzo had given his immortality to you, but when she saw him....It was the scariest thing I've ever seen, Kylar. I mean, I was practically raised by the woman and I've never seen her like that. Hysterical, weeping and screaming—here we are, in the middle of the cloudy night, we'd paddled out to Vos Island with oars wrapped in wool, and she starts wailing, out of her mind. I was so sure a patrol would come that I wanted to get off the island immediately, but she wouldn't leave until he was just how you left him."

Like Kylar cared that Durzo be left on that damned rock. If they were going to dig him up, they could have at least brought him.... *Where? Home? What home did Durzo Blint ever have?*

"How'd he look?" Kylar asked quietly.

"Shit. He looked like he'd been in the ground a week, what do you think?"

Of course he did. *Dammit, Master Blint, why'd you give* me *your immortality? Were you just sick of living? Why didn't you tell me anything?* But then, maybe he had told him in the note he'd given Kylar: the note that had been soaked with blood, illegible. "You want me to break into the Hole and save Logan?"

"Do you know who the Godking keeps as his concubines? Young girls from noble families. Prefers virgins. He guesses how much humiliation and debasement each girl can take. Puts them in tower rooms with balconies where all the railings have been torn off so the jump beckons every day. It's a game for him."

Kylar kept his voice hard. "Get to the point."

"He took Serah and Mags Drake. Serah killed herself in the first week. Mags is still there."

Serah and Mags were practically Kylar's sisters. Mags had always been his pal. Always quick with a laugh, always smiling. He'd been so self-absorbed since the coup that he'd barely thought of them.

Jarl said, "I want you to rescue Logan, and then I want you to assassinate the Godking."

"Is that all?" Coldly amused. It was a tone Kylar had heard Durzo use a hundred times. "Let me guess, Logan first because my odds with the Godking aren't so great?"

"That's right," Jarl said angrily. "That's how I have to think, Kylar. I'm fighting a war, and people better than us are dying in it every day. And you're sitting around because of what some girl thinks?"

"Don't you talk about Elene."

"Or what? You'll breathe heavily on me? You're the dumbass who swore off violence. Yes, I know about that. Let me tell you something. Roth made a lot of people miserable. I'm glad you killed him, all right? He fucked me up bad. But he doesn't hold a candle to his father." Jarl swore. "Look at yourself! I know this hit is impossible. I'm sending you after a god. But if anyone in the world can do it, it's you. You were made for this, Kylar. Do you think you made it through all the shit you made it through so you can sell hangover potions? Some things are bigger than your happiness, Kylar. You can give hope to an entire nation."

"It'll only cost me everything," Kylar whispered. His face was gray.

"You're an immortal. There'll be other girls."

Kylar gave him a disgusted look.

Jarl's expression changed instantly. "I'm sorry. I guess there will be other Godkings and other Shingas too. I just... we need you. Logan will die if you don't come. So will Mags, and so will a lot of other people you'll never know."

It would have been easier if he disagreed with anything Jarl said. Kylar had asked Momma K, "Can a man change?" Here was his answer, and it sucked the life right out of him. "All right," Kylar said. "I'll take the contract."

Jarl smiled. "It's good to have you back, my friend."

"It's bad to be back."

"I didn't want to say it before, but have you done something to piss off the local Shinga?" Jarl asked. He took Kylar's expression to be an admission. "Because one of my sources told me the Shinga put out a contract on a Cenarian wetboy. He didn't know any details, but uh, I don't figure there's all that many Cenarian wetboys hanging around. The longer you're here, the more you put Elene and Uly in danger."

Durzo had taught Kylar that the best way to cancel a contract was to cancel the contract-giver. For Elene and Uly and Aunt Mea and even Braen to be safe, Barush Sniggle had to die.

Kylar stood woodenly and went upstairs. He returned a minute later with a visage as dark as the wetboy grays he wore once again.

Vi looked at the bow in her hands, trying to convince herself to pull back the red-and-black arrow. She was on a rooftop looking into the midwife's home. She'd been there for an hour. Her back was to a chimney, and she'd wrapped herself in shadows. She wasn't invisible by any means, but crouched low in the dying light, with the sun behind her, she was close enough.

She'd come to Caernarvon to escape this. She'd thought the only way to not kill Jarl and still escape the Godking's wrath was to kill Kylar. In the time she was away, Jarl would flee or be killed by another wetboy.

How could he have come here?

She wanted to shoot past him, shoot Kylar and pretend that Jarl wasn't here, pretend that she'd never gotten the note. But she didn't have the shot to take Kylar down, and lies would go nowhere with the Godking. Jarl sat right in front of the window. The window was even open. Vi was using a Talent-tension bow, a bow so powerful that only a person with the Talent could draw it, so the red-and-black traitor's arrow could have punched right through a window, through shutters for that matter. But she didn't even need it.

Jarl sat there, utterly exposed. He never would have made such a mistake in Cenaria, but here he felt safe. He'd fled straight into Death's arms.

Yet she waited. Damn Jarl for his stupidity. If Vi didn't kill him, the Godking would know. He would find her. *Damn you, Jarl. Damn you for your kindness.*

Finish the job. Hu Gibbet liked to torture his deaders first, but he only did it when he was sure he wouldn't be interrupted. Hu Gibbet always finished the job. The perfect shot never comes. Take any shot that kills.

Cursing under her breath to activate her Talent, Vi stood and drew the arrow to her cheek. It moved her out of the silhouette of the small chimney into the dying light. She was shaking, but it was barely thirty paces. "Damn you, Jarl, move!" she said.

She could run away. In Gandu or Ymmur the Godking would never find her. Would he? She couldn't believe it. She had told no one she was coming here, left no sign, and yet he knew. If she fled, the Godking would send her master after her, and Hu Gibbet never failed. For everything that Vi's beauty accomplished for her, the one thing it made nearly impossible was hiding. She'd never worried about disguises. She'd never thought of it as a weakness. Until now.

"Come on, Kylar," she whispered. "Just walk in front of the window. Just once." She was shaking violently now, and not just from the Talent burning in her, not just from the tension of holding the bow drawn for so long. Why did she want Kylar dead so badly?

She saw a leg, a leg dressed in wetboy grays, but no more appeared. Dammit. If Kylar was going out, she was in serious trouble. She'd heard that he could make himself invisible, but that was just the typical wetboy lies. They all bragged about their abilities so they could drive prices up. Everyone wanted to be another Durzo Blint.

But this was Durzo's apprentice, the man who'd killed Durzo. Fear gripped her.

Jarl's face was drawn with compassion, sorrow. At that look—that look she'd seen before when Jarl had taken care of her after Hu Gibbet came in to test the new skills Momma K had been teaching her and found her lacking and beat her senseless and violated her in every way he could imagine—at that look, Vi's vision went blurry. She blinked and blinked, refusing to believe it was tears. She hadn't cried since that night, since Jarl had held her, rocking her, helping her put the fractured pieces of herself back together.

Jarl stood and walked to the window. He lifted his eyes and saw Vi, her dark silhouette limned with sunlight. Surprise lit his eyes, and as it was followed by recognition—what other wetboy had a woman's silhouette?—she could swear she saw her name on his lips. Her fingers went limp and the bowstring slipped.

The red-and-black traitor's arrow leapt across that narrowest of chasms: the distance between a wetboy and her deader. It cut a red path through the air as if the night itself were bleeding.

26

"Elene, I'm sorry," Kylar wrote in a shaky hand. "I tried. I swear I tried. Some things are worth more than my happiness. Some things only I can do. Sell these to Master Bourary and move the family to a better part of town. I will always love you." Taking the ring box from his pocket, he placed it on top of the scrap of parchment.

"What's in the box?" Jarl asked.

Kylar couldn't look back at his friend. "My heart," he whispered and slowly uncurled his fingers from the box. "Just some earrings," he said, louder. He turned.

Jarl saw right through him. "You were going to marry her," he said.

A lump rose in Kylar's throat. There were no words. He had to look away from Jarl's eyes. "Have you ever heard of cruxing?" he asked finally.

Jarl shook his head.

"It's how Alitaerans execute rebels. They stretch them on a wood frame and pound nails through their wrists and feet. To breathe, the criminal has to lift his weight on the nails. It sometimes takes a man a day to die, asphyxiated by his own weight." He couldn't complete the metaphor, though he could feel himself being stretched out, a rebel against fate in a malevolent universe bent on crushing all things good, stretched between Logan and Elene, nailed to each with loyalty owed and gasping under the crushing weight of his own character. But it wasn't just Elene and Logan that stretched him here. It was two lives, two paths. The way of the shadows and the way of the light. The wolf and the wolfhound. Or was it wolfhound and lapdog?

Kylar had thought he could change. He'd thought he could have everything. He'd run headfirst into either/or and chosen both. That was what had driven him to the crux—not the machinations of a trickster god or the implacable roll of Fortune's wheel. Kylar's options had spread further and further apart, and he'd held on until he couldn't breathe. Only one question mattered now: What kind of man am I?

"Let's go," Kylar said, all wolfhound.

Jarl was standing at the window, pensive. "I was in love once," Jarl said. "Or something like it. With a beautiful girl nearly as fucked up as I am."

"Who was she?" Kylar asked.

"Her name was Viridiana, Vi. Beautiful, beautiful—" Jarl looked up and stiffened. "Vi?"

He went down in a spray of blood, an arrow passing fully through the center of his neck. His body dropped to the wood floor like a sack of flour. He blinked once. His eyes were neither afraid nor angry. His expression was wry.

Can you believe that? his eyes asked as Kylar drew him into his lap.

And then Jarl's eyes said nothing at all.

"Can I show Kylar?" Uly asked. She was clutching the very doll that Kylar had picked up a few days before. Elene smiled; Kylar was doing better at being a father than he knew.

"Yes," Elene said, "but you run right home. Promise?"

"Promise," Uly said, and ran.

Elene watched her go, feeling anxious, but she always felt anxious about little things. Caernarvon wasn't like the Warrens. Besides, the house was only two blocks away.

"We need to talk, don't we?" Aunt Mea said.

It was getting late. The sun's rays slanted down on merchants who were packing up their goods and heading home. Elene swallowed. "I promised Kylar. We agreed that we'd never tell anyone, but—"

"Then don't say another word." Aunt Mea smiled and took Elene's arm to guide her back to the house.

"I can't," Elene said, stopping her. "I can't do this anymore."

So she told Aunt Mea everything, from the lie of their marriage to their fights about sex to Kylar's being a wetboy and trying to leave it behind. Aunt Mea didn't even look surprised.

"Elene," she said, taking her hands. "Do you love Kylar or are you with him because Uly needs a mother?"

Elene paused to fully humble herself in the face of the question, to make sure what she would say was true. "I love him," Elene said. "Uly is a part of it, but I really love him."

"Then why are you protecting yourself?"

Elene looked up. "I'm not protecting—"

"You can't be honest with me until you're honest with yourself."

Elene looked at her hands. A farmer's cart loaded with the day's unsold produce rattled past them. The light was fading and the street was beginning to get dark. "We have to get back," Elene said. "Dinner must be getting cold."

"Child," Aunt Mea said. Elene stopped.

"He's a killer," Elene said. "I mean, he's killed people."

"No, you were right. He's a killer."

"No, he's a good man. He can change. I know it."

"Child, do you know why you're talking to me even though you promised Kylar you wouldn't? Because you agreed to something that isn't in your nature. You make a terrible liar, but you tried because you promised. Isn't that what he's done?"

"What do you mean?" Elene asked.

"If you can't love Kylar for the man he is—if you only love him for the man you think he could be—you'll cripple him."

Kylar had been so unhappy. When he'd started going out at night, she hadn't asked, hadn't wanted to know what he did. "What am I supposed to do?" she asked.

"Do you think you're the first woman who's been afraid to love?" Aunt Mea asked.

The words cut deep. It cast a different light on their nightly making out and fighting. She'd thought she was being holy by not making love with Kylar, but she was just terrified. She felt so far out of control already that surrender in the bedroom would have left her powerless. "Can I love him if I can't understand him? Can I love him if I hate what he does?"

"Child," Aunt Mea said. She gently laid a thick hand on Elene's shoulder. "Loving is an act of faith as much as believing in the God is."

"He isn't a believer. An ox and a wolf can't be yoked together," Elene said, knowing she was grasping at straws.

"You think a yoke only refers to wedding rings or lovemaking? You don't need to understand him, Elene, you need to love him until you do." Aunt Mea took Elene's arm. "Come on, let's go eat our dinner."

They walked back to the house together, Elene feeling lighter than she had in months—even if she was going to have to have a big talk with Kylar. She felt a new sense of hope.

Elene threw the door open, but the house was silent, empty. "Kylar?" she said. "Uly?"

There was no answer. The food was cold on the counter, the jelly Kylar had been making congealed and cracked. Her heart clogged her throat. Every breath was an effort. Aunt Mea looked horrified. Elene ran upstairs and clawed at the box of Kylar's wetboy clothes and his big sword. It was empty. There was no sign of anything.

She walked back downstairs, the truth coming to her as slowly as the setting sun.

"Are we going to be all right?" she had asked him.

"After tonight we are," he'd said, unsmiling.

Kylar's wedding ring sat next to the stove. There was no note, nothing else. Even Uly was gone. Kylar had finally given up on her. He was gone.

Vi slung the wiggling child off her shoulder as they came into the stable of the seedy inn where she'd put up her horse. The stable boy lay unconscious and bleeding by the door. He'd probably live. It didn't matter; he hadn't seen Vi before she'd clubbed him with the pommel of her short sword.

The girl squeaked through the rag Vi had tied over her mouth. Vi knelt and grabbed the girl's throat in one hand. She pulled out the gag.

"What's your name?" Vi asked.

"Go to hell!" The girl's eyes flashed, defiant. She couldn't be more than twelve.

Vi slapped her, hard. Then she slapped her again, and again, and again, impassively, the way Hu used to slap her when he was bored. When the girl tried to get away, she clamped her hand down on her throat, the threat explicit: the more you wiggle, the more you choke.

"Fine, Go To Hell, you want me to call you that, or something else?"

The little girl cursed her again. Vi spun her in to her body and clamped a hand over her mouth. With the other hand, she found a pain point in one of the girl's elbows and ground her fingers in.

The girl screamed into her hand.

Why haven't I killed her yet?

The job had gone flawlessly. Kylar had taken Jarl's body after arming himself for hunting. Vi had only seen brief glimpses of blades being sheathed and disappearing—surely it was a trick of the light and the distance, Kylar couldn't really be invisible. Regardless, after a while he'd taken Jarl's body and Vi had gone into the house.

She intended to set a few traps. There was a perfect contact poison that she could smear on the door latch of his bedroom and a needle trap that would fit perfectly in the little box he kept under the bed. But she couldn't do it. Still reeling from Jarl's murder, she walked around the house like a common prowler.

Vi found a note and a pair of earrings that looked expensive—the note said as much—even though they were oddly mismatched, one larger than the other. She pocketed both but didn't touch the thin gold wedding band by the stove. Let the happy little family keep its heirlooms. She wasn't sure what the note meant. Kylar had tried? Tried to protect Jarl?

The door opened, surprising Vi, and the little girl had walked in. Vi bound and gagged her, then stood looking at the mess she'd got herself into.

She was finished. She couldn't kill this child. She couldn't even kill Kylar. No, that wasn't true, she was sure she could still kill Kylar. The only way she could escape the Godking with her life was to please him. He would be more pleased if she delivered Kylar alive. If she delivered Kylar alive, the Godking would never know her weakness. She'd buy herself time to recover whatever it was that had cracked in her as she'd watched Jarl die in a spray of blood.

Galvanized, Vi went back to Kylar's bedroom. She carved the Cenarian Sa'kagé's glyph into the bedside table in a fine, light hand. Beneath it she traced, "We have the girl." When Kylar came back, he'd find his daughter gone and he'd scour the entire house. He'd find it, and he'd follow Vi straight to the Godking.

So now all Vi had to do was figure out how to smuggle a wailing child out of the city.

"Let's try again," Vi said. "What's your name?"

"Uly," the little girl said, tears making her face blotchy.

"All right, Ugly, we're leaving. You can come with me alive or dead. It doesn't matter. You've served your purpose. I'm going to tie your hands to the saddle, so you can jump off the horse if you want, but you'll just get kicked and dragged to death. Your choice. Open your mouth."

Uly opened her mouth and Vi stuffed the gag in. "Be silent," she said. She scowled at the rag. "Say something."

"Mmm?" Uly said.

"Damn." Vi fixed her will on the rag. "Be silent!" she whispered. "Again."

Uly's mouth moved, but no sound came out. Vi pulled out the rag; it wasn't necessary now. It had been a little trick she'd discovered a few years ago by accident. It was spotty, but a merely silent child would be easier to get out of the city than a gagged one. Vi saddled her horse and the second-best horse in the stable.

In half an hour, Caernarvon was fading into the distance, but freedom was still a long way off.

27

Cold fury burned the world white. Kylar sprinted across the roof-top. He reached the edge and leapt, soaring through the night air. He cleared the twenty-foot gap easily and ran up the wall. He pushed off it, grabbed the extended roof beam, and flipped himself up onto it, not even wobbling.

He'd done it all while invisible, a fact that would have pleased him immensely a few days ago. Today, he had no ability to feel pleasure at all. His eyes scanned the dark streets.

Before he'd left, he'd cleaned Jarl's blood from the floor—he wasn't going to make Elene deal with that. He'd taken his friend's body to a cemetery. Jarl wouldn't rot in a sewer like some guttershite. Kylar didn't even have the money to pay a grave digger—*thanks, God*—so he left Jarl and swore to return.

Jarl was dead. Part of Kylar didn't believe it, the part that had thought the soft life of a Waeddryner healer might be his. How could he have believed that? There was nothing soft in a Night Angel's life. Nothing. He was a killer. Death rose in his passage like mud swirling behind a stick dragged across the bottom of a clear, still pond.

There. Two punks were hassling a drunk. Gods, was that the same drunk he'd left to his fate the other night? Kylar dropped from the roof, swung off the next level, and in ten seconds was on the street.

The drunk was already down, bleeding from his nose. One of the punks was tearing the man's purse from his belt while the other stood watch, a long knife in his hand.

Kylar let himself shimmer into partial visibility, muscles gleaming iridescent black, eyes black orbs, face a mask of fury. He only intended to scare the knife-wielder, but as the hoodlum's eyes widened at the sight of him, Kylar swore he saw something so dark in them that it compelled him to act.

Before he knew it, the punch sword was drinking heart's blood. The hoodlum's knife dropped on the ground.

"What are you doing, Terr?" the mugger asked, turning.

A moment later, Kylar had the mugger pinned against the wall by his throat. He had to suppress the urge to kill, kill, kill.

"Where's the Shinga?" he demanded.

Terrified, the man flailed and screamed. "What are you?"

Kylar caught one of the mugger's flailing hands in his own and squeezed. A bone popped. The man screamed. Kylar waited, then squeezed harder. Another bone popped.

The stream of curses was unimpressive. Kylar ground the mugger's hand to pulp, then grabbed his other hand. The man started gibbering as he looked at his mangled hand. "Oh shit oh shit oh shit, my hand."

"Where's the Shinga? I won't repeat myself again."

"You f—no! Stop! Third warehouse down from dock three! Oh, gods! What are you?"

"I am retribution," Kylar said. He cut open the man's neck and dropped him. The drunk gaped at him. He looked like he thought he'd gone crazy.

The warehouse was definitely the Shinga's place, but Barush Sniggle wasn't there. Kylar supposed it was too much to expect. There were, however, ten guards waiting inside the front door. Kylar stared down at them from the ceiling beams, looking for one who might know more than the others.

The presence of the guards was evidence enough that Barush

Sniggle had sent the wetboy who killed Jarl. Kylar had no idea how they'd learned that he was the one who'd made Sniggle wet himself the other night, but killing the wrong man for it was exactly what this Shinga would do.

Kylar dropped behind a man who looked like the leader. He broke the man's right arm and drew the man's sword.

Half of the thugs were down before they grasped the idea that they actually were supposed to fight the invisible man killing them. Those who fought, fought poorly. Dress a thug in armor and give him a sword instead of a cudgel and you don't get a soldier, you get a thug who swings a sword like a piece of wood. They hurried to Death's embrace.

Kylar stood over the leader, the last man alive, and again allowed his eyes and face to become visible. He put one foot on the man's broken arm and touched the sword to his neck.

"You're the wetboy." The man cursed. He was sweating, his broad face pasty. His bushy black beard quivered as he trembled. "He said you were a girl."

"Wrong, tell me," Kylar said.

"The Shinga said he pissed off some Cenarian wetboy. We were supposed to kill you if you came here."

"Where is he?"

"If I tell you, will you let me live?"

Kylar looked into the man's eyes, and curiously didn't feel or imagine—or whatever it had been the other times—the darkness that demanded death. "Yes," he said, though the killing rage was still on him.

The man told him of a hideout, and another trap, an underground room with only one entrance, another ten guards.

With teeth gritted against the white-cold fury, Kylar said, "Tell them the Night Angel walks. Tell them Justice is come."

28

The grate squealed open and Gorkhy's face appeared in the dim light of his torch. He looked pleased. Logan hated the man with all his heart. "Fresh meat, kiddos," Gorkhy said. "Sweet, fresh meat."

Some of the prisoners behind Gorkhy started sobbing. It was a deliberate cruelty to bring them here at this time of day. It was noon; the howlers were shrieking for all they were worth, hot fetid air gusting up out of the Hole like a giant, endless fart. It made the torches dance and the figures of the Holers seem to leap and twist as their sweat gleamed.

Since Logan had jumped down the Hole eighty-two days ago, they had only thrown one prisoner in the Hole. Gorkhy had done it, and he had thrown the man into the Hole—straight into the Hole. The convict's face had smacked wetly against the lip of the Hole and his body had plunged into the abyss. So now the animals and the monsters crowded around the Hole as they did when Gorkhy threw in bread. It wasn't to save the prisoners' lives. It was to save their meat.

"All right, my lovelies," Gorkhy said. "Who's first?"

Keeping an eye on Fin, who was also eyeing him, Logan stayed back from the edge of the Hole. He had the longest reach, but catching a falling body was different from catching falling bread, and Fin had uncoiled his sinew rope from around his body.

There was a scuffle above and curses and a woman flung herself at the grate. Gorkhy tried to intercept her, but she dove under his arms. She dropped headfirst toward the floor, then jerked to a stop as Gorkhy caught her dress.

She screamed and kicked as she hung directly over Logan's head. He jumped and grabbed one of her flailing arms and yanked, but his hand slipped. She dropped a few more feet forward so that she was hanging upside down, ten feet from the stone floor.

"Fin!" Lilly cried. "Get him!" Gorkhy was on his knees, holding on to the girl's dress with one hand and on to the grate with the other. His head was exposed. For Fin, who practiced incessantly with his lasso, it was an easy target.

Gorkhy was cursing, but he was strong. Logan jumped and reached for the girl's hand again, but missed. Fin came running with the lasso in his hand. The rest of the Holers were howling and flinging feces at Gorkhy. Logan jumped again and caught the girl's hand.

Her dress tore and she fell on top of Logan. He was barely able to break her fall, only trying to angle her away from the abyss.

Logan staggered to his feet and saw Gorkhy's face livid in the torchlight, still exposed, just waiting for a noose to drop around his neck, just begging to be dragged into the Hole and torn apart. Turning, Logan saw Fin just feet away, but the man had dropped his lasso. Logan barely had time to see the glittering steel in Fin's hand before Fin stabbed him.

Flesh parted along Logan's ribs and his left arm as he twisted hard to avoid the blade. Fin's hand got caught between Logan's left arm and his body as Logan twisted and Logan heard the knife fall to the stone floor. Logan brought a fist toward Fin's head, but the man ducked, fell to the floor and scurried back. Logan started to go after him, determined to kill the man while he had the chance, but as he moved forward, behind him the Holers closed on the girl.

He couldn't leave her. He knew what they saw when they looked at a young, half-naked woman, dazed from her fall. He'd heard the rapists reminisce about it, tell how many sweets they'd banged. Some of them couldn't even bang Lilly: a willing woman left them limp.

Logan roared with pain and frustration. The animals collapsed backward.

The girl had picked up the knife and was standing now with her back to the wall. She braced herself to keep from falling. From the way she stood, she'd sprained her ankle in the fall.

"Stay back," she said, waving the knife around ineffectually. "Stay back!" Her eyes darted from Logan to the abyss and then to Gnasher.

The girl was shaking. She was pretty in a fragile sort of way, with long blonde hair and fine features. She was barely dirty, though, so she couldn't have been in prison long. Long enough for Gorkhy, though, damn him to the ninth circle of hell. There was fresh blood staining her torn dress between her legs.

Logan held his hands up. "Easy," he said. "I'm not going to hurt you. But we need to move or they'll start falling on us."

Her eyes flashed up the grate and she began scooting along the circular wall.

Gorkhy had been pulled away from the grate by the other guards. The rest of the prisoners were herded to the grate. The first man didn't want to jump in, so they pushed him.

The fifteen-foot fall onto solid rock broke his legs, and the Holers were on him in seconds. To Logan's dismay, Gnasher joined them, flinging aside others and sinking filed teeth into living flesh.

The second man froze at the spectacle he could hear but barely see. The guards pushed him in and he, too, became meat. After that, most of the other prisoners were willing to hang from the grate and drop in themselves.

Logan had no time for it. On another day, he might have fought for meat himself. But he wouldn't feed today, not with this girl here. Her presence made him remember better things. He wanted to weep.

"Gods," he said. "Natassa Graesin." The words escaped his lips. He shouldn't have said anything, but the shock of seeing another noble was too great. At seventeen, Natassa was the second-eldest Graesin daughter. She was his cousin.

Natassa Graesin stared at him, her wide, frightened eyes taking in the tall, emaciated wreck of what had been a huge, athletic body. He was a shadow of what he had been, but though he had withered, he was still tall, unmistakably tall.

He held his hands up to silence her, but he was too late.

"Logan? Logan Gyre?" she said.

He felt his world ending. In all the time he'd been down here, he'd been only King or Thirteen. In the madness of hunger, he'd eventually joined the others who stood around the Hole to catch bread—with his long reach, he got more than most, at the cost of letting Gorkhy know that a tall blond man was in the Hole. But he'd never, never, never used his real name.

Shooting a glance over his shoulder, he saw that new prisoners were still dropping in the hole, sprawling as they hit the ground. In the near-total darkness, they were blind, terrified, whimpering and shrieking and cursing and weeping as they heard the Holers tearing into the fresh meat. The Holers were fighting and Gorkhy was laughing and cheering at the spectacle, taking bets on what would happen with each prisoner, and the howlers were howling. A lot of noise, a lot of confusion, a lot of distractions. Perhaps it had passed without notice.

But one of the new prisoners wasn't whimpering, wasn't confused, wasn't distracted. Tenser Vargun didn't appear frightened, despite the noise and the heat and the stink and the darkness and the violence. His head was tilted toward Logan and Natassa, his eyes squinting against the midnight dark. He looked thoughtful.

29

Elene couldn't breathe. Kylar hadn't only left her; he'd taken Uly. The rejection was complete. Things had seemed to be going so well.

No, things *had* been going so well. Elene couldn't believe it, wouldn't believe it. She scoured the kitchen for some sign. She found a stain on the floorboards, dark against dark wood, hastily cleaned up. Nothing looked like it had been spilled from the cooking, but she couldn't tell what it might be. Then she found a deep, thin gouge in the floor nearby.

She went upstairs. Kylar's wetboy grays were gone, as was Retribution. She was sliding the box back under the bed when she saw the Cenarian Sa'kagé symbol scrawled into the bedside table. "We have the girl," the script below it said, in a careful, neat hand. Elene's heart dropped again.

Someone had taken Uly, and Kylar had gone after them. The revelation brought fear and joy intermingled. Kylar hadn't abandoned her, but Uly had been kidnapped by someone who knew who he was. Someone was trying to trap Kylar. But where had Kylar been when Uly was taken? If someone had grabbed Uly on the street, they might have left a note on the front doorstep, but Elene didn't think they'd dare to break in with Kylar downstairs.

There was a shout from downstairs and pounding on the door. "Open the door. In the name of the Queen, open the door!"

When Elene saw Aunt Mea let the city watch in, her heart seized with fear again. In Cenaria, the guards were considered so corrupt that no one trusted them. But then Elene saw Aunt Mea's obvious relief.

It took almost an hour to sort things out. A neighbor had seen Kylar leave carrying a body over his shoulder, a handsome young man with dark skin, his hair in microbraids, capped with gold beads. Elene knew instantly it had to be Jarl. After Kylar left with the body, the neighbor had gone running for the guards. The guards were only halfway to the house when they were met by the neighbor's wife, who'd seen a woman with a bow enter the house about a minute before Uly returned home, and then leave with the girl. From the evidence, the watch thought the woman was the murderer, thank the God, but they still wanted to talk to Kylar.

Elene lay in bed late that night, mourning Jarl and trying to make sense of it. Why would Jarl come here? Because he was in danger? Because he wanted Kylar to do a job? Just to visit? Elene had to think it was to get Kylar to do a job. Jarl was too important to leave Cenaria on a whim, and if he had left because he was in danger, he'd have had bodyguards. So Jarl had been killed—by accident?—while trying to hire Kylar. Kylar had either agreed to do the job, or he was going out for vengeance. Either way, he'd left before Uly's kidnapping. He might not know about it.

By noon the next day, Kylar still hadn't returned. There was a knock on the door and Elene hurried to answer it. It was one of the guards from yesterday.

"I just thought you should know," the young man said, "we talked to the gate guards as soon as we could, but shifts change and it's hard to get word to everyone. A young woman matching the killer's description left yesterday, headed north. She had a little girl with her. We've already sent men after her, but she's got a good head start. I'm sorry."

After the guard left, Braen and Aunt Mea looked at Elene as if they expected her to burst into tears.

"I'm going after Uly," Elene said instead.

"But—" Aunt Mea began.

"I know, believe me, I know I'm the last person who should go. But what else am I going to do? If Kylar comes back here, tell him where I went. He'll catch up with me, I'm sure. If he's already gone after them, I'll meet him on his way back. But if he doesn't know Uly's been kidnapped, I might be her only chance."

Aunt Mea opened her mouth to protest once more, then closed it. "I understand."

Elene's things fit in a small pack, and by the time she got downstairs, Aunt Mea had packed her enough food for a week. "Is Braen going to say goodbye?" Elene asked.

Aunt Mea took Elene outside. "Braen says goodbye in his own way." There was a horse saddled in front of the shop. It was sturdy and gentle looking. Elene's eyes flooded with tears. She'd thought she was going to walk. "He says he's had some big orders recently," Aunt Mea said, obviously proud of her son. "Now go, child, and may the God go with you."

Kylar was standing over the grave he'd dug and doing his best to get drunk. It was still two hours before dawn. The cemetery was quiet. The only sounds were leaves rattling in the wind and the complaints of night insects. Kylar had chosen this cemetery because it was the richest one on his way out of the city. After killing the Shinga, he'd robbed the man so he had plenty of money, and Jarl deserved the best. If the grave keeper were true to his word, there would even be a headstone here in a week.

They made quite a pair. Jarl laid out on the ground next to the hole, the gore a darker black than his skin, limbs slowly stiffening. Kylar was more blood-spattered than his dead friend, cruor drying into hard ridges on his limbs, cracking as he worked, reconstituting as he perspired. It made him look like he was sweating blood.

The grave was finished. Now Kylar was supposed to say something significant.

He drank more wine. He'd brought four skins and already emptied two. A year ago, two would have flattened him. Now, he wasn't even tipsy. He finished the third skin then dutifully took deep draughts of the fourth until it was gone.

His eyes kept going back to Jarl's corpse. He tried to imagine the wounds closing as his own had so long ago. But they weren't closing. Jarl was dead. He'd been alive one second, and now he was simply not. Kylar finally understood the wry look in Jarl's eyes, too.

The Cenarian wetboy that Shinga Sniggle had ordered killed wasn't Kylar. It was Vi Sovari, and it was Vi Sovari who had killed Jarl with a red-and-black traitor's arrow.

It was just like Jarl to find humor in it. Jarl confessed his love for a woman as she released the arrow that killed him.

"Shit," Kylar said.

There were no words to express the magnitude of the ruin before him. Jarl was no more. This thing in front of Kylar was a slab of meat. Kylar wished he could believe in Elene's God. He wanted to think Jarl and Durzo were in a better place. But he was honest enough to know that was all he wanted—some half-assed good feeling. Even if Elene's God were real, Jarl and Durzo didn't follow him. That meant they got to burn in hell, right?

He climbed down into the grave and pulled Jarl's body in. Jarl's skin was cold, clammy; morning dew was condensing on it. It didn't feel right. Kylar laid him down as gently as he could and climbed back out. He still didn't feel drunk.

Sitting on the pile of soft dirt next to the grave, he realized it was the ka'kari's fault. His body treated alcohol like any poison, and healed him of it. It was so efficient that he'd have to drink massive quantities to get drunk. Just like Durzo had.

And I dismissed him as a drunk. It was yet another way Kylar had misunderstood his master, another way he'd blithely condemned the man. It made everything ache all over again.

"I'm sorry, brother," Kylar said, and realized as the words crossed his lips that Jarl had been exactly that to him: an older brother who looked out for him. Why was Kylar condemned to having revelations about what people meant to him only after they were dead? "I'll make it worth something, Jarl." Making Jarl's sacrifice mean something meant abandoning Elene and Uly and the life that might have been. He'd sworn to Uly that he wouldn't abandon her as every other adult in her life had. And now he was doing it.

Was it like this for you, master? Is this where that ocean of bitterness began? Is giving up my humanity the cost of my immortality?

There was nothing else to do, nothing more to say. Kylar couldn't even weep. As the first birds of morning began singing beauty to the waking sun, he filled the grave.

30

For two days, Uly didn't speak or eat or drink. Vi drove them at a grueling pace along the queen's road heading west and then north. The first night they passed the great estates of the Waeddryner nobility. By the time they stopped, a few hours after sunrise, they were in farmland. The fields were bare, the rolling hills covered with the irregular stubble of harvested spelt.

The first day, Uly waited until Vi had been breathing regularly for about ten minutes, then she bolted for her horse. She hadn't even untied the beast before Vi yanked her away. The second day, Uly waited for an hour. She got up quietly enough that Vi almost missed it. Uly got the tether undone that time, and nearly jumped out of her clothes when she turned to reach for to the horse's head and saw Vi standing behind her, hands on hips.

Both times, Vi beat her. She was careful not to injure the girl. No broken bones or scars for this one. She wondered if she was being too easy on the girl, but she'd never beaten a child before. Vi was used to killing men, used to giving Talent-strength to her muscles and letting her victims deal with the consequences. If she did that with Uly, the child would die. That didn't fit Vi's plans.

By the third day, Uly wasn't doing well. She still hadn't taken a drink. She refused anything Vi offered, and she was losing strength.

Her lips were cracked and parched, her eyes red. Vi couldn't help but feel a grudging admiration.

The girl was tough, no doubt about it. Vi could stand pain better than most people, but she hated not eating. When she was twelve Hu had routinely withheld her food, giving her only one meal a day "so she wouldn't get fat." He'd put her back on full meals when he decided it was all going to her tits. But worse than the starving were the times he'd withheld water because he thought she was being lazy.

The bastard never did grasp the concept of a woman's cramps.

She'd had to pretend the thirst didn't bother her, because she'd known if she let it show, it would have become his favorite punishment.

"Look, Ugly," she said as she made camp in a small valley as the sun began to rise. "I don't give a shit if you die. You are more useful to me alive than dead, but not by much. Kylar will follow me to Cenaria now either way. You, on the other hand, would probably like to see Kylar again, right?"

Uly stared back at her with sunken eyes full of hate.

"And I'd guess he'd kick your ass if you die for no reason. So, hey, if you want to keep starving, you'll die pretty soon. Tomorrow, I'll have to tie you to the saddle, and you might not make it through the night. That inconveniences me, but it hurts Kylar more. If you'd rather die like a kitten than stay alive and fight me, go ahead. But you're not impressing anyone."

Vi put a skin of water in front of Uly and set about securing the horses. She wasn't worried about Uly escaping now. The girl was too weak. But Vi Talent-locked the ropes anyway. She was going to sleep today, dammit.

The rolling hills here were covered with forests broken now and then by a small village in a group of farm fields. The road was still broad and well-traveled, though. They'd made excellent time. There was no way to tell how far ahead of Kylar they were, but Vi had avoided villages and she had no doubt that had given Kylar precious hours on them. Yesterday evening, she'd traded the horses. If Kylar had somehow divined which tracks were theirs among the many, he'd be thrown.

Still, at the rate they'd been traveling, they'd passed numerous other parties, and though she could swaddle herself in a formless cloak that disguised her sex and identity, there was no disguising that Uly was a child. Nor was there any practical way to pass unseen on the barren hills they'd already come through. Usually, they'd just barreled past the traders' wagons and farmers' carts. It was an uneasy balance. They made better time on the road, but they were more likely to be recognized.

Her only contact with Kylar had been when she'd tried to kill him at the Drake house. Ironically enough, King Gunder had hired Vi, who'd tried to assassinate his son, to kill Kylar, who'd tried to protect him.

She'd had Kylar under her hips and under her knife the very day she took the contract. She'd liked him. He'd been surprisingly calm for a man in his situation. Calm and a little charming, if you thought lame humor in the face of death was cute.

And she would have killed him, but she'd hesitated. No, not hesitated. It hadn't been lack of will that stayed her hand that day so much as pride that she'd accomplished such a difficult job so quickly. Hu never complimented her work. Though under duress, Kylar's compliments had seemed genuine, and there weren't that many people a wetboy could talk shop with. So Vi had given in to the temptation Kylar had laid out for her, stalling so obviously that she'd let it work.

Then the do-gooder count had broken into the room and Kylar landed a knife in her shoulder as she escaped. Months later her shoulder still throbbed at times. She'd lost a little flexibility, despite instantly heading to the wytch Hu used for his healing.

Next time, she wouldn't hesitate.

She knew she should feel elated that she'd killed Jarl. She was free now. A master wetboy. Hu would have no say over anything in her life, and if he tried, she could kill him without worrying about the repercussions in the Sa'kagé. That is, if the Sa'kagé survived whatever the Godking had planned.

I killed Jarl. The thought wouldn't go away. Hadn't gone away for two days. *I killed the man who was the closest thing I've ever had to a friend.*

There hadn't been much to the kill. Any child could climb up on a roof and shoot an arrow. She'd wanted to miss, hadn't she? She could have missed. She could have just not taken the shot. She could have gone inside and joined Kylar and Jarl and fought against the Godking. But she hadn't.

She'd killed, and now she was alone again, going somewhere she didn't want to go, taking a little girl against her will, forcing a man she respected to follow her into a trap.

You are a cruel god, Nysos. Could you not leave me with more than dust and ashes? I, who serve you so faithfully. From my knife and my loins flow rivers of blood and semen. Do I not deserve an honored place for that? Do I not deserve one friend?

She coughed and blinked rapidly. She bit her tongue until it threatened to bleed. *I will not cry. Nysos can have his blood and semen, but he will never have my tears. Curse you, Nysos.* But she didn't say it aloud. She had served her god too long to risk his wrath.

She had even made a pilgrimage of sorts—it had been on her way to a kill—to a small town in the Sethi wine country that was holy to Nysos. The harvest festival was dedicated to the god. Wine flowed freely. Women were expected to abandon themselves to whatever passion moved them. They even had an odd form of storytelling where men stood on a stage holding masks and enacting while the audience watched a three-part cycle full of the suffering of mortals and their need for gods to straighten it out, followed by a bawdy, vicious comedy that seemed to make fun of everyone in the village, even the writer of the enactment. The town loved it. They clapped and wailed and sang along drunkenly with the holy songs and fucked like rabbits. For a week, no one was allowed to turn down a sexual advance. For Vi, it turned into a long week. It was one time in her life that she'd felt justified in complaining about being beautiful. She'd taken to wearing baggy clothing in the hopes she would entice fewer men.

All that service, Nysos. For what? For life? Hu's nearing forty, and for all that he says he serves you, the only times a god's name passes his lips is in curses.

By the time Vi came back to where the bedrolls were laid out, Uly had finished the entire bag of water. She looked like she was about to be sick.

"If you throw up on those blankets, you'll sleep in them dirty," Vi said.

"Kylar's going to kill you," Uly said. "Even if you are a girl."

"I'm not a girl. I'm a bitch, and don't you forget it." Vi tossed the bag with their food at Uly, who dropped it. "Eat slow and not much, or you'll puke and die."

Uly took her advice and soon flopped down on her bedroll and was asleep in seconds. Vi stayed up. She was tired, achingly, grindingly tired. She only thought this much when she was exhausted. It did no good to think. It was worthless.

She busied herself making the camp invisible. It was a foggy morning. They weren't far from the road, but they were in a small hollow. The stream came burbling down from the Silver Bear Hills with enough volume that most of the noise the horses might make would be covered, and with the cold camp they'd made, the human presence was barely notable here. She'd done her best to hide the horses behind a thicket. She squatted with her back to a tree and tried to convince her mind how tired her body was.

In the distance, she heard a clatter. It was dampened by the fog, but it could only be one thing: horses. She drew a sword and a knife, and dipped the knife into her poison sheath. She looked at Uly and considered trying to magically silence the girl, but it would expose her and she didn't know if it would work anyway, so she just pressed her back to a tree and peered toward the sound.

Moments later, Kylar appeared, leading two horses. He passed twenty paces away. He must have been riding almost straight through, switching from horse to horse. He barely slowed as he approached the ford. Vi's horse stomped a foot and one of the horses Kylar was leading neighed.

Kylar cursed and jerked the reins. Uly rolled over as Kylar splashed through the stream. The horses climbed the other bank and clattered into the distance. Kylar never even turned his head.

Vi chuckled and lay down. She slept well.

When she woke that evening, Uly was still asleep. That was good. Vi didn't have time to chase the girl. In her place, another kidnapper would have just bound the girl and been done with it. But the strongest ropes weren't the kind that bound hands. Hopelessness was Vi's weapon, not hemp. Ropes of Uly's own devising would bind her forever.

Ropes of my own devising. I know all about that, don't I?

She kicked Uly to wake her, but not as hard as she meant to. The girl's salvation had been so close, and she'd never even known it.

31

The most valuable skill Dorian ever learned turned out to be a simple one: he figured out how to eat and drink without breaking his trance. Instead of having Solon watch him for the inevitable signs of dehydration and wake him, Dorian was able to maintain his trances for weeks.

Though he knew he appeared utterly disconnected from reality, the opposite was true. From his little room in the garrison at Screaming Winds, Dorian watched everything. The Cenarian garrison at Screaming Winds had been bypassed by Khalidor's invasion. Most of the Khalidoran army had simply used Quorig's Pass more than a week east. With the death of Logan's father, Duke Regnus Gyre, the garrison was being led by a young noble named Lehros Vass. He was well-meaning, but he didn't know what to do without a commanding officer.

Solon was giving advice that over the days sounded less like advice and more like orders. If Khalidor attacked Screaming Winds now, they would attack from the Cenarian side, so he shifted the defenses, moved the men and the supplies inside the walls. No one expected an attack, though. The truth was that Screaming Winds now protected nothing. Garoth Ursuul could let them grow old and die here, and all he would lose would be a trade route that hadn't been used for hundreds of years.

Far to the South, Feir was doing less well, though he was tracking

Curoch admirably. Feir had a hard road in front of him, and Dorian could do nothing to make it easier. Sometimes it made Dorian sick. He'd watched Feir die a dozen ways, some of them so shameful he wept even through his trance. At best, Feir would have about two decades and a heroic death in front of him.

As always, Dorian strayed close to his own futures. He'd found a way to do it that didn't risk madness. He simply watched the futures of other people at the places they met him. It didn't work well, though. He would see half a dozen ways a person might interact with him, and how their choices might affect the meeting, but not his own. So he could see what, but not why. He couldn't follow a single line of his own choices to see where it would lead him. Once in a while, he could watch his own face through other people's eyes and guess what he was thinking, but those were rare flashes. It was taking too long, even with his trance stretching over a month, and while he pieced his own life together, everything else changed.

So he started touching his own life directly. He knew several things instantly. First, he was going to be a source of either hope or despair for tens of thousands within a year.

Second, a gaping hole stretched across his possible futures. He traced it back and realized the hole was because in some paths, he would choose to renounce his gift of prophecy. He was stunned. He'd thought of it before, of course. In all his training with the healers, disabling his gift was the only cure he'd been able to find for his growing madness. But Dorian's gift had seemed a gift for the whole world, and he'd gladly borne the consequences because he knew he'd be able to help others avert disaster.

Third, Khali herself was coming to Screaming Winds.

Dorian's heart dropped into his stomach. If she passed the garrison, she would go to Cenaria and take up residence in the hellish gaol they called the Maw. Garoth Ursuul would have two of his sons build ferali. He would use one against the rebel army. There would be a massacre.

Khali and her entourage were still two days away. Dorian had time. He looked back at his own life, trying to figure out how to avert disaster. In a moment, he was swept up in the current. Faces streamed past him, became a maelstrom, sucking him down. His young wife, crying. A girl, hanged. A little village in northern Waeddryn where he might live with Feir's family. A red-haired boy who was like a son to him, fifteen years from now. Killing his brothers. Betraying his wife. Telling his wife the truth and losing her. A gold mask of his own face, weeping golden tears. Marching with an army. Neph Dada. Walking away from an army. Solitude and madness and death, a dozen different ways. Down every path, he could see only suffering. Every time he chose any good for himself, those he loved suffered.

"You knew?" his wife asked. "You knew all along?"

"No!" Dorian shot upright in bed, waking.

Solon flinched in the chair across from Dorian. He gestured, and the lamps in the room lit. "Dorian? You're back! I hope whatever you were doing was important, because I wanted to wake you about a hundred times."

Dorian's head was aching. What day was it? How long had he been catatonic?

His answer was in the air itself. Khali was close. He could feel her.

"I need gold," Dorian said.

"What?" Solon asked. He rubbed his eyes. It was late.

"Gold, man! I need gold!"

Solon pointed to his purse on the table and pulled on boots.

Dorian spilled the gold coins into his hands. It barely even hit his palm before the coins melted into a glob, instantly cooled and wrapped around his wrist. "More. More! There's no time to lose, Solon."

"How much?"

"As much as you can carry. Meet me in the back courtyard, and rouse the soldiers. All of them. But don't ring the alarum bell."

"Dammit, what is it?" Solon demanded. He grabbed his sword belt and strapped it on.

"No time!" Dorian was already running out of the room.

In the courtyard, Dorian could swear he smelled Khali even more strongly, though the scent was purely magical. She was perhaps two miles distant. It was midnight now, and he suspected she'd strike an hour before dawn, the wytching hour, when men are most susceptible to the night's terrors and Khali's delusions.

Dorian tried to untangle what he'd seen. He couldn't imagine the garrison would hold, and if Khali caught him, the results would be as terrible for the world as for him. A prophet, delivered into her hands? Dorian thought of the futures he'd seen for himself. Was it so great a sacrifice to give up seeing those rush inexorably toward him? But if he gave up his visions, he would be blind, rudderless, and useless to anyone else. It also wasn't a simple procedure. He'd described it to Solon and Feir as being like smashing his own brain with a sharp rock in order to stop seizures. Ideally, he could sear one part of his own Talent in such a way that it would eventually heal, but not for years. If Khali captured him, she might think his gift was gone forever, and kill him.

He had begun preparing the weaves before he realized he'd made up his mind. The fact that it was dark and he couldn't replenish his glore vyrden was no problem because the amount of magic he needed was slight. He set up the weaves deftly, sharpening some and setting them aside, holding the prepared portions as if in one hand. As the magic came together, he realized that all his time in his visions, juggling different streams of time and holding place markers at decision points, had paid off in his magic. Not five years ago, he'd come this far with the weave, practicing it to see if he could hold seven strands simultaneously. It had been brutal, especially knowing that letting any one slip could make him an amnesiac, an idiot, or dead. Now, it was easy. Solon came into the yard and saw what he was doing, a look of horror on his face, and even that didn't distract Dorian.

He sliced, twisted, pulled, seared, and covered one section of his Talent.

The courtyard was curiously silent, strangely flat, oddly constricted. "My God," Dorian said.

"What?" Solon asked, his eyes full of concern. "What have you done?"

Dorian was disoriented, like a man trying to stand after losing a leg. "Solon, it's gone. My gift is gone."

32

Three days north of the Silver Bear Hills, Kylar came to the small town of Torras Bend. He'd been pushing hard for six days, barely stopping long enough to rest the horses, and his body ached everywhere from his stint in the saddle. Torras Bend was halfway to Cenaria, at the base of the Fasmeru Mountains and Forglin's Pass. The horses needed the rest, and so did he. South of town, he'd even had to submit to a Lae'knaught checkpoint looking for magi. Apparently, Waeddryn's queen didn't have the will or the power to expel the Lae'knaught either.

He asked a farmer for directions to the town's inn and soon found himself in a warm building filled with the smells of roasting meat pies and fresh ale. Most inns smelled of stale beer and sweat, but the people of northern Waeddryn were fastidious. Their gardens lacked weeds, their fences lacked rot, their children very nearly lacked dirt. They prided themselves on their industry, and the attention to detail of these simple folk was incredible. Even Durzo would have been impressed. All in all, it was a perfect place to rest.

Coming into the common room, Kylar ordered enough food to make the goodwife raise her eyebrows. He sat by himself. His legs were throbbing and his butt was sore. If he never saw another horse again, it would be too soon. He closed his eyes and sighed, only the heavenly odors coming from the kitchen keeping him from going to bed immediately.

In what was obviously a nightly ritual, probably half the men of the village pushed their way through the inn's great oak door to share a pint with their friends before going home. Kylar ignored the men and their inquisitive glances. He only opened his eyes when a stout, homely woman in her fifties set two enormous meat pies in front of him, along with an impressive tankard of ale.

"I think you'll find Mistress Zoralat's ale is as good as her pies," the woman said. "May I join you?"

Kylar yawned. "Ah, excuse me," he said. "Sure. I'm Kylar Stern."

"What do you do, Master Stern?" she said, sitting.

"I'm a, uh, soldier, as a matter of fact." He yawned again. He was getting too old for this. He'd considered saying "I'm a wetboy" just to see what the old goat's reaction would be.

"A soldier for whom?"

"Who are you?" he asked.

"Answer my question, and I'll answer yours," she said, as if he were a recalcitrant child.

Fair enough. "For Cenaria."

"I was under the impression that country no longer existed," she said.

"Were you?" he said.

"Khalidoran goons. Meisters. The Godking. Conquest. Rape. Pillage. Iron-fisted rule. Ring any bells?"

"I guess some people would be deterred by that," Kylar said. He smiled and shook his head at himself.

"You frighten a lot of people, don't you, Kylar Stern?"

"What was your name again?" he asked.

"Ariel Wyant Sa'fastae. You can call me Sister Ariel."

Any vestige of fatigue vanished instantly. Kylar touched the ka'kari within him to be sure it was ready to call up in an instant.

Sister Ariel blinked. Was it because she'd seen something, or had he just let his muscles tense?

"I thought this was a dangerous part of the world for people like you," Kylar said. He couldn't remember the stories, but he remembered something linking Torras Bend with mages' dying.

"Yes," she said. "One of our young and foolhardy sisters disappeared here. I've come to look for her."

"The Dark Hunter," he said, finally remembering.

At tables around them, conversations ceased. Dour faces turned toward Kylar. From their expressions, he could see that the topic wasn't so much taboo as it was gauche. "Sorry," he mumbled, and began attacking a meat pie.

Sister Ariel watched in silence as he ate. He felt a twinge of suspicion, wondering what Durzo would have said if he knew Kylar was eating food served to him by a maja, but he'd died twice already—maybe three times—and lived again, so what the hell? Besides, the pies were good, and the ale was better.

Not for the first time, he wondered if it had been the same for Durzo. He'd lived for centuries, but had he been unkillable, too? He must have. But he had never risked his own life. Was that only because by the time Kylar knew him, the ka'kari had abandoned him? Kylar wondered sometimes if there were a downside to his power. He could live for hundreds of years. He couldn't be killed. But he didn't feel immortal. He didn't even feel the sense of power that, when he was a boy, he thought he would feel once he became a wetboy. He was a wetboy now, more than a wetboy, and he felt like he was still just Kylar. Still Azoth, the clueless, scared child.

"Have you seen a beautiful woman come riding through here, sister?" he asked. Vi had seen where Kylar lived. She would tell the Godking and he would destroy everything and everyone Kylar loved. That was how he worked.

"No. Why?"

"If you do," he said, "kill her."

"Why? Is she your wife?" Sister Ariel asked, smirking.

He gave her a flat look. "The God doesn't hate me that much. She's an assassin."

"So, you're not a soldier, but an assassin hunter."

"I'm not hunting her. I wish I had the time. But she may come through here."

"What's so important that you would abandon justice?"

"Nothing," he said without thinking. "But justice has been too long denied elsewhere."

"Where?" she asked.

"Suffice it to say that I'm on a mission for the king."

"There is no king of Cenaria except the Godking."

"Not yet."

She raised an eyebrow. "There's no man who can unite Cenaria, even against the Godking. Perhaps Terah Graesin can, but she's scarcely a man, is she?"

He smiled. "You Sisters like to think you've got it all figured out, don't you?"

"Do you know that you're an infuriating young ignoramus?"

"Only as much as you're a tired old bag."

"Do you truly think I'd kill some young woman for you?"

"I don't suppose you would. Forgive me, I'm tired. I forgot that the Seraph's hand only reaches beyond its ivory halls to take things for itself."

Her lips pressed into a thin line. "Young man, I don't take well to impudence."

"You've succumbed to the intoxication of power, Sister. You like watching people jump." He raised an insolent eyebrow, bemused. "So color me scared."

She was very still. "Another temptation of power," she said, "is to strike down those who vex you. You, Kylar Stern, are tempting me."

He picked that moment to yawn. It wasn't feigned, but he couldn't have found a better moment. She turned red. "They say the old age is a second childhood, Sister. Besides which, the moment you drew power, I'd kill you." *By the gods, I can't stop. Am I really going to get on the wrong side of half the world's mages because one old lady irritates me?*

Instead of getting angrier, Sister Ariel's face grew thoughtful. "You can tell the moment I draw magic?"

He wasn't going there. "One way to find out," he said. "But it would be a bother to dispose of your corpse and cover my tracks. Especially with all these witnesses."

"How would you cover your tracks?" she asked quietly.

"Come now. You're in Torras Bend. How many of the mages who have been 'killed by the Dark Hunter' here do you think were really killed by the Dark Hunter? Don't be naive. The thing probably doesn't even exist."

She scowled, and he could tell she'd never thought of it. Well, she was a mage. Of course she didn't think like a wetboy. "Well," she said. "You're wrong about one thing. It exists."

"If everyone who's ever gone into the woods has died, how do you know?"

"You know, young man. There's a way for you to prove that we're all crazy."

"Go into the woods?" he asked.

"You wouldn't be the first to try."

"I'd be the first to succeed."

"You're awfully full of braggadocio about the things you'd do if you only had the time."

"Fair enough, Sister Ariel. I accept your correction—until the day Cenaria has a king. Now if you'll excuse me?"

"One moment," she said as he stood. "I'm going to draw the power, but I swear by the White Seraph that I won't touch you with it. If you must kill me, I won't try to stop you."

She didn't wait for him to respond. He saw a pale iridescent nimbus surround her. It shifted quickly through every color in the rainbow in deliberate succession, though some colors seemed somehow thicker than others. Was that an indication of her strength in the various disciplines of magic? He readied the ka'kari to devour whatever magic she threw at him—hoping he remembered what he had done before, and not sure that he did—but he didn't strike.

The nimbus didn't move. Sister Ariel Wyant merely inhaled deeply through her nose. The nimbus disappeared. She nodded her head, as if satisfied. "Dogs find you very odd, don't they?"

"What?" he asked. It was true, but he'd never thought much of it.

"Maybe you can tell me," she said, "why, after days of hard riding, don't you smell of sweat and dirt and horse? Indeed, you have no scent whatsoever."

"You're imagining things," he said, backing away. "Goodbye, Sister."

"Until we meet again, Kylar Stern."

33

$\mathcal{M}$omma K stood on a landing overlooking the warehouse floor. Agon's Dogs, as they'd taken to calling themselves, were training under his watchful eye. The force had shrunk to a hundred men, and Momma K was sure that by now its existence was well-known. "Do you think they're ready?" she asked as Agon labored up the stairs on a cane.

"More training would make them better. Battle will make them better faster. But it will cost lives," he said.

"And your wytch hunters?"

"They're no Ymmuri. Ymmuri can riddle a man with arrows from a hundred paces while galloping away from him. The best I can hope for is ten men who will get in range, stop, shoot, and move on before the fireballs get to them. My hunters aren't worthy of the bows they carry—but they're a damn sight better than anything else we have."

Momma K smiled. He was underplaying his men's capabilities. She'd seen those men shoot.

"What about your rent girls?" Agon asked. "This mission will cost lives. Are they ready for that?" He stood close beside her as they watched his men spar.

"You would have been amazed if you could have seen their faces, Brant. It was like I gave them their souls back. They'd been dying inside, and now they've come back to life, all at once."

"No word yet from Jarl?" Agon's voice was tense and Momma K could tell that, for all that he had clashed with the young man, Agon was worried for him.

"There wouldn't be. Not yet." She put her hands on the rail and accidentally brushed his fingers.

Brant looked at her hand and then in her eyes and quickly away.

She winced and pulled her hand away. Decades ago, Agon had been arrogant, not obnoxious with it but merely full of youthful confidence that he could do pretty much anything better than pretty much anyone else. That was gone now, replaced by a sober understanding of his own strengths and weaknesses. He was a man well tempered by the years. Gwinvere had known men ruined by their wives. Small women who felt so threatened they undercut their husbands for so many years that those men no longer trusted themselves. Such women had made Momma K wealthy. She knew men with perfectly good wives who were regulars, men addicted to the brothels as others were addicted to wine, but much of her business came from men desperate to be considered manly, strong, good lovers, noble.

It was one of the many ironies of the business that they came to a brothel for that.

Men, Momma K believed, were too simple to ever be truly safe from the temptations of a house of pleasure. It had been her business to make sure those temptations were multifaceted, and she'd been good at her business. Her establishments weren't just whorehouses. She had meeting rooms, smoking rooms, dignified parlors, lecturers on all the topics men love. The food and drink were always finer than her competitors' and priced lower. At her best establishments, she brought in chefs and wine masters from all over Midcyru. As a restaurateur, she would have been a dismal failure. The food side of her business operated at a loss every year. But at her houses, men who came for the food stayed to spend their coin other ways.

The few Brant Agons of the world didn't bang her girls for two reasons: they were happy at home, and they didn't walk through the doors in the first place. She was sure Agon had been derided for that. Men who didn't frequent the houses of pleasure were always mocked by those who did.

Brant had conviction, integrity. He reminded her of Durzo.

The thought sent a lance through her stomach. Durzo had been dead three months. Gods, how she missed him! She'd been helplessly in love with Durzo. Durzo was the only man in her life who would ever understand her. She'd been too terrified of that to let love grow. She'd been a coward. She'd starved their relationship of honesty, and like a plant potted in a shallow bowl, the relationship had been stunted. Durzo was the father of her child. He'd only found out a few days before he died.

Momma K was fifty now, almost fifty-one. The years had been kind to her, at least most days they seemed so. She usually looked fifteen years younger than she was. Well, at least ten. If she tried, she thought she still had what it would take to seduce Brant.

Once a whore, always a whore, huh, Gwin? She used to despise old women who clung to their lost youth by their lacquered fingernails. Now she was one. Part of her wanted to seduce Brant just to prove to herself that she still could. But she didn't want to seduce Brant. It had been years since she'd taken a man to her bed. For all the thousands of times it had been work, there had been times she'd liked or admired her lover of the moment. And there had been Durzo. The night they conceived Uly, he'd been so blasted on mushrooms that he hadn't been much of a lover, but to have the man she loved share her bed had filled her to overflowing. She was so shot through with love and grief that she'd wept during their lovemaking. Even in his drugged state, Durzo had stopped and asked if he was hurting her. After that, it had taken all her skill to bring him to completion. Durzo had been a tender man when it came to taking his pleasure.

Now their child was being raised by Kylar and Elene. It was the only deception she didn't regret. With those two, Uly would do well.

But she was tired of deceit. Tired of taking and never giving. She didn't want to seduce Brant. She knew he wanted her, and his wife was probably dead. Probably, but he couldn't know. Wouldn't know. Ever. How long would a man like Brant Agon wait for the woman he loved?

Forever. That's the kind of man he is.

Thirty-some years ago, they'd met at a party, her first ever at a noble's home. He'd fallen instantly in love with her and she'd allowed him to court her, never telling him what she did, what she was. He'd been gallant, confident, determined to make his mark on the world, and so sweetly careful in his courting that he hadn't asked her for a kiss for a month.

She'd indulged in the fantasy. He would marry her, take her away from all the horrors she wanted so desperately to leave behind. She hadn't had that many noble clients, yet. It was possible, wasn't it?

The night of their first kiss, a noble had referred to her as the sweetest harlot he'd ever had. Brant overheard it, instantly challenged the man to a duel, and killed him. Gwinvere had fled. The next day, Brant had learned the truth. He enlisted and tried to get himself honorably killed fighting on the Ceuran border.

But Brant Agon had been too capable to die. Eventually, despite how he despised bootlicking and politicking, his merit had pulled him through the ranks. He married a plain woman from a merchant family. By all accounts, it was a happy marriage.

"How long will it take to get everything ready?" she asked. She would hope Brant's infatuation had died. She would help him dodge the truth. She was good at that, at least.

"Gwin."

She turned and looked him in the eye, her mask in place, eyes cool. "Yes?"

He blew out a great breath. "I loved you for years, Gwin, even after..."

"My betrayal?"

"Your indiscretion. You were what? Sixteen, seventeen? You deceived yourself first, and I think you suffered for it more than I did."

She snorted.

"Regardless," he said. "I bear you no ill will. You are a beautiful woman, Gwin. More beautiful than my Liza ever was. You are so brilliant that I feel I have to sprint just to keep up with you jogging. I felt quite the opposite with Liza. You...affect me profoundly."

"But," she said.

"Yes. But," he said. "I love Liza, and she has loved me through a thousand trials, and she deserves all that I have to give. Whether or not you have tender feelings for me, while I have hope that my Liza lives, I would ask—beg—that you would help me remain true to her."

"You've chosen a hard road," she said.

"Not a road, a battle. Sometimes life is our battlefield. We must do what we know to do, not what we want to do."

Gwinvere sighed, and yet somehow felt lighter. Dodging Brant's attraction could have so easily turned into dodging his presence, and she needed to work closely with him now. *Is honesty so easy? Could I have just said, "Durzo, I love you, but I fear you'll destroy me"?* Brant had just offered her his vulnerability, confessed her effect on him, and yet seemed not weaker but stronger for it. *How was that? Is truth so powerful?*

She swore then, in her own heart, that she would not tempt this man for her own vanity. Not in her voice, not in accidental touches, not in her dress, she would lay down every weapon in her arsenal. The resolution made her feel oddly...decent. "Thank you," she said. She smiled companionably. "How long till they're ready?"

"Three days," Brant said.

"Then let us make the night run red."

34

Solon dropped the two leather five-hundred-weight bags he carried and grabbed Dorian as the prophet tottered. At first, he didn't understand what Dorian had said.

"What are you talking about?"

Dorian pushed Solon's steadying arm away. He put on his cloak and sword belt and picked up two pairs of manacles. "This way," he said, grabbing one of the bags from Solon and heading down the open road away from the wall.

The land leading to the wall was rocky, barren ground. It had been cleared of trees out to a hundred and fifty yards, and though the road was broad enough for twenty men abreast, it was rutted and pitted from the wear of many feet and wagons over ground that alternated between soil and solid rock.

"Khali is coming," Dorian said before Solon could ask what was happening again. "I gave up my prophetic gift in case she captures me."

Solon couldn't even answer.

Dorian stopped beneath a black oak that grew on a rocky outcropping that hung over the road. "She's here. Not a half a league away." Dorian didn't even take his eyes off the tree. "It'll have to do. Make sure you only step on rock. If they see tracks, they'll find me."

Solon didn't move. Dorian had finally gone crazy. The other times it had been obvious: he'd simply been catatonic. But now, he seemed so rational. "Come on, Dorian," Solon said. "Let's go back to the wall. We can talk about this in the morning."

"The wall won't be there in the morning. Khali will strike at the wytching hour. That gives you five hours to get the men out of there." Dorian hoisted himself up on the ledge. "Throw the bags up to me."

"Khali, Dorian? She's a myth. You're trying to tell me that a goddess is half a league from here?"

"Not a goddess. Perhaps one of the rebel angels expelled from heaven and given leave to walk the earth until the end of days."

"Right. I suppose she's brought a dragon? We can talk about—"

"Dragons avoid angels," Dorian said. Disappointment etched his features. "Are you going to abandon me now when I need you? Have I ever lied to you? You thought Curoch was a myth too, before we found it. I need you. When Khali comes through the wall, I'll go out of my mind. You've seen me when I thought I could use the vir for good. That was like one part wine and ten parts water; this is pure liquor. I will be lost. Her very presence brings out the worst. The worst fears, the worst memories, the worst sins. My hubris will come out. I might try to fight her, and I'll lose. Or my lust for power will break me and I'll join her. She knows me. She will break me."

Solon couldn't take the look in Dorian's eyes. "What if you're wrong? What if it is the madness you've warned about for so long?"

"If the wall stands at dawn, you'll know."

Solon threw the bags up to Dorian and then climbed carefully up the rock, making sure he didn't leave so much as a footprint.

"What are you doing?" he asked as Dorian smiled at him and poured the gold onto the ground. Next Dorian pulled on the manacles and the iron chains holding them together tore apart as if they were made of paper. He dropped a manacle onto the pile of coins and it fell into the coins as if they were liquid. The other three manacles followed and the pile of coins shrank each time. Dorian reached through the gold and pulled out each of the manacles, now sheathed in gold, and placed one on each of his wrists. He stretched the iron of the second pair and locked those manacles around his thighs just above the knee.

It was amazing. Dorian had always said that his power with the vir had dwarfed his Talent, yet here he was, molding gold and iron artfully and effortlessly.

In another moment, Dorian had shaped the rest of the coins into four narrow spikes and what looked like a bowl. He stopped, and now he concentrated. Solon could feel the brush of spells flowing past him, sinking into the metal. After two minutes, Dorian stopped and spoke under his breath to the black oak.

"There will be a contingent with her, the Soulsworn," Dorian said. "They've given up much of what it is to be human to serve Khali. But they aren't the danger. She is. Solon, I don't think you can defeat her. I think you should take the men away from here. Take them somewhere where their deaths might accomplish something. But...if she makes it to Cenaria, Garoth Ursuul's sons will make two ferali. They will use them on the resistance. This I have seen."

"You didn't really do it, did you? You didn't really destroy your gift," Solon said.

"If I don't see you again, my friend, may the God go with you." Dorian said. He fused the gold spikes to the manacles and knelt behind the tree. He slid the spikes into the wood with unnatural ease. His hands were set high and far apart. As he knelt there, obviously ready to pray his way through whatever ordeal he thought was coming, Solon felt a stab of envy. This time, it wasn't for Dorian's power or Dorian's lineage or Dorian's simple, humble integrity. He envied Dorian's certainty. Dorian's world was very clear. To him, Khali wasn't a goddess or a figment of the Khalidorans' imagination or just an ancient monster who'd conned the Khalidoran people into worshipping her. She was an angel who'd been expelled from heaven.

In Dorian's world, everything had a place. There was a hierarchy. Things fit. Even a man with Dorian's vast powers could be humble, because he knew others were far above him, even if he never met one of them. Dorian could name evil without fear and without rancor. He could claim that some did evil or served it without hating them. Solon had never known anyone like that. Except perhaps Count Drake. Whatever happened to him? Did he die in the coup?

"What does all this do?" Solon asked, picking up what had been a gold bowl. Now, it was something between a helmet and a mask. It would fit completely over Dorian's head, with only two small holes in the nose for breathing. He turned it over. It was a perfect sculpture of Dorian's face, weeping tears of gold.

"It will keep me from seeing her, from hearing her, from shouting out to her, from moving from this place. It will keep me from indulging in the last temptation—believing myself strong enough to fight her. I hope it will also keep me from using the vir. But I can't bind myself magically. I need you to do it for me. After she's passed, I'll be able to escape when the sun rises and refills my Talent, so you needn't worry for me. If you need your gold, it will be here."

"You're leaving, no matter what."

Dorian smiled. "Don't ask where."

"Good luck," Solon said. There was a lump in his throat that reminded him of how good it had felt not to be alone again. Even fighting with Dorian and Feir had been better than peace without them.

"You've been a brother to me, Solon. I believe we'll meet again, before this is done," Dorian said. "Now hurry."

Solon fit the gold helmet over Dorian's head and bound it with the strongest magic he could, completely emptying his glore vyrden to do it. He'd do no more magic until sunrise. It wasn't a comforting thought. As he climbed down from the rock outcropping, he swore that he saw bark growing over Dorian's arms where they otherwise would have been exposed.

From the road, Dorian was invisible. "Goodbye, brother," Solon said. Then he turned and strode toward the wall. Now he just had to convince Lehros Vass that he wasn't stark raving mad.

35

The Godking perched on the fireglass throne he'd ordered cut from the rock of the Maw. To him, the sharp-edged blackness was a reminder, a goad, and a comfort at once.

His son stood before him. His first *son,* not just the seed of his loins. The Godking spread his seed far and wide. He never considered the weeds that took hold to be sons. They were just bastards, and he gave them no thought. The only ones who mattered were the boys who would be Vürdmeisters. The training, though, was more than most could survive. Only a few boys out of scores of wytchborn survived to become his aethelings, his throne-worthy sons. Each of those had been given an uurdthan, a Harrowing to prove his worth. So far, only Moburu had succeeded. Only Moburu would he acknowledge as his son. And still not yet his heir.

The truth was, Moburu pained him. Garoth remembered the boy's mother. An island princess of some sort, captured in the days before the Sethi Empire had destroyed Garoth's attempt at a navy. He'd been intrigued by her, and while an endless procession of other women born high and low, willing and not, made its way through his bedchamber, he'd actually tried to seduce her. She'd been as passionate as he was calculating, as hot as he was cold. She'd been exotic, enticing. He'd tried everything except magic. He'd been certain

with a young man's certainty that no woman could long resist
him.

After a year, she still held onto her haughty disdain. She despised
him. One night he'd lost his patience and raped her. He'd meant
to have her strangled afterward, but was oddly ashamed. Later, Neph
had told him the woman was pregnant. He'd put the child out of his
mind until Neph told him the boy had survived the trials and was
ready for his uurdthan. Garoth had given Moburu an uurdthan he'd
been sure would be the death of him. But the man had completed that
task as easily as every other Garoth had put before him.

The worst part of all was that the heir presumptive to Khalidor's
throne didn't even look Khalidoran. He had his mother's eyes, her
throaty voice, and her skin—her Ladeshian skin.

It was a bitter gall. Why couldn't Dorian have made it? Garoth
had held such high hopes for Dorian. He'd liked Dorian. Dorian had
achieved his uurdthan and then had betrayed Garoth. Garoth had held
lower hopes for the one who'd called himself Roth, but at least Roth
looked Khalidoran.

Moburu wore the regalia of an Alitaeran cavalry officer, red bro-
cade on gold with a dragon's head sigil. He was intelligent, quick-
witted, utterly self-assured, roughly handsome despite his Ladeshian
skin (Garoth grudgingly admitted), reputed to be one of the best riders in the cavalry, and ruthless. Of course. He stood as a son of the
Godking should. He wore humility as naturally as a man wore a dress.

It irked Garoth, but it was his own fault. He had designed his seeds'
lives so that those who survived would be exactly what Moburu was.
His problem was that he'd designed all those tests to present him with
candidates. He had hoped to have a number of sons. If he did, their
attention would be fixed on each other. Brother would plot against
brother for their father's favor. But now, with Dorian gone, Roth dead,
and none of the others beyond their uurdthan, Moburu was alone. The
man's ambition would force him to turn his eyes on the Godking himself soon. If he hadn't already.

"What news from the Freeze?" the Godking asked.

"Your Holiness, it is as bad as we thought. Maybe worse. The clans have already sent out the summons. They've agreed to truces so they can winter close enough to the border to join the war band at spring. They're spawning krul, and maybe zel and ferali. If they've learned to do that, they'll be increasing their numbers for the next nine months."

"How did they find a spawning place in the Freeze, for Khali's sake? Under the permafrost?" Garoth swore.

"My lord," his son said. "We can counteract that threat easily enough. I've taken the liberty of ordering Khali brought here. She'll come through Screaming Winds. It's faster."

"You did what?" The Godking's voice was icy, dangerous.

"She'll massacre one of the Cenaria's most formidable garrisons—saving you a headache. She'll arrive in a few days. Beneath this castle is perfect spawning ground. The locals call it the Maw. With Khali here, we can breed an army such as the world has never seen. This ground is steeped in misery. The caverns beneath Khaliras have been mined for seven hundred years. The krul our Vürdmeisters can produce there are nothing compared to what's possible here."

The Godking's muscles were rigid, but he allowed nothing to show on his face. "Son. Son. You have never spawned krul. You have never forged ferali or bred ferozi. You have no idea what it costs. There's a reason I used human armies to conquer the highlanders and the river clans and the Tlanglang and the Grosth. I've solidified our rule within and expanded our borders four times—and never once used krul. Do you know how people fight when they know that if they lose their entire families will be eaten? They fight to the last man. They arm the children with bows. Their women use kitchen knives and pokers. I saw it in my youth, and it gained my father nothing."

"Your father didn't have the vir you do."

"There's more to it than vir. This conversation is over." Moburu had never dared speak to him this way before—and ordering Khali brought here without asking!

But Garoth was distracted. He had lied. He had made krul, ferozi, and even ferali. Ferali had killed his last two brothers. He'd sworn then: never again. Never again with any of the monsters except for the few breeding pairs of ferozi he'd been working on to someday send into the Iaosian Forest for Ezra's treasures. But those he'd already paid for. They required nothing more of him.

But Moburu might be right. That was the worst of it. He had gotten used to treating Moburu as a partner, a son in the way other fathers treated their sons.

It had been a mistake. He'd shown indecision. Moburu was surely already plotting for his throne. Garoth could kill him, but Moburu was too valuable a tool to throw away carelessly. Curse him. Why hadn't his brothers turned out? Moburu needed a rival.

The Godking lifted a finger. "I've changed my mind. Think out loud for me, son. Make your case."

Moburu paused for a moment, then swelled with self-confidence. "I'd admit that our armies could probably counter the wild men from the Freeze. Even if the clans stay together, our Vürdmeisters would tip the balance in our favor. But to do that, we have to send every capable meister north. Quite honestly, there couldn't be a worse time. The Sisters grow suspicious and frightened. Some of them are saying they need to fight us now before we grow any stronger. We know the Ceurans will seize any weakness to come pouring over the border. They've wanted Cenaria for hundreds of years."

"The Ceurans are split."

"There's a brilliant young general named Lantano Garuwashi who's gathering a large following in northern Ceura. He's never lost a duel or a battle. If we send our armies and our meisters north, attacking us could be just what he needs to unify Ceura. Unlikely, but possible."

"Go on," the Godking said. He knew all about Lantano Garuwashi. Nor was he worried about the Sisters. He'd personally arranged for their present political crisis.

"It also seems the Sa'kagé is much better established and more capably led than we had believed. It's obviously the work of this new Shinga, Jarl. I think it shows that he's moved into a new phase of—"

"Jarl is dead," Garoth said.

"That can't be. I haven't found any sign—"

"Jarl has been dead for a week."

"But there haven't even been rumors of that, and with the level of organization we've found...I don't understand," Moburu said.

"You don't have to," the Godking said. "Go on."

Oh, Moburu looked less confident now. Good. He obviously wanted to ask more, but didn't dare. He floundered for a moment, then said, "There are rumors that Sho'cendi is sending a delegation to investigate what they call the alleged Khalidoran threat."

"Your sources call it a delegation?" Garoth asked, smiling thinly.

Moburu looked uncertain, then angry. "Y-yes, and if the mages decide we're a threat, they could return to Sho'cendi and come back with an army by spring—the same time all our other threats may materialize."

"Those delegates are battlemages. Six full battlemages. The Sa'seuran believe they've found and lost Jorsin Alkestes' sword, Curoch. They think it may be here in Cenaria."

"How do you know that?" Moburu asked, awed. "My source sits just outside the High Sa'seuran itself."

"Your brother told me," the Godking said, pleased with this turn of the conversation. He was back where he belonged. In control. Alive. Moving the world on the fulcrum of his desires. "He's one of the delegates."

"My brother?"

"Well, not a brother yet. Soon. I suppose you can guess his uurdthan. It is somewhat more difficult than your own."

Moburu absorbed the insult, and Garoth could see it sank deep. "He is to recover Curoch?" Moburu asked.

Garoth smiled his thin-lipped smile. He could see Moburu thinking. A son who recovered Curoch would be highly favored, highly powerful. Indeed, one of Garoth's ulcers had Curoch's name on it. If any of his sons recovered Curoch, that son might not hand it over. Curoch would give him enough power to challenge Garoth himself. Moburu would think of that immediately. But Garoth already had plans for that. Many plans, from the most facile—bribes and blackmail—to the most desperate—a death spell that might throw his consciousness into the murderer's body. That was not a spell one could safely test, so the best thing was to keep the sword out of his sons' hands.

"But you have raised some excellent points, son. You have become valuable to me." Oh, how it grated to say that to this half-breed. Son! "I will grant your wish. You will build me a ferali."

Moburu's eyes widened. Oh, he had no idea. "Yes, Your Holiness."

"And Moburu?" Garoth let the silence sit until Moburu swallowed. "Impress me."

36

You want us to flee, and you won't say why? Is that supposed to impress me?" Lord Vass asked.

Three hundred soldiers had gathered in the dark courtyard, the moon a sliver in a night sky aflame with stars. Three hundred soldiers dressed for battle, bundled against the fierce cold that had already descended on these mountains, though summer's heat had barely lost its edge in Cenaria City. Three hundred soldiers and their commander—who wasn't Solon. Three hundred men who were watching the exchange between Solon and Lehros Vass.

"I admit," Solon said quietly, "that it sounds weak. But I only ask for a day. We leave for one day, and then we come back. If I'm wrong, it's not like there are any looters who will have taken anything. We're the only people in these godforsaken mountains aside from the high-landers, and they haven't raided the wall in three years."

"It's abandoning our post," the young lord said. "We're sworn to hold this wall."

"We have no post," Solon snapped. "We have no king, we have no lord. We have three hundred men and an occupied country. Our oaths were to men now dead. Our duty is to keep these men alive so they can fight when we have a chance. This isn't the kind of war where we gloriously charge the enemy lines with our swords waving."

Lord Vass was young enough that he flushed with anger and embarrassment. Of course, that was exactly the kind of war he had in mind, and it had been a mistake to belittle it. How long had it been since Solon had lost those illusions of war?

The men weren't moving a muscle, but they all saw the anger on Lord Vass's face, the red made redder in the flickering torchlight.

"If you would have us leave, I demand to know why," Lord Vass said.

"A contingent of Khalidoran elites known as the Soulsworn is coming. They're bringing the Khalidoran goddess Khali to Cenaria. They'll attack the wall at the wytching hour."

"And you want to leave?" Vass asked, incredulous. "Do you know what it will mean when we capture the Khalidoran's goddess? It will destroy them. It will give our countrymen hope. We'll be heroes. This is the place to stop them. We have the walls, the traps, the men. This is our chance. This is just what we've been waiting for."

"Son, this goddess..." Solon gritted his teeth. "We're not talking about capturing a statue. I think she's real."

Lehros Vass looked at Solon, first incredulous, then indulgent. "If you need to run away, you go ahead. You know where the road is." He chuckled, giddy with his own grandeur. "Of course, I can't let you go until you give me my gold back."

If Solon told him where his gold was now, Vass would have his men go get it immediately. Dorian would be left helpless.

"To hell with you," Solon said. "And to hell with me too. We'll die together."

Sister Ariel Wyant sat five paces from the first magical boundary that separated the Iaosian Forest from the oak grove. For the past six days, she'd had her eye on what appeared to be a plaque twenty feet inside the forest. It didn't look like it had been there long: undergrowth hadn't covered it yet.

Her first hope in all her examinations of the ward had been that Ezra had made the ward hundreds of years ago. With another magus, she would have expected the weaves to disintegrate after so much time. Weaves always disintegrated. But with Ezra *always* didn't mean always. The proof shimmered just beyond mundane sight before her.

The second hope was that, given Ezra's power and the power of the other magi of his era, he would be defending himself against opponents far more powerful than any alive today. Sister Ariel didn't have the arrogance to think herself equal to those Ezra would have expected. She could only hope that her light touches against the weaves would be beneath notice. Termites were tiny, but they'd destroyed many a mighty house.

So for six days, she'd examined and reexamined the weaves that divided the Iaosian Forest from the oak grove. It was as beautiful as a black widow's web. There were traps both large and small. There were weaves that were meant to tear apart with the faintest touch, weaves that were meant to be unraveled, weaves that couldn't be broken with double Ariel's strength. And each had a trap.

Ariel could guess exactly what Sister Jessie had done. She'd probably tried to conceal her Talent. For the first day, it looked like a perfect strategy. It was a strategy that would have worked, had Ezra been simple. Sister Jessie was weak enough that she could compress her Talent and then shield it. That would make her Talent invisible to other Sisters or to male Seers—now there was a strange thought, how many times had Talented women used exactly that strategy to hide themselves or their Talented daughters from Sisters who came to recruit for the Chantry? Ariel shook her head. It wasn't time to get distracted. The problem was that Ezra's weaves didn't just register Talent. As nearly as Ariel could tell—and she had to guess because of the complexity and delicacy of the weaves—Ezra's weaves detected mages' bodies.

Everyone knew that mages were different from regular people, but not even Healers today understood exactly how magic changed a mage's flesh. That it did so was undeniable. Mages aged differently, sometimes more slowly the more Talented they were, but sometimes not. Regardless, their very flesh was altered in subtle ways by their constant interactions with magic. Apparently Ezra knew exactly what those ways were. Sister Ariel should have guessed that. Among no few other achievements, he had been a Sa'salar, a Lord of Healing. He had created the Dark Hunter—created a living being!

Oh, Sister Jessie, did you walk right through this wall of magic? Did you really think yourself cleverer than Ezra himself? How many mages' bones litter this damned forest?

She was letting her mind get off the problem at hand. She was still alive. She had made it past the first barrier. Now she needed to do something with that accomplishment. She needed to get that damned gold plaque. It was stuck, twenty feet away, just at the top of a small hillock. It was so close, and yet she had no hope of getting it. Her examination of Ezra's traps had left her convinced of it. It would take her years to dismantle his traps. Years, if ever. Even if she had the time, she would never be sure that she hadn't missed something. She could never be sure how many other layers of protection were left. Ezra might have spun this ward in a few days. He might have intended that this layer be penetrated by weak mages. Sister Ariel could spend her whole life dismantling traps and never uncover Ezra's real secrets.

If she'd come here as a younger woman, she might have thought it a worthy use of her life. But as a younger woman, she'd been much more idealistic. She'd believed in the Chantry with the kind of foolish faith that most people reserve for their religion. If Ezra did possess devastatingly powerful artifacts, would Ariel really want to deliver those to the Speaker? Would she trust Istariel with something that would multiply her power ten times?

Stop it. Ariel, you're letting your mind wander again.

She looked at the plaque. Then she started laughing. It was so simple. She stood and started walking back to the village.

She returned an hour later with a full stomach and a rope. Master Zoralat had been kind enough to show her how to make and throw a

lasso. For the last two days she'd wondered how to get the plaque—
and for two days she'd thought of only magical means. Stupid stupid
stupid.

The next several hours proved her clumsy as well. How many times
in her life had she sneered at the men who worked the Chantry's stables? This was the kind of exercise every Sister should be exposed
to—in front of all the stable hands in the Chantry.

The day ended and she still hadn't lassoed the plaque. She did her
cursing in the forest and went home. The next day she returned, her
arm and shoulder aching. It took her another three hours, during
which she cursed herself, cursed the rope, cursed Ezra, cursed her
lack of exercise, and just cursed—but all silently.

When the lasso finally dropped around the plaque, she could swear
the gold glowed briefly. She wanted to extend her senses to see what
had just happened, but it was too far away. She decided there was
nothing to do but pull the damned thing in.

At first, the plaque wouldn't move. It was somehow stuck. Then,
as Ariel pulled, part of the hillock shifted and rolled over, freeing the
plaque. It wasn't a hillock; it was Sister Jessie's body. She'd been dead
for weeks. Mold grew over her bright robes, obscuring the bloodstains.
It looked like a claw had torn away half of her head in a single terrible
swipe. Since her death, no animals had disturbed her body: there were
no bears or coyotes or ravens or other carrion feeders in Ezra's Wood,
but the worms were well into their work.

Sister Ariel looked away, allowing herself a moment to be a woman
confronting an acquaintance's mutilated body. She breathed slowly,
glad that Jessie's body was as far away as it was. She'd been this close
for days, and she'd never even smelled decay. Was that a trick of the
wind, or magic?

The plaque had been clutched in Sister Jessie's hands.

Sister Ariel carefully walled up all the emotions she felt and set
them aside. She would examine them later, allow herself tears if tears
must come. For now, she might be in danger. She looked at the plaque.

It was too far away to tell what symbols if any were on its surface, but there was something about it that chilled her to the bone.

The square plaque had hooks embedded in the rope. They looked as if they had formed when the lasso had landed to help her pull it out.

She pulled the plaque close to the ward but kept it on the far side. There was no telling what pulling something that might be magical through the barrier would do. The script was Gamitic, but Ariel found she remembered it surprisingly well.

"If this is the fourth day, take your time. If it's the seventh, pull this through the ward now," the script said.

The runes went on, but Ariel stopped and scowled. It wasn't at all the sort of thing someone would usually write on a plaque. She wondered to whom the words could possibly have been addressed. Perhaps this plaque had been part of some ancient test? A rite of passage for mages? How had Sister Jessie interpreted it? Why had she thought it was so important?

She read on: "Days at the ward, Horse Face. You're a lousy throw, by the way."

Ariel dropped the rope from nerveless fingers. She'd been called Horse Face when she was a tyro. She tried to translate the words another way, but the Gamitic runes made it clear that it was a personal name, a specific insult, not generic.

Looking at the way the plaque had caught on the rope now, she was suddenly sure that it had *grabbed* the rope. As if it was sentient. The hooks weren't equally placed on opposite sides of the plaque. Instead, it was as if they had grown in response to the lasso's touch.

The plaque glowed and Sister Ariel stumbled backward in fright.

It was a mistake. Her foot caught in a loop of the rope and as she fell, she yanked the plaque through the ward.

She scrambled to her feet as quickly as her fat limbs would lift her. The plaque was no longer glowing. She picked it up.

"Prophecy," it said, the Gamitic runes dissolving into common as she touched the plaque. "Not sentience."

She swallowed, not sure she believed it. The script continued to appear before her, as if written by an invisible quill. "If this is the seventh day, look two stadia south."

Stadia? Perhaps units of measure didn't translate. How far was two stadia? Three hundred paces? Four hundred?

Fear paralyzed Sister Ariel. She'd never been the type for adventures. She was a scholar, and a damned good one. She was one of the more powerful sisters, but she didn't like charging into things she didn't understand. She turned the plaque over.

"Wards in trees," Jessie al'Gwaydin had written in a panicked hand. "Don't trust him."

Oh, perfect.

Sister Ariel was rooted to the ground. The words Sister Jessie had written could only have been written with magic. Surely Sister Jessie wouldn't have used magic inside the wood. It would have been suicide.

She *is* dead.

It could all be a trap. The plaque might have triggered something as it was pulled through the ward. There might be a trap in the trees to the south where the plaque was trying to get her to go. Maybe she should go write down everything, ignore the trap, play by her own rules.

But Sister Ariel didn't go back to Torras Bend to write in her journal. She'd studied the ward to the south. If there had been a trap, she'd already triggered it.

There was a time and a place for haste. Apparently, that was now and here.

37

So you're kind of a pain in the ass. Why'd Kylar take you in?" Vi asked.

They'd been on the trail for a week, and if Uly wasn't the best company, at least she was more interesting than the horses and the trees and the little villages they had to avoid. Vi wasn't making conversation, she was gathering much information. Kylar was coming to kill her.

"He did it because he loves me," Uly said, as defiant as usual. "Someday he's going to marry me."

She'd said such things before, and it had immediately aroused Vi's suspicions, but after asking a few questions that left Uly puzzled, Vi had realized her suspicions were wrong. Kylar wasn't a pedophile.

"Yes, yes, I know. But he couldn't have loved you before he knew you, could he? You said that when he took you out of the castle was the first time you saw him."

"I thought he was my real father at first," Uly said.

"Hmm," Vi said, as if she weren't very interested. "Who are your real parents?"

"My father's name was Durzo but he's dead now. Kylar won't talk about him. I think my mother is Momma K. She always looked at me funny when we stayed with her."

Vi had to grab the back of her saddle to steady herself. Nysos, that was it! She knew Uly looked familiar. Uly was Durzo and Momma K's daughter! No wonder they'd concealed her. It also explained why Kylar had taken her in.

Inexplicably, the thought made her ache. She couldn't imagine taking in one of Hu's bastards. For that matter, she couldn't imagine Hu caring about one of them. Suddenly Uly was twice as valuable to the Godking. Holding Uly would mean controlling Momma K.

Maybe it would be enough to free Vi from his clutches. But Vi knew better. The Godking rewarded his servants well. Any vice she had, she would be allowed to indulge to satiety. He'd give her gold, clothes, slaves, whatever she wanted. But he'd never give her freedom. She'd proven herself too valuable for that.

The more Vi learned about Kylar, the more she despaired. She needed Uly to talk, because she needed to know everything about her enemy she could. Everything she learned was from a twelve-year-old girl who had a crush on the man, but Vi was good at sifting truth from opinion. Still, Kylar was sounding more and more—fuck!

She wasn't going to think about that again. It just left her feeling worse. Damn this trail. Damn this long trip. One more week and she could wash her hands of this. Maybe she wouldn't even stick around for her payday, much as she deserved it. She'd drop off the girl with a note about what she'd done, and she'd disappear. She'd killed Jarl. She'd deliver Kylar and Momma K to the Godking. Surely he wouldn't waste his resources sending someone after her then. Even if he did, he wouldn't come after her with the fury he would have if she betrayed him. She could disappear. There were only a few people she feared, and all of them were too valuable to be sent after her.

One of them was Kylar, but he wouldn't survive long. Maybe he'd killed Roth Ursuul, thirty elite highlanders, and some wytches—Uly seemed to know a lot about that—but he'd never survive the Godking.

Vi would head to Seth or Ladesh or deep into the mountains of Ceura where her red hair wouldn't be so unusual. She'd never spread her legs for another man, and she'd never take another contract. She didn't know what a normal life looked like, but she'd give herself time to figure it out. After this.

She pulled the scrap of note she'd taken from Kylar's house and read it again. "Elene, I'm sorry. I tried. I swear I tried. Some things are worth more than my happiness. Some things only I can do. Sell these to Master Bourary and move the family to a better part of town. I will always love you."

"Hey, Ugly." Vi said, "what did Elene and Kylar fight about?"

"I think it was about how the bed wasn't creaking."

Vi furrowed her brow. What? Then she burst out laughing. "Well, that's normal enough. Was that all?"

"Why, what's it mean?" Uly asked.

"Fucking. Men and women fight about it all the time."

"What's fucking?" Uly asked.

So Vi told her as explicitly as possible, and Uly looked more and more horrified.

"Does it hurt?" Uly asked.

"Sometimes."

"It sounds gross!"

"It is. It's messy and sticky and sweaty and smelly and gross. Sometimes it even makes you bleed."

"Why do girls let them do that?" Uly asked.

"Because men make them. That's why they fight about it."

"Kylar wouldn't do that," Uly said. "He wouldn't hurt Elene."

"Then why'd they fight about it?"

Uly looked sick. "He wouldn't do that," she said. "He wouldn't. I don't think they ever did it anyway 'cause the bed never creaked and Aunt Mea said it would. But Aunt Mea said it was fun."

The bed never creaked? "Whatever. Is that all they fought about?" Vi asked.

"She wanted him to sell his sword, the sword Durzo gave him. He didn't want to, but she said it proved he still wanted to be a wetboy.

But he didn't. He really wanted to be with us. It made him really mad when she said that."

So he wanted out, too. That's what he meant in the note when he said he tried. He tried to leave.

Nysos! Kylar might not even know she'd taken Uly. She didn't know if that was a good thing or not. It did explain why he'd gone charging past them in the fog that morning, though. He would have been sure she'd return to Cenaria as quickly as possible.

Several hundred paces ahead, Vi saw the forest change. No, not change. It transformed as abruptly as if the earth had been split with an axe. On the near side, the forest was like what they'd been riding in for days. On the far side, enormous sequoys grew. They must be near Torras Bend. It didn't mean much to her, but it looked like the riding would be easier under those great trees. There was almost no undergrowth in a forest that old.

They were only fifty paces from the sequoys when an old woman stepped out from the trees in front and to one side of them. She looked as startled as Vi felt. She was holding a glowing sheet of gold in her hands.

Glowing gold could only mean magic. The woman was a mage.

"Stop!" the old woman yelled.

Vi snapped her body back in the saddle and yanked the reins of Uly's horse out of her hands. As she sat back up, she jabbed her heels in and looked toward the mage. The woman was running heavily, awkwardly—and not toward Vi and Uly. She was running away from the old forest and she had flung aside the glowing gold sheet.

What the hell? It was strange, but not so strange that Vi stopped. In all the world, the only people she had to fear were wetboys, wytches, and mages.

The horses charged for the forest, almost throwing Uly out of the saddle.

The mage was only thirty paces away now, almost even with them. She ran a few more steps, and Vi could have sworn that the woman was emerging from something like a vast, nearly invisible bubble covering the forest.

The woman brought up her hands and spoke. Something crackled and whipped forward. Vi dropped her body as far on the opposite side of her horse as she could. There was a concussion nearby and Uly flew off the horse.

Vi didn't stop to look. She grabbed a throwing knife from an ankle sheath and threw it as she brought herself back up into the saddle. It was a long throw—twenty paces at a target she couldn't see before she released the knife—but it was really only meant as a distraction. Vi looked back.

Uly was lying on the ground, unconscious.

There was no hesitation. A wetboy doesn't hesitate. A wetboy acts, even if it's the wrong action. Vi couldn't stay still, it made her a target. She dug her heels into her horse's flanks again. The horse lunged forward—

And promptly crashed into the ground, its front legs cut out from under it.

Vi pulled her feet from the stirrups. She would land in a ball, roll free of the horse, draw throwing knives—except the horse fell faster than she expected. She slapped into the ground hard, her body flipping over as she skidded on her back. Her head kissed an iron-hard root and black spots swam before her eyes.

Up, damn you! Get up! She got on her hands and knees and tried to stand, eyes watering, head ringing.

"I'm sorry, I can't let you do that," the old woman said. She looked like she actually meant it.

No. It can't end like this.

The beefy old woman raised a hand and spoke. Vi tried to throw herself to one side, but she didn't make it.

38

It was two small cuts. A line along the ribs, and a matching line across the inside of his arm. Neither was deep. The knife had cut skin but not muscle. Even together, they were nothing a clean bandage and some fresh air wouldn't have seen heal in a few days.

But in the Hole, nothing was clean. Fresh air was only a memory.

Logan recognized the signs, but there was nothing he could do. He was hot and cold already, shivering and sweating. The odds were, he wouldn't come out of the fever. After all the time he'd spent in the Hole, he was a shadow of his former self. Cheeks sunken, eyes bright, face skeletal, his tall frame now skin and bone.

If he survived, he could get worse yet, he knew. For all that he'd starved, Logan still didn't have the malnourished, emaciated look that those who had been in the Hole for years had. His body was clinging to its strength with a stubbornness that surprised him. But the fever cared nothing for that. It would take days, at the least, to fight off the fever. Days of total vulnerability.

"Natassa," he said. "Tell me again about the resistance."

The younger Graesin daughter had a hunted look in her eyes. She didn't respond. She was looking across the hole at Fin, who was gnawing on sinews to add to his rope.

"Natassa?"

She sat up. "They move around. There are a number of estates that welcome them in the east, especially—especially the Gyres'. Even the Lae'knaught have helped."

"Bastards."

"Bastards who are our enemy's enemy."

She said that like she'd said it before. Damn, she had said it before, hadn't she?

"And our numbers are growing?"

"Our numbers are growing. We've been conducting raids, small groups going and doing anything they can to hurt the Khalidorans, but my sister wouldn't let us try anything big yet. Count Drake has set up informants for us in every village in eastern Cenaria."

"Count Drake? Wait, I asked that before, didn't I?"

She didn't respond. Her eyes were still on Fin. Fin had killed four of the newcomers in the last three days. Three days? Or was it four now?

Count Drake was part of the resistance. That was great. Logan hadn't known if the man had made it out alive.

"I'm glad Kylar didn't kill him, too," Logan said.

"Who?" Natassa asked.

"Count Drake. He betrayed me. He's the reason I'm down here."

"Count Drake betrayed you?" Natassa asked.

"No, Kylar. Dressed all in black, called himself the Night Angel."

"Kylar Stern is the Night Angel?"

"He was working for Khalidor all along."

"No, he wasn't. The Night Angel's the only reason there's a resistance at all. I was there. We were all herded into the garden and he saved us. Terah offered him whatever he wanted to escort us out of the castle, but he only cared about you. He left us to try to save you, Logan."

"But he—he killed Prince Aleine. He was the one who started all of this."

"Lady Jadwin killed Aleine Gunder. She's been given a portion of his estates as her reward."

It didn't seem possible. After everything had been stripped away from him, Natassa was giving him back his best friend. He'd missed Kylar so much.

Logan laughed. Maybe it was the fever. Maybe he'd imagined that she said that because he wanted it so much. He was so sick that the entire world hurt. Everything was fuzzy, so fuzzy. He thought he was going to start blubbering like a little girl.

"And Serah Drake? Was she with you, too? She's part of the resistance? Kylar saved her?" Logan asked. He'd asked that before, hadn't he?

"She's dead."

"Did she . . . did she suffer?" He hadn't dared ask that before.

Natassa looked down.

Serah. His fiancée, not so long ago. She seemed part of another life. Another world. He had loved her once. Or thought he loved her. How could he have loved her when she'd barely crossed his mind in all the time he'd been down here?

She'd betrayed him. She'd slept with his friend, Prince Aleine Gunder, when she had never even slept with him—the man she said she loved. Had that been it? Had that betrayal extinguished his feelings for her? Or had he ever loved her at all?

He'd thought that he was finally understanding love on his wedding night.

Everyone who's infatuated thinks he understands love. But Logan couldn't help it. What he'd felt for Jenine Gunder—the fifteen-year-old girl he'd been so sure was too young and immature for him—had seemed like love. Maybe she'd been snatched away before he'd had time to see her flaws, but Jenine Gunder—Jenine Gyre, his wife, if only for a few tragic hours—was the woman who had haunted his thoughts. He'd dreamed of her in the moments before sleep yielded to the hard stone and cruel stink and howling and heat of the Hole—her full smile, her bright eyes, her golden curves in candlelight as he had seen her just once, so briefly, before the Khalidoran soldiers had broken into the room, before Roth had cut her throat.

"Oh, gods," Logan said, putting his face in his hands. Suddenly, the grief rose up in him. His face contorted and he couldn't stop the tears. He'd held her, her body so small and vulnerable against him, as she'd bled. Gods, how she bled! He told her everything would be all right. He'd spoken peace to her, and that was all the protection he could give her, because he could do nothing else.

Someone wrapped an arm around him. It was Lilly. Gods. Then Natassa hugged him, too. It made it worse. He was sobbing uncontrollably. Everything was fuzzy and getting fuzzier. He had held off grief for so long, but he couldn't do it anymore.

"I'll be with you soon," he'd told Jenine. It was true now. He was going to die here. He already was dying.

He looked at Natassa's face, and she was weeping with him. The poor girl; she'd been captured, betrayed by someone in the resistance and put down here with these monsters. Logan didn't know how much she wept for him and how much she wept for herself. He didn't blame her. She had to know that once he was gone, the Holers would take her.

Even Lilly was crying. He wouldn't have imagined she was capable of it. Why was she crying? Was she afraid that once the Holers had Natassa—who was younger and prettier—that she'd lose her power and her position? That she would be killed?

Looking at Lilly's face, Logan hated himself for the cynicism of that thought. He'd been down here too long. The look on her face wasn't fear. It was love. Lilly wasn't weeping for herself; she was weeping for him.

Who am I to deserve such devotion? I'm not worthy of this.

"Help me up," he said, his voice raw.

Lilly looked at Natassa, and her tears ceased. She nodded. "Up we go."

Everyone in the Hole was looking at Logan now. Some with curiosity, some with hunger. Fin looked positively jubilant.

"All right, you fucks!" Logan said. It was the first time he'd used profanity, and he could see that some of them noticed. Well, the crazier they thought he was, the better.

"Listen up. I've kept a little secret from you because I didn't know what fine upstanding felons you all are. I've kept a little secret that might make a big difference——"

"Yes, yes, we know," Fin said. "Our little King thinks he's Logan Gyre. He thinks he really is the king!"

"Fin," Logan said. "There's two good reasons for you to shut your shit hole. First, I'm dying. I've got nothing to lose. If you keep that tooth-filled anus of yours shut, I'll die and you won't have to do a damn thing. But if you keep talking, I'll come kill you. I might be weak, but I'm strong enough to drag your poxy asshole down the hole if I don't mind falling in myself. Believe me, if we start fighting, there's more than one person down here who'll make sure we both go in."

"And the second reason?" Fin practically hissed. He was uncoiling his rope, adjusting the noose on the end of it.

"If you don't shut up," Logan said, "It'll be your fault that I throw this down the hole." He reached inside his belt, and pulled out an iron key. "It's the key to the grate," Logan said.

Instant hunger filled every eye. "Give it here!" someone said. The Holers started pressing close, and Logan staggered toward the hole. He held the key out over the darkness and swayed back and forth, in not completely feigned dizziness.

The threat quieted the Holers.

"I'm feeling real sick, real dizzy," Logan said. "So if you all want this key to go to its little home up there, you'll listen real close."

"How could you have held onto it for all this time?" Nine-Finger Nick demanded. "We could have escaped months ago!"

"Shut up, Nick," someone said.

Logan looked around, trying to see where the greasy Khalidoran duke was, but the faces were a blur. "If we want to use the key, we have to work together. Do you all understand? If one person does the wrong thing, we all die. The worst thing is, we have to trust each other. It will take three of us to reach the lock." They started murmuring, some volunteering, others objecting.

"Shut up!" Logan said. "We do this my way, or I throw away the key! If we do this my way, we'll all get out. Understand? Even you, Fin. Once we get up into the Maw, I have a plan that will get at least half of us out. Maybe all of us. They've been doing construction at the other end of this level, and I think we can use that as long as we kill Gorkhy before he raises an alarm. But you all have to do exactly what I say."

"He's crazy," Nick said.

"It's our only chance," Tatts said. "I'm in." Everyone looked at Tatts in wonder. It was the first time anyone had heard the tattooed Lodricari speak.

"Good," Logan said. "We need three people to make a tower to reach the grate. Gnasher will be the base, I'll be second, and Lilly will unlock the grate. From there, we've got two options—and which one we choose is up to Fin."

Fin looked even more suspicious.

"First option, all of you who are light enough and strong enough to climb up the three of us can get out, but I won't let Fin climb out. So me and Gnasher and Fin will die."

"If anyone's going, I'm going," Fin said. "You're not—"

"Shut up, Fin!" someone said, suddenly brave at the prospect of freedom.

"Second option, Fin gives Lilly his rope. She can tie it to something up there and we all climb out. Fin, it's your rope, so it's your choice. Oh, and if I don't get out, I'm not telling you my plan to get out of the Maw."

Everyone looked at Fin. Logan was suddenly sweating again. *Come on, body, just a little longer.*

"You can use the rope," Fin said. "But you want to use my rope, I'm going to be part of the tower. I'll open the grate."

"Forget it," Logan said. "No one here trusts you. If you get out, you'll leave us here."

There was mumbled agreement to that, even from some of the Holers on Fin's side.

"Well I'm not climbing up that toothy freak. You want my rope, I'm part of the tower, and that's final."

"Fine," Logan said. He'd figured it would be this way all along. He'd just needed to offer the first position so Fin could feel that he'd won something. "I'll be the base. You be second. Lilly opens the grate." Logan handed her the key. "Lilly," he said loudly enough for everyone to hear. "If Fin tries anything, you throw the key down the hole, got it?"

"If anyone tries anything, I throw the key down the hole," she said. "I swear by all the gods of hell and pain and the Hole."

"We do this one at a time," Logan said. "I'll tell you who goes next." He drew the knife and handed it to Natassa. "Natassa, anyone comes close before their turn, you stick them with this, all right?" Again, he said it loudly so everyone would know.

"Natassa will be the first out. She'll tie the rope to something up there so we can all climb out. Fin and me will be the last, but everyone's going to get out. We've paid for our crimes."

Fin walked around the hole, uncoiling the sinew rope from around his body. He rolled it into big loops with an almost frightening ease. He claimed to have strangled thirty people before he was caught, not counting islanders and women. Underneath the ropes, he looked like anyone who'd been in the Hole for a long time. Scrawny, skin deep brown with dirt, reeking, his mouth bloody sometimes from the scurvy that every long-time Holer suffered.

He smacked his lips as he stepped close to Logan and sucked blood through his teeth. "We'll settle us later," he said. He took the coiled rope and settled it around his neck.

Logan wiped the sweat off his brow. He wanted to kill the man now. If he grabbed the rope and shoved, maybe.... Maybe. It wasn't worth the risk. He was too weak, too slow now. He should have tried this plan earlier, but earlier, Fin would never have come this close to him. Fin would have expected Logan to try to kill him any other time, and before Logan had regained the knife, trying it would have made him too vulnerable.

Bracing himself against the wall with his hands, Logan squatted. Fin edged close to him, sneering and swearing under his breath. He finally put a foot on Logan's thigh, stepped onto his back, and then up onto his shoulders, walking his own hands up the sheer wall.

Surprisingly, the weight wasn't that bad. Logan thought he could make it. He just had to lock his knees and lean on the wall, and he could make it. There was no way he'd be able to climb up the rope on his own strength, but maybe his friends would pull him out. If he went out last, he'd tie the rope around himself and Lilly and Gnash and Natassa could pull him out. If only he'd stop shivering.

"Hurry," he said.

"You're too damn tall," Lilly said. "Can you squat down?"

He shook his head.

"Shit," she said. "Fine. Ask Gnasher to help. You're the only one he listens to."

"Ask him what?" It should be obvious, he knew, but he wasn't thinking clearly.

"To lift me," Lilly said.

"Oh. Gnash. Pick her up. No, Gnash, not like that." It took some coaching, but finally, Gnash understood, and squatted beside Logan while Lilly climbed up onto his back and then stood on his shoulders. Then she put the key in her teeth and started trying to transfer over.

Logan was much taller than Gnasher, so Lilly had to step up onto Logan's shoulder, where Fin was already standing. The uneven weight made Logan sway.

"Stay still," Fin hissed. He cursed Logan repeatedly as Natassa put a hand on Logan's shoulder, trying to brace him.

Logan felt cold wash over him. "Go," he said. "Just hurry."

Lilly's weight pressed down again on his left shoulder, then weight shifted back and forth above him as she and Fin tried to balance.

Logan couldn't tell what they were doing. He squeezed his eyes shut and held onto the wall.

"You can do this," Natassa whispered. "You can do this."

The weight shifted suddenly, hard to the right, and the Holers gasped. Logan sagged and then fought, his right leg shaking with the exertion.

The burden suddenly lightened and there were little gasps around the Hole. Logan squinted up and saw that Lilly was on Fin's back, and she had grabbed the grate above her with one hand, stabilizing herself and taking some of her weight.

Then they heard the sound they dreaded. It was the sound of leather and chain mail clinking and protesting, curses floating freely, a sword tapping on the rocks. Gorkhy was coming.

39

The wytching hour had come. An icy wind scoured clouds through the mountains' teeth. It was cold, too cold for snow. The wind cut through cloaks and gloves, made swords stick in their scabbards, made the men shiver at their posts. The clouds looked like phantoms scurrying over the killing fields and rushing up and over the walls. Thick wide braziers of coal that were burning all along the walls did nothing to stave off the chill. The heat was carried off and swallowed into the night. Beards froze and muscles stiffened. Officers barked at the men to keep moving, shouting over the familiar scream of the wind.

Those high screams were usually the subject of endlessly retold jokes and comparisons to the men's last bedchamber conquests, sometimes done with imitations. Regnus Gyre had never disciplined the men for howling into those winds. It staved off fears, he said. Anywhere else, it would be a distraction, would make the men unable to hear invaders, but you couldn't hear a thing at Screaming Winds anyway.

No one howled tonight. Tonight those screams seemed ominous. And if the men's hearing was bad, their sight wasn't much better. The swirling, racing clouds were thick enough and obscured the moon and stars so fully that they'd be lucky to see fifty paces out. The archers would only be useful to about that distance anyway, with this wind. It had been Regnus's nemesis. No matter how much the archers trained, shooting into that damn inconstant wind, their accuracy never improved much. One or two had an uncanny sense of when the wind would gust and could hit a man-size target at sixty paces, but that wasn't nearly the advantage a garrison usually got from holding a wall.

Solon had taken a position on the opposite side of the first wall from Vass, hoping that if worst came to worst, he'd be able to help the men without Vass's interference.

He couldn't hate the boy. Armies were full of men like Lehros Vass, and he was a good enough man. Better than most. He was just a soldier who needed a commanding officer, and the times had conspired to make him one instead. It was a cruel trick of fate that would probably make Vass be remembered as a bold idiot who'd gotten his men slaughtered, rather than as a heroic soldier.

The waiting was the worst. Like every soldier, Solon hated the waiting. It was good to be an officer when it came time to wait. You could fill your time encouraging the men to stand strong. It kept you from having the time to worry yourself.

Solon thought he saw something through the swirling clouds and darkness. He stiffened, but it was nothing. "It's time. Remember, don't look directly at her," he told the men near him. He pulled out the beeswax plugs he'd been rolling in his fingers to warm, and jammed one in his ear, then paused.

He thought he saw something again, but it wasn't the outline of a man or a horse, but an enormous square—no, it was nothing. Around him, other men were leaning forward, squinting into the darkness.

Then his skin began prickling. Like most male mages, Solon had little talent as a Seer. The only magic he could usually see was his own. But he could feel magic, especially when it was close, and always when it was used against him. Now he felt as if he had walked outside on a humid day. The magic wasn't intense, but it was everywhere. It was so diffuse that if Dorian hadn't put him so much on edge, he would never have noticed it. "Do any of you know how to tie knots well?"

The soldiers exchanged puzzled looks. Finally, one of them said, "I practically grew up on a fishin' boat, sir. I reckon I know 'bout every knot there is."

Solon grabbed the coil of rope tied to a bucket that the soldiers used to refill the water cisterns at the top of the wall. He cut the bucket free. "Tie me up," he said.

"Sir?" The soldier looked at him like he was crazy.

Is that how I looked at Dorian? Sorry, friend.

The magic was thickening.

"Tie me to the wall. Tie me so I can't move. Take my weapons."

"I, sir, I—"

"I'm a mage, dammit, I'm more susceptible to what she's—dammit! She's coming!" Soldiers were turning, staring at him. "Don't look at her. Don't believe what you see. Damn it, man, now! The rest of you, shoot!"

That was an order more of them were comfortable with. Even if Lehros Vass was angry at them in the morning, the most they'd have to do is go fetch their arrows in the killing ground before the walls.

The former sailor looped the rope around Solon expertly. In moments, Solon's hands were tied behind his back, secured to his feet, and only after that was his cloak bound around him so he wouldn't freeze. Then the man bound him to the winch they used to raise the bucket.

"Now a blindfold and my other earplug," Solon said. The man had bound him facing over the wall. Solon should have told him to make sure he couldn't face her. "Hurry, man."

But the soldier didn't respond. He was looking over the wall into the darkness, as was everyone else.

"Elana?" the soldier said. "Elly, is that you?" His face flushed and his eyes dilated. He threw his cloak off. Then he jumped off the wall.

He was halfway to the ground before he flailed wildly, suddenly aware, trying to find something to save himself. The rocks broke his body cruelly and the wind swallowed the sound of his death scream.

There was a sudden flurry of arrows as men began obeying Solon's earlier command to start shooting as soon as anything strange happened. The fog billowed and he saw the vast wagon being drawn forward, surrounded by Khalidoran soldiers, pulled by six aurochs. Solon's heart leapt as he saw a dozen Khalidorans cut down by the first wave. The aurochs took several arrows and didn't even falter.

But the rain of arrows was slowing.

Across the wall, Solon saw men flinging themselves off the wall. Others were shaking their heads, each lost in a private vision, bows held in limp hands.

Don't look, Solon. Don't look.

I won't believe it. Just a quick—

The magic roared past him as he were flying at tremendous speed. And then calm.

He blinked. He was standing in the Hall of Winds. The magnificent jade throne shone green like the waters of Hokkai Bay. Upon the throne sat a woman he barely recognized. Kaede Wariyamo had been sixteen when he'd left the Islands. Though he'd known from the times he'd played with her when they were both young that she would be beautiful, her transformation had made him awkward. She'd reproached him for avoiding her. But he'd had no choice. He knew he had to leave forever, but he'd never been prepared for what the sight of her would do to him.

Twelve years later, she had grown in grace and confidence. If he hadn't known her so well, he never would have seen the slight apprehension in her eyes—will he still think I'm beautiful?

He did. Her olive skin still glowed, her black hair poured around her shoulders like a waterfall, her eyes still gleamed with intelligence and wisdom and mischief. Perhaps there used to be less wisdom there and more mischief, but those lips looked like they still held three lifetimes of smiles. And if she had the faintest smile lines around her eyes and lips—what a tribute to a life well lived. To him, they were a mark of distinction.

His eyes swept over her body, clad in a light blue silk nagika, cut to emphasize the perfection of each curve, bound at the waist by a narrow belt of gold, the silk looped up over one shoulder. Her stomach was still flat, athletic. There were no stretch marks. Kaede had never borne children. His eyes lingered on her exposed breast.

Perfect. She was perfect.

He was interrupted by her laugh. "Have you been on Midcyru so long you've forgotten what breasts look like, my prince?"

Solon blushed. After so many years of seeing women treat ordinary parts like they were erotic, and erotic parts like they were ordinary, he was thoroughly confused. "I apologize, Your Majesty." Remembering himself, he tried to kneel, but something was interfering with his motion.

It didn't matter. All that mattered was before him. He couldn't take his eyes off her.

"You've been a hard man to find, Solonariwan," Kaede said.

"It's just, just Solon now."

"The empire needs you, Solonariwan. I won't make any demands of you besides the—besides producing an heir, and if you require rooms for a mistress, it will be arranged. The empire needs you, Solon. Not just for your family. For you. I need you." She looked terrifically fragile, as if the wind would break her. "I want you, Solon. I want you as I wanted you twelve years ago and as I wanted you before that, but now I want your strength, your fortitude, your companionship, your…"

"My love," Solon said. "You have it, Kaede. I love you. I always have."

She lit up, exactly like she had when she was little and he'd given her a special present. "I've missed you," she said.

"I've missed you," he said, a lump rising in his throat. "I'm afraid I was never able to explain why I had to leave—"

She stepped close to him and put a finger on his lips. Her touch sent shockwaves through him. His heart thundered against his ribs. Her very scent suffused him. His eyes couldn't find a place to rest as he looked at her. Every beautiful line and curve and color and tone led to another and another.

Smiling, she put a hand on his cheek.

Oh gods. I'm lost. *She had that same uncertain, wavering look that she'd had that last day, when she kissed him and he'd nearly torn her clothes off. She kissed him and her lips were all the world. She started tentatively, just touching that exquisite softness against his lips, and then drawing him out. She was suddenly aggressive, just as she had been that day, as though her passion had only been building for all the time he was gone. Her body pressed up against him and he moaned.*

She broke away from him, breathing hard, her eyes fiery. "Come to my chambers," *she said.* "This time, I swear my mother won't break in on us."

She climbed up a tall step and looked at him over her shoulder as she took a few steps away, her hips swaying. She grinned devilishly and brushed the nagika strap off her shoulder. He tried to step up after her, but he slipped back to his place on the floor.

Kaede slipped the gold belt off her waist and dropped it carelessly. Solon strained to climb up that damned step. Something was cutting off his breath.

"I'm coming," *he said, wheezing.*

She shimmied and the nagika dropped to the floor in a silk puddle. Her body was all bronze curves and shining waterfalls of black hair.

He coughed. He couldn't breathe. He'd thrown this away once, and he wasn't going to give it up now. He coughed again and again and dropped to his knees.

Kaede was just down the hall, smiling, the light playing over her lean body, her long long legs, her slim ankles. He climbed back to his feet and strained against the ropes again.

Why is she smiling? *Kaede wouldn't smile when he was choking to death.*

Kaede wouldn't be like this at all. *Her mannerisms weren't similar to the girl he had known, they were exactly the same, fitted to an older face.*

A woman who'd been a queen for ten years wouldn't let down all the barriers that fast. She was everything he'd hoped or imagined— the real Kaede would be furious with him.

The vision disappeared all at once, and Solon was back on the wall. He was staring over the edge, only the ropes keeping him from falling to his death.

Around him, men were dying horribly. One's stomach had swollen to three times its normal size and he was still reaching into the air, as if shoving food down his throat. Another was purple, screaming at someone who wasn't there, but he was no longer screaming words. His voice was a wreck and every once in a while, he coughed and blood flew out of his mouth, but he never stopped screaming. Another was shrieking, "Mine! It's mine!" and beating the stone wall with his hands as if they were attacking him. His hands were bloody stumps, ruined, but he never stopped. Others were lying down, dead, with no indication of what had killed them.

Many had killed themselves by one means or another, but some had been scorched with magic or exploded. The wall ran red with their already freezing blood. The gate had been blown apart while he'd been in his trance and dark figures were marching toward them now, driving the team of aurochs pulling the enormous wagon.

It was Khali. Solon had no doubt of that.

"Has Dorian gone mad yet?" a woman's voice asked. "That was my little gift, you know."

Solon looked, but couldn't see the source of the voice. He wasn't sure it wasn't coming from inside his own head. "He's completely cured, actually."

She laughed; it was a deep, throaty sound. "So he is alive."

Solon wanted to crumple. They'd thought Dorian was dead. Or at least they didn't know. "Let's get this over with," Solon said.

She chuckled. "You've been told many lies in your life, Solonariwan. They lied to you when you were growing up. They lied to you at Sho'cendi. They stole from you. I'm not going to offer you power, because the truth is, I can't give you power. The vir doesn't come from me. That's just another lie. I wish it did. The truth is, the vir is natural, and it's vastly more powerful than your pitiable Talent. The truth is, Dorian's Talent was weak before he used the vir, and you know how powerful his Talent is now."

"It's enslaving. Meisters are like drunks looking for their next glass of wine."

"Some of them, yes. The fact is, some people can't handle drink. But most people can. Maybe you'd be one of the people who can't, like Dorian, but I wouldn't bet on that. The truth is, Dorian always liked his special place in the sun, didn't he? He liked having you look up to him. Having everyone look up to him. And what would he be without his power, without his extra gifts? He'd be so much less than you, Solon. Without the vir, he'd have no gifts, and his Talent would be minuscule compared to yours. So where would that put you if you used the vir? Even if you just used it once, just to unlock the hidden Talents you don't even know you have? What could you do with that kind of power? Could you go back to Seth and make things right? Take your place with Kaede on the throne? Take your place in history?" She shrugged. "I don't know. I don't really care. But you're pathetic, you magi. You can't even use magic in the dark. Really."

"Lies. It's all lies."

"Is it? Well, then, you hold on to your weakness, your humility. But if you ever change your mind, Solonariwan, this is all you have to do. The power is there, and it's waiting for you." And then she showed him. It was simple. Instead of reaching toward a source of light, the sun or a fire, or instead of reaching into his glore vyrden, he just had to reach toward Khali. A little twist and it was there. An ocean of power, being constantly fed from tens of thousands of sources. Solon couldn't understand it all, but he could see the outlines. Every Khalidoran prayed morning and night. The prayer wasn't empty words: it was a spell. It emptied a portion of everyone's glore vyrden into this ocean. Then Khali gave it back to those she willed, when and as much as she wanted. At heart, it was simple: a magical tax.

Because so many people were born with a glore vyrden but lacked the capability or the teaching to express it, Khali's favorites would always have ample power—and the people would never even know they were being robbed of their very vitality. That didn't explain the vir, but it did explain why the Khalidorans had always used pain and torture in their worship. Khali didn't need the suffering, she needed her worshippers to feel intense emotions. Intense emotions were what allowed marginally Talented people to use their glore vyrden. Torture was simply the most reliable way to spark emotions of the right intensity. Whether the torturer and tortured and spectators felt disgust, loathing, fear, hatred, lust, or delight made no difference. Khali could use them all.

"My Soulsworn will find you now, and you'll die," Khali said. "You emptied your glore vyrden already, didn't you?"

"Begone," he said.

She laughed. "Oh, you're a good one. I think I'll keep you." Then her voice was gone, and Solon crumpled to the stones. Khali was in Cenaria. The Ursuuls would make ferali and the rebels would be massacred. All his service here had been for nothing. All he had just learned was for nothing. He should have gone home to Seth twelve years ago. He'd failed.

He opened his eyes and saw one of the Soulsworn, draped in heavy sable cloaks, their faces obscured behind blank black masks, picking through the dead along the wall. Now and then one would stop, draw a sword and dispatch someone. They wiped their swords afterward, so the blood wouldn't freeze their blades to the inside of their scabbards.

They were coming toward him. There was nothing he could do. He was bound and the horizon was barely gray. No weapons. No magic. The vir was his only way out. Even if it was suicide, at least he could take a lot of them with him.

Maybe he could outsmart her. If he could just survive—and how stupid to be killed by some thug in a costume—he could fight Khali. She wasn't invincible. She wasn't a goddess. He'd talked to her. He'd understood her. He could fight her. He just needed the power to do it.

Solon's heart thudded in his chest. It was exactly what Dorian had said he himself would be tempted to do. Solon had thought the temptations had stopped, but this was the last one. The hardest one. Dorian was right. He'd been right about everything.

O God…Sir, if you are there…I despise myself for praying now when I've got nothing to lose, but shit, if you just help me to live through—

Solon's prayer was interrupted as a heavy corpse fell on him. Solon opened his mouth and took a deep breath. He was just exhaling when warm blood from the corpse poured into his mouth. It was metallic and already thickening.

He almost threw up as the blood spilled over his chin, down his neck, through his beard, but he froze as he heard a foot scuff on stone nearby.

The Soulsworn pulled the body off him, but didn't walk away.

"Look at this one, Kaav," he said with a thick Khalidoran accent.

"Another screamer. Love it when they do that," a second voice said. "Must have pissed off the men, huh? Must have been one of the first to go if they tied him up like that."

The first Soulsworn stepped close and bent over Solon. Solon could hear the man's breath hissing through the mask over his face. The man stood and kicked Solon in the kidney.

Pain lanced through him, but he didn't make a sound. The man kicked him again and again. The third time, Solon's body betrayed him, and he tensed his muscles. It was just too hard to lie limp.

"He's still alive," the man said. "Kill him."

Solon's heart leapt into his throat. It was over. He had to grab the vir and die.

Wait. The thought was so calm, so simple and clear that it seemed to come from outside of him.

Solon held still.

The second I hear steel, I'll...He didn't know. He'd take the vir? Then Khali would have him.

The other man grunted. "Shit, my blade's froze. Coulda swore I got it cleaned off."

"Ah, forget it. Between the cold and the bleeding he'll be dead in five minutes. If he coulda gotten out of the ropes he would have when She came through."

And they walked away.

40

When Vi woke, bound tightly at wrists, ankles, elbows, and knees, the first thing she saw was a middle-aged woman with thin, graying brown hair, a thick slab of body, the stance of a woman who had never worn anything but practical shoes, a round, lined face, and piercing eyes. The maja was staring at her. A fire was burning behind Vi, and a small bundle near her that was probably Uly, bound and trussed like she was.

"Fock eww," Vi said. She was gagged. Not just some little gag of a handkerchief tied around her mouth, a serious gag. It felt like a rock had been wrapped in a handkerchief and stuffed in her mouth, then thin leather ties wrapped every which way around her face, guaranteeing she couldn't speak.

"Before we start, Vi," the woman said. "I want to tell you something very important. If you do escape from me—which you won't—do not run into the forest. Have you ever heard of the Dark Hunter?"

Vi scowled as well as she could with her mouth stuck partially open, then decided she had nothing to lose by letting the old woman talk. She shook her head.

"That would explain why you were rushing headlong into death, I suppose," the woman said. "I'm Sister Ariel Wyant Sa'fastae. The Dark Hunter was created some six hundred and maybe fifty years ago by a magus named Ezra, perhaps the most Talented magus who ever lived. Ezra was on the losing side of the War of Darkness. He was one of Jorsin Alkestes' most trusted generals, the kind of man who seemed to be able to do everything, and everything he did he did superlatively. I'm sorry, superlatively means he did everything excellently."

"I oh wha ih eenz, idj," Vi said, though it was a lie.

"What? Never mind. Ezra created a creature that sensed magic and certain kinds of creatures that are now extinct—krul, ferozi, ferali, blaemir, and what have you—for which you may thank whatever gods your superstitions support. He created his perfect hunter too well, and he couldn't control it. It began killing anyone with the Talent, escaping while Ezra slept. Finally, they battled—of course no one knows what happened because no one was there. But the Talented children of Torras Bend stopped dying and no one ever saw the Dark Hunter again, nor Ezra. However, whatever Ezra did, it didn't kill the Dark Hunter. He only walled it in. Here. About ten paces north of where I regrettably had to kill your horse is the first ward. That ward marks you for death.

"Every magus or maja or meister to attempt Ezra's Wood in six hundred years has died. Powerful mages carrying potent artifacts died, those artifacts in turn lured other mages, and so forth. Whatever happens in the wood—even if the Dark Hunter is a myth—whatever happens there, no one comes back." Sister Ariel paused and then her voice became bright and cheery, "So, if you escape, don't go north." Ariel scowled. "You'll pardon me if I'm not doing this right. I've never kidnapped anyone before—unlike you."

Shit.

"Oh yes, Ulyssandra was rather eager to tell me all about you, wetboy."

Double shit.

"But about that. You're not a wetboy, Vi. You're not even a wetgirl. Oh, there have been such things, but what you are is a *maja uxtra kurrukulas,* a bush mage, a wild mage—"

"Ock ew! Ock ew!" Vi thrashed against her bonds. It was no use.

"Oh, you don't believe me? A wetboy, Vi, even of the female variety, can use her Talent without speaking. So if you are a wetboy, why don't you escape?"

There was nothing, nothing in all the world that Vi couldn't stand as much as feeling helpless. She'd rather have Hu paw her hair. She'd rather have the Godking mount her. She bucked on the ground, tearing her skin against the ropes. She tried to scream. It made part of the handkerchief go down her throat. She gagged and coughed and for a moment, she thought she was going to die. Then she regained her breath and lay limp.

Ariel scowled. "I really don't like this. I hope you'll realize that someday. I'm going to take off your gag, understand? You can't get away from me, even with your Talent, and you'll have to learn that sooner or later, so we might as well make it clear now to spare you as much pain as possible. But before you fight me, I do expect your first words to be curses or lies or an attempt to use magic, so before you do that, I'd like to ask you a question."

Vi's eyes burned holes in the woman. The bitch. Just let her take out that gag.

"Who is the extremely talented Vürdmeister that put this spell on you?"

Thoughts of escape evaporated. It was a bluff. It had to be a bluff. But how?

Nysos. What did the bastard do to me? It was just what the Godking would do, put some fucking spell on her. Hadn't she imagined something of the sort when she was in the throne room? What if it hadn't been her imagination?

"Because that spell is really something," Sister Ariel said. "I've been studying it for the past six hours while you've been unconscious, and I still can't tell what it does. One thing I do know is that it's trapped. And he's—it definitely bears the marks of being a man's magic—he's anchored it in some interesting ways. I'm considered strong among my sisters. One of the stronger magae to attain the colors in the last fifty years. And it's too strong for me to break, that's clear immediately. You see, there are weaves you can unravel and there are weaves you have to burst—Fordaean knots if you will—are you familiar with Fordaean knots? Never mind. This spell has both. The traps might be unraveled. But the core weave will have to be broken most carefully. Even if I could do it myself, it would probably leave you with some permanent mental damage."

"Nnn ga."

"What? Oh." Sister Ariel stayed seated cross-legged and murmured. The bonds fell from Vi's face. She spat out the handkerchief—it *had* been wrapped around a rock, the bitch!—and breathed. She didn't grab her Talent. Not yet.

"The rest?" she asked, gesturing to her other bonds.

"Mm. Sorry."

"It's a little hard to talk to you lying on my side."

"Fair enough. *Loovaeos.*"

Vi's body was pulled upright and scooted backward to a tree.

"So that's your bait? A bluff about some spell on me that we won't be able to take off until we get to the Chantry—where it just so happens it will be impossible for me to escape?"

"That's it."

Vi pursed her lips. Was it her imagination, or was there a slight glow around Ariel? "That's pretty good bait," she admitted.

"Better than we offer most girls."

"You always kidnap girls?"

"Like I already said, this is my first time. It doesn't usually come down to kidnapping. The sisters who do the recruiting have lots of ways to be persuasive. I was deemed too tactless for such work."

Big surprise. "What's the usual bait?" Vi asked.

"Just to be like the recruiters, who tend to be beautiful, charming, respected, and—not least—always get their own way."

"And the hook is?" Vi asked.

"Oh, we're continuing the fishing metaphor?"

"What?" Vi asked.

"Never mind. The hook is servitude and tutelage. It's like an apprenticeship, seven to ten years of service before you become a full Sister. Then you're free."

Vi had had enough of apprenticeship to last her for ten lives. She sneered. *Keep her talking. I might as well learn what I can.* "You said I'm not really a wetboy. I do all the wetboy stuff."

"Have trouble with the Embrace of Darkness, don't you?"

"What?"

"Invisibility. You can't do it, can you?"

How did she know that? "That's just a legend. It drives up prices. No one goes invisible."

"I can see you're going to spend a lot of time unlearning things you think you know. True wetboys can go invisible. But mages don't do invisibility. Your Talent has to practically live in your skin. Invisibility requires a total body awareness so profound that it extends to feeling how light is touching every part of your skin. What you are is something different—in fact, something forbidden by a treaty a hundred and thirty—umm—thirty-eight years old. The Alitaerans would be shall we say highly overwrought if we'd trained you this way. You see, if you mastered a few more things, you'd be a warmage. Oh, you're going to cause the Speaker a few headaches, I can see that already."

"Fuck you," Vi said.

Sister Ariel leaned over and slapped her. "You will speak civilly."

"Fuck you," Vi said without intonation.

"Let's settle something now, then," Sister Ariel said, standing. *"Loovaeos uh braeos loovaeos graakos."* Vi was yanked to her feet. Her bonds dropped away. A dagger flew from her pack and dropped at her feet.

Vi didn't reach for the knife. She didn't stop to take the time. She cursed her Talent into a titanic punch into Sister Ariel's stomach.

The force of the blow blasted Sister Ariel off her feet. She flipped over the fire and skidded across the dirt on the other side, but Vi didn't move. She didn't even try to run. She was looking at her drooping hand.

It was like she'd punched steel. Bones were sticking out of her skin. Her knuckles were a mass of blood. Her wrist was broken. Both bones in her forearm had snapped. One of them was pressing against the skin from underneath, threatening to jut out.

Sister Ariel stood and shook her big, loose dress. Dust puffed out. She snorted as she looked at Vi, who was cradling her arm.

"You should really strengthen your bones before you strike with your Talent."

"I did," Vi said. She was going into shock. She sat—or maybe fell.

"Then you shouldn't punch an armored maja." Ariel tsked as she looked at Vi's destroyed hand. "It seems you've more Talent than sense. Not to worry, that's common enough. We know how to deal with it. The truth is, Vi, that your body magic is untrained, undefined, and no match for any schooled sister. You could be so much more. Do you even know how to heal yourself?"

Vi was shaking. She looked up dumbly.

"Well, if you ever want to use your hand again, I can heal it. But it hurts and I'm slow."

Vi offered up her arm, mute.

"Just a second, I need to ward Uly's ears. Otherwise your screams will wake her."

"I won't—I won't scream," Vi swore.

As it turned out, she lied.

Logan froze. Another time, he might have tried to get everyone down to build their tower again once Gorkhy was gone, but he knew he'd never summon the strength to try it again.

"What's going on down here?" Gorkhy demanded.

What? We've been silent. How did he hear anything?

Pressing in to the wall as much as he could, Logan looked up and saw that Fin was doing the same thing, and, sitting on his shoulders, Lilly was too.

Torchlight slanted through the grate as Gorkhy came the last few feet. From where he was standing now, Lilly was only a few feet from his shoes. With the sheer edges of the Hole below the grate, though, the torchlight wouldn't fall on Lilly unless he stepped closer.

They heard Gorkhy sniffing, and the torchlight shifted as he leaned forward. He cursed them. "Animals. You stink worse than usual." Gods, he was smelling Lilly. "Why don't you wash yourselves?"

This could go on for a while. If it was a bad day, he'd empty his bladder onto them. Logan shook with rage and weakness. There was no reason for a Gorkhy. There was no understanding it. Gorkhy gained nothing by tormenting them, but he did, and he loved it.

Go away. Just go away.

"What's going on down there?" Gorkhy said. "I heard some noise. Whatcha doin'?"

The torch shifted again and light dipped perilously close to Lilly. Gorkhy was walking around the grate, holding up the torch, staring as deeply into the Hole as he could. He was moving counterclockwise, away from them first.

The Holers were frozen. None of them were cursing or fighting or talking or anything. It was a dead giveaway. Only Natassa moved, away from Logan.

The light cut a path across the grate and lit up Lilly's entire head.

"GO TO HELL, GORKHY!" Natassa shouted.

The torch shifted away from Lilly suddenly. "Who's... ah, it's my little girl? Isn't it?"

"You see my face, Gorkhy?" Natassa asked. Clever girl. "This is the last thing you're ever going to see, because I'm going to kill you."

Gorkhy laughed. "You got a mouth on you, don't you? But then, you already showed me that before we sent you down there, didn't you?" He laughed again.

"Fuck you!"

"Did that too, ha ha. You were the hottest little thing I've had in years. You been letting the rest of them boys have a piece? I was your first, though. You never forget your first. You'll never forget me, will ya?" He laughed again.

Logan marveled at Natassa's courage. She was taunting the man who had raped her, just to give them a chance.

"How's Lilly takin' it? I'm sure all them boys would rather stick you than that old whore. How's it going, Lilly? Competition get fierce all the sudden? Where are you, Lilly?" He shifted again, searching the depths for Lilly.

"I threw that bitch down the hole," Natassa said.

Logan was shaking so hard he could barely stand.

"No shit? You are a little wildcat, aren't you? I bet you even tempt our virginal little King, don't you? You banged her yet, King? I know Lilly was a little scabby for you, but this is some fine meat, eh, King? Where are you?"

Across the Hole, Tatts said, "Fuck you," into his hands. Muffled, it sounded almost like Logan. At the quick thinking, Logan felt a rush of warm feeling for the Holers. Gods, they were all in this together, and they'd get out together, too.

Gorkhy laughed. "All right, well, it's been fun. You all let me know when you're hungry. I got extra steak tonight, and I'm so full I don't think I could force another bite down."

Logan had no strength left. He wanted to cry out, his body felt so weak. He couldn't even feel himself standing. He just knew that if he tried to move he'd collapse. His body was bathed in cold sweat. His vision was blurring.

Logan heard ragged breathing, breaths of relief, a moment later.

"He's gone," someone said. It was Natassa. She was standing next to Logan again, and her eyes were full of fierce tears. "Just hold on, Logan. We're close."

Something rattled loudly on the grate.

"What are you doing?" Fin hissed. "Lilly, what the hell—"

"I didn't even touch it! I swear!" she said.

"Get down!" Logan cried.

But it was too late. There was already the sound of running steps and a moment later Gorkhy was over the grate, Lilly and Fin and Logan fully lit by his torch. With savage speed, he smashed Lilly in the face with the butt of his spear. All of them collapsed.

Even as the bodies landed on him, crushing him to the sloping stone floor, Logan saw his treasure—the key he had saved for months—fly free of Lilly's hand. It rang as it bounced off the stone floor, gleaming in the cutting light of the torch—and fell into the hole.

Every one of his hopes, every dream, was tied to that key. As it disappeared into the hole, it dragged them along with it.

A second of fragile peace passed as every eye watched the key disappear. Then one by one, the Holers grasped the new reality—which was just like the old reality before they'd known the key existed. Fin was punching someone—it had to be Lilly because when he got to his knees, he was holding his rope. Then he punched Logan in the face.

Logan couldn't stop him. Fin was too strong; all of Logan's strength was exhausted. He fell limp.

There was an inhuman snarl and a solid form slammed into Fin, sending him flying, tumbling right to the edge of the hole.

It was Gnasher, and he crouched over Logan, baring his teeth.

On his hands and heels, Fin scrambled to get away from Gnasher. When Gnasher didn't follow, Fin stood slowly.

Logan tried to sit up, but his body refused to obey. He couldn't even move. The world swam before his eyes.

"I get the new bitch first," Fin said.

Gods be merciful.

"You'll be the first to die, you asshole!" Natassa screamed. She was trembling, holding the dagger like she had no idea what to do with it.

The Holers—the fucking animals!—surrounded her on three

sides. She retreated to the edge of the hole, slashing at the air with the dagger.

Above them, Gorkhy was laughing. "Sweet meat, boys, sweet meat!"

"No," Logan said. "No. Gnash, save her. Save her, please."

Gnasher didn't move. He was still snarling, making everyone stay away from Logan.

Natassa saw it. If she could only get to Logan's side of the Hole, everyone's fear of Gnasher would keep them back. But Fin saw it too. He unlimbered a coil of rope into a lasso.

"You can make this easy, or you can make it hard," Fin said, smacking bloody lips.

Natassa looked at him, her eyes fixed on the lasso in his hands as if she'd forgotten the dagger in her own. She looked across the hole and met Logan's eyes.

"I'm sorry, Logan," she said. Then she stepped into the hole.

The Holers cried out as she fell out of sight.

"Shut up and listen!" Gorkhy screamed. "Sometimes you can hear 'em hit bottom."

And the bastards, the animals, the monsters, they did shut up and listen, hoping to hear a body smash against the rocks below. They were too late. The Holers grumbled the customary curses about lost meat, and looked over to Lilly. Logan's tears were as hot as his fever.

"Now who the fuck's Logan?" Gorkhy shouted. "King, was she talkin' to you?"

Logan closed his eyes. What did it matter anymore?

41

*I*t's time, Fatty," Ferl Khalius said. "He's not crazy enough to follow us across this."

They were fourteen hundred feet up Mount Hezeron, the tallest mountain on the Ceuran border. So far, the hike had been arduous, but the worst exposures had been of a dozen feet. From here, there were two ways over the mountain: through the notch to one side, or straight across the face. Ferl had nearly started a brawl at the last village by asking which way a brave man in a hurry would go.

Some of the villagers maintained that the face was never a good option, but that it would be especially bad this time of year. Even a light dusting of snow or freezing rain would make the path suicide. Others had maintained that going over the face was the only way to make it through the mountains before the snows hit. Getting stuck in the steeps and the deeps that made the devil's pass through the notch would be certain death if it snowed.

And snow was coming.

Baron Kirof wasn't doing well. He was so scared of heights he'd been crying. "If—if he'd be crazy to follow us, what does that make us?"

"Eager to live. I grew up in mountains tougher than this." Ferl shrugged. "Follow or fall."

"Can't you leave me?" Baron Kirof was pathetic. Ferl had brought him along because he didn't know what would happen when he fled, and he'd wanted a bargaining chip. But maybe it had been a mistake. The fat man had slowed him down.

"They want you alive. If you stay here, that Vürdmeister will blast me off the rock. If you're with me, he might not."

"Might not?"

"Move, Fatty!"

Ferl Khalius looked at the dark clouds grimly. His tribe, the Iktana, was a mountain tribe. He was one of the best climbers he knew, but he'd never liked climbing. Battle he liked. Battle made you feel alive. But climbing was arbitrary, the mountain gods capricious. He'd seen the most devout clansman plunge to his death when he'd put his weight on a stone that had held Ferl—who was heavier—only a moment before. In battle, a stray arrow might kill you, of course, but you could move, you could fight. Death might still come, but it wouldn't find you scared, clinging to a bit of rock with slick fingers, praying against the next blast of wind.

This traverse wasn't the worst he'd seen. It climbed perhaps a hundred feet and its entire length was narrow, maybe three feet wide. Three feet was pretty damn wide. It was the sheer drop that made that three feet seem ever so much smaller. Knowing that if you slipped you had absolutely no chance of catching yourself, that stumbling meant certain death, that did things to a man.

It was doing things to Fatty Kirof.

The baron, unfortunately, had no idea why he was important. Ferl hadn't been able to find out anything either. But Fatty was important enough that the Godking had sent a Vürdmeister after them.

"You're going first, Fatty. I'll take all the gear, but that's all the mercy you get."

It wasn't mercy. It was practicality. Fatty would go slower with a pack, and if he fell, Ferl didn't want to lose his supplies.

"I can't do it," Baron Kirof said. "Please." Sweat was coursing down his round face. His little red whiskers quivered like a rabbit's.

Ferl drew his sword, the sword he'd given so much to protect, the sword that would make him a clan warlord. It was everything a warlord could want, a perfect sword, down to the highland runes on the steel that Ferl recognized but couldn't read.

He gestured with the sword, a little shrug that said, "Take your chances with the path, or take your chances with the sword."

The baron started onto the path. He was muttering too low for Ferl to hear him, but it sounded like he was praying.

Surprisingly, Fatty made good time. Ferl had to slap him once with the flat of his blade when he froze up and started scooting. They didn't have time to scoot. If they weren't far enough away from the Vürdmeister when he made it out of the trees, Ferl was dead. He'd chosen to go behind Fatty because it was the only way to keep the man moving, but it meant that he was exposed to whatever magic the Vürdmeister threw at them. If they weren't far enough away to make the Vürdmeister worry that he would kill the baron, it would be all over.

The view was breathtaking. They were past the middle of the exposure, and they could see forever. Ferl thought he could see Cenaria City, far to the northwest. It made it seem that they'd hardly covered any ground at all. But Ferl wasn't interested in the cloudless expanses to the north. He was interested in the slight prick he'd just felt on his skin. Snow.

He looked up. The leading edge of the black wall of clouds was directly above them.

Fatty stopped. "The path is getting narrower."

"The Vürdmeister's out of the woods. We've got no choice."

The baron swallowed and started shuffling forward, his face pressed to the rock, his arms spread-eagled.

Behind them, the Vürdmeister was standing with his fists on his hips, furious.

Ferl looked ahead. Another thirty paces, and just one more hard section where the ledge narrowed to a foot and a half across. Fatty was sucking down the thin air, frozen.

"You can do this," Ferl told him. "I know you can."

Miraculously, Fatty started moving, shuffling, but with confidence, as if he'd found some well of courage in himself that he'd never known he had. "I'm doing it!" he said.

And he did. He made it past the narrowest part of the ledge and Ferl followed hard on his heels, kicking gravel out into space and trying not to follow it.

The ledge began to widen and Fatty turned to walk rather than shuffle—even though the ledge was still less than three feet wide. He was laughing.

Then there was a blur of green past them and the ledge exploded in front of them.

As the smoke blew away in the icy winds, the clouds opened up and it started snowing. Big, fat flakes were driven in circles and horizontal lines by the wind. Fatty and Ferl both stared at the gap in front of them.

It was barely three feet across, but there was no room to run for the approach. The far side didn't look stable, either.

"If you do this," Ferl said, "I'll never call you Fatty again."

"Go bugger yourself," Fatty said—and jumped.

He scrambled on the other side, but he made it.

Another missile hit the rock over Ferl's head and rock chips cut his face and rained down over him. He shook his head to clear his eyes, lost his balance, and then found it again, all in a moment. He took two steps and leapt.

The ledge crumbled under his feet faster than he could scramble up it. He threw out his arms, grabbing for anything.

A hand grabbed his. The baron yanked him to safety.

Gasping, Ferl bent over at the waist, hands on his thighs. After a moment, he said, "You saved me. Why'd you—why?"

The baron's answer was lost as the rock behind them exploded again.

Ferl surveyed the rest of the ledge. It was another thirty paces before they would disappear around a corner from the Vürdmeister. The ledge from here on was five feet wide or wider, too wide for one of the missiles to demolish, but they were still exposed, and Ferl sure as hell wasn't going to stay in the back anymore. He sheathed his sword and grabbed the baron, turning him around.

"This is the only way we get out of this," he said.

"It's fine," the baron said. "I'm not climbing back across that ledge, and I have no idea what to do in the wilderness anyway. I'm with you."

They started backing up together, Ferl looking at his feet and then at the Vürdmeister across the face from them. The young man had a glowing green missile circling slowly around his body. He knew his quarry was getting away from him. The missile started spinning faster and faster.

Ferl forced the baron closer to the edge in a silent threat.

The missile slowed and they could see the Vürdmeister's mouth moving in inaudible curses. Ferl extended his middle finger to the man in a silent salute. A moment later, laughing, the baron copied the gesture.

Then a stone shifted under Ferl's heel as he stepped backward. He was slipping, pulling Baron Kirof right on top of himself.

There was only one thing to do. He pushed the baron toward the edge as hard as he could, propelling his own body to safety.

He landed on his butt on the ledge. He could see the baron's fingers clinging to the edge. Ferl rolled close and saw the baron's eyes as round as saucers.

"Help!" the baron shouted.

Ferl didn't move.

In the end, Fatty was simply too fat. He held on for a moment longer, then his spindly arms couldn't hold him anymore. His fingers slipped off the rock.

The fall took a long time, but Fatty never screamed. Together, Ferl and the Vürdmeister watched him sail to the rocky shores of death.

On the other side of the mountain, the Vürdmeister's face seemed to fall as far as the baron's body. The Godking was not understanding of failure.

Ferl scooted back from the edge and around the bend. He congratulated himself on having the foresight to keep the pack.

42

The Gyre estate at Havermere had undergone huge changes since Kylar passed through with Elene and Uly on the way to Caernarvon. Then, it had been nearly empty. Without a lord to protect them, some of the farmers had moved away. The coming harvest and this year's fortunate lack of Ceuran or Lae'knaught raids were the only reasons the rest stayed.

Now, the estate was filled to overflowing, and it took Kylar only a moment to guess why. The resistance had moved its base to Havermere. They were a few days' hard ride outside Cenaria, which put them close enough to strike at patrols but far enough to flee if the God-king mustered a large force against them. The richness of the harvest and the resources of the Gyre household—which included hundreds of the best horses in the country, a substantial armory, and walls that would be defensible at least against anyone who wasn't using magic—made it a perfect base. Kylar wondered if they had seized it by force, or if the Gyre steward had welcomed the army in.

He paused as he first caught sight of the company in the early morning darkness. If he wanted to, he could probably avoid detection—or at least interference. They probably hadn't seen him yet, not in this light, though he had no idea how good their sentries were. Finally, he figured he might as well find out what was happening in Havermere.

If Logan were still alive and Kylar managed to rescue him, this would be where they would come. If he could let Logan know what was waiting for him, all the better.

Still, before he rode on, he fixed his Durzo disguise to his face. It was much easier than the only other disguise he'd constructed—Baron Kirof—and probably less dangerous. The rebels who knew Baron Kirof would want to kill him. The rebels who knew Durzo would probably pretend they didn't—no one in their right mind would admit to knowing a wetboy. And it was better than going as himself.

A Kylar Stern who showed up in the rebel camp was a Kylar Stern who was committing himself to their cause. Besides, he didn't know yet if the Kylar persona was safe. Elene had told Lord General Agon, and Kylar didn't know if Agon had passed the word along.

So here he was, sitting on his horse, trying to fix Durzo's face to his. It wasn't easy, even though he'd spent days—weeks—perfecting the disguise. The problems were manifold.

First, you had to remember the face perfectly. Even after years of looking at Durzo Blint, that was harder than Kylar would have imagined. He'd spent weeks after initially starting the project remembering just how the little lines at the corners of Durzo's eyes turned down, placing the pocks that had pitted his cheeks, getting the shape of the eyebrows right, adjusting the wisps of his thin beard. Then, when he'd thought he had that perfect, he'd realized he was only beginning.

A static face wasn't a disguise. He needed to anchor every moving spot of that face to his, so that it moved almost the same way. Almost. The fact was, even after ten years of being raised by Durzo and years of picking up little mannerisms from him, Kylar's facial expressions weren't much like Durzo's. So, the Durzo face glowered when he frowned, smirked when he smiled, and sneered when he grimaced, plus a hundred other things that he'd added as they occurred to him during long hours spent making faces at himself in the mirror.

Even then, the disguise wasn't complete. Durzo had been tall. Kylar was just pushing average. So after making his disguise, he projected it upward a good six inches. When someone tried to stare Durzo in the eye, he was looking over Kylar's head. It took a lot of discipline to remember to stare at the person's neck so Durzo would be looking back into their eyes. That was one thing Kylar hadn't fixed yet: he'd tried to make it so he could look wherever he wanted and Durzo's eyes would follow from six inches higher, but he hadn't figured out how yet.

And of course, if anyone tried to touch the face or the shoulders he projected, the illusion was destroyed. Kylar had tried to make the illusion ethereal, so something that touched it would slip right through. It hadn't worked. The Talent mesh—or whatever it was—was physical. If anything thicker than rain hit it, it broke apart. Kylar had tried to take that the other way, too, and give it physical form, so that light touches against it might feel resistance like a real face or real shoulders would provide. That hadn't worked either.

All in all, it was a damned lot of work for what turned out to be a mediocre disguise. Now Kylar understood why Durzo had preferred makeup.

He nudged his horse's flanks with his heels, and they descended into Havermere.

The sentries didn't appear surprised to see him riding out of the dawn, so maybe their perimeter was better than he'd thought. "State your business," a tough-looking teenager said.

"I'm a native of Cenaria but I've lived in Caernarvon for the last few years. I heard things had settled down for the most part. I've got family in Cenaria and I'm going to see if they're all right." It was quick, and he'd probably explained too much, but a nervous trader would probably do the same.

"What's your trade?"

"I'm an herb merchant and apothecary. Normally, I'd take the opportunity to bring some herbs along with me, but my last cargo was destroyed by bandits. The bastards burned my wagon when they found it didn't have any gold in it. Tell me, who did that help? Anyway, I can make better time this way."

"Are you armed?" the young man asked. He seemed more relaxed, though, and Kylar could tell he believed him.

"Of course I'm armed. Do you think I'm mad?" Kylar asked.

"Fair enough. Go ahead."

Kylar rode into the camp that was spread out before Havermere's gates. It was well-organized, laid out in neat rows with toilets at regular intervals away from the cooking pits, numerous permanent or semi-permanent buildings, and clear lanes for foot and horse traffic. But it wasn't very military. Some of the structures looked like they were planning on staying through the winter, but the fortifications around the camp were laughable. From the looks of things, all the nobles and their personal guards had taken residence in the Gyre estate, while the soldiers and civilians who had thrown in their lot with the rebels were out here, trying their best to make do.

Kylar was looking at a wood building, trying to divine its purpose, when he almost rode down a man wearing a pince nez and limping on a cane. The man looked up and appeared as shocked as Kylar was.

"Durzo?" Count Drake asked. "I thought you were dead."

Kylar froze. It was so good to see Count Drake alive that his control of the disguise almost wavered. The count looked older now, careworn. He'd walked with a limp since Kylar had known him, but he'd never needed a cane before.

"Is there some place we can talk, Count Drake?" Kylar barely stopped himself from calling him "sir."

"Yes, yes of course. Why are you calling me that? You haven't called me Count Drake in years."

"Uh…it has been a while. How did you get out?"

Count Drake squinted at him, and Kylar stared at Count Drake's chest, hoping that Durzo's eyes were meeting Count Drake's. "Are you well?" Count Drake asked.

Dismounting, Kylar extended his hand and clasped Count Drake's wrist. The man clasping his wrist back felt real, solid, the way Count Drake had always felt. He was an anchor, and Kylar was overwhelmed between an urge to tell him everything and shame just as strong.

The danger in talking to Count Drake was that everything became clear as he listened. Decisions that had seemed so muddy became suddenly simple. Something in Kylar shied away from that. If Count Drake really knew him, he'd stop loving him. A wetboy doesn't have friends.

Count Drake led him to a tent near the center of the camp. He sat in a chair, his leg obviously stiff. "It's a little drafty, but if we're still here we'll shore it up before winter."

"We?" Kylar asked.

The joy leached out of the count's eyes. "My wife and Ilena and I. Serah and Magdalyn didn't—didn't make it out. Serah was a comfort woman. We heard…she hanged herself with her bed sheets. Magdalyn is either a comfort woman or one of the Godking's concubines, last we heard." He cleared his throat. "Most of them don't last very long."

So it was true. Kylar hadn't thought Jarl was lying, but he hadn't been able to believe it. "I'm so sorry," Kylar said. Words were totally inadequate. Comfort women. Bound into the cruelest, most dehumanizing form of slavery Kylar knew: magically sterilized and given a room in the Khalidoran barracks for the convenience of the soldiers— a convenience used dozens of times a day. His stomach churned.

"Yes. It's a, an open wound," Count Drake said, his face gray. "Our Khalidoran brethren have given themselves over to the worst appetites. Please, come inside. Let's talk about the war we have to win."

Kylar stepped inside, but the churning in his stomach didn't stop. It intensified. As he saw Ilena Drake, the count's youngest daughter, who was now fourteen, that guilt crushed in on him. God, what if they'd caught her, too?

"Could you heat up some ootai for us?" the count asked his daughter. "You remember my daughter?" he asked Kylar.

"Ilena, right?" Ilena had always been his favorite. She had her mother's cool complexion and white-blonde hair and her father's penchant for mischief, untempered by her father's years.

"Pleased to meet you," the girl said politely. Damn, she was becoming a lady. When had that happened?

Kylar looked back to the count. "So what's your title or your position here?"

"Titles? Position?" Count Drake smiled and spun his cane on its point. "Terah Graesin has been bargaining off titles, trying to tie families into the rebellion. But when it comes to actually getting things done, she's glad to have my help."

"You're joking."

"Afraid not. That's why we're still here—what is it? Three months since the coup? She's only allowed small raids against supply lines and poorly defended outposts. She's afraid that if we get handed a big loss the families will back out and swear their allegiance to the Godking."

"That's no way to win a war."

"No one knows how to win a war against Khalidor. Nobody's fought successfully against an army reinforced with wytches in decades," Count Drake said. "There are reports that the Khalidorans are having troubles along the Freeze. She's hoping that most of them will be sent home before the snows block Screaming Winds."

"I thought we held Screaming Winds," Kylar said.

"We did," Count Drake said. "I even got news from my friend Solon Tofusin to signal them when we were ready to march for war. The garrison there had the best Cenarian troops in the realm, veterans, every one."

"And?" Kylar asked.

"They're all dead. Killed themselves or lay down and let someone slit their throats. My spies say it was the work of the goddess Khali. That just adds to the duchess's caution."

"Terah Graesin," Ilena said, "does most of her campaigning on her back."

"Ilena!" her father said.

"It's true. I spend every day with her maids-in-waiting," Ilena said, scowling.

"Ilena."

"Sorry."

Kylar was shaken. It was impossible. Gods were superstition and madness. But what superstition would drive hundreds of veterans to suicide?

Ilena hadn't taken her eyes off Kylar since he came into the tent. She looked at him like he was going to try to steal something.

"So what's the plan?" Kylar asked, taking ootai from the frowning girl. Too late, he realized he wouldn't be able to drink it—Durzo's lips were in the wrong place.

"So far as I can tell," the count said, pained, "there isn't one. She's talked about a big offensive, but I'm afraid she doesn't know what to do. She's been trying to hire wetboys; there was even a Ymmuri stalker here a few weeks ago—scary sort—but I think she's trying to stack the deck but not play the game. She's gathering an army, but she doesn't know what to do with it. She's a political creature, not a martial one. She doesn't have any military men in her circle."

"It sounds like this is going to be the shortest-lived rebellion in history."

"Stop encouraging me." Count Drake sipped his ootai. "So what brings you here? Not work, I hope?"

"What kind of work do you do?" Ilena asked.

"Ilena, be silent or be gone," Count Drake said.

At her expression, which was at once wounded and peeved, Kylar coughed into his hand and looked away to keep from laughing.

When he looked up, Ilena's expression had changed altogether. Her eyes were bright and wide.

"It is you!" she said. "Kylar!"

She threw herself into his arms, knocking the delicate ootai cup from his hands and utterly smashing the illusion as she hugged him.

The count was shocked into silence. Kylar looked at him, aghast.

"You big oaf, hug me!" Ilena said.

Kylar laughed and hugged her. Gods, it felt good—really, really good—to be hugged. She squeezed as hard as she could, and he picked her up as he hugged her. He pretended to squeeze as hard as he could. She squeezed harder until he cried out for mercy. They laughed again—they'd always hugged like that—and he set her down.

"Oh, Kylar, that was so the slam," she said. "How did you do that? Can you teach me? Will you, please?"

"Ilena, let the man breathe," her father said, but he was grinning. "I should have recognized the voice."

"My voice! Oh, sh—darn!" Kylar said. Altering his voice would either require some great acting—which seemed to be beyond him—or more magic. That meant more hours working with a single disguise. When would he find the time to do that?

"Well," the count said, tucking away his pince nez and picking up the pieces of his shattered ootai cup, "it would seem we need to talk. Shall Ilena be excused?"

"Oh, don't make me go, father."

"Um, yes," Kylar said. "See ya, squirt."

"I don't want to go."

Count Drake gave her a look and she wilted. She stomped her foot and marched out.

Then they were alone. Count Drake said gently, "What happened to you, son?"

Kylar picked at a ragged fingernail, stared at a few splinters of the shattered ootai cup on the ground, looked anywhere but at those accepting eyes. "Sir, do you think a man can change?"

"Absolutely," Count Drake said. "Absolutely, but usually he just becomes more himself. Why don't you tell me everything?"

So Kylar did. Everything from the Jadwin estate to breaking his oaths to Elene and Uly, and the raw, gnawing sore that left in his stomach. Finally, he was finished. "I could have stopped it," he said. "I could have ended the war before it began. I'm so sorry. Mags and Serah would be safe if I'd killed Durzo before..."

The count was rubbing his temples as tears leaked down his cheeks. "No, son. Stop that."

"What would you have done, sir?"

"If I knew stabbing Durzo in the back would save Serah and Magdalyn? I'd have stabbed him, son. But it wouldn't have been the right thing to do. Unless you're a king or a general, the only life you have the right to sacrifice for the greater good is your own. You did the right thing. Now let's talk about this little jaunt to the Maw. Are you sure this rumor is true?"

"The Shinga came to tell me himself—and died for it."

"Jarl's dead?" Count Drake asked. It was a blow, Kylar could see.

"You knew about Jarl?" Kylar asked.

"He'd been talking with me. He was planning an uprising to give us a chance to split Ursuul's forces. The people believed in him. They loved him. Even the thieves and killers were beginning to believe they could have a new start."

"Sir, after I rescue Logan..."

"Don't say it."

"I'm gonna go after Mags."

Count Drake's face was gray once more, hopeless. "You save Logan Gyre and you do it fast. Ulana will be sorry she missed you, but you have to go now."

Kylar stood and replaced the Durzo mask. Count Drake watched and his face regained some life. "You know, you have tricks that are— well, the slam."

They laughed together. "One more question," Kylar said. "I've been thinking that it might be good for rumors to get out that Logan is alive before he shows up. I mean, it will give the people something to hope for and it will make it easier for him to consolidate power when he does appear. Should I tell Terah Graesin he's alive?"

"It's a little late for that," a voice said from the opening of the tent. It was Terah Graesin, in a lavish green dress and cloak lined with new mink. She was smiling a thin smile. "Why Durzo Blint, I haven't seen you in ages."

43

*U*sually Garoth summoned his concubines to his rooms, but sometimes he liked to surprise them. Magdalyn Drake had entertained him for a long time, but as always, his interest was beginning to wane.

Tonight, he'd woken, hours past midnight, with the infernal itch and a headache and an idea. He would enter silently and wake Magdalyn roughly. He loved Magdalyn's scream. He would beat her savagely and accuse her of plotting against him.

If she begged and swore it wasn't true like most frightened women would, he'd throw her off the balcony. If she cursed him, he would bang her, matching her defiance with an equal degree of brutality, and she would live another day. Before he left, he would hold her tenderly in his arms and whisper that he was sorry, that he loved her. Decent women always wanted to see something good in him. He shivered in anticipation.

He extended the vir through the closed door, hoping to detect the even sound of her breathing in sleep. Instead he felt something different. She was awake.

Garoth opened the door, but she didn't notice him. She was sitting on her bed, facing the open door to her rail-less balcony. She was dressed only in a thin nightgown, but she didn't seem to feel the cold air blowing in the open door. She was rocking back and forth.

He swore loudly. She didn't respond. He touched her skin and it, too, was cold. She must have been sitting like this for hours.

Other concubines had pretended madness in an attempt to escape his attentions. Maybe Magdalyn Drake was the same. Garoth slapped her and she fell off the bed. She didn't cry out. Grabbing a fistful of dark hair, Garoth dragged her onto the balcony.

Coming right to the edge, he pulled her to her feet. He grabbed her throat in one thick hand and pushed her back until her toes were barely on the edge. His fingers wrapped almost all the way around her throat. He took care to choke her as little as possible, but if he released her, she would fall.

Her eyes finally came into focus. The shadow of death tended to have that effect on people.

"Why?" Magdalyn asked sadly. "Why do you do this?"

He looked at her, confused. The answer was so obvious that he wasn't sure he'd understood the question. "It pleases me," he said.

And strangely—but Magdalyn Drake had always been a strange girl, it was part of why she appealed to him—Magdalyn smiled. She pulled toward him, but not like a woman dangling off a precipice would pull toward her only hope of life.

She kissed him. If it was an act, it was a damn convincing one. If her mind had broken, it had broken in an intriguing way. Magdalyn Drake kissed him, and Garoth swore it was with real desire. His arousal came back stronger than ever as she climbed him, her lean young legs wrapping around his waist.

He thought of taking her back inside, but it was impossible to stay fully in control, about to make love with a woman who might be trying to kill him. She kissed her way to his ears.

"I've been listening to you and Neph," she said, washing her hot breath back in his ear.

He usually didn't let his concubines talk while he fucked them, unless they were cursing him, but Garoth didn't want to destroy this fragile insanity.

Magdalyn kissed him again, then pulled away. She leaned back. Holding him with her legs, she let go of his neck and leaned back. He grabbed onto her hips to keep her from plunging to her death. Upside down, she waved her arms above her head, looking over the castle and the city below, laughing.

Garoth's pulse pounded loud in his ears. He didn't even care who might be watching. Whatever kind of madness this was, it was intoxicating.

She shimmied her hips and said something again.

"What?" he asked.

"Let go," she said.

She seemed to have a tight grip with her legs, so he let go, ready to catch her with the vir if need be. He wasn't going to let this end without taking his pleasure. Not now.

Magdalyn tugged her nightgown free from where it was trapped between their bodies and stripped it off. She dropped it over the edge, laughing again as the flimsy cloth spun toward the flagstones below.

Then she sat up and kissed Garoth again, pressing her young body against him. She stripped his robe back roughly. Then she burrowed into him, moaning as her skin touched his, warm against warm in the cold night air.

She nuzzled his neck. "I heard you talking about the Night Angel," she said. "Kylar Stern."

"Mmm."

"I want you to know something," she whispered into his ear, making him shiver. What the hell was she saying? "Kylar's my brother. He's coming for me, you dirty fucker, and if I don't kill you, he will."

She bit his carotid artery as hard as she could and tried to throw them both off the edge.

The vir reacted before Garoth could, exploding at his neck. The vir lashed from his limbs, flinging him inside even as Magdalyn Drake spun out into space.

He stood shakily and summoned Neph.

The Vürdmeister found him standing on the balcony, looking at the ruin of the young woman crushed in the courtyard below.

"Take care of her, Neph. Tell Trudana I expect the best," the God-king said, greatly moved. "Hers was a great spirit."

"Shall I..." The Lodricari coughed his fake cough and Garoth hated him anew. "Shall I send in another concubine?" He pointedly didn't look toward the evidence of Garoth's continued arousal.

"Yes," Garoth said tersely. *Curse you, Khali, yes.*

"If you'll excuse us, Count Drake," Terah Graesin said. "I have need of your quarters."

Count Drake limped out on his cane as several guards took up position outside the tent.

Kylar was still reeling. Terah Graesin knew Durzo. That meant he was supposed to know her, and he didn't. If she knew Durzo, that meant she knew Durzo through his work. That meant she had hired him.

"So," she said. "Logan's alive. That's...terrific." Terah Graesin had a silky, low voice. It was reputed to be sexy, but then, everything about Terah Graesin was supposed to be sexy. Kylar didn't see it. Oh, she was pretty. She had a wide mouth, full lips, and the kind of figure that was unattainable for the majority of noblewomen who spent their days doing nothing more strenuous than issuing orders to the servants. Maybe it was that she was a little too self-consciously good-looking. She wore lots of makeup—expertly applied and subtle, but lots—and had tweezed her eyebrows down to tiny lines. The truth was, she held herself like he ought to admire her, and it pissed him off.

What pissed him off more was that to look her in the eye with his disguise, he had to stare straight at her admittedly perky breasts. Dammit, why were breasts so intriguing?

"So who's paying you to save Logan Gyre?" she asked.

"You don't really expect me to answer that," Kylar said. The only card he had to play was that Blint tended to be blunt and secretive. If she knew him, she'd know that much.

"Master Blint," she said, seeming to come to a decision, but still speaking in that same consciously sexy voice, "you're the only man I know who's killed two kings. How much can I pay you to kill a third?"

"*What?!* You want me to kill the Godking?"

"No. Simply don't save Logan Gyre. I'll double whatever your employer is paying."

"What?" Kylar asked. "Why? You need all the allies you can get right now. Logan would bring thousands to your banners."

"The problem is . . . well, can you keep a secret, Durzo?" She smiled.

"Would you trust a murderer with your secrets?"

"I knew you'd say that!" she said triumphantly, almost giggling. "You said the same thing last time, remember?"

"It's been a while," Kylar said, his throat constricting.

"Well, I'm glad you remembered long enough to kill my father." Kylar blinked.

"Tell me, did you do it before or after you killed King Gunder?"

"I'm paid to kill, not to talk about it." *Gods! Her own father?*

"And that's why I can trust you. Though I will remind you that I've already given you money for not killing me—so you can't do to me what I did to my father."

"Of course not." It took him a second to puzzle it out. She must have met Durzo when the wetboy had taken a job for her father, Duke Gordin Graesin. Perhaps Gordin had hired Durzo to kill King Davin? Duke Graesin must have thought Regnus Gyre would become king after King Davin died, thereby making Gordin's other daughter Catrinna a queen. Logan's mother, Catrinna Graesin, had been Terah's half-sister, though older than Terah by almost twenty years.

"So why let Logan die?" he asked.

"Because I don't give up things that belong to me easily, Durzo Blint. As you know."

"Don't you think you might want to worry about taking the throne from the Khalidorans before you worry about murdering your allies?"

"I don't need a civics lesson. Are you interested in making money for doing nothing, or do you wish to make me your enemy? I will be queen one day, and you'll find me an implacable foe."

"Seven thousand crowns," Kylar said. "How do I know you're good for it? If the Khalidorans wipe you out, I'm not getting stiffed."

She smiled. "Now there's the Durzo Blint I remember." She pulled a fat ring off her finger with an even fatter ruby in it. "Please don't pawn it. It belonged to my father, and it's not worth even half of the eight thousand I'll give you for it after I take the throne. There'll be a bonus if you bring me proof of Logan's death."

"Fair enough," Kylar said.

"I foresee some of my allies becoming ... problematic in the future. I'll have other jobs for you. That is, if you haven't lost your edge."

"What's that supposed to mean?"

"When you didn't answer my summons a month ago, I had to go elsewhere."

"You'll never find anyone as good as me." That, at least, was classic Durzo Blint.

Terah Graesin licked her lips and her eyes filled with sudden hunger. Kylar didn't recognize the look, but he didn't like it, whatever it was. She smiled.

What is she waiting for? Me to make a pass at her? The moment passed.

"Well, then, good day," she said in a level tone that didn't tell Kylar whether he was right or wrong. She stepped close to him to kiss each of his cheeks. It put his real face right at level of her chest, but he was lucky. She didn't lean close enough to touch either his real lips with her breasts or his phantom cheek with her lips. The illusion stayed intact.

As soon as she was gone, he fled. He jumped on his horse and went north out of the camp, worried that Terah might have someone watching the western exit. He shifted his disguise so that Durzo's face was where his own was, rather than above it so that he could see the guards' expression. The guards let him out without question, however, and when he was a mile out, he began to let down his guard. His heart was still pounding as he thought about what this meant for Logan. Even if he got his friend out of the Maw, the road ahead wouldn't be easy. At least now he would know who his enemies were.

Kylar entered a thin stretch of trees when something whispered coolly in his mind: ~*Duck.*~

"What?" he said aloud.

An arrow drove through Kylar's chest.

It rocked him back in the saddle, but his horse kept walking, oblivious. Kylar coughed blood. He'd made so many mistakes. Durzo would never have forgiven him for his carelessness. Letting down his guard, going back to the path when he'd worried someone might have been sent after him, taking his own horse rather than stealing someone else's. It only took one mistake to get you killed, and he'd made many.

Gods, his lungs burned.

~*I told you to duck.*~

A shadowy form stepped out from behind a tree and took his horse's reins in one hand, holding a sword in the other.

The wetboy let down his shadows—they weren't nearly as good as Durzo's, never mind Kylar's. It was Scarred Wrable. "Well, son of a bitch," the wetboy said. "Durzo Blint? Shit."

"Howdy, Ben," Kylar said. Son of a bitch was right. He'd kept the Durzo disguise—and if he'd kept it at Durzo's height, Ben Wrable would have shot his arrow right over Kylar's shoulder.

It was taking more and more effort to maintain the Durzo disguise, and Kylar was painfully aware that it was important he do so. If Terah thought she'd killed Durzo, Kylar could still come back. That had its own set of problems, but far fewer than revealing that he was both Durzo Blint and Kylar Stern and immortal.

"Shit, Durzo! I didn't even know it was you. That uppity Graesin bitch said 'special job, easy, pay ya double.' What the hell you riding on the path for, D?"

"Just..." Kylar coughed. "Made a mistake."

"It only takes one, I guess. Shit, buddy. I woulda fought ya at least."

"I would have killed you," Kylar said. He was stirred by a sudden panic. What if this was his last life? He had no guarantee that he would come back. The Wolf had never explained it. Gods, he'd been totally crazy when he'd let Baron Kirof kill him for money.

"Probably." Scarred Wrable swore again. He'd gained his nickname from the innumerable scars he had on his face. He'd come to Cenaria as a child from somewhere in Friaku and spent time as a slave. He was one of the few men who'd gained his freedom from the fighting pits. Kylar thought the scars were self-inflicted, but the man spoke without an accent. Whatever rituals he practiced he'd learned from rumors about the Friaki, not from observation. "How am I supposed to brag about this, Durzo? I just shot you with a goddam arrow. That's no way to kill the world's greatest wetboy."

"Seems to be working all right." Kylar coughed.

"Shit," Ben said, disgusted.

"Make something up," Kylar said. He sprayed more blood again as he coughed. He'd forgotten dying was so much fun.

"I can't do that," Wrable said. "It dishonors the dead. They haunt you if you do that."

"I feel really fucking sorry for you," Kylar said. He was slipping out of the saddle. He hit the ground with a thump and smacked the back of his head on the ground, but whatever he'd done, the disguise held.

Ben scowled. "Wait," he said, working it out. Scarred Wrable had never been the brightest torch on the wall. "You mean, you mean it would honor you more if people thought you'd been killed in heroic combat?" Scarred Wrable asked. He liked the idea. "You'd let me say that and not haunt me? I'd make you sound good, I swear."

"Depends," Kylar said. His vision was already beginning to white out. "Are you going to hack anything off my corpse?" That would be just his luck. He'd wake up without a head or something. How would that work? Would he die for real if someone took his head?

"The bitch did want proof."

"Take her the ring. Take my horse, my clothes, whatever you need, but leave my body alone, say you're superstitious or something and you can tell the story however you want. Just put my body..." Kylar lost the thought. His head was getting thick. He thought he could feel his heart laboring as blood spilled inside his chest.

"Fair enough. You ready, friend?" Ben asked.

Kylar nodded.

Ben Wrable stabbed him through the heart.

44

I've been working on the web," Sister Ariel said. "It's trapped in some really interesting ways. Who put it on you again?"

"How about if I tell you, you let me go?" Vi said. *Not very subtle, are you, Bitch Wytch?*

They were heading back to the trail after taking a huge detour around the rebel camp at Havermere. Vi could tell that Sister Ariel had wanted to go into the camp but thought that it would give Vi chances to escape.

"Why are we going west?" Vi asked. "I thought the Chantry was northeast."

"It is. But I still haven't finished what I was sent to do," Ariel said.

"What was that?" Uly asked. She was sitting on the cantle behind Vi right now, and both of them were leashed magically. Vi was glad that Uly asked the question. Sister Ariel answered Uly's questions. That probably had something to do with Vi's repeated escape attempts, which had left them both bruised and irritable.

"I'm looking to recruit someone special, and I'm hoping I can find a woman who fits the bill in the rebel camp. Unfortunately, I don't trust Vi as far as I can throw her."

"That's pretty far," Uly said.

Vi scowled. Not only had Ariel left her with the scratches from where she'd landed in brambles, but afterward she'd spanked her. Life in the saddle was a sore life.

"So I don't count as someone special?" Vi said. "You already said I'm vastly talented. Or whatever." She sneered as she said it, but she was curious—and, strangely, a little hurt that she didn't measure up.

"Oh, you're both very special. But neither of you qualifies for what I need," Ariel said. The bitch was enjoying being mysterious.

"What do you mean, both of us?" Vi asked.

"I'm taking you both to the Chantry, but neither of you can fulfill—"

"Why are you taking us both?"

Ariel looked at Vi, puzzled. Then she laughed. "Uly's Talented, Vi."

"What?" Vi was incredulous.

"Oh, it's rare to find Talented women, I don't deny it. But if only one woman in a thousand is Talented, that doesn't mean that you only find two Talented women together once in a million times. You see?"

"No," Uly said. Vi didn't either.

"People with the Talent tend to feel an affinity for each other, even if neither of them knows why. We frequently find them together, which is great for us . . . usually. Perhaps you're too young for this much truth, Ulyssandra, but that affinity is probably the only reason why an otherwise heartless murderer didn't add you to her already overburdened conscience."

"You mean she would have killed me? Would you, Vi?" Uly asked.

Vi was glad the girl was sitting behind her so she couldn't see the guilt written all over her face. Why did she care what Uly thought?

"You can look at it in a negative light or a positive one, Ulyssandra," Sister Ariel said. "Negative: she normally would have killed you. Positive: she didn't—and she's had many opportunities to change her mind since then and still hasn't. You might even say Vi likes you."

"Do you like me, Vi?" Uly asked.

"I'd like to kick you in the head," Vi said.

"Don't take it too hard," Sister Ariel said. "With the way she was raised, Vi's a—well, let's be charitable—let's call her an emotional cripple. She's probably only poorly able to differentiate between most of her emotions, feeling comfortable only with rage, anger, and condescension because they make her feel strong. Indeed, I'd guess her interactions with you may well be the first positive ones she's had in her entire life."

"Stop it," Vi said. Ariel was cutting her into pieces and scoffing at the bits.

"This is positive?" Uly said.

"She doesn't shy away from your touch, Uly. When you ride with her, she's at ease. For anyone else, she'd be constantly on guard."

"I'll kill the little wench the first chance I get," Vi said.

"Bluster," Ariel said.

"What's that mean?" Uly asked.

"It means horseshit," Vi said.

"So you just keep being nice to her, Uly," Ariel said, ignoring Vi, "because probably no one else in your tyro class will like her very much."

"In *our* class?" Vi asked. "You're putting me with the children?"

Sister Ariel looked surprised. "Why yes. And you should be nice to Ulyssandra, because she's got more Talent than you do. And none of your bad habits."

"You cruel, cruel bitch," Vi said. "I know what you're doing. You're trying to break me, but I'll tell you what. Nothing can break me. I've been through everything."

Sister Ariel turned her face to the setting sun that limned the treetops of a small copse in front of them. "That, my dear, is where you're wrong. You are already broken, Vi. You were broken years ago and you healed hunched. And now you're broken again and trying to heal even more hunched. I won't let that happen. I'll break you one more time if I have to so you don't have to be a cripple anymore. But I can't make the choice to be healthy for you. And I don't promise a lack of scars. But you can be a better woman than you are now."

"A woman who looks a lot like you?" Vi sneered.

"Oh no. You're more passionate than I ever was," Sister Ariel said. "I'm afraid I'm a bit of an emotional cripple myself. Too much brain, they say. Too comfortable in my own mind. I never had to come out. But I was born this way; you were made. And you're right; you'll not learn what you need to know from me."

"Were you ever in love?" Uly asked.

Vi wondered where the hell that came from, but the question must have been a good one because it hit Sister Ariel like a shovel across the face.

"Huh. That's a—a very good question," Ariel said.

"He left you for someone who wasn't so cold and ugly, didn't he?" Vi asked, with a little twist of satisfaction.

Ariel said nothing for a moment. "I see you aren't without claws," Ariel said, quietly. "Not that I expected any less."

Uly jabbed her fingers into Vi's ribs to chastise her, but Vi ignored her. "So you never got around to your point. Why are we going west?"

"There's a sister who lives this way. She's going to nursemaid you two while I scout out the rebel camp for a suitable woman."

"What are you looking for?" Uly asked.

"We should start looking for a place to set up camp. It's getting dark. Looks like we're not going to make it to Carissa's tonight," Sister Ariel said.

"Aw, please?" Uly said. "It's not that dark and we don't have anything else to talk about."

Sister Ariel seemed to chew it over. She shrugged. "I'm looking for a highly Talented woman who is ambitious, charismatic, and obedient."

"Ambitious and obedient? Good luck," Vi said.

"If she were willing to be obedient to the Speaker, she'd have personal instruction, a rapid rise through the ranks, a lot of attention and power—but all those are easy. The problem is that she has to be new because we have to be sure of her loyalties, and she has to be married. A woman whose husband is Talented would be the real gem."

"So when you find this married woman, you're going to kidnap her?" Vi asked. "Isn't that a little risky?"

"Another person might have said immoral, but...well, a truly kidnapped woman wouldn't cooperate. Ideally, we'd like to have the man on the premises. Just sticking a wedding ring on a woman's hand isn't going to cut it. The more permanent and steady the marriage appears, the better."

"Why not have Vi do it?" Uly asked. "She doesn't want to be stuck in classes with me and the other twelve-year-olds anyway."

Ariel shook her head. "Believe me, I thought of her first, but she's totally unsuited to the task."

"You mean as a student or a wife?" Vi asked.

"Both. No offense, but I've known men who married the wrong woman, and they were all miserable. I'm sure we could ask some man to marry you, and we'd get lots of takers. You're a beautiful woman and around beautiful women men tend to think with their—" she looked at Uly and cleared her throat—"irrational side. Even if we could bribe the right fool, and believe me, the Chantry would—they won't put some man's happiness ahead of the Chantry's welfare—even then it wouldn't happen. Vi isn't trustworthy. She isn't obedient. Nor is she intelligent enough—"

"You really are a bitch," Vi said, but Sister Ariel ignored her.

"—and besides, she'd probably try to run away, which would destroy her usefulness to us and waste all our effort. So, like I said, totally unsuitable."

Vi stared at her hatefully. She knew the whole discussion had just been a ploy to cut her down, tell her how unworthy she was, but the intelligence comment had cut deeper than anything. For all the times that she'd been complimented in her life—men did a lot of that when they were trying to get up your skirts—whether the compliments had been crass or poetic, they had always been about her body. She was smart, dammit.

Sister Ariel stared right back at her. Then she seemed to look deeper.

"Stop!" she said.

Vi stopped. "What?"

Sister Ariel nudged her horse awkwardly until after a few attempts she got it to move beside Vi. She reached out and grabbed Vi's face in both of her hands.

"That son of a bitch," Ariel said. "Don't let anyone heal this, do you understand? He's—wow—look at that. If anyone touches this with magic, there are weaves of fire that will be unleashed around all of the major blood vessels in your brain. And that looks suspiciously like... have you lost control of your body at any time you can remember?"

"What do you mean, like pissed myself?"

"You'd know what I mean if it had happened. I'm going to have to see if Sister Drissa Nile will come back. She's the only one I'd let touch this."

"Who's that?" Uly asked.

"She's a healer. The best with tiny weaves that I know. Has some little shop in Cenaria, last I heard."

"You're not going to tell me anything else about this weave that's supposed to kill me?" Vi said.

"Not unless you tell me who set it."

"You can go—"

"If you curse me one more time, you'll regret it," Sister Ariel said.

The last punishment had been bad enough and the satisfaction for cursing small enough that Vi choked back her words.

They had entered the copse of trees when Vi spotted something partly hidden under leaves off the side of the path, something like dark hair glowing in the dying sunlight.

Uly followed her gaze. "What's that?"

"I think it's a body," Vi said. And then, as they left the path to take a closer look, her heart soared. It was indeed a body—a death that meant life for her. It was freedom and a new start. The dead man was Kylar.

45

Elene's whole body was in pain. She'd been riding as hard as she could bear for six days, and she still hadn't made it to Torras Bend. Her knees hurt, her back hurt, her thighs were in agony, and she still wasn't gaining any time on Uly and Uly's kidnapper. She knew that because she asked everyone she passed on the road if they'd seen a woman and child riding hard to the north. Most of them hadn't, but those who had remembered. If anything, Elene had been falling behind. And it was all up to Elene now.

The guards of the city watch had passed her yesterday, going back to Caernarvon. They'd assured her that a woman, especially a woman encumbered with a child, couldn't have ridden faster than they had. They had given up and gone home. One look at their faces and she knew she would have no luck convincing them otherwise. They were tired and probably under orders not to cross the Lae'knaught who sometimes wandered this far east. Elene let them go. What mattered more than the city watch was Kylar. He'd come this way, too. At some point, he'd passed the kidnapper and Uly—because he hadn't been looking for them.

But she was almost to Torras Bend. Tonight she would sleep in a bed. Bathe. Then she would find out if the kidnapper had headed toward Cenaria, as Elene suspected. And have a hot meal. Elene was daydreaming when she saw the Lae'knaught.

They straddled the road in the middle of some of the largest wheat fields south of Torras Bend. If Elene had wanted to go around them, she'd have to go miles to the east and risk crossing into Ezra's Wood, which was supposed to be haunted. As it was, it was too late. They'd already seen her, and the knights had horses saddled and ready to give chase.

Elene approached them directly, suddenly acutely aware of being a woman traveling alone. There were six men, all armed, and as she neared, all of them stood to intercept her. Over chain hauberks, they wore black tabards emblazoned with a golden sun: the pure light of reason beating back the darkness of superstition. She'd never come across the Lae'knaught, but she knew Kylar didn't think much of them. They professed not to believe in magic, but hated it at the same time. Kylar said they were nothing more than bullies. If they really hated Khalidorans, he'd said, they would have come to Cenaria's aid when the Godking invaded. Instead, they'd hovered like vultures, picking up recruits among the fleeing Cenarians and scavenging off Cenarian lands.

One of the standing knights stepped forward. He held his twelve-foot ash lance carefully. It looked too long to use on foot, but Elene knew that once mounted, all of the knights' awkwardness would vanish. "Halt, in the name of the Bringers of the Freedom of the Light," he said. Elene guessed he couldn't be more than sixteen. As Elene stopped, he stepped forward and grabbed the reins. She wasn't sure what they were so nervous about, and then she realized what should have been immediately obvious. When they saw a woman traveling alone, they saw vulnerability. No normal woman would travel alone, therefore, she must not be a normal woman. She must be a wytch. Elene's stomach tightened.

"Thank goodness," Elene said, sighing as if with relief. She almost said thank the God, but she didn't think the Lae'knaught believed in gods, either. "Can you help me?"

"What is it? What are you doing alone on these roads?" one of the older ones asked.

"Have you seen a young woman, maybe with red hair, traveling with a young girl? Maybe two days ago? No?" Elene slumped, and the sudden pained look on her face was real, even slumping hurt after how much she'd ridden. "I guess she would certainly have avoided you, given what she is. You're certain you didn't see anyone, maybe trying to avoid you by traveling farther east?"

"What are you talking about, young lady? What's happened? How can we help?" the knight asked. From the change in his voice, Elene knew he no longer saw her as a threat. Acting weak and vulnerable had done the trick.

"I've come from Caernarvon," Elene said. "We were originally from Cenaria, but we left as soon as those awful men and their wytches invaded. We were making a new life, Uly and me—Uly's the little girl, my ward. Her parents were killed by the wytches.... We thought we were safe in Caernarvon, but she was kidnapped, sirs. I just had to follow her. The city watch came a way, but then they turned back. I'm afraid I'll never catch up."

"It's just like those damn Sisters, kidnapping a child," the youngest knight said. "That letter said—"

The older knight barked, "Marcus!"

The men were all looking at each other, and Elene knew that her near-truths had not only worked, but that they knew something more. The knights withdrew, leaving the young Marcus standing and looking at her scars awkwardly. Then he realized he was staring, and coughed into his hand.

The older knights returned after a few minutes. The eldest spoke again, "Usually, we'd like to take you to the underlord to tell him all this yourself, but I can see that time is crucial. In fact, we'd love to go with you to help, but our orders are to stay south of Torras Bend. Politics. The thing is, there was a messenger this morning. We intercept all correspondence from Chantry wytches. Well, here. We've already made a copy." He handed her a letter.

"Elene," the letter read in a looping, flowing script, "Uly is safe now, I have taken her from the custody of the woman who took her from you, but I'm afraid I can't send her home. Uly is Talented, and she is on her way to the Chantry, where she will receive the best tutelage in the world and material advantages beyond what you could hope to provide. I understand that you have no reason to believe that this letter is from me. If you wish, you may go to the Chantry to see Uly yourself, or even take her home, should you both wish it. As soon as she arrives safely at the Chantry, she will write to you. I apologize, and if other events weren't so pressing, I would deliver this message myself. Sincerely, Sister Ariel Wyant Sa'fastae."

She had to read the letter two more times before she could grasp what it was saying. Someone had kidnapped Uly from her kidnapper? Uly was Talented?

In the end, the letter changed nothing. Elene still had to go to Torras Bend and find out what the villagers knew. If what it said was true, she would have to go north and on to the Chantry. If not, she'd have to head west, to Cenaria. Still, the kidnapper wouldn't have known that Elene was following her. It wasn't like she'd been closing in on them.

"Damn wytches," the young knight said. "Always kidnapping little girls, turning them away from the Light and into more like themselves."

"Marcus!"

Elene was suddenly relieved she'd told the truth to these men. If her story hadn't lined up with the letter, things would have gone very differently. "No, it's all right," she said. "I'll have to press on hard if I've hope of finding Uly before she gets in their clutches."

"Be careful," the older knight said. "Not all of these villagers love the Light."

"Thank you for your help," Elene said. With that, she rode on toward Torras Bend, her mind awhirl.

46

*W*henever Ariel saw something she thought was fascinating or puzzling, she had a curious talent for memorizing it. It had been an enormous benefit when studying, of course, because she was able to picture whole sections of scrolls and find whatever she needed.

She was lucky enough now to not be looking at the corpse. She was looking at Vi's and Uly's faces—and each face's expression was locked in the vault of her memory. Vi's was all exhilaration, a thrill that might just have come from seeing death. Ariel hoped that wasn't it. She hoped there was more to it than that, that Vi had had some personal reason to want Kylar dead. If not, Vi might be less useful than she thought. For now, she disregarded Vi's expression. She put it away to examine another time. It was Uly's expression that truly intrigued her.

Kylar had been a father figure to the girl. Uly was a tenderhearted child. She hadn't grown up in the Warrens or any other place where she had to see death on a daily basis. The sight of her adoptive father stripped to his underclothes and lying dead by the side of the road should have left her shocked. She should look distant or in denial— not curious. Had she just not recognized him yet? Then Uly's expression shifted to something Ariel thought was elation. Elation? Surely that couldn't be right. Why would the girl be happy?

Ariel was interrupted as she realized she was having her own emotions about seeing Kylar dead. She tried to label them as quickly as possible so she could file them away and get back to the task at hand. Disappointment, yes. She'd been planning something clever for Kylar and it wasn't going to work now. A little bit of grief. Kylar had seemed like the kind of man she would like. Curiosity at how such a capable man had let himself be killed. Some sorrow for how it would affect Uly—*good enough, that will do.* Having labeled her emotions, she set them aside.

Uly looked up and saw Ariel staring at her. "He's not dead," Uly said. "He's just hurt."

"Girl," Vi said. "I've seen lots of dead people. He's dead."

"He'll get better."

It sounded like denial, and Vi obviously took it as such, but it wasn't.

Sister Ariel unrolled the mental scroll to examine the expression on Uly's face and watch it change. Curiosity to elation. Curiosity to elation. Uly saw that he was dead—it was obvious from how pale he was that he'd been here for quite some time, maybe a day—but Uly wasn't surprised and she wasn't worried. Why? Did she really believe he'd get better?

Sister Ariel reached out with her Talent and touched Kylar and realization whooshed over her—no, it crashed over her like a ten-foot wave, leaving her breathless and sputtering. Her magic was sucked from the air into Kylar's body, channeled a hundred different ways to join in the healing that was going on within him.

The magic would have baffled her. The magic combined with Uly's expression that said she'd seen this before and was elated, that told her everything.

Kylar was a creature out of legend. A legend no Sister believed. Until now.

"You're right, Uly," Sister Ariel said gently, meeting Vi's gaze as if to say "play along." "How about we set up camp and you can start on our dinner while Vi and I tend to his wounds? She and I know more about healing, and you can make sure there's dinner ready for him when he wakes up."

Ariel dismounted and helped Uly down.

"I don't want to go. I want to stay here," Uly said.

"Uly," Vi said. "The best way you can help is to get dinner ready. You'll get in the way here."

"Come on, child," Ariel said. She led Uly away as Vi got off her horse and began pulling leaves away from Kylar's body. Ariel turned and mouthed "start digging." Vi nodded.

If she'd had time to think, Ariel wouldn't have played such a desperate hand. A thousand factors were in play and playing too fast for her to calculate the odds.

She took Uly about twenty paces into the woods and bound her and gagged her with magic, setting her on the far side of a tree trunk. "I'm sorry, child. It's for the best."

"Mmm!" Uly said, her eyes wide, but the sound was barely a whisper.

Ariel came around the tree just in time to see Vi vault onto her horse's back and gallop off into the woods. Ariel shouted and threw a ball of light whizzing past her, but didn't put any heat into it. She wasn't going to light the forest on fire just to scare the girl. Besides, she might have accidentally hit her.

In moments, even the sound of hoofbeats faded. Sister Ariel shook her head and made no attempt to follow.

So much for the obvious part of the gamble. What Vi did now was the real trick. *Good luck, Vi. May you come back to us ready to heal.*

She hoped that someday she might sit with Vi in her chambers at the Chantry and laugh about what they'd done today, but she didn't think it would happen. Not after what she'd just done. Passionate women tended to hate women like Sister Ariel. Or at least they hated being coldly manipulated—but what choice did Ariel have?

"And now you," she said, turning. "My undying warrior. How do you work?"

*   *   *

"I didn't see you last time," Kylar told the Wolf. "I thought maybe I was done with you." The Wolf was sitting in his throne in the Ante-chamber of Mystery, his lambent yellow eyes weighing Kylar. The indistinct ghosts who populated the indistinct chamber murmured beyond Kylar's hearing. The whole place still unnerved him.

He couldn't feel the floor beneath his feet. He couldn't see the ghosts when he looked directly at them. Couldn't tell if the chamber actually had walls. His skin prickled, but he couldn't have said if it was warm or cold here. He couldn't smell. Aside from his voice, he heard noth-ing. He had a sense of noise, voices, the scuff of feet beyond his hear-ing, but that was only an intuition. He was disembodied and somehow he'd carried along some of his senses but not all of them, and none of them reliably. Only a few things were clear here: the Wolf, and the two doors. One was plain wood with an iron latch, the other gold with light leaking around the edges.

"I was too furious to bear the sight of you," the Wolf said.

He didn't look much happier now. Kylar couldn't think of anything to say. Furious? Why?

"It took Acaelus fifty years to rack up three deaths. You've done it in less than six months. You took money for a death. Money. Wasn't the price for that blasphemy enough? Will you never learn?" the Wolf asked.

"What are you talking about?" Kylar could sense that the ghosts or whatever the insubstantial people were who crowded the chamber had gotten very quiet.

"You sicken me."

"I don't—"

The Wolf held up a burn-scarred finger and the weight of the small man's authority was such that Kylar stopped immediately.

"Acaelus took money once, too, after his first wife died. I think he didn't really believe in his immortality until then. He took money twice and did something worse once. After that, I showed him what it cost. It stopped him, as it should be stopping you. If you persist in throwing lives away, I will make you rue every day of your interminable life."

It was like a bad dream: the frowning tribunal holding him to a standard he didn't understand, declaring his guilt, the looming watchful figures, the doors of judgment, the threat of a truth he couldn't bear. He would have shaken himself, pinched himself—if he'd had a body to shake or pinch. If he didn't remember being killed.

"I don't know what you're talking about. What the hell am I supposed to do?" Kylar asked bitterly. "What am I for?"

Light flashed in those hard gold eyes and the world telescoped. Perspectives changed and Kylar felt suddenly awkward. Fat and uncoordinated, he was seated in a small chair. His fingers were short and pudgy and wailing filled his head. His head itself seemed almost unbearably heavy. He flailed and realized he was the one screaming.

He was back in a body, but it wasn't his. He was a baby. In front of him, the gray-haired man, now a giant, held a spoon full of gruel. "OPEN WI—IDE!" the Wolf crooned, pushing the gruel toward Kylar's face.

Kylar snapped his screaming mouth shut.

Light flashed once more and he was back in his own body.

The man smiled wolfishly at him. "You are nothing but a fat, awkward child in the land of giants. You close your mouth instead of eating. You speak when you should listen. What are you for? Any answer I gave you'd reject. So why should I waste my time? You're as arrogant as your master ever was, and you don't have a shred of his wisdom. I find you wanting."

"What am I supposed to do?"

"Better. Do better."

Part of Ariel wished she could slow whatever was happening in Kylar's body. As it was, he was almost recovered. As she watched, the arrow in his chest wobbled and began to shift. Then it quivered and began to rise out of his body as if being pushed from within.

With an audible plop, the arrowhead broke through skin that had already healed flush around the shaft. The arrow fell to the side and Ariel grabbed it and put it in her pack next to the gold tablet for later study.

The skin over Kylar's heart the arrow had just broken was knitting together so quickly she could see it. In moments, it was smooth once more, unscarred. Sister Ariel reached out with her magic, but as soon as it touched Kylar's body it was absorbed. A tremor passed through him and his heart started beating. A long moment later, his chest rose and he coughed violently, spitting half-congealed lumps of blood out of his lungs. Then the coughing passed. Sister Ariel tried to watch without touching, but the streams of magic were so fast she couldn't begin to understand them. She put a hand close to his body, and the air felt cold there. The grass beneath him was wilted and white.

It was like his whole body was sucking up energy in any form and using it to heal him. What would happen if he were put in a cold, dark room? Would the healing stop? How the hell was he translating all that energy into magic? How was he doing it at all, much less unconsciously?

Gods, studying such a man might even tell the sisters about the afterlife. That was something they'd given up on long ago, considering it outside the realm of experimentation. Kylar could change everything.

She pooled magic in a white ball in her hands and brought it close to his body to watch the way the magic was sucked in like water down a drain.

Amazing.

Now this, this was a puzzle she could devote her life to solving.

The last of the magic dissolved from her hands and Kylar's eyes flicked open.

Sister Ariel raised her hands. "I'm not here to hurt you, Kylar. Do you remember me?"

He nodded, his eyes darting around like a wild animal's. "What are you doing here? What's happened? What did you see?"

"I saw you dead. Now you live again. Who killed you?"

Kylar seemed to deflate, too tired or too rattled to bother with a denial. "It doesn't matter. A wetboy. Nothing personal."

"A wetboy like you and Vi?"

He stood, feigning stiffness. She knew he was feigning it because she could see that he was in absolutely perfect condition now. "Graakos," she whispered under her breath, armoring herself.

"What do you want, wytch?" he asked. Abruptly, the tendrils of magic she'd extended toward him vanished. Not just vanished; they blew apart like smoke in strong breeze. He'd done that—scattered her magic. His eyes glittered dangerously. Would her magical armor disappear just as easily? For the first time in decades, Sister Ariel was in danger from a man.

"I want to help you, if your cause is just," she said.

"You mean if I'll help you in return?"

She shrugged, willing herself to calmness. "What are the extents of your powers, young man? Do you even know?"

"Why would I tell you?"

"Because I already know you're Kylar indeed. You're the killer who is killed. The undying dier. What's your real name? How did you get this power? Were you born with it? What do you see when you're dead?"

"Shouldn't have told you my name, should I? You overeducated types will be the death of me. Or the ruin of me, at least."

Having seen how the healing worked, Ariel knew the shell of this man, his body, wouldn't change, wouldn't age in a thousand years. Kylar might be centuries old, but no matter how she looked at him, she saw a young man behind those cool blue eyes. A young man's bravado, a young man's invincibility. He'd certainly evinced a young man's foolishness in telling her so much already. "How old are you?" she asked.

He shrugged. "Twenty, twenty-one."

"So the Society's wrong?"

"The Society?" Kylar asked.

Drat. How can I be so subtle with Vi and so clumsy with this boy?
She knew why, though. She wasn't used to dealing with men. She'd
spent too much time cloistered in the company of women. She understood women. Even if they could be terrifically illogical, over the
years she'd learned to gauge when illogic was about to strike. Men
were a different matter entirely. It would have been, well, logical, that
she would feel more at home in the company of men, but it wasn't the
case. Still, every word Kylar said was teaching her volumes. He hadn't
lied about his age. That felt true—but who didn't know their exact
age? Was that because he couldn't remember how long he'd been in
this incarnation? She felt that it was something different. Still, she
shouldn't have said anything about the Society. Now she'd have to tell
him more. If she refused to share, so would he.

" 'Lo, the long night passes and he is made new.' That Society," she
said. Kylar was rubbing his eyes like they felt funny. He seemed overwhelmed, which was good, because she didn't want to explain how
she knew about the Society. "They believe you come back from the
dead and they hope to learn how. Apparently, their belief is justified.
And what more could a man hope for but to conquer death?"

"Lots," Kylar snapped. "I'm immortal, not invincible. It's not always
a blessing." He was still disoriented. He looked like he was regretting
every word he said. He wasn't stupid, this one. Reckless, maybe, but
not stupid. "So, Sister, what do you plan to do about me? Chain me
and bring me to the Chantry?"

As he said it, it spun a fantasy out for Ariel. What temptation! Oh,
she'd never try to chain him with magic. But she had something better
than magic. She had Uly. A few lies about how Uly would die if she
weren't taken to the Chantry immediately, a subtle weave to make Uly
sick a few times, and Kylar would come with her of his own accord.
Kylar's existence would be hidden from most of the sisterhood. Only
Istariel would know. Ariel herself would study the man.

Oh, the challenge of it! The sheer intellectual puzzle. The depth of the magical complexity! It was intoxicating. She would be part of something great. Kylar wouldn't lead a bad life. They'd provide him with everything he asked for. The best food, the best apartments, training with the swordmasters, visits with Uly, whatever entertainments they could bring to him, and doubtless they'd be curious to breed him with Sisters to see what gifts his progeny had. For his sake, they would surely choose the most attractive women. Most men would find such duties quite pleasant. He would have whatever he wanted but freedom. He was immortal! What were a few decades for him? One single lifetime of pampered luxury and the knowledge that by resting in opulence he would change the course of history. He would have meaning and purpose, just by indulging.

What might happen if the sisterhood—if Ariel herself—unraveled his secrets? Perfect healing for anyone injured, without scars. Immortality! How powerful would the Chantry become if they could choose to whom to give a thousand years of youth?

What would that do to the world?

She, Ariel Wyant, had finally found a puzzle worthy of her gifts. No, not a puzzle, a mystery. She would take her place in history as the woman who gave humanity eternal life. It was breathtaking, and—she realized after far too long—terrifying.

She laughed under her breath. "I see now why the Society has gotten nowhere with you. The temptations are simply too great, aren't they?"

The young man didn't answer. He seemed to have determined that anything he said would tell her more. At the same time, it seemed to her that he thought she knew things that he wanted to know.

"You said in Torras Bend that you were a Cenarian soldier," Ariel said. "But it doesn't seem like you're with the rebels. From how long your body was lying here, I'd guess you didn't even stop at the camp for orders. So here's the deal. You tell me what you're really doing, and I'll help you. You do happen to be alone in the woods, in your undergarments, in the cold, without a horse, without money, and without weapons. I'm sure the being without weapons part isn't a problem, but the rest certainly are."

"Oh, so we're friends now?" Kylar asked, arching an eyebrow. "To me, the question seems to be why I don't kill you to keep the Chantry from finding out about me."

"You're immortal, not invincible," Ariel said, smirking. "If I needed to, I could kill you a dozen times as I dragged you to the Chantry. Neither of us knows if by killing you with magic I might disrupt the delicate balances that bring you back to life, so that's a risk for both of us, isn't it? Of course, after killing you with magic once, I could kill you manually thereafter. And of course, you might kill me. So it's a conundrum for me as well. I might end up with a bag of meat for all my troubles. You might end up dead. Permanently dead."

"If you tell the Chantry of my existence, I'll have every Sister in the world on the lookout for me. For the rest of a very long life. Maybe for me it's better to take the risk once, with one Sister, than to have to deal with every newly frocked tart looking to make a name for herself for all eternity."

"So you'd murder me in cold blood?" she asked.

"Call it preemptive self-defense."

She stepped closer to him and peered into the cool blue eyes. He was a killer, yes. A wetboy, yes. But was he a murderer? The saddest thing about all he'd said was that he was right. If he wanted freedom, if he prized secrecy as much as he or his predecessor or predecessors had, he should kill her. If the Chantry learned he existed, they would never rest until they had him. He was uniquely suited to elude them, but who wanted to live a hunted life? He could escape for five years or fifty, but not forever. The Chantry would never give up. Never. He would become every ambitious Sister's greatest ambition, the greatest test and greatest prize imaginable.

Ariel pictured Istariel interrogating this man. She was shocked to see how ugly the scene became. Istariel would want immortality—not for the Chantry, for herself. She wouldn't pursue a slow, studied method of experimentation. Istariel hated growing old, hated losing her beauty, hated stiff joints and the smell of growing old. To Istariel, Kylar would be an obstacle, defying her, condemning her to death by refusing to yield his secrets.

And what if they pried his secrets from him? What kind of stewards of immortality would the Sisters be?

The answer was disheartening. Who was pure enough and wise enough to know to whom to grant everlasting life? Who, having received the gift, could be trusted not to abuse it?

"You must be a good man, Kylar," she said quietly. "Don't let your gift corrupt you. I won't share your secret with the Chantry. At least not until I can speak with you again. I know you have no reason to trust me, so here." She drew a knife from her belt and handed it to him. "If you must kill me, do so." She turned her back.

Nothing happened.

After a long moment, she turned around. "Will you let me help you?" she asked.

He looked weary. "Logan Gyre is alive," he said. "He's in the Maw's deepest pit, a place called Hell's Asshole."

"You think he's still alive?"

"He was a month ago. If he made it through the first two months, he's made it through the hardest part. I'd guess he's still kicking."

"And you mean to bring him out?"

"He's my friend."

Ariel breathed slowly to get hold of herself. She wanted to berate this boy for his idiocy. How dare he endanger the ka'kari for a mere king? "Do you know what it will mean if Garoth Ursuul gets his hands on your ka'kari? What it will mean for the world?" Sister Ariel asked. It might be terrible for the world for the Chantry to unlock Kylar's secrets; it would be apocalyptic if the Khalidorans did.

"Logan's my friend."

Ariel bit her tongue, literally. If Istariel ever found out what she was about to do, expulsion from the Chantry would be the least of Ariel's punishments.

"Well, then. All right." She exhaled. "I'm going to help you. I think I can do something really special. I think, yes. Don't ask another Sister to do this. It will only be possible because of how much I've already seen of you. But hold on. I need you to take a note to someone."

"What are you doing?" Kylar asked as she found a scrap of parchment and scribbled on it, then magically sealed it.

"Either trust me or don't, Kylar. If you don't trust me, kill me. Since you've already decided not to do that, you might as well make yourself internally coherent and trust me." He blinked at the rush of words, but she continued anyway. "I can get you to the city by tomorrow night, maybe tomorrow afternoon."

"It's a three-day ride—"

"But you have to promise me two things. Promise you'll deliver this letter first, and promise you'll rescue Logan second. Swear it."

"What's in the letter?"

"It's to a healer named Drissa Nile, and it's not about you. Events you'll put into motion will require changes in the Chantry's position. Our people need to know how to react if you save Logan Gyre, you understand?" It wasn't the whole truth, of course, but she wasn't going to tell him the letter was mostly about her clever plan for Vi, which did concern Kylar. "When you get to the city, eat a huge meal and sleep for as long as your body needs. It'll still put you ahead by a day or two."

"Hold on, hold on," Kylar said. "I don't want Logan to rot in there any longer than I have to, but why do you care that I save a day or two?"

Ah, yes. Reckless, not dumb.

"Vi's ahead of you. She's heading for Cenaria."

"That bitch! Going to report her successful hit, no doubt. Wait, how do you know where she's heading?"

"She was traveling with me." Sister Ariel winced.

"What?!"

"You have to understand, Kylar. She's enormously Talented. I was taking her back to the Chantry. She escaped me just after we found your body. She thinks you're dead." Now the tricky part. "Jarl is the one who told you about Logan being alive?"

"Yes, why?"

"Did she...did she torture Jarl before she killed him?"

"No. She didn't talk to him at all."

And the hook—letting the lie sit in the water as if you had no interest in it, not fleshing it out so much that it looked too good: "Then I don't know how she knew, but she said something about the king and a hole. I think she knows about Logan."

Kylar's face paled. He'd bought it. Now he'd go after Logan immediately, rather than trying to kill Vi.

Light! Sister Ariel had thought that she loved studying. She'd always been comfortable in her cloistered life. Now she understood why Sisters left the Chantry to do work in The World. That's what they called it, The World, because the Chantry was another reality entirely. Ariel thought she didn't care what happened in The World, thought that books would always be more fascinating than some petty kingdom's petty politics. But right now, she felt so alive. Here she was, sixty-some years old, thinking on her feet, gambling futures—and loving it!

"She's only got a few minutes on me. I can catch her and kill her now! Let me have your horse!"

"It's dark, Kylar, you'll never—" Stupid! She'd been thinking like a Sister, not like an assassin. She'd just given him more reason to kill Vi.

"I can see in the dark! Give me your horse!"

"No!" she said. *He can see in the dark?*

A change came over Kylar in an instant. One moment, he was a furious young man, his intensity such that despite standing in his undergarments in the cold he still looked formidable. The next moment, his entire body flashed iridescent. The coruscation went beyond the visible spectrum into the magical, leaving Ariel's eyes watering. When she blinked them clear, Kylar was utterly changed.

In Kylar's place stood an apparition, a demon. Every curve and plane of Kylar's body was sleeked in black metal, his face a mask of fury, his muscles exaggerated but not his power. Ariel realized she was seeing the Angel of the Night in all its fury. She was denying the avatar of retribution his chance to mete out justice.

There was no dissembling, no clever deception in her fear. She stumbled backward and put a hand on her horse—as much to steady herself as to keep the frightened beast from bolting.

"Give. Me. The horse," Kylar said.

So Ariel did the only thing she could do. She drew a sliver of magic and killed the horse. *That's two innocent beasts I've killed for Vi.*

Kylar leapt some inhuman distance into the woods as soon as Ariel touched her magic. But as the horse crumpled to the earth, she released the magic and raised her hands.

She didn't even see him move, but a second later Kylar was standing in front of her, the point of her knife an inch from her eye. Light! Had she thought she enjoyed this? Gambling futures looked different when your own was on the table.

"Why protect a murderer?" the black-sleeked demon asked.

"I'm trying to redeem Vi. I won't let you kill her until I've tried."

"She doesn't deserve a second chance."

"And who are you to say that, immortal? You get as many second chances as you want."

"It's not the same thing," Kylar said.

"I'm only asking you to save Logan first. If you don't accept my help, you'll be lucky to get to Cenaria this week."

The glowering mask disappeared into his skin, but he still looked furious. "What do I have to do?"

She smiled, hoping he couldn't see how her knees were trembling.

"Hold onto your trousers," she said.

47

Applying the last touches of kohl around her eyes, Kaldrosa Wyn looked deep into the mirror. *I can do this. For Tomman.*

She couldn't have said why, but she wanted to look perfect tonight. Maybe it was just that tonight would be her last night. Her last night whoring or her last night, period.

The costume was pure fantasy, of course. A Sethi woman would never wear such a thing on deck, but for tonight it was perfect. The trousers were so tight that she hadn't even been able to get them on until Daydra had laughingly told her that she couldn't wear underclothes beneath them. ("But you can see right through them!" "And your point is...?" "Oh.") For some reason, they exposed not just her ankles but even her calves—horrifying!—while the blouse was just as tight and sheer, with a lacy flounce at the wrists—ridiculous!—and down the front an open V that reached to her navel. Buttons on the shirt suggested it could be closed, but even if Kaldrosa could have stretched the tiny piece of fabric over her slender frame—she'd tried—there were no buttonholes.

Momma K had been very pleased with Master Piccun's work. She insisted that being scantily clad was sexier than naked. Tonight, Kaldrosa didn't mind. If she had to run, she'd be harder to grab in this than in skirts.

She came into the foyer and soon the other girls came out of their rooms. Everyone was working tonight except for Bev, who was too scared. Bev was pretending to be sick and was staying in her room all night. Kaldrosa almost panicked when she saw them. All of them looked fantastic. Every one of them had spent extra time on makeup and hair and clothes. By Porus' spear. The Khalidorans would notice. They'd have to notice.

Her suitemate, Daydra, who'd saved her more than once by calling for bashers when she heard Kaldrosa scream her codeword, smiled at her. "Here goes nothing, huh?" Daydra said. Daydra looked like a new woman. Though barely seventeen, she'd been a successful prostitute before the invasion, and tonight wasn't the first time that Kaldrosa saw why she had done so well. The woman glowed. She didn't care if she died.

"You ready?" Kaldrosa asked, knowing it was a dumb question. Their floor was going to be opened to clients in just a few minutes.

"So ready I've told all my girlfriends at the other brothels."

Kaldrosa froze. "Are you insane? You'll get us all killed!"

"Didn't you hear?" Daydra asked quietly, her face somber.

"Hear what?"

"The palies killed Jarl."

The breath whooshed out of Kaldrosa. If she'd held onto any slim hope for the future, it had been because of Jarl. Jarl and his radiant face, his talk of expelling the Khalidorans and going legitimate, of building a hundred bridges across the Plith and eliminating all the laws that bound the Warren-born and the slaveborn and former slaves and the impoverished to the city's west side. Jarl had spoken of a new order, and when he spoke, it sounded possible. She'd felt powerful in a way she never had before. She'd hoped.

And now Jarl was dead?

"Don't cry," Daydra said. "You'll mess up your makeup. You'll get all of us crying."

"Are you sure?"

"The whole city's talking about it," Shel said.

"I saw Momma K's face. It's true," Daydra said. "So you really think any lightskirt's going to rat us out to them? After they killed Jarl?"

The last door on the landing opened and Bev came out wearing her bull dancer costume, ponytails wired up into twin horns, midriff bare, and short pants. The dancer's knife at her belt didn't look like the usual blunted blade. Bev was pale but resolute. "Jarl was always kind to me. And I'm not going to listen to that damned prayer of theirs one more time."

"He was good to me, too," another girl said, choking back tears.

"Don't start," Daydra said. "No tears! We're gonna do this."

"For Jarl," another girl said.

"For Jarl," the rest of the girls repeated.

A bell tinkled that told the girls their guests were coming.

"I told some other girls, too," Shel said. "I hope that's all right. As for me, I get Fat Ass. He killed my first suitemate."

"I get Kherrick," Jilean said. Under her makeup, her right eye was still a puffy yellow.

"Little Dick's mine."

"Neddard."

"I don't care who I get," Kaldrosa said. She clenched her jaw so hard it hurt. "But I'm taking two. The first one's for Tomman. The second's for Jarl."

The other girls looked at her.

"Two?" Daydra asked. "How are you gonna do two?"

"I'll do what I have to. I'm getting two."

"Fuck it," Shel said. "Me too, but I'm taking Fat Ass first. Just in case."

"I'm in," Jilean said. "Now shut up. We're on."

The first man up the stairs was Captain Burl Laghar. Kaldrosa's heart stopped beating. She hadn't seen him since she'd moved in to the Craven Dragon to escape him. She stood frozen until he came to stand in front of her.

"Well, if it isn't my little pirate bitch," Burl said.

She couldn't move. Her tongue was lead in her mouth.

Burl saw her fear and stuck his chest out. "See? I knew you were a whore before you did. I could tell you liked it the very first time I banged you in front of your husband. And here you are." He smiled and was obviously disappointed that none of his sycophants were with him to laugh. "So," he said finally. "You happy to see me?"

Inexplicably, the fear vanished. It was just gone. Kaldrosa smiled impishly.

"Happy?" she said, grabbing the front of his trousers. "Oh, you have no idea." And she led him to her room. For Tomman. For Jarl.

That night, a gray-haired cripple climbed to the roof of the manse that had briefly belonged to Roth Ursuul but was now infested with hundreds of Rabbits. He balanced on his crutch in the moonlight and screamed into the night, "Come, Jarl! Come and see! Come and listen!" As the Rabbits gathered to watch the madman, a wind kicked up off the Plith. Tears shining in his eyes like stars, the general began reciting a dithyramb of hatred and loss. He sang a threnody to Jarl, a dirge for the hope of a better life. The words swirled with the wind and not a few Rabbits felt that not only the winds but the spirits of the murdered were gathering to the general's voice, rising with the cadences of vengeance.

The humbled general screamed and shook his crutch at the heavens as if it were a symbol of every Rabbit's impotence and despair. He screamed at the very moment the winds fell still.

The Warrens answered. A scream rose. A man's scream.

As if released by that sound, the winds roared. Lightning cracked against the castle looming to the north, and the light painted the general black against the sky. Black clouds covered the moon and rain lashed down.

The Rabbits heard the general laughing, crying, defying the

lightning, waving his crutch at the heavens as if conducting a wild chorus of rage.

Screams rose that night from the Craven Dragon as never before. Women who had refused to scream for their clients before now screamed loudly enough to make up for all their previous silence. Beneath those screams, the grunts and whimpers and soft cries and begging of dying men were never heard. Forty Khalidorans died at the Craven Dragon alone.

Momma K's plot had been for one brothel, after which she planned to smuggle the girls out of the city. It was supposed to make the Khalidorans think twice about brutalizing the working girls. But the plan, whipped up by the news of Jarl's death, spread like wildfire. One brothel owner invented a holiday as an excuse to serve lots of ale cheap to get his customers as drunk as possible. He called it Nocta Hemata. The Night of Passion, he claimed, smiling broadly at his guests. Another brothel owner who'd worked with Jarl for years confirmed that it was an old Cenarian tradition. The Night of Abandon, he said.

Across the city, fueled by drugged food and excessive drink, brothels celebrated an orgy unlike any ever seen. The air filled with shrieks and screams and wild ululations. Screams of terror, screams of vengeance, frenzied screams of blood lust and blood debts repaid. Men, and women, and even the small men and women in children's bodies who were the guild rats killed with savagery too terrible to comprehend. Bereaved men, women, and children stood over bloodied Khalidoran corpses and called upon the ghosts of their dead beloved to see what vengeance they had wrought, called upon Jarl to see what retribution they had exacted from the flesh of the enemy. Dogs howled and horses panicked at the feral smells of blood and sweat and fear and pain. Running men and women poured through the streets in every direction. There was too much blood for even the torrents of rain to wash away. The gutters ran red.

Soldiers arrived to find the doors of brothels adorned with dozens of small trophies, one cut from each rapist's body. But every brothel was empty of all but corpses. In the early hours of the morning, gangs of aggrieved husbands and boyfriends tore apart the drugged Khalidorans who had escaped the brothels and were wandering, trying to find their way out of the Warrens. Even the fully armed and lucid units sent to investigate wandered into ambushes. Rocks were thrown from rooftops in storms, archers picked off soldiers from a distance, and every time the soldiers charged, the Rabbits who had spent months learning to disappear did it again. It was like attacking ghosts, and every narrow twisting alley had a perfect place for an ambush. The Khalidorans who entered the Warrens didn't leave.

That night, the Godking lost 621 soldiers, 74 officers, three brothel owners who had acted as informants, and two wytches. The Rabbits didn't lose a soul.

Forever after, both sides would call it the Nocta Hemata, the Night of Blood.

Logan woke. He didn't move. He just let the fact wash over him until he was sure it was true. He was alive. Somehow, he had survived unconsciousness and delirium. Here.

He remembered snippets of Gnasher roaring, standing over him. Of Lilly putting a damp rag over his forehead. Between those fragments, like pus in a suppurating wound, were nightmares, garish beasts of his lost life, of dead women and gloating, ghoulish Khalidoran faces.

When he moved, he knew he wasn't out of the woods. He had a kitten's strength. Opening his eyes, he struggled to sit up. Around the Hole, he heard muttering. It sounded like everyone else was as surprised as he was. People who got sick down here never survived.

A meaty hand grabbed him and pulled him to a sitting position. It was Gnasher, grinning his fool's grin. A moment later he was kneeling, hugging Logan, crushing the wind out of him.

"Easy, Gnash," Lilly said. "Let him go." Logan was surprised when Gnasher actually let go of him immediately. Gnasher didn't listen to anyone but him.

Lilly smiled at him. "Good to see you're back."

"I see you made a new friend," Logan said, feeling jealous and guilty for it.

She dropped her voice. "You should have seen him, King. He was magnificent." She grinned her gap-toothed smile and rubbed Gnasher's knobby head. He closed his eyes, his filed teeth showing as he smiled broadly. "You did good, didn't you, Gnash?"

"Yehhss," he said, his voice rising oddly through the middle of the word.

Logan almost fell over. It was the first time he'd heard Gnasher speak.

"You can talk?" he asked.

Gnasher smiled.

"Hey, whore," Fin called from across the Hole. He had uncoiled most of his sinew rope and was adding a newly braided section to it. Logan saw that there were now only seven Holers left. "Time for you to get back to work."

"You'll wait'll I'm good and ready," Lilly said. "I haven't let any of 'em have a throw since you got sick," she told Logan.

"What's that sound?" Logan asked. He hadn't noticed it at first because it was so constant, but there was some sort of chipping sound and a low murmuring echoing down into the Hole from elsewhere in the Maw.

Before she could answer, Logan felt something shift in the air. The Holers looked at each other, but every face was blank. Something had changed, but no one could tell what.

Logan felt weaker, sicker. The air seemed thicker than it had been before, oppressive. He was once more aware of the stench and the foulness of the Hole—smelling it for the first time in months. He felt as if he were for the first time aware of the sludge covering the surface of life. He was being covered in filth and there was no escape. Every breath filled him with more toxins, every movement stroked more filth along his body, ground oil deeper into every pore. Just to exist was to let that scum be pressed into him, to let darkness pierce his skin so deeply that it tattooed him, making filth forever part of him, so anyone who ever saw him would see every evil he'd ever done, every unworthy thought he'd ever entertained.

He was barely even aware of the noise clattering through the Maw. Prisoners were screaming, begging for mercy. The screams spread and rose in pitch and desperation as the prisoners closer and closer to the Hole started joining the screaming. Beneath the high-pitched wails, Logan heard that clattering sound again, as of iron wheels grinding against rock.

Around the Hole, hardened murderers were curled into the fetal position, holding their hands over their ears, pressing up against the wall. Only Tenser and Fin didn't cower. Fin looked to be in raptures, his ropes lying limp on his lap, his face upturned. Tenser saw Logan staring.

"Khali has come," Tenser said.

"What is it?" Logan asked. He could barely move. He wanted to throw himself in the Hole to end the horror and the despair.

"She is god. The very stones here drip with a thousand years of pain and hatred and despair. The entire Maw is like a gem of evil and here is where Khali will make her home, in the blackest depths of unmined darkness." Then he began chanting, over and over, *"Khali vas, Khalivos ras en me, Khali mevirtu rapt, recu virtum defite."*

Tatts was next to Tenser and he seized the man. "What are you saying! Stop it!" He grabbed Tenser by the throat and dragged him to the edge of the Hole.

Instantly, black webs sprang up all over Tenser's arms and Tatts's eyes bulged. He choked. His mouth worked and his throat made little gasping sounds. He stumbled back from the Hole, releasing Tenser, and fell to his knees. Tatts's face was red, veins bulging in his neck and forehead and he gasped for no apparent reason.

Then he dropped to the ground, heaving great breaths.

Tenser smiled. "You great tattooed ass, no one lays a hand on a prince of the empire."

"What?" Nine-Finger Nick asked for all of them.

"I'm an Ursuul and my time with you is done. Khali has come, and I'm afraid she's going to be needing all of you. That is our prayer: *Khali vas, Khalivos ras en me, Khali mevirtu rapt, recu virtum defite.* 'Khali come. Khali live in me. Khali take this my offering, the strength of those who oppose you.' A prayer that is answered today. Khali is now a Holer. You will live in her holy presence. It is a great honor, though I confess, not one highly sought."

Above, Logan heard the sound of what could only be wagon wheels reach the third level of the Maw.

"Why are you here?" Nick asked.

"That doesn't concern you, though it is my doing that we're all still here." Tenser was smiling like this was the best thing that had ever happened to him.

"What?" Nick asked.

"You bastard," Lilly said. "You made the key not fit the lock. You knocked it out of my hand. You summoned Gorkhy, you fuck!"

"Yes, yes, yes!" Tenser laughed. He held a hand out and red light burst from it. The Holers shrank back, blinking eyes that hadn't seen light in months. The red light floated up through the bars high above.

Far down the hall, someone cried out, seeing the light.

Behind Tenser, Fin picked up a loop of his rope.

"Don't even think it," Tenser said. He grinned ghoulishly. "Besides, Khali's presence won't mean death for all of you. You, Fin, you may do very well in her service. The rest of you will do well to follow his example."

An old man shuffled into sight above the bars. The grate flipped open and Logan recognized Neph Dada. Before the Vürdmeister could see him, Logan scooted into his little niche.

Tenser rose through the air gently as the Vürdmeister's magic lifted him. He laughed all the way.

The grate slammed shut and Logan poked his head out. A spotlight of red light blinded him, pinned him in place. "Oh," Tenser Ursuul said, "And don't think I've forgotten you, King. I can't wait to tell my father that I found Logan Gyre hiding in the deepest depths of his own dungeon. He'll love it."

48

Garoth Ursuul was not pleased to see his aetheling. He hadn't summoned Tenser and despite all the precautions Neph Dada had taken—bringing Tenser to Garoth's private chambers and magically tearing out the tongues of any servant they passed so they couldn't speak of what they'd seen—this castle still had too many eyes. It was all too likely that someone had seen Tenser come. Certainly the prisoners in the Maw would have seen him leave.

In Garoth's estimation, there was an even chance that Tenser had just destroyed his usefulness. Garoth didn't like his aethelings to take liberties. No one made decisions for the Godking.

Tenser saw the displeasure on Garoth's face and hurried through the end of his story.

"I, I thought Logan might make a perfect sacrifice for Khali, may her name be revered forever, as she takes her new home," Tenser said, his voice quavering. "And I figured that by now Baron Kirof must have been captured...."

"You did, did you?" Garoth asked.

"He hasn't?"

"Baron Kirof plunged to death from a mountain pass, trying to escape," Neph said. "His body was not recoverable."

Tenser's mouth moved like a fish's as he tried to absorb the news.

"Your guilty verdict will have to stick," Garoth said. "It doesn't matter. These Cenarians have not appreciated my mercy anyway. They will be a lesson for future conquests. Your usefulness, boy, is at an end. The Cenarians are not pacified. You have failed your uurdthan."

"Your Holiness," Tenser said, falling to his knees. "Please. I'll do anything. Use me however you like. I'll serve with my whole heart. I swear. I'll do anything."

"Yes," Garoth said. "You will."

On his own merits, Tenser was nothing special. He'd survived his training, barely. But he was not a son of Garoth's soul. He never would be. He would never be his heir. But Tenser didn't know that. More importantly, Moburu didn't either.

"Neph, where is the virgin queen?"

"Your Holiness," the wizened Vürdmeister said, "she awaits your pleasure in the north tower."

"Ah yes." Not that Garoth had forgotten, but he wouldn't have Neph know how much the girl intrigued him.

"I could send for her immediately if it pleases you to sacrifice her," Neph said.

"The pair of them would be a nice offering for Khali as she takes her new *ras*, wouldn't they?" Garoth asked. But he wouldn't surrender Jenine, and he needed Tenser to distract Moburu. "My seed, I have . . . great hopes for you," Garoth said. "The death of Baron Kirof wasn't your fault, so it pleases me to give you a second chance. Go make yourself presentable so you look like my son, and then fetch this Logan Gyre. I won't have him escape from under my nose a second time. I will give you your new uurdthan anon."

As soon as the door closed behind Tenser, Garoth turned to Vürdmeister Dada. "Take him to the Maw and have him build a ferali beside his brother's. Help him and praise his work in front of Moburu. Do as much of it yourself as you must. Now send in Hu Gibbet."

*   *   *

"I'm not sure how this is going to work," Sister Ariel said. The woods were fully dark now, except for the light of her magic. "If I saw correctly, this form of magic should be especially easy for you to absorb. Just take in as much as you can."

"Then what?" Kylar said.

"Then you run."

"I run? That's the most ridiculous thing I've ever heard." *You speak when you should listen,* the Wolf's voice echoed in his head. He gritted his teeth. "Sorry. Tell me more."

"You won't get tired....I think. You'll still pay a price for whatever of your own magic you use, but you won't pay nearly as much for what you take from me," Sister Ariel said. "I'm ready, are you?"

Kylar shrugged. The truth was, he felt more than ready. His eyes were tingling the same way they'd tingled when he'd first bonded the ka'kari. He rubbed them again.

I'm getting more powerful. The thought was a revelation. He'd been learning to control his Talent better during his training on the rooftops, but this was different. This was different, and he'd felt it before.

He'd felt it every time he'd died. Every time he died, his Talent expanded, and something was changing in his vision, too. The thought should have been exhilarating. Instead, he felt the cold fingertips of dread brush down his naked back.

There must be a cost. There must be. Of course, it had already cost Kylar Elene. The thought made him ache anew. Maybe the costs were merely human ones.

The Wolf had spoken of Durzo committing a blasphemy even worse than taking money to die. Had Durzo committed suicide? Yes. Kylar was sure of it. Had it been just for curiosity? A lust for power? Or had he felt trapped? Suicide was impossible.

To a man as unhappy, as lonely, as isolated as Durzo had been, being bound to life would surely be odious. *Oh, master, I'm so sorry. I didn't understand.* And just like that, the raw wound that was Durzo's death tore open again. Time had done little to heal Kylar. Even knowing he had released Durzo from an existence he didn't want was no consolation. Kylar had murdered a legend, murdered a man who had given him everything, and he had done it with hatred in his heart. Even if Durzo had intended it as a sacrifice, Kylar hadn't killed him for mercy. He'd murdered him for raw vengeance. Kylar remembered the sweet bile of fury, of hatred for every trial Durzo had put him through, that bile had saturated him, kept him strong as he clung wounded to the ceiling of that tunnel in the stacks.

Now Durzo was truly dead, released from the prison of his own flesh. But it felt lonely and raw and unjust. Durzo's reward for seven centuries of isolation and service to some goal that he didn't understand shouldn't have been death. It should have been an unveiling of the worth of that goal. It should have been reunion and communion commensurate with seven hundred years of isolation. Kylar was just coming to understand his master now, and now that he wanted to make things right, there was no Durzo to make it right with. He'd been clipped out of the tapestry of Kylar's life, leaving an ugly hole that nothing could fill.

"I can only hold the full measure of my Talent for so long, young man," Sister Ariel said, sweat beading on her forehead.

"Oh, right," Kylar said.

A pool of concentrated light burned in Sister Ariel's hands. Kylar put his hand in it, willing the power into himself.

Nothing happened.

He brought the ka'kari up to the skin of his palm. Still nothing happened.

It was strangely embarrassing to look so inept. "Just let it happen," Sister Ariel said.

Just let it happen. That pissed him off. It was that falsely wise crap that teachers pulled. Your body knows what to do. You're thinking too much. Right.

"Will you look away for a sec?" he asked.

"Absolutely not," Sister Ariel said.

He'd done this before while wearing the ka'kari as a second skin. He knew it could be done.

"I can't hold this for much longer," Sister Ariel said.

Kylar drew the ka'kari into a ball in his hand and palmed it, holding his hand palm down over the pool of magic in the sister's hands. He thought it was quick enough she didn't see it. *Come on, please work!*

~Since you ask so nicely...~

Kylar blinked at that. Then the pooled magic winked out like a candle in a high wind. Kylar only had a moment to be unnerved before the thought was obliterated. Where the metallic sphere touched his palm, Kylar felt like he was holding lightning. He lost control of his body as it arced through him, freezing him in place, ignoring his desire to pull away—pullawaypullaway!—before he fried.

Sister Ariel was pulling back, but the ka'kari stretched between them, sucking magic like a lamprey sucking blood.

Kylar felt himself filling, gloriously filling with magic, with power, and light, and life. He could see the very veins in his hands, the veins in the few remaining leaves overhead. He could see life squirming and wriggling everywhere in the forest. He saw through the grasses to the fox's burrow, through the bark of the fir tree to the woodpecker's nest. He could feel the kiss of starlight on his skin. He could smell a hundred different men from the rebel camp, tell what they'd eaten, how much they'd worked, who was healthy and who sick. He could hear so much it was overwhelming, he could barely pull the strands apart. The wind made leaves clang against each other like cymbals, there was a roar that was the breathing of two—no, three large animals—himself, and Sister Ariel, and one other. The leaves themselves were breathing. He heard the heartbeat of an owl, the thunderous wallop of...a knee hitting the ground.

"Stop! Stop!" Sister Ariel said. She was slumped on the ground, and still magic flowed from her.

Kylar yanked the ka'kari back and took it into his body.

Sister Ariel fell, but he didn't even notice her. Light—magic—life—dazzled, bled, exploded from every pore on his body. It was too much. It hurt. Every beat of his heart scoured his veins with more power. His body was too small.

"GOOOOO," Sister Ariel said. It was ludicrously slow. He waited while her lips moved and the whisper thundered forth. "SAAVE…" Save? Save what? Why didn't she just say it? Why was everything so slow, so interminably, so damnably slow? He could barely hold himself still. He was bleeding light. His head throbbed. Another chamber of his heart compressed while he waited and waited. "THE…"

Save the king, his impatience supplied. He had to save the king. He had to save Logan.

Before Sister Ariel spoke again, Kylar was running.

Running? No, running was too pedestrian a term. He was moving twice the speed of the fastest man. Three times.

It was sheer joy. It was sheer moment, for there was nothing but the moment. He dodged and twisted, he looked ahead as far as his glowing eyes could see.

He was moving so fast that the air began to battle against him. His feet couldn't gain the traction they needed to push him faster. He threatened to leave the earth.

Then he saw a camp ahead, right in the middle of his path. He jumped and he did leave the earth. A hundred paces he flew. Two hundred. Straight at a tree.

He threw the ka'kari forward and jerked as he slammed through the three-foot-wide trunk. Wood exploded in every direction, but he kept going. Behind him, he heard the tree cracking and beginning to fall, but he was already too far away to hear it land.

So he ran. He extended the ka'kari before him so it cut the wind, extended it behind him so that it pressed his feet to the earth so he could run faster still.

The night faded, and he ran. The sun rose, and still he ran, a glutton devouring miles.

*   *   *

Sister Ariel crawled back to the tree where she'd bound Ulyssandra. It took a long time, but she had to. She wasn't sure if she slept that she would ever wake up. Finally, she reached Uly. The little girl was awake, her eyes red, tear tracks covering her cheeks. So she knew Kylar had awakened, and that Sister Ariel had concealed her, betrayed her.

There was nothing Sister Ariel could say. There was nothing either of them could do, anyway. Sister Ariel had loosed Vi and Kylar like twin hunting falcons. There was no calling them back now. If Uly were still here when Ariel woke, she'd take the girl to the Chantry. It would be a long trip, and it might give her some time to think about what she'd just experienced.

By all the gods, the boy had sucked her dry and still had room for more. Her! One of the most powerful women in the Chantry! He was so young, so blithe and terrifying.

It took all her willpower to unbind Uly. Touching magic now was like drinking liquor while hung over. But in a moment, it was done, and she collapsed.

49

Somehow, Logan had believed that there was something special about him. He'd had everything taken from him. His friends had been taken, his wife taken, his hopes taken, his freedom taken, his dignity taken, his naïveté taken. But his life had been spared.

Now that would be taken, too. The Godking wouldn't leave him down here. Logan had already died once and been resurrected. This time, Garoth Ursuul would want to see Logan die with his own eyes. There would doubtless be torture first, but Logan couldn't care.

If he'd been stronger, he would have tried one last desperate plan, but his fever had left him a shell. At the least, he could throw away his own life to kill Fin. He could have done it—before the fever. He'd just never been willing to make that sacrifice while he still had hope. He'd always wanted to preserve his own life, and so now he'd lost his life and gained nothing. Not even for his friends.

Logan brooded in the darkness. Mercifully, whatever Khali was, it had moved further away, and the smothering feel that had so suffused the Maw was now just a dull pressure. Everything that had seemed so unbearable about the Hole—the stink, the heat, the howling—was again familiar, if not comfortable.

"Bitch, come here," Fin said.

Lilly stood and patted Logan's shoulder. She whispered to Gnasher, probably telling him to watch over Logan, and then she left.

Of course she left. He didn't even blame her, though it made him feel even more empty and desolate. Lilly had to be practical. The sentimentality of all the books Logan had once loved died when it came within smelling distance of the Hole. Lilly was a survivor. Logan was going to be dead within an hour or two. Life went on. Logan's heart might blame her, but his mind couldn't. In any other circumstance, he would have condemned himself for eating human flesh.

Then Gnasher got up and walked away.

Do I reek so much of death? It wasn't fair to blame Gnasher and not blame Lilly, but Logan did. He suddenly hated the simple, misshapen man. How could he leave? After all he'd lost, Logan wanted to at least believe he had gained a friend or two.

Gnasher probably didn't even know Logan was going to die. He'd just gone to play with the end of Fin's sinew rope—Fin was too busy banging Lilly to pay him any mind. Logan looked at Gnash and tried to see him with pity. The simpleton was surely here for less reason than Logan was. He hadn't betrayed Logan, he just saw a chance to play with something new. Fin never let anyone touch his rope.

Logan smiled as he saw Gnasher sit down and grab the rope in both hands, squeezing it as hard as he could with all the concentration in the world, as if it were going to get away from him. The man truly lived in a different world.

Logan was aware of the other Holers staring at him. He could tell what they were thinking. King. He'd called himself King as a grim joke when he'd jumped down here—a stupid, insane joke, but the joke of a man who'd just watched his wife bleed to death. It was taking them some time to absorb the fact that it was all real.

Tatts stood and walked over. He squatted beside Logan. Beneath the grime that covered his skin, his dark tattoos looked like vir. He sucked at his gums and spat blood; the scurvy was getting to him, too.

"I would have liked it," Tatts said, speaking for only the third time

Logan had ever heard. "If you'd been the king. You got balls like no royal I ever heard of."

"Balls!" Fin paused in his rutting and propped himself up on his hands and laughed. He was a gruesome sight, sweating and dirty, his mouth bloody, the sinew rope half undone, half still wrapped around his naked body. "Someone else is gonna have his balls soon enough."

Logan looked away, still embarrassed to see Lilly doing what she needed to do to survive, so he almost missed it. Lilly shoved and Fin cried out and Logan saw him at the edge of the Hole on his side, precariously balanced, arms scrambling.

Then Lilly kicked him in the groin with all her strength and he fell in the Hole.

Lilly flung herself away from the coils of rope that snapped taut beneath her. Tied to Fin, coil upon coil disappeared down the Hole.

Gnasher's arms jerked out and his entire body jumped forward. Then again and again as the sinew rope jerked Fin to a stop, dropped again, stopped again, and then began unwinding at great speed as gravity uncoiled the rope wrapped around Fin's body.

Finally, Fin's body must have hit bottom, because the weight on the rope eased.

Lilly cried out and hugged Gnasher and kissed him. "You did perfect! Just perfect!" She turned to Logan. "You, on the other hand, could have been a lot more helpful."

Logan was stunned. He'd tried to think of ways to kill Fin for— well, for however long he'd been in this hell. Now he was just gone. Gone, and Logan hadn't done a thing.

"Now listen to me," Lilly said. "All of you. We're fucked. We always have been. We all done what we done, and ain't one of us worth trusting. But King ain't one of us. We can trust him. We ain't got but half a chance, and to have even that, it needs all of us."

"What're you asking?" Nine-Finger Nick asked.

"We had a key. Now we've got Fin's rope. But we got no time. I say we lower King and Gnash into the Hole. King cuz we can trust him and he saw where the key fell, and Gnash because he's the only one strong enough to climb back up the rope if he needs to. They go down and take a look around, see if they can find a way out from down there or find the key. One way or the other, it might give us a chance to get out before the palies come back."

"Why don't we all climb down?" Nick asked.

"Cuz we all got to hold the rope, idjit. There's no place to tie it."

"We could tie it to the grate," Nick said.

"Fin's body's still tied to it. We'd have to make a tower three people high and then lift Fin's body weight—it's impossible. After King goes and unties Fin's body, we can do that. Then all of us can get out. Or if there's no way out down there, he might find the key and we'll be able to make a rush up here."

"We'd have to go past that...thing," Nick said, fearful.

"Nobody said it was a good chance," Lilly said. "You want to stay, you die for sure."

Tatts nodded. He was in.

"I still say we lower someone else," Nick said.

"I got us the rope," Lilly said. "We do it my way or not at all."

"Come on, Lill—"

"Would you trust us to hold the rope with you on it, Nick? We let it go and we'd get your cut of the food."

That shut Nick up.

"Can you trust us, King?" Tatts asked.

"I trust you." *I don't have anything to lose.*

It took them a few minutes to explain it to Gnasher, and even then Logan wasn't sure the man understood. They got the rest of the Holers arranged holding the rope. Lilly stood at the front. She told the Holers that even if they let go, she wouldn't. If they wanted to keep her sexual favors, they'd better not let go.

"I owe you everything," Logan told her. Lilly was anything but a beautiful woman, but right now, she looked radiant. She looked proud of herself for the first time Logan had ever seen.

"No, I owe you, King. When you came down here, I told you to hold onto something good, but you're the one who showed me how. I'm more than this, no matter what I done. If I die now, it don't matter. I ain't good, but you are, and I'm helping you. No one can take that away. You just promise me, King, when you get it all back and go to your fancy parties, you remember. You're the king of us criminals, too."

"I won't forget." He stepped up to the edge to the Hole. "Lilly, what's your real name?"

She hesitated as if she almost didn't remember, then said shyly. "Lilene. Lilene Rauzana."

He straightened his back and spoke, "By the powers vested in our person and in our royal office, be it known that Lilene Rauzana is absolved of all crimes committed heretofore and that all penalties thereof are commuted. Lilene Rauzana is innocent in our sight. Let the record of her wrongs be taken as far as the east is from the west. So let it be written, so let it be done."

It was a ridiculous thing for a man in rags to say to a prostitute. Somehow though, it was right. Logan had never had more power than at this moment, when he had the power to heal. The Holers didn't even mock.

Lilly's eyes spilled tears. "You don't know what I done," she said.

"I don't need to."

"I wanna make it right. I don't wanna be like I been—"

"Then don't. As of now, you're innocent."

With that, Logan stepped into the Hole.

50

It turned out that Sister Ariel Wyant Sa'fastae had stayed in Torras Bend for several weeks, and the villagers knew her well. Though few people were comfortable having a Sister in their presence, she had struck them as scholarly, absent-minded, and kind. The description was an immense comfort to Elene. It meant the letter was probably legitimate.

That left her with a problem. Did she go north, toward the Chantry after Uly, or did she go west, after Kylar?

She'd decided she had to go after Uly. Cenaria wasn't safe for her. Her presence would make Kylar's work harder to accomplish, and she couldn't help him. The Chantry was safe, if intimidating, and Elene could at least make sure that Uly was safe—if not take her home.

So she'd continued north the next morning. Aside from nearly exhausting her small savings, a night in a bed had only seemed to remind her body of all its aches, so she wasn't making good time. She'd get to the Chantry faster if she made her horse go faster than a walk, but the very thought of a canter made Elene groan. The mare's ears flicked up, as if wondering what she was saying.

Then Elene saw the rider, forty paces away. He wore black armor, though no helmet, and he carried neither sword nor shield. He was hunched over in the saddle on a small, long-haired horse. The man's hand was pressed to his side, covering a wound, his pale face spotted with blood.

As Elene pulled her mare to an abrupt stop, he looked up and saw her. His lips worked but no words came. He tried again. "Help. Please," he said in a hoarse whisper.

She flicked her reins and came to his side. Despite the pain on his face, he was a handsome young man, barely older than she was. "Water," he begged.

Elene grabbed her water skin, then paused. The young warrior had a full wineskin dangling from his saddle. His pallor wasn't the paleness of blood loss; he was Khalidoran.

His eyes lit with triumph even as she dug in her heels. He snatched the rein nearest him. Elene's mare danced in a circle that the man's smaller horse quickly followed. Elene tried to jump out of the saddle, but her leg was trapped between the horses.

Then his mailed fist flashed. It caught her above the ear. She fell.

It was a descent into Hell. Logan was still too weak to do even half of the work in lowering himself, but Gnasher seemed content to do almost all of it, lowering them hand under hand. Logan just watched.

The first twenty feet was sheer black fireglass that made up the Hole, utterly smooth and featureless. Then the Hole opened up in an enormous chamber.

Iridescent green algae clung to the distant walls and gave off just enough light to see dimly, and it was as if they'd plunged into an alien world. The rotten-eggs smell was sharper down here, and puffs of heavy smoke rolled up toward them, obscuring Logan's view of thousands of stalagmites jutting unevenly from the invisible cavern floor. The howlers were quiet, and Logan prayed they would stay that way. Over the months, he'd lost his confidence that the sound was merely wind rising through the rocks.

Gnasher was beginning to breathe heavily, but he maintained the same pace, hand under hand. All around them except from directly beneath the Hole itself, stalactites glistened like icy knives and the sound of water dripping from their tips lay just beneath the rush of wind. The wind barely moaned as it rose from the depths.

They descended for two more minutes before Logan saw the first corpse. It was desiccated from the hot dry winds, but it must have been a Holer who had fallen, been pushed, or jumped decades or centuries ago. The body rested, impaled for so long on a stalagmite that the rock was growing over it, the stone slowly entombing the man.

Then there were others. Gnasher had to slow his descent several times to push off from stalagmites, and each time, they saw inmates who'd never had rope. Some were even older than the first, their bodies gashed from hitting several stalagmites on the way down. Some were missing body parts, having had them sheared off by the rock or fallen off through the years, but the slickness of the stalagmites had prevented rats from getting to them, and the sere wind had kept them from rotting. The only unrecognizable bodies were the few along the wetter areas by the wall that had become homes for the algae. These glowed green, like ghosts trying to pull out of the wall.

Finally, they began reaching ledges, most of them too far off to one side for Logan and Gnash to reach, but on one against a wall, he saw a corpse seated. His dried-out bones were intact. Somehow this man had lived through the descent, whether he'd used a rope or just fallen and been spared through some miracle. Then he'd died down here. His empty eye sockets stared a question at Logan, "Can you do better?"

Suddenly, the sinew rope shook. Logan looked up, but there was only blackness. His vision below was blocked by Gnasher.

"Let's hurry, Gnash."

The big man protested wordlessly.

"I know, you're doing great. You're doing fantastic, but I don't know how long Lilly can hold the rope. We don't want to end up like these guys, do we?"

Gnasher went faster.

They passed another ledge and Logan saw that the ground around the base of the stalagmites was thick with soil rather than bare rock. Soil? Here?

Not soil. Human waste. Generations of criminals had been kicking their feces into the Hole. Among the spires of rock, not all of it was dried, so the entire area smelled like an open sewer with rotten eggs mixed in.

Logan started to turn away when he saw something glint as they passed right next to another ledge. He looked again and couldn't see anything.

"Stop for a second, Gnasher."

Logan reached his hand into the six-inch deep layer of shit and groped around. Nothing. He pushed his arm in up past the elbow, ignoring the slime that oozed all over his skin. There.

He pulled out a lump of something and wiped it against his other arm. It was the key.

"Amazing," he said. "A miracle. We aren't going to die down here after all, Gnash. Now let's get to the bottom and untie Fin's body, then we can try to climb back up. They might even be able to pull us up."

As it turned out, they were close to the bottom, or at least another ledge. There was a steam vent nearby that billowed acrid smoke over them, obscuring everything below and killing the luminescent algae, so Logan couldn't see far enough to tell where they were. If, indeed, such a question had any meaning in hell.

Gnasher stopped and grunted. He stepped away from the rope, spreading his fingers out to ease the pain in them. Logan put his feet back on semisolid ground—the sewage here was only a few inches deep—with a sigh. He hadn't held nearly as much weight as Gnasher had, but he was still exhausted.

Then he saw the rope. It was loose.

"Gnasher," Logan called, his throat tight. "How long's there been slack in the rope?"

Gnasher blinked at him. The question didn't mean anything to the simpleton.

"Gnash, Fin's alive! He could be—AH!"

Something sharp stabbed into Logan's back and he fell.

Fin more fell than jumped on top of him. The convict moved like he'd dislocated his hip, and he was bleeding from his head, his mouth, both shoulders, and one leg. In his right hand, he held the broken, bloodied tip of a stalagmite. As he fell on Logan, he began slashing. He was injured and pitifully weak, but Logan was weaker.

Fin's sharp rock bit into his chest, gashed open his forearm as he tried to block, cut from his forehead past his ear. Logan tried to throw Fin off the ledge, but he was too weak.

There was a feral roar louder than the roar of a sudden eruption of the vent below them. Hot steam and fat drops of boiling water flew past them a moment before Gnasher hit.

He knocked Fin off of Logan and bit his nose, rising a moment later with a bloody chunk in his filed teeth. Fin screamed a bubbly scream. Before he could scream again, Gnasher grabbed Fin's dislocated leg, pulling him away from Logan.

The wounded man screamed again, louder, higher. He reached out, tried to grab anything to get away from Gnasher. Then Fin's body caught between two stalagmites. Gnasher either didn't see or didn't care. He had decided to pull Fin away from Logan, and that was what he was going to do. Logan saw the misshapen man's shoulders bunch, the muscles stringy knots of power. Gnasher braced his feet and roared as Fin screamed.

There was a rending sound as the dislocated leg gave way. Gnasher stumbled and fell as he ripped Fin's leg off and sent it sailing into the abyss.

Fin locked hateful eyes on Logan as he gasped his last breaths, his life's blood spurting from his torn hip, his face ghost-pale. "See you . . . in hell, King," he said.

"I've already done my time," Logan said. He held up the key. "I'm leaving."

Fin's eyes flared with hatred and disbelief, but he didn't have the strength to speak. The hate slowly left his open eyes. He was dead.

"Gnash, you are amazing. Thank you."

Gnash smiled. With his filed, bloody teeth, it was a gruesome sight, but he meant well.

Logan trembled. He was bleeding pretty badly. He didn't know if he'd make it, even if they ran into no problems getting out of the Hole and out of the Maw. But there was no reason for Gnash to die, too, or Lilly. And Gnash wouldn't climb the rope without him, he knew that.

"All right, Gnash, you're strong. Are you strong enough to climb out of here?"

Gnasher nodded and flexed. He liked being called strong.

"Then let's get out of this hell," Logan said, but even as he grabbed the rope, he felt a slackness in it. A moment later, the entire length of the sinew rope fell around them. There would be no climbing out. There would be no using the precious key. There would be no escape. The Holers had dropped the rope.

"Where the hell are they?" Tenser Ursuul demanded. The Holers barely recognized him in his fine tunic with his face shaved and his hair washed.

"Where do you think they are? They escaped," Lilly said.

"They escaped? Impossible!"

"No shit," Lilly said.

Tenser flushed, embarrassed in front of Neph Dada and the guards accompanying him.

A magical light bloomed in the Hole, illuminating everyone. It even dipped to the cutout where Logan had so frequently hidden. There was no one there.

"Logan, Fin, and Gnasher," Tenser said, naming those missing. "Logan and Fin hated each other. What happened?"

"King wanted—" Lilly started to say, but something cracked across her face and sent her sprawling.

"Shut up, bitch," Tenser said. "I don't trust you. You, Tatts, what happened?"

"Logan wanted to build another pyramid. He wanted to attract Gorkhy and see if we could grab his legs and get the key off of him. Fin wouldn't go for it. They fought. Fin threw Logan in the Hole, but then Gnasher attacked him and all of them fell in."

Tenser cursed. "Why didn't you stop them?"

"And fall in myself?" Tatts said. "Anyone who's tangled with Fin or Logan or Gnash gets killed, buddy—Your Highness. You were down here long enough to know that."

"Could they have survived the fall?" Neph Dada asked in his icy voice.

One of the newer inmates yelped and everyone looked at him. "No," he shouted. "Please!" A bright ball of magical light stuck to his chest and another to his back and lifted him over the Hole. Then he fell.

Everyone crowded around the hole, watching the light disappear into the darkness.

"Five...six...seven," Neph said. The light winked out right before eight. He looked at Tenser. "No, then. Well, I can't say your father will be pleased."

Tenser cursed. "Take them, Neph. Kill them. Do whatever you do, but make it painful."

$\mathcal{H}$u Gibbet crouched on the roof of a warehouse deep in the Warrens. In a more prosperous time, it had been used to store textiles. Later, smugglers had used it. Now, it was a crumbling ruin that housed guild rats of the Burning Man guild.

None of that mattered to Hu, except for the inconvenience of having to kill the ten-year-old boy who was standing guard. Or maybe it had been a girl. Hard to tell. The only thing that mattered to Hu was a slab of stone on the floor by one crumbled wall. It looked like it weighed a thousand pounds and it was as weathered as all the other stones, but it opened on hinges that not even the guild rats knew about. It was the second exit for one of the largest safe houses in the city.

Right now, if Hu's source was correct, the safe house held approximately three hundred whores, enough food and water to keep them for a month, and the real prizes: Momma K and her lieutenant, Agon Brant. Hu didn't expect those two to be here, not really. But he could always hope.

He always had trouble with the big jobs. A big job required such balance. The pleasure in so much blood threatened his professionalism. It was so easy to get caught up in the sheer joy of it—watching blood spill or dribble or spurt, blood in all its glorious hues, the red red blood fresh from the lungs, the black blood from the liver, and every shade in between. He wanted to bleed every body dry to please Nysos, but on the big jobs he couldn't usually take the time. It made him feel like he was doing things halfway.

Plus it always left him depressed. After he'd killed and bled thirty or thirty-two at the Gyre estate, he hadn't been the same for weeks. Even all the killing during the coup couldn't satisfy him. It was all a letdown. The Gyre estate had been the best. He'd still been in the estate when the duke got home. He'd watched Regnus Gyre run from room to room, mad with grief, slipping in the Nysos-pools Hu had left in every hall. He'd been so excited by watching that he couldn't even kill the duke, though he knew the Godking wished it.

He'd finished that job the next night, of course, but that had been nothing. Not even close.

This job wouldn't be too hard. There would be some tight moments early on. First, he had to get in. He'd kill the children if he had to, but guild rats were slippery. They knew every hole in the Warrens the size of a walnut and could fit into it with room to spare. It would be better not to give them the chance to warn anyone.

After he got in, there would be a guard or two on the back exit. It was an exit that had never been used, and there was only so long a man could stare at a wall before he got bored and tired, so the guards there might well be asleep.

Then Hu would need to kill the guards at the front exit without raising an alarm. Then he'd have to block or destroy the front exit. After that point, it wouldn't matter if the whores found out he was there or not. He could handle whores.

Then… well, the Godking had told him that he had twenty-four hours to do whatever he wanted. "Hu," the Godking had said, "make me a cataclysm."

The Godking planned to open up the place afterward and march every noble in the city through it. When the bodies were starting to get ripe, they'd start marching the rest of the city through it. The residents of the Warrens would go last. Then the Godking would have a public ceremony. People selected at random from among the Rabbits, the artisans, and the nobility would be sent into the massacre site. While they were inside, the Godking's wytches would seal the exits.

Garoth Ursuul expected it would provide a forceful deterrent to future rebellion.

But Hu felt uneasy. He was a professional. He was the best wetboy in the city, the best in the world, the best ever. He treasured that position, and there was only one thing that could threaten it: himself. He'd taken stupid risks at the Gyre estate. Idiotic risks. It had all worked out, but the fact remained that he'd been out of control.

There had just been too much blood. Too much thrill. He'd walked like a god through an orgy of worship that was death. He'd felt invulnerable during the hours he'd butchered the Gyres and their servants. He'd spent time displaying the bodies. He'd hung up several by their feet and cut their throats to bleed them to create that glorious lake of blood in the last hallway.

His job was to kill, and he'd gone dangerously beyond that. Durzo had been a killer. He took lives with the impersonal precision of a tailor. Durzo Blint would never have put himself at risk. It was why some people had considered him Hu's equal. Hu hated that. He was feared, but Blint was respected. His niggling worry was that the judgment was deserved.

That was why three hundred might be his undoing. The beast within would come out. Three hundred might be too much.

No. He was Hu Gibbet. Nothing was too much for Hu Gibbet. He was the best wetboy in the world. Tactically, this job wouldn't be nearly the challenge some other jobs had been, but when people whispered his name, this would be what they remembered. This would be his legacy. They would remember this all over the world.

The guild rats were all asleep, huddled together in clumps against the cold. Hu was about to drop through the hole in the roof when he saw something.

At first, he thought he was imagining it. It began as a whisper of wind, a puff of dust scattered in the moonlight. But the dust didn't settle, and there was no wind tonight. Still, the dust seemed to swirl in one place, gathering in one of the patches of moonlight in the warehouse near the children.

One of the children woke and gave a little cry, and in a second, every child in the guild was awake.

The whirlwind became a tiny tornado. Though there was still no wind, something was taking shape, black specks obscuring and spinning at a dizzying pace to a height of six feet. The tornado glowed an iridescent, scintillating blue. Sparks shot out and danced across the floor and the children cried out.

Taking shape through the tornado was a man, or something like a man. The figure flashed blue, spraying light in every direction, and not even Hu was fast enough to cover his eyes.

When he looked again, a figure unlike any he had ever seen stood before the children who were cowering wide-eyed on the floor. The man appeared to be carved from glossy black marble or shaped from liquid metal. His clothes weren't so much clothes as skin, though he appeared to wear shoes and was sexless, his whole body was unrelieved black and every contour was crisply defined. He was lean and every muscle was etched, from his shoulders to his V of a chest to his stomach to his legs. There was something funny about his skin, though. At first, the man or demon or statue made of flesh had reflected light like burnished steel. Now, only parts of him gleamed: the crescents of his biceps, the horizontal slashes of his abdominal muscles. The rest of him faded from glossy black to matte black.

Most frightening was the demon's face. It looked even less human than the rest of it. The mouth a small gash; cheekbones high; hair a disheveled, spiky black; brows prominent and disapproving above overlarge eyes out of a nightmare. The eyes were the palest blue of the coldest winter dawn. They spoke of judgment without pity, of punishment without remorse. As the figure studied the children, Hu became more and more certain that the eyes were actually glowing. Wisps of smoke curled out from them from whatever infernal fires burned within that hellish figure.

"Children," the figure said. "Be not afraid." There were gulps all around, and despite the words, every guild rat looked on the verge of bolting. "I will not harm you," the demon said. "But you are not safe here. You must go to Gwinvere Kirena, the one you know as Momma K. Go and stay with her. Tell her the Night Angel has returned."

Several children nodded, wide-eyed, but they all seemed frozen to the ground.

"Go!" the Night Angel said. He stepped forward through a shadow that cut the moonlight on the warehouse floor and an eerie thing happened. Where the shadow cut across the Night Angel, the demon disappeared. An arm, a diagonal slash of his body, and his head disappeared—except for two glowing spots that hung in space where his eyes should be. "Run!" the Night Angel yelled.

The children bolted like only guild rats can.

Hu knew that he should kill this Night Angel. Surely the Godking would reward him. Besides, the demon blocked Hu's entrance to his assignment. The Night Angel stood between him and more than three hundred succulent kills.

But it was hard to breathe. He wasn't afraid. It was simply that he didn't do jobs for free. He'd kill this angel, but he'd leave for now, make the Godking pay him for it. If the Night Angel knew about the underground chamber, it was already too late. If the Night Angel didn't know about the chamber, the whores would still be there tomorrow. He'd go get a contract on the Night Angel today and come back tomorrow and kill all the whores and the Night Angel too. It was completely logical. Fear had nothing to do with it.

The Night Angel turned his face up and as his eyes locked on Hu Gibbet's, they flashed from a smoldering blue to a fiercely burning red. In the next moment, the rest of the Night Angel vanished except for the burning red points of light.

"Dost thou desire thy judgment this night, Hubert Marion?" the Night Angel asked.

Cold dread paralyzed him. Hubert Marion. No one had called him that in fifteen years.

The Night Angel was moving toward him. Hu was on the verge of fleeing when the Night Angel stumbled. Hu stopped, puzzled.

The ruby eyes dimmed, flickered. The Night Angel sagged.

Hu dropped to the floor and drew his sword. The Night Angel drew itself up once more by an act of will, but Hu read exhaustion there. He attacked.

Their swords rang in the night, then Hu's kick blew through a block and connected with the Night Angel's chest. The creature flew back, its sword flying from its hand. It landed in a heap and began to shimmer.

In moments, the Night Angel was gone. In its place lay a man, naked, barely conscious.

It was Kylar Stern, Durzo's apprentice. Hu cursed him, his fear bleeding into outrage. It was all tricks? Illusions?

Hu stomped forward and slashed at Kylar's exposed neck. But his blade went completely through the man's head without resistance— shattering the illusion. Hu had barely stopped the slash when he felt a rope tighten around his ankles and yank him off his feet.

Fingers dug into his right elbow, hitting the pressure point and enervating his arm. A hand grabbed his hair and smacked his face against the floor again and again, breaking his nose with the first smack. On the third time, Hu's descending face came down on a rock. It ripped into his eye. Then he was rolling over and over.

He thrashed with all his Talent and hit nothing. Then his arms were behind his back and with a swift jerk upward, both shoulders were dislocated. Hu screamed. When he next thought to thrash, he found his arms and legs tied together.

From his remaining eye Hu caught sight of Kylar Stern, wobbling, clearly exhausted, but still pulling Hu across the floor by his cloak. Hu thrashed again, trying to kick something, anything, trying to stand.

Kylar dropped him on his back and Hu screamed again as it put pressure on his bound, dislocated shoulders. Kylar stood over him.

Whatever the black skin had been, illusion or something else, Kylar obviously didn't have the power to hold it now. He stood naked, but his face was as much of a mask as the mask had been. Hu gathered his Talent to try another kick.

Kylar's foot streaked down first, breaking Hu's shin. Hu screamed against the exploding blackness of pain that threatened to make him fall unconscious, and when he looked again, Kylar was kicking a section of the floor. It came open on unseen hinges. Inside, a hidden water wheel turned, driven by the flowing waters of Plith River. Hu realized it must be the mechanism that opened the huge door of the safe house, its mighty gears currently disengaged, spinning slowly.

"Nysos is the god of waters, right?" Kylar asked.

"What are you doing?" Hu shouted, hysterical.

"Pray," Kylar said, his voice pitiless. "Maybe he'll save you." Kylar did something with Hu's cloak. For a moment, nothing happened. Then the cloak tightened around his neck. It started dragging him across the floor.

"Nysos!" Hu screamed through the strangling tightness. "Nysos!"

The cloak pulled him into the water and for a long, blessed moment, the tension around his neck vanished. Hu kicked his good leg and found the surface. Then the cloak tightened and drew him into the gear. The disengaged gear pulled him out of the water by his throat and then flipped him over, dragging him back under the water again. He couldn't breathe. It dragged him out of the water again, flipped him again, and pulled him back under the water.

This time, he kicked as he came out of the water. It gave him enough slack to suck in a great breath, then he was flipped and plunged under the water once more. Hu tried to fight his bonds, but any pressure he put on his shoulders was agony. His arms were tied so tightly he couldn't pop his shoulders back into their joints and his good leg kicked against nothing but water.

He screamed again as he came out of the water, but the gear ground on. Up, down, up, down.

Kylar watched Hu Gibbet pulled from the water and then pulled under, over and over, sometimes begging, sometimes coughing up dirty river water. He felt no remorse. Hu deserved it. However Kylar knew what he knew, he knew that. And maybe it was as simple as that.

Swaying on his feet, Kylar looked for the switch to open the safe house. He hadn't been faking his exhaustion. He was just lucky that he'd had enough Talent left to fool Hu. In a fair fight, Hu would have taken him. Kylar had no illusions about that. But Durzo had taught him there was no such thing as a fair fight. Hu let himself be taken by surprise because he thought he was the best. Durzo had never considered himself the best; he just thought everyone else was worse than he was. It might seem like the same thing, but it wasn't.

Finally Kylar found what he was looking for. He grabbed a plank beside the rock and pulled it up.

The spinning gear slid sideways until its teeth met another gear's. They grated for a moment, then meshed together and turned. Hu was pulled inexorably out of the water one more time. He screamed. His head caught between the great teeth of the gears and his scream pitched abruptly higher. The gears stopped, straining.

Then Hu's head popped like a bloody pimple. His legs jerked spastically and his whole body arched out of the water. Then his corpse flopped to the side and the gears turned on, blood staining the water.

The enormous rock lifted, revealing a tunnel into the earth. An alarm bell clanged in the depths.

In moments, a pair of guards thundered up the steps, spears in their hands.

"Have to...evacuate," Kylar said. He wobbled and neither man made a move to help him. "Godking knows you're here. Tell Momma K." Then he passed out.

52

Feir Cousat huddled as much of his bulk behind a tree as he could. It was two hours before dawn, and the figure lying beside the fire had been still for hours. In just a few moments, Feir would know whether all his gambles had paid off.

His search for Curoch had taken him to Cenaria, through the camps of the Khalidoran highlanders, and into the mountains on the Ceuran border. His hope and his despair for weeks had been that he hadn't even heard a whisper of a special sword. That meant if he was on the right track, Curoch might be held by a man who had no idea what it was. That scenario was vastly preferable to the idea of trying to take it from a Vürdmeister. Any Vürdmeister with the ability to use Curoch would have the ability to kill Feir a hundred ways.

What was more likely was that he was on the wrong track. He'd made a dozen guesses as he'd narrowed his list of possibilities. First, he'd taken a Khalidoran uniform and stitched messengers' insignia on it and sat at lots of campfires. When they'd been in school, Dorian had taught him Khalidoran, so even when the conversation lapsed into the old tongue—all young Khalidorans were bilingual; the Godking thought they could better rule if they knew the schemes of those they conquered—he knew what they were saying.

Because they hadn't immediately found Curoch, and Feir guessed

rumors would have spread about that if they had, he figured someone must have taken the sword. He found the units that had done the
cleanup detail on the bridge. Most of the men had been from units
nearly destroyed in the fighting. Later they'd been lumped into a
new unit and sent home guarding the wagons taking loot back to
Khalidor—the very wagon train he and Dorian and Solon had been
following.

Because Dorian had sent him south, Feir knew that the sword
hadn't gone with the baggage train. So he'd asked after anyone from
those units who hadn't gone home, and he'd found one.

Finding where Ferl Khalius had gone was an entirely different matter. In fact, Feir had never found the man. Instead, he'd followed a
Vürdmeister who had been sent south. The Vürdmeister tracked Ferl
Khalius and Feir tracked the Vürdmeister. He'd watched the Vürdmeister throw missiles at Ferl Khalius and the lord he'd kidnapped.
The Vürdmeister lost interest as soon as the lord fell from the heights
of Mount Hezeron.

While the Vürdmeister used his signal stick to tell the Godking of
his failure, Feir had crept close. The falling snow and the concentration required to work magic had covered Feir's approach. As soon as
the Vürdmeister was finished, Feir killed him.

Then he'd done something he would never do again. He'd crossed
the broken ledge, in the snow. He'd jumped across a five-foot gap,
from slick snow to slick snow. There had been places steep enough
that his feet slid back as far as he climbed. He'd ended up using magic
to melt some of the ice just long enough to take a few more steps. He'd
made it, but it had been close.

Curoch was worth it.

He drew his sword and stepped forward in a modified *zshel posto,*
a fighter's stance for keeping balance and agility on slick ground. In a
few quick steps, he was over the man. His sword dipped and stabbed
through the figure's chest—a chest made of snow wrapped in a cloak.

Feir cursed and whipped around as the real Ferl Khalius charged out of the woods, Curoch held high. Feir barely had time to move. The highlander's slash would have cut through Feir, except that he had thrown himself to one side. As it was, Curoch knocked the blade from his hand.

"Naw much honor in stobbin' a sleeping mon," Ferl said with a thick Khalidor accent.

"The stakes are too high for honor," Feir said. He had thought the man had no idea he was being followed. "Give me the sword," Feir said, "and I'll let you live."

Justifiably, Ferl looked at him like he was crazy: he was armed, Feir wasn't. "Me give it ta you? This is a warchief's sword."

"A warchief? That sword is worth more than your entire clan and every other clan for a hundred miles put together."

Ferl didn't believe him, but he didn't care, either. "It's mine."

Three points of white light, each smaller than Feir's thumbnail, appeared before him and whizzed at Ferl Khalius. The man wasn't half bad, but there was only so fast anyone could move a sword.

The two missiles that Ferl blocked with the sword blasted off into the night. The third missile went right below Ferl's hands into his belly. Feir reached out with difficulty—magic at a distance was never his strength—and yanked the missile up. It burned a path to Ferl's heart.

The highlander fixed his eyes on Feir and toppled sideways.

Feir picked up Curoch without elation. He'd been right. All his guesses and gambles had paid off. If anyone ever heard this story, the bards would make it a legend. He'd just recovered one of the most powerful magical artifacts ever created.

So why did he feel empty?

It had been so easy this time. Slow, but easy. Maybe Ferl had been right. It hadn't been honorable, but when one person had Curoch, the fight was never fair.

But that wasn't it, either. He'd recovered this damn sword three times—three! He could be declared the Official Finder of the Blasted

Sword. He had it, but he could never use it. He was mediocre and he'd made the mistake of being friends with the great.

Solonariwan Tofusin Sa'fasti had been a prince of the Sethi empire. His Talent put him in the top ranks of all living mages. Dorian was another prince, a Vürdmeister and more. He was a magus of the kind that came along once a generation. Feir was a cordwainer's son with middling Talent and a good hand with a sword. He'd been an apprentice smith when his Talent had been discovered, and he'd later attended the Maker's school and then been hired as a smith and blades instructor at Sho'cendi, where he'd met Solon and Dorian.

Dorian had disavowed his birth, and neither he nor Solon had been officially granted any special treatment. But that, Feir knew, didn't mean they'd gotten no benefit from their noble birth. No matter what happened to Dorian or Solon, they knew that they were something special. They knew they mattered. Feir never had that. He was always second place, if not third.

The signal stick flashed and Feir pulled it out. The young Vürdmeister he'd killed had kept a translation key on him. Evidently it had been the first time he'd been entrusted with a signal stick, so Feir had been able to translate the flashes of light into letters, but they were still in code, and in Khalidoran. Breaking that code was simple. The first letter was its Khalidoran letter plus one, the second was the letter plus two, and so on. But the letters were spelled out rapidly, and Feir had nothing to write on, and his Khalidoran vocabulary was limited.

The Godking was using them exactly the way Feir would have. He was coordinating distant troops and meisters. It was simple and yet an enormous advantage. His commands were delivered instantly, while his opponents had to wait hours or days for messengers. In those days or hours, situations changed, plans changed.

No wonder he's devastated every army to come against him.

"Gather...north...of..." the signal stick flashed. Then it paused and the blue modified to red. What the hell did that mean? Feir spelled out the letters and on a hunch, transliterated them into Common.

"P.A.V.V.I.L.S. G.R.O.V.E." Pavvil's Grove. It turned blue and went too rapidly for Feir to catch, but it repeated one section twice. "Two days. Two days." Then it went dark.

Feir let out a long breath. He'd passed through Pavvil's Grove on his way south. It was a small logging town that produced some of Cenaria's only oak. There was a plain north of the town suitable for a battle. Clearly, the Godking had a plan to wipe out the rebel army there.

Feir could get there in two days. But it was still two hours until dawn. Did the Khalidorans count a day from dawn or from midnight? Did two days mean two, or three?

Feir cursed. He could break an obscure cipher in another language, but he couldn't count to three. Great.

The signal stick turned yellow—something it had never done before. "Vürdmeister Lorus report..."

Oh, no.

The stick flashed, "Why...going...south?"

Feir blanched. So the signal sticks didn't just communicate, they transmitted his position. That wasn't good.

"Punishment will...when you return." My punishment will be decided when I return? "...Lantano...rumored to be near you. Any sign?"

Feir wanted to grab his own ignorance by the neck and shake the life out of it. What was rumored to be near him?

"Vürdmeister? Lorus? Failure to respond will..."

Feir threw the stick away and scurried backward. Nothing happened. A minute passed. Still nothing happened. He was beginning to feel silly when the signal stick exploded with such force that it shook snow from the trees for a hundred paces.

Well, that'll wake the neighbors.

The neighbors. That wasn't a pretty thought. And Lantano? The name sounded familiar.

Feir climbed a rock hill nearby to get a better view of his surroundings. He almost wished he hadn't. Four hundred paces to the south an army was camped, with perhaps six thousand men. The usual camp followers added perhaps four thousand to that: wives and farriers and smiths and prostitutes and cooks and servants.

The army's flags bore a stark black vertical sword on a white field: Lantano Garuwashi's sigil. That was the name, Feir remembered: a general who'd never been defeated, a commoner's son who had won sixty duels. If the stories were to be believed, sometimes he fought with wood practice swords against his opponents' steel to make things interesting.

The neighbors had definitely heard the noise, and a knot of ten horsemen was riding toward Feir right now. At least a hundred others followed.

53

$\mathcal{K}$ylar opened his eyes in an unfamiliar room. It was getting to be an all-too-common occurrence. This rendition was small, dirty, cramped. The bed smelled as if the straw hadn't been changed in twenty years. His heart raced as he prepared himself for whatever might come next.

"Relax," Momma K said, coming to stand near his bed. It was a safe house doubtless, on the north side of the Warrens by the smell.

"How long?" Kylar asked, his voice a croak. "How long have I been out?"

"Nice to see you, too," Momma K said, but she smiled.

"A day and a half," a man's voice said.

Kylar sat up. The speaker was Lord General Agon. That was a surprise. "Well, looks like the huge new wall around the city isn't the only thing that's changed."

"Amazing what the bastards can do when they try something constructive, isn't it?" Agon said. He had a crutch and moved like his knee pained him.

"It's good to see you, Kylar," Momma K said. "The rumors have already started about how the Night Angel killed Hu Gibbet, but the only people who know that it was actually you are my guards. They've been with me a long time. They won't speak." So his identity was safe, but Kylar wasn't going to be distracted. He'd come too far, too fast, and given too much with only one thing in mind. "What do you know about Logan?"

Momma K and Agon looked at each other.

"He's dead," Momma K said.

"He's not dead," Kylar said.

"The best information we have—"

"He's not dead. Jarl came to tell me, all the way to Caernarvon."

"Kylar," Momma K said, "the Khalidorans found out who Logan was yesterday. As best we can tell, he either was killed by another inmate because of it, or he threw himself down the Hole to avoid what the Godking would do to him."

"I don't believe it." *Yesterday? While I was sleeping? I was this close?*

"I'm sorry," Momma K said.

Kylar stood and found a new set of wetboy grays piled on the foot of the bed. He began getting dressed.

"Kylar," Momma K said.

He ignored her.

"Son," Agon said, "it's time to open your eyes. No one likes that Logan's dead. He was like a son to me. You can't bring him back, but you can do some things that no one else can."

Kylar pulled on his tunic. "And let me guess," he said bitterly. "You two already have some ways you want to put my talents to use?"

"In a few days, Terah Graesin's army will meet the Godking's army just north of Pavvil's Grove. She'll get there first and have the advantage both of terrain and numbers," Momma K said.

"And the problem is?"

"That the Godking's going for it. After the Nocta Hemata, he should be twice as careful as he ever has been, but he's walking straight into this. Kylar, our spies have only caught hints, but I'm sure this is a trap. Terah Graesin won't listen. She wouldn't fight until the Godking presented her with a fight she couldn't lose. Now she has that, and nothing will stop her. All we know is that he's doing something magical, and it's big."

"Don't say it," Kylar said.

"We want to hire you for a hit, Kylar," Momma K said. "A hit worthy of the Night Angel. We want you to kill the Godking," Momma K said.

"You're insane."

"You'll be a legend," Agon said.

"I'd rather be alive." It was eerie. It was exactly what they'd wanted him to do before he left the city. It was exactly what Jarl had died to ask. Kill the Godking. Redeem all the pain and waste of his wetboy training. One kill, and he could hang up the sword, satisfied that he'd done more than his part. One kill that would save thousands. It had the feel of destiny.

"Even if Logan is still alive, it won't be any good to save his life if you let his only chance to have a kingdom be destroyed," Agon said. "If he's survived this long, he can make it for another day or two. Kill the Godking and save the kingdom, then go looking for our king."

Kylar selected weapons from the wide array Momma K had prepared for him, and secreted them about himself in silence.

"You'll doom us all," Agon said. "You have the kind of power I'd die for, and you won't use it to help us. Damn you." He turned on his heel and hobbled out of the room.

Kylar looked at Momma K. She didn't leave, but she didn't understand, either.

"It's good to see you again, too, Momma," Kylar said. He took a deep breath. "I left Uly with Elene. They're both going to be all right. I left them with enough money that they'll be taken care of for the rest of their lives. And Elene will love her. I did the best I could. . . . Jarl . . ." Suddenly, tears were hot in his eyes.

Momma K put a hand on Kylar's arm and he looked down.

"I know it doesn't make sense," he said. "But I swore to leave this behind me. I broke that vow for Logan. That cost me Elene's love and Uly's trust. I didn't abandon them so I could steal another life, but so I could save a life. Do you understand?"

"Do you know who you remind me of?" Momma K asked. "Durzo. When he was younger, before he lost his way. He would be proud of you, Kylar. I...I'm proud of you, too. I wish I could believe that the fates wouldn't be so cruel as to make you sacrifice everything just to find Logan dead, but I don't have that kind of faith. But I tell you what I do believe in. I believe in you." She hugged him.

"You're different," he said.

"It's all your fault," she said. "Next I'll go senile."

"I like it," he said.

She put her hands on his cheeks and kissed his forehead. "Go, Kylar. Go and please do come back."

Logan had fallen asleep twice now, each time expecting that he wouldn't wake up. He had stopped eating: he wouldn't touch Fin's body. He had stopped smelling the thick, corrosive air. He had stopped noticing Gnasher's little moues of concern. He had stopped bleeding, too, but it was too late. He had no strength.

After Gnasher had helped him sit up against a stalagmite, Logan saw another crushed body lying broken in the gloom not ten feet away. It was Natassa Graesin. The screams of the howlers didn't frighten her now. Her limbs were mangled but her face looked at peace. Her eyes held no accusation. They held nothing.

The most passion Logan could wake was simple regret. He was sorry for Natassa, who'd never even told him how she ended up down here. He was sorry for all the things he would never do. He had never truly desired the throne. He'd always suspected that being a king was far harder than it looked. In the Hole, he'd sometimes regretted that he wouldn't be remembered as someone who mattered.

Now, as he sat with his back propped against the stalagmite that would someday flow over his body and entomb him for eternity, he wished for simpler things. He missed sunlight. He missed the smell of grass, of fresh rain, of a woman. He missed Serah Drake and all her trivialities. He missed his wife. Jenine was so young, so smart, so pretty. She had been a diamond found and then lost forever. He missed Kylar, his best friend. Another diamond stripped away, found, and lost.

Logan wished for love and children and the running of his estates. A simple life, a big family, a few close friends. That would give him all the immortality he needed.

For a while, he prayed to the old gods. There was nothing else to do, and Gnasher wasn't much for conversation, but the old gods had nothing to say. He even prayed to Count Drake's One God. He wasn't sure how one was supposed to pray to the god of all things. Why would He care? Logan gave it up.

Mostly, he tried to ignore the pain.

He was about to close his eyes to try to die again—or sleep, whichever—when Gnasher started howling. It was a high, piercing, irritating sound unlike anything Logan had ever heard.

The vent belched acrid smoke, and the figure Logan glimpsed for an instant was devoured in the thick cloud and darkness. Then, as the cloud dissipated, a demon strode out of it.

For the first time Logan had ever seen, Gnasher showed fear. He retreated to Logan's side and crouched, whimpering, but that was as far as he would retreat. The simple man's loyalty knew no bounds.

The demon walked forward slowly, its glowing blue eyes fixed on Logan. Was this a howler? Or was this Death, finally come to claim him? Logan wasn't afraid.

"Well, shit, man," Death said with a familiar voice. "I thought I was going to have to climb all the way up the Hole to find you."

"What are you?" Logan croaked.

The demon's face shimmered and melted off of Kylar's face. Logan was sure he'd finally gone crazy.

"Sorry, I forgot about the face," Kylar said. He was half-grinning his crazy smirk to cover his concern. "You, ah, look like the south end of a northbound horse." It was one of Logan's old lines—gods!—from back when he barely knew a tenth of the curses he'd learned in the Hole. Kylar smirked again. "Is, ah, the big guy here going to be all right?"

Gnash was trembling all over, and even Logan couldn't tell if it was from anger or fear. "Gnash," Logan said, "he's a friend. He's here to help." Gnasher's expression didn't change, but he didn't move to attack. "It really is you, isn't it?" Logan asked.

"Here to save the day," Kylar said. When Logan failed to respond, he came over and checked Logan's body. The expression on his face was grim. "Well, what's one more miracle, huh? You're still kicking," he said to himself.

Logan felt himself drifting away from consciousness as Kylar helped him to his feet. Kylar was speaking, and part of Logan realized that he was just trying to keep Logan with him. He did his best to listen to Kylar's voice and ignore the voices of pain and death calling to him.

"...because it's damn near impossible to get into the Maw now. Not like the old days...they say someone or something has taken up residence. I mean, 'residence,' like the Maw's a palace or something."

"Khali," Logan whispered.

Kylar was taking them deeper into the Hole. Logan stumbled again, and when he opened his eyes, he found he was lashed to Kylar's back. That couldn't be right. Even with all the weight Logan had lost, Kylar shouldn't have been able to carry him this easily. But the sensation didn't fade. Kylar was picking his way farther and farther down. There was no path and no luminous moss down here, but Kylar moved surely, and kept talking, his voice itself warding off Logan's terror of the dark.

"...was in the Stacks once, and I remembered how the pipes seemed to go down into the very center of the earth. I figured that the Maw goes down and the stacks' pipes go down and they're right next to each other. I thought that if I went deep enough, the tunnels might connect.

"You ever seen the inside of those pipes in the Stacks, Logan? Sheer metal, going straight down just about forever. Big windmill blades spinning as they catch the rising air. I figured I could take the slow way down or the fast way. You know me, you can guess which I took. I grabbed a shield, made myself a little sled with hand brakes so I could steer a little. . . . I tell ya, it was a helluva ride. I almost made it all the way down, too. Good thing I'd lost most of my speed before that last fan. I was sure it was turning faster. I pity the poor bastards who'll have to climb down to fix it."

Then Kylar stopped. He breathed deeply. "I'm not going to lie to you. This is the bad part. We have to go under water. This is the line, Logan. This is what separates the Hole from the Stacks. The water's hot, and it's tight, and it's going to feel like you've been buried. I promise you, if you can make it through this death, you'll come out into a new life. You just hold your breath, and I'll do all the work."

"Gnasher," Logan said.

"Gnasher? Oh, the big guy? Uh, he doesn't look like he likes water much, Logan."

Logan couldn't see Gnasher. It wasn't just dark down here. It was utterly black. There wasn't even lighter blackness. It was a single, unalleviated, embracing darkness. It was hot, wet, heavy, oppressive darkness that seeped into his very lungs. He had no idea how Kylar was seeing Gnasher, but Logan wouldn't leave him here.

"Will you . . . come back and get him?" Logan asked.

There was a long silence.

"Yes, my king," Kylar said finally.

"I'm . . . I'm ready."

"You just count. I got through in about a minute. It might take us a little longer together."

A minute?

"Before we go . . . I'm sorry, Logan. I'm sorry for all of this and for how much of it's my fault. I'm sorry I didn't tell you what I was. I'm sorry that I didn't kill Tenser when I had the chance. I'm . . . just sorry."

Logan said nothing. He couldn't find the words and the strength to give Kylar what he deserved.

Kylar didn't wait. He began taking great breaths and Logan followed his example. A moment later, they plunged into the water together. Logan leaned close to Kylar's body, trying not to get in the way of his arms, trying to make his body streamlined in the water.

The water was hot, stinging hot, and clearly Kylar didn't mean for this to be a leisurely swim. Logan felt them turn upside down, and then Kylar must have been grabbing on to rocks to pull them down, because they were moving fast. In fact, they were moving faster than Logan thought was possible underwater. He knew Kylar was strong: he'd wrestled and sparred with him, but the speed they were moving shouldn't have been possible with the mass Kylar was pulling through the water.

Ten. Eleven. The water was pressing on every side, tight and constricting. Some part of Logan marveled that Kylar had done this already, alone, without any sure idea that the tunnels did connect, or how long of a swim it would be. At fourteen seconds, Logan's lungs were already burning.

He held on, trying not to hold on too hard, trying to preserve his strength. The pain was nothing, he told himself.

It was twenty seconds before he felt them level off. His back scraped against rock. It felt different, though he couldn't have said what sense told him so. He thought they had entered a tunnel, and from how Kylar was moving, it was a narrow tunnel.

Forty. Forty-one. Now the pain was undeniable. The air was pressing its way up his throat, begging for release. It hammered at him. Just a little release, just a little.

At fifty, they got stuck. Abruptly, all forward motion ceased. The shock of it made Logan open his eyes. Hot, sour water attacked his eyes and he coughed. An enormous bubble of life-giving air rushed from his lungs.

Kylar pulled and pulled. Logan felt something tearing, whether it was his ragged tunic or his skin, he didn't know, but then they were moving again.

He had less than half a lungful of air. Kylar was moving at incredible speed again, but they still weren't heading upward.

Then Logan felt Kylar turn, but his friend didn't push upward. Instead, in a frenzied motion illuminated with blue magical light, he drew a short sword from his belt. Logan was thrown this way and that as Kylar slashed and stabbed at something flashing like silver lightning in the water.

There was no way he could take any more. Kylar started moving upward, but Logan couldn't make it for another twenty seconds. He couldn't hold on that long.

At sixty-seven seconds, he let the last of his air go.

They were moving up so fast he felt it play against his face as they shot up. They passed the bubble.

His lungs burned. He surrendered and breathed.

Scalding water poured into his lungs—followed by air. Logan coughed and coughed and the hot, acrid stuff shot from his nose and mouth. It seared his sinuses, but a moment later, sweet cool air replaced it.

Kylar untied him and lowered him gently to the ground. Logan lay on his back, just breathing. It was still dark, but high overhead, up the metal tubes of the Stacks, he saw the twinkle of distant torches. After the black waters, it felt like stepping into a universe of light.

"My king," Kylar said. "There's something in the water. Some giant, terrible lizard. If I go back, I don't know if I'll return. You're in no shape to make it out alone. Without me, you'll die here. Do you still want me to retrieve the simpleton?"

Logan wanted to say no. He was more important to the kingdom than Gnasher. And he was afraid to be left alone. Life was suddenly so close, and he didn't want to die.

"I can't abandon him, Kylar. Forgive me."

"You'd only need forgiveness if you'd asked me to leave him," Kylar said, and then he dove into the water.

He was gone for five agonizing minutes. When he broke the surface of the water, he was swimming at such great speed that it carried him into the air. He landed on his feet. He'd made a harness of the rope and had pulled Gnasher behind him. Now he grabbed the rope and pulled it in rapidly.

Gnasher virtually flew clear of the water. He took a deep breath and smiled at Logan. "Hold breath good!" he said.

Kylar swept Logan into his arms as something huge broke through the water behind them. Something slapped into Kylar and sent all three of them sprawling.

Then the chamber was lit with iridescent blue light that came from Kylar himself. He was darting about, flipping from stalagmite to stalagmite, using them to change direction unpredictably. Fear clamped down on Logan's throat. Whatever Kylar was fighting, it was huge. Enormous webbed hands crashed through stalagmites like they were twigs. Rocks rained down everywhere as Logan curled into a ball. Great gusts of air burst from a maw visible only as the teeth and eyes reflected Kylar's blue fire. Silvery-green light blinked on and off.

The most terrifying thing was being unable to see. The battle raged mere paces away, and Logan could do nothing, not even observe it. He heard clanging and guessed it was Kylar's sword ringing off of the creature's hide, but had no idea. He had no idea how Kylar was fighting it at all in this pitch black, and no hope of fighting it for himself. He didn't even know how big it was, or what it looked like.

He lost sight of Kylar—or Kylar disappeared, because even the beast paused and snorted. It began sniffing the air, its huge head weaving back and forth.

Suddenly, it shot toward Logan and Gnasher. Logan threw his hands out and felt slimy hide rush past his fingers. Stalagmites crashed down everywhere. Then it pulled back and turned its head. A light as silvery cold as the moon bloomed in its green-marbled eyes and then the great snuffling head turned.

The slimy snout slid past Logan's cheek as the beast's head turned.

It sniffed and sniffed. Logan's fingers brushed a broken chunk of stalagmite and he grabbed it. The motion attracted the creature. It pulled back and the light from its eye illumined Logan like torchlight. The great cat's eye turned to him and came into focus.

Logan buried the jagged rock into that great eye and ground it back and forth. Luminous green-silver light spilled on Logan with the creature's blood. The eye went out like a blown candle and a howl filled the chamber, echoing back from the great distances all around. A moment later, a dark figure blurred past Logan and attacked the blind eye.

The creature shrieked again and thrashed backward. An enormous splash sounded, and then all was quiet.

"Logan," Kylar said, his voice shaking with the aftereffects of adrenalin, "was that...was that Khali?"

"No. Khali's...different. Worse." Logan laughed uncertainly. "That was just a dragon." He laughed again like a man set free from his senses. Then all light faded.

When he woke, the three of them had been fitted with harnesses, and Kylar was hoisting them all by a rope that must have been attached to a pulley high above. They were ascending the central shaft of the Stacks. It was a huge metal tube, thirty paces across, and all of the enormous fans had been stopped. How did Kylar manage that?

The trip took several more minutes, and the whole time, Logan was aware of his arm burning and tingling where the creature's eye blood had spilled on him. He didn't have the courage to look at it.

"We have a man inside who helped me," Kylar said. "The Sa'kagé is now one of your most important allies, my king. Maybe your only ally."

A few minutes later, they reached a section where the pipes turned horizontal. With great care, Kylar untied Logan and then Gnasher. He cut the ropes and let them fall into the abyss. The pulley followed. He led them down the narrowing horizontal section until they reached a door. Kylar tapped on it three times.

The door opened and Logan found himself face to face with Gorkhy. "Logan, meet our inside guy," Kylar said. "Gorkhy, your money is—" "You!" Gorkhy said. His face showed the same disgust Logan felt. "Kill him," Logan croaked.

Gorkhy's eyes bulged. He grabbed at the guard's whistle he carried on a lanyard around his neck. Before it reached his lips, though, his head spun free of his body. The corpse dropped without a sound.

It was that fast, that easy. Kylar dragged the body down the tunnel to drop it into the shaft and returned a minute later. Logan had just ordered his first kill.

Kylar didn't ask for an explanation. It was an eerie, awesome, awful thing. It was power, and it felt disconcertingly ... wonderful.

"Your Majesty?" Kylar said, opening the door out of the shaft, out of the nightmare. "Your kingdom awaits."

54

*W*hen Kaldrosa Wyn and ten of the other girls from the Craven Dragon emerged from Momma K's safe house, the Warrens were changed. There was a nervous excitement in the air. The Nocta Hemata had been a triumph, but repercussions were coming. Everyone knew it. Momma K had told the girls they needed to leave her subterranean safe house because the secret of its existence had leaked. Somehow, the Night Angel had saved them all from being slaughtered by Hu Gibbet.

Kaldrosa had heard rumors of the Night Angel before, right after the invasion, but she hadn't believed them. Now they all knew he was real. They'd seen Hu Gibbet's body.

Momma K had told them she would smuggle them out as quickly as possible, but moving three hundred women out of the city was going to take time. They had ways to get around or under the Godking's new walls, but it wasn't easy. Kaldrosa Wyn's group was supposed to go tonight. Momma K had told them that if they wanted to stay in the city, if they had husbands or boyfriends or family to go back to, all they had to do was not show up at the rendezvous tonight.

The Warrens were quiet, expectant, as the women made their way to the safe house. They were conspicuous, of course, all of them still dressed in their rich whoring clothes. Master Piccun's designs seemed obscene in the broad daylight, in the context of open streets. Worse, some of the girls' costumes were stained with brown-black smears of dried blood.

But the women passed no guards, and it was soon clear that the Khalidorans didn't go into the Warrens now. The residents who saw them looked at them strangely. One alley they tried to traverse was blocked by a building that must have been knocked down during the Nocta Hemata itself, and it forced Kaldrosa Wyn and the others to walk straight through the Durdun Market.

The market was busy, but as the former whores passed through it, a wave of silence preceded them. Every eye was on them. The girls set their jaws, ready for the derision their clothing would surely evoke, but nothing happened.

A stout fishwife leaned over her stall and said, "You done us proud, girls."

The women were caught off guard. The approval hit them like a slap in the face. Everywhere it was the same. People everywhere nodded in greeting and acceptance, even the women who a week ago would have sneered at rent girls even as they envied their good looks and easy lives. Even as the Rabbits waited for the Godking to crush them, as they knew he must, they shared a unity forged of persecution. The Rabbits had surprised themselves with their own bravery that night, and somehow, the whores bore their standard.

The gloriously solitary two-day ride to Cenaria had only one problem. There was no irritating child. No domineering hag. No verbal sparring. No humiliation. But the time gave Vi an opportunity to see how flimsy her plans were.

The first plan was to go to the Godking. It had seemed great for about five minutes. She'd tell him that Kylar was dead. She'd tell him Jarl was dead. She'd ask for her gold and she'd leave.

Right. Sister Ariel's musings about the spell on Vi were far too

specific to be guesses. They were also far too plausible. Vi would either
have a short leash or a long leash, but she'd have a leash. Garoth Ursuul
had promised to break her. It wasn't the kind of promise he'd forget.

In truth, Vi felt broken already. She was losing her edge. It was one
thing to feel bad for killing Jarl. Jarl had kept her alive. He'd been a
friend and someone who would never demand the use of her body. He
hadn't been a threat, physically or sexually.

Kylar was a different matter altogether, and yet even now, riding
slowly through the streets of Cenaria, her hood close around her face,
Vi couldn't stop thinking about him. She was actually sorry he was
dead. Maybe even sad.

Kylar had been a damn good wetboy. One of the best. It was a
shame he'd been killed with an arrow, probably from hiding. Not even
a wetboy could stop that.

"That's it," Vi said aloud. "Could happen to anyone. Makes me
realize my own mortality. It's just a shame."

It wasn't just a shame. That wasn't what she felt, and she knew it.
Kylar had been kind of cute. If you could think "kind of cute" with a
mental sneer. Kind of charming. Well, not that charming. But he did try.

Really, it was Uly's fault. Uly had talked and talked about how
great he was. Fuck.

So maybe she'd entertained a whim that Kylar could be the kind
of man who could understand her. He'd been a wetboy, and somehow
he'd left it and become a decent person. If he could do it, maybe she
could, too.

Yes, he was a wetboy, but he was never a whore. *You think he could
understand that? Forgive it? Sure. You go ahead with your little
crush, Vi. Bawl your eyes out like a little girl. Go ahead and pretend
you could have been an Elene, making a little home and having a
little life. I'm sure it would have been great fun to suckle brats and
crochet baby blankets.*

*The truth is, you didn't even have the courage to admit you had a
crush on Kylar until you knew he was safely dead.*

All the things Vi had always hated about women were suddenly showing up in herself. For Nysos' sake, she even missed Uly. Like some sort of fucking *mother*.

Well that was nice. Boo hoo. Do we feel better now? Because we still have a problem. She sat on her horse outside Drissa Nile's shop. The Bitch Wytch had said the weaves were dangerous, but Drissa might be able to free Vi from the Godking's magic. Looking at the modest shop, Vi thought the smart money was on the Godking.

The Godking would make her a slave. Drissa Nile would either free her or kill her.

Vi went inside. She had to wait half an hour while the two diminutive, bespectacled Niles took care of a boy who'd been splitting firewood and buried an axe in his foot, but after his parents took him home, Vi said that Sister Ariel had sent her. The Niles closed shop immediately.

Drissa seated her in one of the patient rooms while Tevor drew back a section of the roof to let sunlight in. They looked alike, baggy clothes over short, lumpy bodies, graying brown hair as straight as sheaves of wheat, spectacles, and single earrings. They moved with the easy familiarity of long partnership, but Tevor Nile clearly deferred to his wife. They both appeared to be in their forties, but scholarly Tevor seemed perpetually befuddled, while Drissa left no doubt that she was aware of all things at all times.

They sat on either side of her, holding each other's hand behind her back. Drissa rested her free hand on Vi's neck, and Tevor laid his fingers on the skin of her forearm. Vi felt a cool tingle in her skin.

"So, how do you know Ariel?" Drissa asked, her eyes sharp through her spectacles. Tevor seemed to have completely sunk into himself.

"She killed my horse to keep me from going into Ezra's Wood."

Drissa cleared her throat. "I see—"

"Gwaah!" Tevor yelled. He jerked backward and fell off his stool, smacking the back of his head against the stone of the fireplace.

"Don't touch anything!" As fast as he fell, he was on his feet again.

Vi and Drissa stared at him, baffled. He rubbed the back of his head. "By the hundred, I nearly incinerated all of us." He sat down. "Drissa, look at this."

"Oh," Vi said. "Ariel said it was trapped in some interesting ways."

"Now you tell me?" Tevor asked. "Interesting? She calls this interesting?"

"She said you were the best with small weaves."

"She did?" Tevor's demeanor changed in an instant.

"Well, she said Drissa."

He threw his hands up. "Of course she did. Damn Sisters can't admit a man might be good, not even for a second."

"Tevor," Drissa said.

He was abruptly calm. "Yes, dear?"

"I'm not seeing it. Can you lift it—"

She exhaled all at once. "Oh my. Oh my. Yes, don't lift it."

Tevor didn't say anything. Vi turned to see what his expression was.

"Please hold still, child," Drissa said.

For ten minutes, they worked in silence. Or at least Vi thought they worked. Aside from something like feather brushes on her spine, she felt nothing.

Finally, Tevor grunted as if satisfied.

"Are we done?" Vi asked.

"Done?" he said. "We haven't started. I was inspecting the damage. Interesting? I'll say it's interesting. There are three side spells protecting the primary spell. I can get them. Breaking the last one is going to hurt, a lot. The good news is that you came to us. The bad news is that by touching the weave, I've disrupted it. If I can't break it in perhaps an hour, it will blow your head off. You might have said it was a Vürdmeister who put the spell on you. Any other surprises?"

"What's the primary spell?" Vi asked Drissa.

"It's a compulsion spell, Vi. Go ahead, Tevor." The man sighed and sank back into himself. He didn't seem to be able to speak while he was working. Drissa, on the other hand, had no problem. Vi could see her hands beginning to glow faintly even as she spoke. "It's going to start hurting soon, Vi, and not just physically. We can't numb you to the pain because he's trapped that area of your brain. Numbing you is one of the first things a healer would do, usually, so he's made it lethal. Hold still now."

The world went white and stayed white. Vi was blind.

"Just listen to my voice, Vi," Drissa said. "Relax."

Vi was breathing quick, shallow breaths. Suddenly, the world returned. She could see.

"Four more times and we'll have the first spell," Drissa said. "It might be easier if you close your eyes."

Vi snapped her eyes shut. "So, uh, compulsion," she said.

"Right," Drissa said. "Compulsion magic is very limited. For the spell to hold, the caster must have authority over you. You have to feel you owe the caster your obedience. It would be worst with a parent or a mentor, or a general if you were in the army."

Or a king. Or a god. Holy hells.

"Regardless," Drissa said, "the good news is that you can throw off a compulsion if you can throw off that person's hold over you."

"Brilliant," Tevor said. "Bloody brilliant. Mad and sick, but genius. Did you see how he's anchored the traps in her own glore vyrden? He's making *her* sustain *his* spells. Horribly inefficient, but—"

"Tevor."

"Right. Back to work."

Vi's stomach muscles convulsed like she was throwing up. When it passed, Vi said, "Throw it off how?"

"Oh, the compulsion? Well, we should be able to break it this afternoon. It is a little tricky, though. If you try to untie it the wrong way, you just make it tighter. It won't be a problem for you."

"Why's—" Vi's convulsing stomach cut off the rest of her question.

"Magae are forbidden the use of compulsions, but we learn to protect ourselves from them. If you didn't have us, to throw off the compulsion requires an outward sign of an inward change, a symbol to show you've changed your loyalties. You'll have that covered too, as soon as you take the white dress and the pendant."

Vi looked at her blankly.

"When you enroll in the Chantry," Drissa said. "You do intend to enroll in the Chantry, don't you?"

"I guess," Vi said. She hadn't really thought about the future, but the Chantry would be safe from the Godking.

"Two. Ha," Tevor said triumphantly. "Tell her about Pulleta Vikrasin."

"You just like that story because it makes the Chantry look bad."

"Oh, go on, ruin the story," Tevor said.

Drissa rolled her eyes. "Long story short, two hundred years ago the head of one of the orders was using compulsion on her subordinates, and they didn't find out until one of the magae, Pulleta Vikrasin, married a magus. Her new loyalty to her husband broke the compulsion and led to several sisters being severely punished."

"That was the worst rendition of that story I've ever heard," Tevor said. He looked at Vi. "That marriage not only probably saved the Chantry, but in the twisted minds of those spinsters it also confirmed that a woman who married would never truly be loyal to the Chantry. I can't wait until the Chattel gather and—"

"Tevor. One more?" Drissa said. Again the little man went back to work. "Sorry, you'll get more than enough Chantry politics soon. Tevor's still bitter about how they treated me after we got ringed." She pulled at her earring.

"Is that what those mean?" Vi said. No wonder she'd seen so many earrings in Waeddryn. They were wedding earrings.

"Besides a few thousand queens out of your purse, yes. The ring-smiths tell women that the rings will make their husbands more submissive, and they tell men that they'll make their wives more, shall we say, amorous? It's said that in ancient times a ringed husband could be aroused by no woman but his wife. You can imagine how well they sold. But it's all lies. Maybe it was true once, but the rings now barely have enough magic to seal seamlessly and stay shiny."

Oh, Nysos. Kylar's note to Elene suddenly made a lot more sense. Vi hadn't stolen some expensive jewelry; she'd stolen a man's promise of his undying love. Vi had a sick feeling in her stomach again, but this time she didn't think it had anything to do with Tevor's magic.

"Are you ready, Vi? This one's really going to hurt, and not just physically. Lifting compulsion will make you relive your most significant experiences with authority. I'm guessing it won't be pleasant for you."

Good guess.

Drissa Nile was the only one who could help now. Logan was in bad shape. Getting him off of Vos Island had been easy enough, but it had taken time and Kylar wasn't sure how much of that Logan had left.

Logan had been stabbed in the back, and he had all kinds of cuts, including some along his ribs and arm that were red, inflamed, and filled with pus.

Few mages had made the city their home for the last couple of decades, but Kylar was starting to believe that the Chantry never abandoned any corner of the world. He knew of a woman in town who had a great reputation as a healer, and if anyone was a mage in the city, she was. It'd better be so; if anyone needed healing magic, it was Logan. Especially with that stuff on his arm.

Kylar wasn't even sure what it was, but it seemed to have burned its way into the flesh. The strangest thing was that it appeared not to have fallen randomly on Logan's arm, like he would have expected from gushing blood, but in a pattern. Kylar didn't even know if he should put water on, cover it, or what. Anything might make it worse.

And what the hell had that thing been? In repayment for the many cuts it had given him, Kylar had taken a fang from the beast, but his survival had been as much luck as skill. If there hadn't been so many stalagmites in the chamber, the creature's speed would have overmatched anything Kylar could do. Its skin was impregnable, even with all the strength of Kylar's Talent. He'd guessed that its eyes would be vulnerable, but it had already protected them from him three times before it got distracted by Logan and Gnasher. And the swim—that thing speeding after him under the water—had been sheer terror. He'd probably dream of it for the rest of his life.

Regardless, saving Logan was the best thing he'd ever done. Logan had needed to be saved, had deserved to be saved, and Kylar had been the only one who could save him. This was Kylar's purpose. This redeemed his sacrifices. This was why he was the Night Angel.

He crossed into the Warrens with his odd cargo and loaded them into a covered wagon. Then he drove to Drissa Nile's shop.

The place was in the wealthiest location in the Warrens, right off the Vanden Bridge, and it was fairly large, with a sign above it that read "Nile and Nile, Physickers," over a picture of the healing wand for the illiterate. Like Durzo before him, Kylar had avoided the place, fearing that a mage might recognize what he was. Now he had no choice. He pulled up in back of the shop, grabbed Logan from the bed of the wagon, and carried him to the back door with Gnasher following him.

The door was locked.

A small surge of Talent took care of that. The latch burst and wood splintered. Kylar carried Logan inside.

The shop had several rooms off a central waiting area. At the sound of the latch bursting through the frame, a man was emerging from one of the patient rooms where Kylar glimpsed two women talking before the physicker closed the door. A quick glance confirmed that the front door was barred, too.

"What are you doing?" the physicker asked. "You can't break in here."

"What the hell kind of physicker locks his doors in the middle of the day?" Kylar asked. As he looked into the physicker's eyes, he knew the man wasn't a criminal, but he did see something else, a warm green light like a forest after a storm when the sun comes out.

"You're a mage," Kylar said. He had thought that this man had simply been a front, a male physicker that Drissa Nile had used to take away the attention from her own too-miraculous cures. He was wrong.

The man went rigid. He wore spectacles, and the right lens was much stronger than the left, giving his suddenly widened eyes a disconcertingly lopsided appearance. He said, "I don't know what you're talking—" Kylar felt something brush him quickly, try to probe him, but the ka'kari didn't allow it. The mage never finished his sentence. "You're invisible to me. It's like—like you're dead."

Shit. "Are you a healer or not? My friend's dying," Kylar said.

For the first time, the man turned his bespectacled eyes to Logan. Kylar had thrown a blanket over the king to ward him from curious eyes. "Yes," the man said. "Tevor Nile at your service. Please, please put him on the table there."

They went into an empty room. Tevor Nile threw the blanket back and clucked. Kylar had laid Logan on the table face down. The physicker sliced open Logan's blood- and dirt- and sweat-encrusted rag of a tunic to look at the gash on Logan's back. He was already shaking his head.

"It's too much," he said. "I don't even know where to start."

"You're a mage, start with magic."

"I'm not a—"

"If you lie to me one more time, I swear I'll kill you," Kylar said. "Why else a hearth that size in a room this small? Why else the retractable section of roof? Because you need fire or sunlight for magic. I'm not going to tell anyone. You have to heal this man. Look at him. Do you know who he is?"

Kylar rolled Logan over, throwing away the rag of a tunic.

Tevor Nile gasped, but he wasn't looking at Logan's face. He was looking at the glowing imprint on his arm.

"Drissa!" he shouted.

From the next room, Kylar could hear the sound of the two women talking. "...you think? What do you mean you think? Is it gone or isn't it?"

"We're fairly certain that it's gone," a woman said.

"DRISSA!" Tevor yelled.

A door opened and closed and then their door opened and Drissa Nile's irritated face appeared. Like her husband, she had a wizened look, despite being maybe in her late forties. Both were small and scholarly, wearing spectacles and shapeless clothes. As with her husband, Kylar saw no taint of evil in her, but there was definitely that something extra there that he thought was magic.

Two mages married to each other. In Cenaria. It was an oddity, certainly, especially here. Kylar could only believe that it was the most fortunate oddity possible. If two mage healers couldn't fix Logan, no one could.

Drissa's irritation disappeared the second she saw Logan. Her eyes went wide. She came close and stared from his glowing arm to his face and back again in wonder.

"Where'd he get this?" she asked.

"Can you help him?" Kylar demanded.

Drissa looked at Tevor. He shook his head. "Not after what we just did. I don't think I've got enough power in me. Not for this."

"We'll try," Drissa said.

Tevor nodded, submissive, and Kylar noticed the rings in their ears for the first time. Gold, both of them, matching. They were Waeddryners. If it had been any other circumstance, he would have asked them if those damn rings really did hold spells.

Tevor drew back the section of roof to let the cloudy morning sunlight in. Drissa touched the wood already stacked in the hearth and it began blazing. They took up positions on either side of Logan and the air above him shimmered.

Kylar brought the ka'kari up within him to his eyes. It was like putting spectacles on a man nearly blind. The weaves over Logan that had been just barely visible to him were suddenly clear.

"Do you know herbs?" Drissa asked Kylar. At his nod, she said, "In the great room, get Tuntun leaf, grubel ointment, silverleaf, ragweed, and the white poultice on the top shelf."

Kylar came back a minute later with the ingredients, plus a few others he thought would be helpful. Tevor looked at them and nodded, but didn't seem capable of speech.

"Good, good," Drissa said.

Kylar began applying the herbs and poultices while Drissa and Tevor worked the weaves of magic. Over and over, he saw them dipping a weave as thick as a tapestry into Logan, adjusting it to fit his body, raising it above him, repairing it, and dipping it into his body again. What surprised him, though, was the way some of the herbs responded.

He'd never considered that normal plants might react to magic, but they obviously did. The silverleaf that Kylar had packed into the stab wound on Logan's back turned black in seconds—something he'd never seen it do.

For Kylar, it was like watching a dance. Tevor and Drissa worked together in perfect harmony, but Tevor was tiring. Within five minutes, Tevor was flagging. His parts of the weaves were getting shaky and thin. His face was pale and sweaty. He kept blinking and pushing his spectacles back up his long nose. Kylar could see the mage's exhaustion, but could do nothing about it. Critiquing a dancer was different from being able to step in and do better. That was what he wished he could do. He wasn't sure how he knew, but it seemed that Drissa was attempting smaller and smaller changes in Logan each time, and he still had some things terribly wrong in him. Looking at him through the healing weave, his entire body seemed to be the wrong color. Kylar touched him, and he felt hot.

Kylar felt impotent. He had Talent here. Talent to spare, even after everything, he still had Talent. He willed the ka'kari back, willed himself to be unshielded, tried to will all that magic into Logan. Nothing happened.

Take it, damn you. Get better!

Logan didn't stir. Kylar couldn't use the magic; he didn't know how to form any weave, much less one as complex as what the Niles were doing.

Tevor looked at Kylar apologetically. He patted Kylar's hand.

At the contact, light blazed through the entire room. It burned beyond the magical spectrum into the visual, throwing their shadows on the walls. The weaves over Logan, which had been flagging, dimming, fading into nothing just a moment before, now burned incandescent. Heat flashed through Kylar's hand.

Tevor gaped like a fish.

"Tevor!" Drissa said. "Use it!"

As Kylar felt the Talent flood out of him, he felt his magic all the way through Tevor being pulled down into Logan's body. It was out of his control. Tevor was directing Kylar's Talent completely. Kylar realized that Tevor could turn that magic to kill him, and having submitted like this, Kylar wouldn't be able to stop him.

Sweat broke out on Drissa's face and Kylar could feel the two mages working feverishly. They ran magic through Logan's body like a comb through tangled hair. They touched the glowing scar on his arm—still glowing, hours later—but there was strangely nothing wrong. It wasn't something they could fix. The healing magic moved right past it.

Finally Drissa breathed and let the weave dissipate. Logan would live, in fact, he was probably healthier than when he'd gone into the Maw.

But Tevor didn't let go of Kylar. He turned and stared at him, eyes wide.

"Tevor," Drissa said, warning.

"What are you? Are you a Vürdmeister?" Tevor asked.

Kylar tried to draw the ka'kari up to sever the connection, but he couldn't. He tried to ready his muscles with Talent strength, but he couldn't.

"Tevor," Drissa said.

"Did you see? Do you see this? I've never—"

"Tevor, release him."

"Honey, he could incinerate us both with this much Talent. He—"

"So you'd use a man's own magic against him after he submitted it to you? How do the Brothers look on that? Is that the kind of man I married?"

Tevor dropped his head and his hold on Kylar's Talent simultaneously. "I'm sorry."

Kylar shivered, drained, empty, weak. It was almost as disconcerting to get control of his Talent back as it was to give it away. He felt like he'd gone two days without sleeping. He barely had the energy to be excited that Logan was going to make it.

"I think we'd better see to you and your simple friend. Your wounds can use more mundane treatments," Drissa said. She lowered her voice, "The, ahem, king should wake this evening. Why don't you come with me to another room?"

She opened the door and Kylar stepped into the waiting area. Gnasher had curled up in a corner and was sleeping. But directly in front of Kylar was a beautiful, shapely woman with long red hair. Vi. She was staring at him down the length of a bare sword. Its tip touched his throat.

Kylar reached for his Talent, but it slipped through his fingers. He was too tired. It was gone. There was nothing he could do to stop her.

Vi's eyes were red and puffy like she'd just gone through a wringer, though how or why Kylar had no idea.

She stared down the length of steel for a moment that seemed to stretch and stretch. He couldn't read the look in those green eyes, but it was something wild.

Vi stepped back three measured and balanced steps, Valdé Docci, the Swordsman Withdraws. She knelt in the center of the room, bowed her head, pulled her ponytail to one side, and laid the bare sword across her hands. She raised the sword in offering.

"My life is yours, Kylar. I surrender to your judgment."

55

Seven of the eleven rent girls had left the safe house to see if they had families they could go back to. Six had come back, weeping. Some were now widows. Others were simply rejected by fathers and boy-friends and husbands who could see only whores and disgrace.

Kaldrosa's courage failed her; she never left the safe house. For some reason, she'd been able to face death. She'd emasculated Burl Laghar and watched him bleed to death, tied to her bed, screaming into a gag. Then she'd moved the body, put fresh sheets on the bed and welcomed in another Khalidoran soldier. He was a young man who'd always had sex first and afterward was half-hearted in the beatings and the invocation. He always seemed disgusted with himself. She asked, "Why do you do it? You don't like hurting me. I know you don't."

He couldn't look her in the eye. "You don't know what it's like," he said. "They have spies everywhere. Your own family will turn you in if you make the wrong joke. He knows."

"But why beat up whores?"

"It's not just whores. It's everyone. It's the suffering we need. For the Strangers."

"What do you mean? What strangers?"

But he wouldn't say any more. A moment later, he stared at the bed sheets. Blood in the mattress was soaking through the fresh sheet.

Kaldrosa stabbed him in the eye. The whole time, even when he came after her, bleeding, roaring, furious, she'd never been afraid.

Facing Tomman, though, that was too much. They'd fought bitterly before she left for Momma K's. He would have forcibly restrained her except that he'd been beaten so severely he couldn't get out of bed. Tomman had always been jealous. No, Kaldrosa couldn't face him. She'd leave with the others and go to the rebel camp. She didn't know what she'd do there. They were inland and nowhere near a river, so jobs as a captain would likely be scarce. In fact, if she couldn't obtain clothes that covered her up more, honest labor of any kind would be scarce. Still, after Khalidorans, being a rent girl for Cenarians might not be too bad.

There was a knock on the door and all the girls tensed. It wasn't the signal knock. No one moved. Daydra picked up a poker from the fireplace.

The knock sounded again. "Please," a man's voice said. "I mean no harm. I'm unarmed. Please, let me in."

Kaldrosa's heart leapt into her throat. She went to the door in a fog.

"What are you doing?" Daydra whispered.

Kaldrosa opened the peep window, and there he was. Tomman saw her and his face lit up. "You're alive! Oh gods, Kaldrosa, I thought you might be dead. What's wrong? Let me in."

The latch seemed to lift itself. Kaldrosa was helpless. The door burst open and Tomman swept her into his arms.

"Oh, Kally," he said, still delirious with joy. Tomman had always been a little slow. "I didn't know if—"

He only noticed the other women gathered around the room then, their expressions either joy or jealousy. Though he was hugging her and she couldn't see his face, Kaldrosa knew that he must be blinking stupidly at the sight of so many beautiful, exotic women all at the same time, and all of them scarcely wearing anything. Even Daydra's virginal dress breathed sensuality. His hug was slowly stiffening, and Kaldrosa was limp in his arms.

Tomman stepped back and looked at her. His hands flopped off of her shoulders like a fish onto the deck, spastically.

It really was a beautiful costume. Kaldrosa had always hated her skinny figure; she thought she looked like a boy. Wearing this, she didn't feel scrawny or boyish; she felt trim, nubile. The open-fronted shirt not only showed that she was tanned to the waist, but also conspired to give her cleavage and expose half of each breast. The scandalous trousers fit like a glove.

In short, it was exactly the kind of thing Tomman would have loved to see Kaldrosa wearing in their home—for the brief interludes that extended between when she surprised him with it and when he caught her after chasing her around the house.

But this wasn't their home, and these clothes weren't for Tomman. His eyes filled with grief. He looked away.

The girls went very quiet.

After an aching moment, he said, "You're beautiful." He choked and tears cascaded down his face.

"Tomman..." She was crying too, trying to cover herself with her arms. It was a bitter irony. She was trying to cover herself from her husband's eyes, when she had flaunted herself for strangers she despised.

"How many men have you been with?" he asked, his voice cracking.

"They would have killed you—"

"So now I'm not man enough?" he snapped. He wasn't crying now. He'd always been brave, fierce. It was one of the things she loved about him. He would have died to save her from this. He'd never realized he would have died and then she'd have had to do this anyway.

"They hurt me," she said.

"How many?" His voice was hard, brittle.

"I don't know." Part of her knew that he was like a dog crazed with pain, snapping at its master. But the disgust on his face was too much. She was disgusting. She surrendered to the deadness and despair. "A lot. Nine or ten a day."

His face twisted and he turned away.

"Tomman, don't leave me. Please."

He stopped, but he didn't turn. Then he walked out.

As the door swung gently shut, she began keening. The other girls went to her, their hearts broken anew as her grief mirrored theirs. Knowing she would not be comforted, they went to her because she had no one else who would, and neither did they.

56

Momma K stepped into the physickers' shop as Kylar swept the sword up into his hand, but she was too late to stop him.

Vi didn't move. She knelt motionless, her shiny red hair pulled out of the sword's path to her neck. The sword descended—and bounced off. The shock of the collision rang the sword like a bell. The sword whisked out of Kylar's nerveless grip.

"You will not do murder in my shop," Drissa Nile said. Her voice carried such power, and her eyes such fire, that her diminutive frame might as well have been a giant's. Even though Kylar had to look down to meet her eyes, he was intimidated. "We've accomplished an excellent piece of healing with this woman, and I'll not have you spoil it," Drissa said.

"You healed her?" Kylar asked.

Vi still hadn't moved. She faced the floor.

"From compulsion," Momma K said. "Am I right?"

"How did you know that?" Tevor asked.

"If it happens in my city, I know," Momma K said. She turned to Kylar. "The Godking bound her with a magic that forced her to obey direct orders."

"How convenient," Kylar said. His face contorted as he crushed the tears that were rising. "I don't care. She killed Jarl. I mopped up his blood. I buried him."

Momma K touched Kylar's arm. "Kylar, Vi and Jarl practically grew up together. Jarl protected her. They were friends, Kylar. The kind of friends that never forget. I don't believe anything less than magic could have compelled her to hurt him. Isn't that right, Vi?" Momma K put her hand under Vi's chin and brought her face up.

Tears streamed down Vi's face in mute testimony.

"What did Durzo teach you, Kylar?" Momma K asked. "A wetboy is a knife. Is the guilt the knife's or the hand's?"

"Both, and damn Durzo for his lies."

There was a knife on Kylar's belt, but he'd already tested its edge. Sister Drissa had blunted it, as he had guessed she might. But she didn't know about the blades up his sleeves. Nor could she stop the weapons that were his hands.

Vi saw the look in his eyes. She was a wetboy. She knew. He could get a knife out and across her throat in the time it took Drissa to blink. Let the healer try to cure death. Vi's eyes were black with guilt, a mishmash of dark images he couldn't comprehend. A short rush of black figures passed through his mind's eye. Her victims?

~She's murdered fewer people than you have.~

The thought hit him like a shot in the solar plexus. Some guilt. Some judge.

And the look on her face was all readiness above the tears. There was no self-pity, no avoidance of responsibility. Her eyes spoke for her: *I killed Jarl; I deserve to die. If you kill me, I won't blame you.*

"Before you decide, you have to know there's more," Vi said. "You were a secondary target. After.... After Jarl, I couldn't do it—"

"Well, that's commendable," Momma K said.

"—so I kidnapped Uly, to make sure you'd follow me."

"You what?" Kylar said.

"I figured you'd follow me back to Cenaria. The Godking wants you alive. But Sister Ariel captured me and Uly. When we found you, I thought you were dead. I thought I was free, so I escaped Sister Ariel and came here."

"Where's Uly?"

"On her way to the Chantry. Uly's Talented. She's going to be a maja."

It was horrifying and yet perfect.

Uly would be a Sister. She'd be taken care of, educated. Kylar had imposed Uly on Elene. Elene hadn't chosen to have a daughter who was more the age of a little sister. It wasn't a burden that had been fair for Kylar to ask her to assume. This way, and with the fortune that Kylar had left her, Elene would be free to have her own life again. It was all logical.

He had a niggling doubt that he wasn't thinking the way Elene would think, he could do nothing about that. Finding out that the damage had been minimized—hadn't it?—eased his mind.

A sudden fire lit in Momma K's eyes at the thought of her daughter being taken to the Chantry, but Kylar couldn't tell whether she was upset that her daughter had been taken or pleased that her daughter would certainly become a woman of consequence. Either way, Momma K quickly smothered it. She wasn't about to let strangers know Uly was her daughter.

If he got through this, Kylar would go to the Chantry and see Uly. He wasn't angry that they'd taken her from Vi. If anything, he owed them. And for a girl who was Talented, going to the Chantry wasn't really optional. It was supposed to be dangerous for a child to learn on her own. But if Uly didn't want to stay and they tried to keep her, Kylar would tear down the White Seraph around the Sisters' ears.

But just thinking about Uly made him think about Elene, and thinking about Elene threw his emotions into turmoil, so Kylar asked, "Why are you so eager to save Vi?" Momma K never worked on just one level.

"Because," Momma K said, "if you're going to kill the Godking, you'll need Vi's help."

Say one thing for Curoch: the mages are wrong. It wasn't in the form of a sword for purely symbolic reasons. The son of a bitch could cut.

It was a good thing, too. The sa'ceurai were implacable. They were called *sa'ceurai*, Old Jaeran for "sword lords," for good reason.

Nonetheless, Feir was a Blade Master of the Second Echelon. The first clash left three of the Ceuran warriors dead and gave Feir a short, tough pony.

Soon, Feir's height and weight proved a liability again. The pony tired and slowed. In the darkness, Feir let it go. Unfortunately, the little warhorse was trained too well. It stopped and waited for its rider the moment it was released. Feir solved that problem tying a small weave of magic under its saddle that randomly prickled. It would keep the beast running for hours. If he were lucky, the sa'ceurai would lose his trail and follow the horse.

He was lucky. It bought him a number of hours—hours on foot. It brought him to the crest of the mountain. He had cut a sapling before he'd hiked above the tree line, and now he was working on the wood with Curoch. The sword had an edge like he couldn't believe, but it wasn't a plane, or a chisel. Right now, he needed both and a few other tools besides.

Dorian once told him about a sport the more suicidal highland tribes practiced. They called it *schluss*. It consisted of strapping small sleds to one's feet and going downhill at incredible speeds. Standing. Dorian contended that they could steer, but Feir hadn't figured out how. All he knew was that he had to go faster than the Ceurans pursuing him, and there was no way he could build a full sled in the time he had.

What he couldn't accomplish with the blade, he accomplished with magic: he was a Maker, after all. Wood chips flew as the sun rose.

But he had skylined himself like a fool, standing right at the edge of the mountain so that his figure was clearly visible for miles. The sa'ceurai saw him before he saw them. They had dismounted and were walking on top of the snow with broad woven bamboo shoes strapped to their feet. The gait they had to assume to keep from tripping over the snowshoes was comical—until Feir realized how fast it let them travel. They would cover in a few minutes what had taken Feir half an hour lumbering through the snow.

He worked faster. He almost forgot to turn up the front tip of each long, narrow sled. He shook his head. He'd caught that mistake, what else had he missed? He didn't have time to fashion proper fasteners, so he wove a web of magic around his shoes and feet and bound them directly to the wood planks. He stood—

—and immediately caught an edge and fell.

Damn, why'd I square the edges? He should have left them curving like a boat's hull.

Standing was embarrassingly difficult. Feir cursed as the Ceurans came closer. He was a Second Echelon Blade Master—and he was this clumsy? This was madness. He should have just run downhill.

He rolled over onto his butt and finally used the length of the planks to lever himself into a squat. He stood and tried to step forward. The schlusses, which he had smoothed and polished, did exactly what they were supposed to do: they slid back and forth, and Feir barely moved.

Feir looked over his shoulder. The sa'ceurai were a bare hundred paces back now. If it came to a fight, the schlusses would doom him. He stumbled, caught an edge, and threw his foot to the side to catch himself. He staggered—and slid forward.

The joy was as great as he'd felt when he'd been named a Maker in the Brotherhood. He turned each schluss outward and pushed forward.

It worked until he got to the edge and started moving downhill faster than he could step. Each schluss went the way he had pointed it: out. His legs stretched until they could stretch no more and he pitched forward on his face.

The mountain was steep and the snow mercifully deep. Air was scarce as Feir flipped over and over through the powder. He was dimly aware that he needed to point the schlusses downhill. After six or seven rolls, it happened.

Suddenly Feir burst out of the omnipresent snow. The snow was at least three feet deep, but he was on top of it.

His heart was a thunder in his chest. He was headed straight down-hill at incredible speed. In moments he was going faster than the fast-est horse, and then faster and faster still. Controlling the two schlusses independently was almost impossible, so he quickly lashed them together with magic, both front and back, giving each a little leeway.

There were more crashes, and sometimes the snow wasn't as for-giving. Finally, Feir learned how to steer. He steered around a rocky death and looked downhill for the first time, squinting against the white. He blinked. *What is that line in the snow?*

He shot over the precipice. For two seconds, there was no schluss of sleds on snow. The world was silent except for the blast of wind in his ears.

Then he landed. He crashed through a world of white powder, flip-ping, arms and legs pulled every which way. Then the miracle hap-pened again and he popped out of the snow to fly downhill once more. His heart hammered. He laughed.

He had Curoch. He was safe. The Ceurans wouldn't follow him down the mountain. Doing so would put them in Cenaria. He'd escaped!

"Incredible," Lantano Garuwashi said. He was a big man for a Ceuran. His red hair hung thick and long with dozens of narrow sections of differently colored hair bound in. In Ceura, it was said that you could read a man's life in his hair. At a boy's clan initiation, his head was shaved bald except for one forelock. When the forelock had grown the length of three fingers, it was bound with a tiny ring and the boy declared a man. When he killed his first warrior, the forelock was bound again at the scalp and he became sa'ceurai. The shorter the span between the two rings on their forelocks, the better. Thereafter, when the sa'ceurai killed an enemy, he bound the slain man's forelock to his own hair.

At first, a few warriors had thought Lantano only had one ring, because his first two were right on top of each other. He killed his first opponent at thirteen. In the seventeen years since, he'd added fifty-nine locks to his own hair. Had he been born a little higher, all of Ceura would have followed him. But a sa'ceurai's soul was his sword, and nothing could change that Lantano had been born with an iron sword, a peasant sword. Lantano was a warlord because Ceuran tradition allowed any man of excellence to lead armies, but for Lantano it had become a trap. As soon as he stopped fighting, his power ended. He'd begun fighting for Ceura's regent, Hideo Watanabe. Then, when the regent ordered him to disband, he became a mercenary instead. Desperate men flocked to his banners for one reason: he never lost.

The giant was becoming a speck in the distance.

"War Master, do you wish us to follow?" a stump of a man with a score of locks tied in his balding hair asked.

"We'll try the caves," Lantano said.

"Into Cenaria?"

"Just a hundred sa'ceurai. It'll be a cold winter. Killing this giant will give us a tale to keep us warm."

57

$\mathcal{M}$omma K wanted Agon and his army to take Logan to the rebel camp. If he were to be king, he needed an army. Kylar refused to leave his friend, at least until Logan was conscious. When Kylar fainted, Agon asked Momma K if they should load Logan into the wagon. Momma K cursed and railed but said no.

They never asked Vi's opinion. She was content. She wanted to atone for what she'd done, but she didn't want to think.

Even as she sat with Kylar and Momma K and Agon, a part of her urged her to kill them. The Godking rewarded those who served him well. She could wipe out all the greatest threats to the Godking's rule in one minute.

She didn't obey that thought. She'd been judged innocent. She'd come completely clean.

Almost. She'd realized only lately that perhaps the most damaging thing she'd done to Kylar was something that had seemed trivial at the time, a small gesture of contempt. She'd pocketed the note and pair of earrings Kylar had left for Elene.

It was only today that she'd learned they were wedding rings. Drissa and Tevor had explained the custom at length. Between taking those and the note, Vi had left Elene with nothing.

She hadn't been brave enough to tell Kylar about that, had she?

It was just too much truth. She could have accepted Kylar killing her, but she didn't know what to do if Kylar despised her. If he knew her, he would despise her. There was no way love could overcome so much.

Love? What am I thinking? Limit yourself to fighting and fucking, Vi. You're good at those.

The door to a patient room opened and Kylar came in. Logan stepped in from another.

For the first time, Vi saw Kylar smile. It did something strange inside her when he smiled like that—and he wasn't even looking at her. He bowed deeply. "Your Majesty," Kylar said.

"My friend," Logan said. He was achingly thin, his bones poking at his skin. Despite that, he had an unmistakable aura of rallying health. Dressed richly once more, he was handsome despite his ordeal. He crossed the distance quickly and hugged Kylar.

"I'm sorry," Kylar said. "I came too late that night. I found blood and I thought...I'm so sorry."

Logan squeezed Kylar silently, heaving great breaths until the emotions died down. Finally, he stepped back and held onto Kylar's shoulders.

"You've done so well, my friend. I'm the one who's sorry. I'm sorry I ever doubted you. Someday soon we will have to talk. You—you did some things down there that..." Logan looked around, aware of the others. "That I'm really curious about. And I seem to have some holes in my memory, like how I got this."

He pulled back his sleeve and Vi and Momma K gasped. Sunken into his arm was something like a glowing silvery-green tattoo. He didn't show the whole thing, but to Vi the lines looked stylized and abstract, not random.

"Your Majesty," Drissa Nile said. "I would be...very cautious about showing that."

"I'm sorry to press you," Momma K said, "but we have to make some decisions."

"You mean I have to make some decisions," Logan said, his tone whimsical.

"Yes, Your Majesty, pardon me."

Logan addressed Kylar first. "You have done us greater service than we could demand or hope for. I won't order you, but we deem it most meet for . . ." He got a faraway look and let the sentence trail off.

"Sire?" Kylar asked.

Logan snapped back into the present. "Odd. I've been cursing with the worst of the Holers for months, and now I'm back to 'deeming' and judging what is 'meet.'" He shook his head and smirked ruefully. "Kylar, it comes down to this. If you can kill the Godking before our armies close for battle, we might avert battle altogether. I ask you to do this, but I won't order it. You've already made enormous sacrifices to save me. And I know that you don't trust this woman, but if she can help, use her help. Her surrender when she could have killed us is proof enough of her good intentions for me. Vi is as much a weapon as you are, and I can let none of the weapons in my small arsenal lie idle."

"You think that's the right thing to do?" Kylar asked.

Logan gave him a measured look. "Yes."

"Then it's done," Kylar said. "What are you going to do?"

"I'm going to ask Terah Graesin for my army. Then I'm going to take back our country."

"It won't be that simple," Momma K said.

Logan smiled a wan, distant smile. "It never is."

58

Elene woke with a blinding headache. She couldn't move her arms or legs; when she tried, her feet and hands tingled. Opening her eyes, she saw three other captives, bound hand and foot as she was. Another rope bound them to each other. They lay in the darkness, their forms lit only by the flickering light of the Khalidorans' fire. Elene lay nearest to the six Khalidorans, who were laughing and drinking, slipping between words Elene understood and what she guessed must be Khalidoran.

She didn't dare move too much and alert them, so all she could see of them was the young man who'd captured her. From the conversation, she picked up that his name was Ghorran. The others mocked him for getting hurt by some woman.

For a moment, the gravity of Elene's situation threatened to overwhelm her. Kylar didn't know she was here. No one knew she was here. No one was going to come save her. These men could do anything they wanted to her, and there was nothing she could do to stop them. Her chest tightened with fear and she couldn't think, couldn't breathe.

Then she started praying, reminding herself that the God knew she was here. It was a small thing for the God to save her. Eventually, she calmed. By that time, several of the soldiers had gone to their blankets to sleep, leaving Ghorran and someone she couldn't see talking in hushed tones.

"I don't think Vürdmeister Dada has even told His Holiness what we're doing," Ghorran said. "There's a reason Black Barrow is forbidden ground. If His Holiness finds out, what happens to us?"

"Neph Dada is a great man, and most zealous in his service of Khali. If he serves her, and His Holiness does not, whose side would you rather be on?" the other asked.

"I heard he wants to raise a Titan, is that what you're saying?"

The other man laughed quietly. "The Vürdmeister wants to do a hundred things. Of course he wants a Titan, but that isn't why he needs untouched young women, is it?"

"*Khalivos ras en me*," Ghorran said, awed. "Khali come live in me."

"Indeed."

"Is it possible?"

"The Vürdmeister thinks so."

Ghorran breathed a curse. "Then what about the boy? What's he for?"

"Mm, not that important. They'll kill him and see what they can raise from his body. The meisters just want the corpse fresh."

Elene had heard of Black Barrow; it was an ancient, dead battlefield. It was said nothing grew there to this day. But she couldn't understand any of the rest of it, except that Vürdmeister Neph Dada had something planned for her that was worse than slavery. She lay her head back down and saw that the captive nearest her was awake. He was a young boy. He looked terrified.

59

$\mathcal{M}$omma K had saved Logan's life today.

His little army, consisting of Lord General Agon, Momma K, and Agon's Dogs, was riding into the rebel camp to cheers. It would have been much different if Momma K hadn't planted rumors that Logan was returning after triumphing over the worst horrors of the Maw. Without the rumors as forerunners, the band would have been greeted as an unknown army, and Terah Graesin could have had Logan killed. Doubtless, many tears would have been shed afterward about the terrible mistake.

The old, naive Logan wouldn't have believed that Terah Graesin would do such a thing. Logan the Holer knew differently. He was a changed man, quieter, sobered. He knew all too well what people would do when they were threatened.

And Terah Graesin had to see Logan as a threat. She'd rallied support for the last three months. She'd survived assassination attempts and lost family members. She'd assembled an army and had brought it to the eve of battle. All to be queen.

Logan's appearance threatened to make her ambition implode on the eve of her triumph. His legitimacy was unquestionable: he'd come from the nation's leading family, he'd been declared the Gunders' heir, and he'd married into the Gunder family. Numerous families had sworn fealty to Terah Graesin only because they had thought they were free of their earlier oaths to the Gyres.

Any other time, Logan would have gone to Havermere and sent missives to all the families in the realm, including the Graesins. He would have given Terah a chance to see her coalition falling apart, and then offered her a suitable position.

This wasn't any other time. The rebel army was assembled less than a mile from the Godking's. The Cenarians outnumbered the Khalidoran army two to one. The Khalidorans had meisters and Vürdmeisters, but it still looked like a sure victory.

To Logan, Agon, and Momma K, it looked like a Cenarian massacre in the offing. So here he was, riding at the head of his tiny army of a hundred into the heart of the rebel camp.

He was lucky it was an overcast day, because after three months in the Hole, his eyes couldn't handle full daylight. Squinting didn't lend itself to a particularly regal look.

They were nearing the cluster of the nobles' pavilions when a group of a dozen horsemen rode out to meet them. They were led by an officer carrying an unstrung Alitaeran longbow like a staff. Logan and his army came to a stop.

"Declare yourself," Sergeant Gamble said.

"This," Agon said loudly enough for the man and the bystanders to hear, "is King Logan Gyre, by law and tradition heir to the throne and now king of our great land. The king is dead, long live the king."

It was a declaration of war, and the word would blaze through the camp within minutes. Momma K had already sent word to Logan's steward, and the Gyre men-at-arms were already positioned nearest the noble pavilions. They cheered.

"The queen will see you now, my lord," Sergeant Gamble said.

Logan dismounted in front of Terah Graesin's pavilion. When Momma K and Agon Brant made to follow him, the guards stopped them. "Only you, sir," one of them said.

Logan stared at the man. He said nothing. For a moment, he let the

beast rise within. He had not lived through hell to be stopped by a
guard. The feeling flew past determination to rage. He felt his forearm
tingle.

The guard stepped back and swallowed. "My lord," he said weakly,
"only nobles are—"

Logan stared at him and the words dried up. Momma K and Agon
followed him inside.

The queen's pavilion was huge. Tables and maps and nobles were scattered liberally around the interior. Some of the men looked positively
comical, their fat squashed into armor they hadn't donned in twenty
years. Black and white tiles sat in two bowls on one of the tables. *By
the gods, they're voting on their battle plan.* Beside Momma K, Brant
Agon made a strangled sound of outrage.

Momma K was looking around the room as quickly as she could,
counting allies, potential allies, and sure enemies. She knew she
could give Logan a crown if he gave her two weeks to work her special brand of truth. With only one day until a major battle against the
one enemy everyone hated, the odds changed drastically. Her only
hope was that someone disposable would attack her or Logan or Brant
Agon first. Then she could ruin him, and making an implacable foe of
him wouldn't hurt Logan too much.

"Why Logan Gyre, how the mighty have fallen," Terah Graesin
said, emerging from behind several taller lords, sashaying across the
luxurious rugs. "Who would have expected you to appear in the company of whores and has-beens? Or is it cripples and cunts?"

The nobles snickered.

"Looking to get into the business?" Momma K asked.

You could have heard a feather drop in the sudden silence. Momma
K couldn't care less about their shock. Terah Graesin had greeted
Logan with claws out. That wasn't good.

A young man pushed forward from the crowd. "If you speak like that again, I'll kill you myself," Luc Graesin said. He was Terah's brother, seventeen years old, handsome, and a damned fool.

Oh, Luc, you have no idea. I know your secret. I could end you right now.

Except that she couldn't. Here, now, wild truths delivered without prelude wouldn't be believed. Terah Graesin would only dig in her heels. "Pardon me," Momma K said, "Titles are switching hands so fast recently, I'd forgotten I was speaking to a duchess."

"Queen!" Luc said. "Your queen!"

Momma K lifted her eyebrows as if he were trying to put one over on her. A little reminder to everyone how far and how fast Terah Graesin was attempting to rise. "But here stands the rightful king," Momma K said. "Designated heir by King Gunder IX and received by common acclamation. The man to whom you've already pledged fealty." But she knew she'd already lost. She saw it in the defiance, the absolute hatred, in Terah Graesin's face.

"That's enough, Gwinvere," Logan said.

She smiled her acquiescence. She stepped back, her head down, abruptly meek.

"May I remind everyone," a voice near the maps said, "that tomorrow we face the Godking and his wytches?" It was Count Drake, ever the peacemaker.

"We need no reminders," Terah Graesin said. "We have our army, we have our battlefield, we have the advantage, and in a few more moments, we'll have our battle plan."

"No," Agon said.

"Excuse me?" Terah asked, indignant.

"You have His Majesty's army," Agon said. "My lords, many of you were there at the feast before the coup. Garret Urwer, your father died beside me in the north tower. As did your uncle, Bran Braeton. They died going to save our king, Logan Gyre. You were there—"

"Enough!" Terah Graesin cried. "We know what the mad king said."

So the king had been insane when he'd designated Logan his heir.

It wasn't a perfect line of attack, but it was good enough. Given time, Momma K would have reminded everyone of the timing of the coup, of the irrelevance of the king's sanity to the legality of his decrees, and of Logan's marriage to Jenine. Given time, Momma K could have orchestrated pressure from all sides to get Terah to surrender her claim. Now all that was immaterial. She simply had to wait for the inevitable.

"My lady," Duke Havrin Wesseros said, "they say only what would be said in backrooms and great rooms throughout the kingdom if there were time. It seems to me that we all have decisions to make now, and little time in which to make them."

"I won't hear their lies," Terah hissed.

"Don't you see?" Duke Wesseros said. "If you won't hear them out, Logan will leave, and he won't leave alone. He'll take half of our army with him, maybe more. Does anyone fancy taking on the Khalidorans with half an army?"

Closer. But you're worried about the wrong person leaving.

Agon said, "As you say, the king was mad when he died. The Sa'kagé poisoned him at the feast."

"Poisoned? You murdered him, Brant!" Garret Urwer cried out.

"Yes, I killed him," Agon said. "I won't justify that deed now. What's important is that Khalidor wished to wipe out the royal family to cause exactly this. They wished to split any resistance before it could begin. King Gunder saw that coming, which is why—not the night of the coup, when he was poisoned, but earlier in the day—he married his daughter Jenine to Logan. Many of you have sworn oaths to Lady Graesin. But your fealty was already owed to Logan Gyre. Thus, you're released from your oaths to the duchess."

"I release none of you!" Terah Graesin shrilled.

Pandemonium broke out. Nobles were screaming at each other, gathering in clumps to talk with their advisers and the lords closest to them, some pressing toward Terah Graesin, others pressing toward Logan. Logan watched it all, impassive. He understood, too.

"Hold on," Duke Wesseros said. He looked a lot like his sister

Nalia, the last queen. He'd been out of the city checking on lands the Lae'knaught had seized in eastern Cenaria when the coup had occurred. He raised his hands and gradually the nobles quieted. "The hour grows late, and an army waits for us," Duke Wesseros said. "Stand to the side of the man or the woman you would have rule us."

"Why don't you vote with the stones instead, that people may vote for who they truly wish to lead?" Momma K said. Inwardly, she cursed. She should have let one of the other lords suggest it, but Wesseros had brought up voting so quickly that Momma K hadn't had the chance. All the talk was worth nothing if they didn't have a blind vote.

"Tomorrow we must stand on the field of battle. I think today we have the courage to stand in a tent," Terah Graesin said. Clever bitch.

Silence fell again, and then people started moving.

Momma K had been depressingly accurate in her estimations of who would end up where. For the most part, the minor nobles looked like they would prefer to go to Logan but didn't dare defy their lords, which was why Momma K had wanted the blind vote. Terah had concentrated her bribes on the powerful.

As it was, they had a three-way split. Logan, Terah, and undecided.

"As I suspected," Duke Wesseros said. He led the undecided camp. "The rhetoric has done nothing. With the assassinations of the Gunders, only three great families are left in our country, and here we stand. It seems to me that there is a golden mean, a middle way. Logan Gyre, Terah Graesin, with the fate of all your countrymen at stake, will you put aside your own selfish ambitions?" The buffoon. The idiot. The pox-ridden windbag. He thought he was being smart. If the duke hadn't created a third camp, Logan at least would have had a majority. They would still have had a chance.

"What are you talking about?" Terah asked.

Logan already knew. Momma K could see it in his stony face.

"This night, on the eve of a battle that will determine the future of our land, will you split our forces, or will you join them? Logan, Terah, will you marry tonight?"

Terah looked around the room quickly, judging who stood with her. Her support was eroding. She looked at those who stood defiant on Logan's side, those who stood passive with Duke Wesseros. Then she looked at Logan. It wasn't the look a woman gives a suitor. It was a probe for weakness.

"For the country I love, yes," Terah Graesin said.

"Logan?"

"Yes," Logan said woodenly. Gods help him.

60

They had erected a platform so the entire army could see the wedding. Men had already gathered from their fires, and their officers were beginning to organize them into ranks for the ceremony as the moon rose. Besides the army, several thousand commoners and camp followers had crowded around the platform.

"Logan," Count Drake said, closing the flap of the little tent where Logan was getting ready, "You can't do this."

For a long moment, Logan didn't answer. When it emerged, his voice was low and stern, "What else can I do?"

"The One God says he will provide an escape from every temptation."

"I don't believe in your god, Drake."

"Truth doesn't depend on your belief in it."

Logan shook his head slowly, like a bear emerging emaciated after months of hibernation. "Marrying Terah is no temptation. My father married a beautiful, poisonous woman and I saw what it did to him."

"A lesson you would do well to heed. The difference being that your mother wasn't capable of nearly as much destruction."

Logan's eyes flashed, the bear slowly raising his head to tower above all others. "If there's a way out that doesn't destroy us, you tell me what it is! I don't want to marry—"

"I didn't say marriage was the temptation."

"Then what is?"

"Power," Count Drake said, thumping his cane.

"Damn it, man! It's marry her or doom us all. You think I haven't figured out a way to get the majority of these people to follow me? I have! I could take maybe two-thirds of them and leave. That would leave a third to die. You want me to ask thousands to die so I can avoid a bad marriage?"

"No, Logan." Count Drake leaned on his cane. He looked like he needed its support. "My question is, can you be the king that you need to be with such a queen beside you? Terah Graesin was caught off guard today. You caught her in a moment of weakness. That won't happen again."

"Well, thank you for illustrating the bleakness of my future," Logan said. "But if you can't help me escape it, help me get dressed."

"My king," Count Drake said, "sometimes the way out of a hole isn't climbing."

"Get out," Logan said.

Count Drake bowed and left sadly.

Logan lifted the circlet and put it on his head. Momma K had seen to it that he looked a king. He had been shaved, his hair cut, his body anointed with oils and adorned with furs. He was dressed in a fine dark gray tunic and cloak trimmed with white samite. He'd reached the age of majority immediately before the coup, but he'd forgotten to choose his own sigil. Now he saw that Momma K had chosen one for him. It incorporated the Gyres' white gyrfalcon on a field sable, but his falcon wore broken chains on its feet, and the sable field was a black circle reminiscent of the Hole. The gyrfalcon's wings were spread. It was a worthy sigil. His father would have been proud.

What would you do, father? As a young man, his father had married to save the family. With the benefit of hindsight, would he have done it again?

The tent flap opened and Momma K stepped inside. She looked at him with a shallow but genuine compassion. She couldn't understand.

She'd never loved as Logan had loved. To her, it must look like this was the obvious choice. Marry Terah, deal with the problems later. In his position, Momma K would scheme and manipulate and have Terah killed if it came to it.

"It's time," she said.

"The sigil is perfect," Logan said. "Thank you."

"Did you notice the wings?" she asked. "The wingtips extend beyond the circle, Your Majesty. The gyrfalcon will always fly free."

Together, they walked up onto the platform. It was a circle almost the same size as the Hole. It was a circle to symbolize the perfect, eternal, unbreakable nature of marriage. As Logan climbed, with thousands of eyes turned on him, to take his place right at the center, where the fall to death had been, his heart lurched. He felt sick, claustrophobic. He remembered stretching over the Hole, stretching as far as he could. For what? For pissed-on bread he wouldn't give to an animal.

Music began playing and his pissed-on bread stepped up daintily onto the platform.

Part of Logan was ravenous for her, as he had been ravenous in the Hole. For the past three months, he'd been so weak, so starved, so preoccupied with surviving that he'd barely spared a thought for sex. Before the Hole, it seemed he'd barely spared a thought for anything else. Now that he was out and regaining his strength, that old Logan was coming back. Terah Graesin was tall and lithe, her curves almost boyish, but her smile was all woman. She moved like a woman who knew what men liked and knew that she had it. The starving, greedy part of Logan wanted to fuck her.

And pissed-on bread always looked so good, until you tasted it. But at least it filled you up, no matter how you felt about it afterward. At least he'd have sex. By all the gods; at twenty-one, he was still a fucking virgin!

The irony of the thought made him smile grimly. Terah saw the smile and smiled back. She did look fantastic. Her hair was teased up into—well, something fancy. Logan wondered how many tailors had been cursing at each other for the last two hours as they'd somehow altered one of her dresses into a wedding dress. It was the traditional green of fertility and new life, slim cut to Terah's slim body, with ornate groom ties up the back, and a long expanse of leg exposed that was certainly not traditional but welcome nonetheless. It was completed with a stylish veil symbolizing chastity that worked perfectly with the dress, if not so well with the woman in it.

Well, I'll have as much sex as I want, if her reputation is at all deserved. The thought sloshed in his stomach like warm piss. No, better not to think about her reputation.

Whatever he felt, Terah Graesin somehow pulled off what he had thought was impossible. She was sexy and regal at the same time—to her it was all power, whether it came from her status or her personality or her body. They were all tools to impose her will.

Power. Count Drake said the temptation was power.

Terah came to stand beside him and took his hand shyly. The people cheered. It was just like Jenine Gunder had taken his hand when her father had announced their marriage. Logan swallowed his rising gorge. For Jenine, it had been a spontaneous act. Terah had been at that dinner. She'd seen what Jenine had done and how people had approved. She was imitating Jenine deliberately.

"Relax," Terah said. "You're five minutes away from everything you ever wanted."

You're a fool if you believe that, Terah. Logan painted a smile on his face and willed his body to relax. No, it wasn't what he would have chosen, but he would be able to change everything. He could defeat King Ursuul. He could root out the Sa'kagé. He could abolish the poor laws. He could...

That was it. That was what Count Drake meant. That was the temptation of power. He'd turned his ambition in his own mind. *It isn't for me,* he'd told himself, *it's for the people.* But that wasn't altogether true, was it? He'd liked ordering Gorkhy's death; he'd liked dismissing the count: Logan spoke and things happened. People obeyed. He'd been so powerless for so long in the Hole that the idea of never being subject to anyone was honey on his tongue.

Fine, Count Drake, I understand. Now where's the way out?

It was too late. On one side stood a hecatonarch in his rich cloak—a hundred colors for the hundred gods. On the other stood a man in simple brown robes, a patr of the One God. Duke Wesseros took his place in the middle. Terah had made sure that their marriage would be performed in triplicate. The cheering crescendoed as fifteen thousand people shouted themselves hoarse for the couple they thought would save them.

"May I address the people?" Logan asked.

"Absolutely not," Terah said. "What kind of a ploy is this?"

"It's not a ploy. I just wish to speak to those who will bleed and die for us. I haven't had the chance to do that."

"You're going to set them against me," Terah said.

"How about," Duke Wesseros said, "how about Logan swears not to say anything negative about you? And if he does, I'll step in and stop him? Is that acceptable, my lord?"

"Yes."

"My lady?" Duke Wesseros said. "He is their king."

"Make it quick."

"Logan, five minutes," Duke Wesseros said. He stepped close and lowered his voice. "And may the spirit of Timaeus Rindder inspire you."

It was a contingent declaration of support. Timaeus Rindder had been an orator of such skill he'd turned a chariot race loss into a coup, though he had been bound by exactly the restrictions that Duke Wesseros had put on Logan. In framing the rules the way he had, Duke Wesseros was saying, "If you can get the people on your side, I'll come, too."

"My friends, tomorrow we will stand together in the clash and roar of battle." Logan had barely spoken the first sentence when his words were doubled and redoubled in volume. He paused, then saw Master Nile standing near the front, smiling. Logan pretended that it wasn't important, and in a moment, everyone else did, too. "Tomorrow, we will face a foe whose face we know. You have seen his face darkening your doors. You have seen his boots muddying your floors. You have seen his torches setting fire to your fields. You've felt his fists and whips and scorn, but you refused to yield!"

Logan's nerves and self-criticism—*Could I have said that better? Is my voice steady? Why is it so hard to get a full breath?*—faded as he looked at the upturned faces of the people who would be his people. He'd had no idea just a few months ago who the Cenarian people were. He'd known and loved the Gyres' smallfolk, but had shared the noblemen's fashionable disdain for the unwashed masses. How easy it was to ask a nameless, faceless mob to die.

"My friends, I spent the last three months in the depths of Hell's Asshole. I was trapped with the shit and the stink of humanity. I spent my time fearing death and things worse than death. They took my clothes. They took my dignity. I saw the good suffer with the evil. I saw a woman violated and a woman kill herself so she wouldn't be violated again. I saw good men and bad make their deals with the darkness. And I made my own. To survive.

"My friends, I was imprisoned beneath the ground. You were imprisoned above it. You knew the fears I knew. You saw the horrors I saw, and worse. We had friends killed. We knew that to resist was to die... and my friends, my people, we looked at the odds against us and we saw no hope. We fled. We hid." Logan paused, and the people were silent.

"Were you there with me?" Logan asked. "Did you feel rage? Did you feel powerless? Did you watch evil and do nothing to oppose it? Were you ashamed?"

The men and women didn't look to the left or the right, afraid that their neighbors would see the tears in their eyes. Their heads nodded, yes, yes.

"I was ashamed," Logan said. "Let me tell you what I learned in the Hole. I learned that in suffering, we find the true measure of our strength. I learned that a man can be a coward one day and a hero the next. I learned that I'm not as good a man as I thought I was. But the most important thing is this: I learned that though it costs me dearly, I can change. I learned that what has been broken can be made new. Do you know who taught me that? A prostitute. In a bitter woman who made her living in shame, I found honor, courage, and loyalty. She inspired me and she saved me.

"Today, there are women here who taught you the same lessons. Many of you are ashamed of your mothers and your wives and your daughters who were raped, who were pressed into sexual slavery at the castle, who sold themselves in brothels so they might survive. You've shunned them, rejected them.

"But I say your wives, mothers, and daughters have shown us how to fight. They gave us the Nocta Hemata. They have given us courage. They have shown us the road from shame to honor. Let every woman who fought that night stand forth!"

A few women stepped forward immediately. Bolstered by their courage, others emerged. Men moved aside silently. In moments, a crowd of three hundred women gathered in front of the platform. Some let tears fall, but their backs were straight, their chins high. Men in the ranks were openly weeping now. Not just the men who must have known this small sample, but men from the countryside, men who must have known their own women to be shamed and dishonored, men who were now ashamed of themselves.

"Today," Logan said. "I declare you the inaugural members of the Order of the Garter. A garter, because you have taken shame and turned it to honor. Display it with pride and tell your grandchildren of your courage forever. And no man shall ever join your order unless he displays the highest levels of heroism and courage."

The people cheered. It was the best thing Logan had ever done.

"I'm afraid," Logan said, quieting the crowd, "that your garters aren't ready yet. It seems we don't have all the materials on hand. You see, we're going to make them out of the Khalidoran battle flags."

They cheered.

"What do you say, men? You think we can help them out?"

They cheered louder.

"Now brothers, please, welcome your beloved. They need you. And sisters, welcome these shamed and broken men. They need you.

"There are just a few more things for me to say." Logan breathed deeply. He'd gone longer than he intended already. He hadn't established the Order of the Garter to gain support. It was just something that needed to be fixed. But somehow, wherever he looked, he saw faces full of hope.

"A few months ago, I didn't want to be king," Logan said, "but something changed me in the Hole. Before the Hole, I could see you as a mob. Now, I see you as brothers and sisters. I can ask you to bleed with me, to die with me, and I do. Many of us will bleed tomorrow, and some of us will die." He looked down at the Hole on which he stood. *Is this your way out, Count Drake? Oh, father, would this make you proud?* "I can ask you to bleed to throw off your chains, but I cannot ask you to bleed for my ambition."

The crowd quieted.

"In the Hole, I learned that a man or woman may wield power over life and death, but there is no power over love. My friends, I love you and this nation and the freedom we will win. But I feel no love for this woman. I will not marry Terah Graesin, not this day, not ever."

"What?" Terah Graesin yelled. She stepped forward. "Stop him, Havrin!"

But Duke Wesseros held her back and Master Nile didn't amplify her voice. "Terah," the duke said, "if you try to stop him now, it'll be civil war right here."

A roar was going through the crowd and men were looking at their neighbors, unsheathing their weapons, and trying to see who would join which side.

"STOP!" Logan cried, and his voice boomed over the assembly. He held his hands up. "I won't have a single man die to make me king, much less a thousand." He turned. "Lady Graesin, will you swear fealty to me?"

Her eyes flashed and this time Master Nile did amplify her voice. "Not if it cost a thousand thousand lives!"

Logan held his hands up to forestall the furor. "My friends, we have no hope of defeating Khalidor if we are not united. So," he turned to Terah Graesin, who looked less than beautiful with a rage-splotchy face, "grant me that you will establish the Order of the Garter and that you will pardon my followers of all crimes up to this day . . . grant me that, and I will swear fealty to you."

Terah Graesin hesitated only a moment. Her eyes were wide with disbelief, but she recovered before any cry could go up. "Done," she said. "Swear it now."

Logan knelt and reached toward the center of the platform where Terah stood. In the perfect inverse of a gyrfalcon stretching its wings beyond the black circle of submission and imprisonment, he reached his hand back in. It made all the difference.

Sometimes the only way out of the Hole isn't climbing. He touched her foot in the oath of submission.

"In recognition of your valor," Queen Graesin said in a tone that dripped poison. "You will have the honor of leading the first charge. Your honeyed words will doubtless impress the Vürdmeisters."

61

$\mathcal{K}$aldrosa Wyn stood with hundreds of women at the front of the crowd, all of them in various states of shock, disbelief, and tears. There were too many emotions to hold them all in. Usually Kaldrosa Wyn hated crying. Now, her tears were a relief.

She felt as if her heart had just tripled in size. Duke Gyre amazed her. Here was a man who set aside the greatest ambition in the world for love. He'd cracked the hard shell of bitterness she'd been growing around her heart. He'd turned them from whores to heroes. He was a saint, and that bitch was going to send him to his death.

Then the throng was around her and the other women, men pushing into the lines, looking for their spurned beloved. Next to Kaldrosa, Daydra was sobbing. A bear of a man pushed through the mob to get to her, and as she saw him, her cries crescendoed. He was an older man, her father, and his eyes were streaming, snot dribbling into his great bushy moustache. Before he could say a word, Daydra fainted. He caught her as she fell and lifted her into his arms as easily as a baby. Another couple embraced next to Kaldrosa, just squeezing, squeezing.

Kaldrosa tried not to hate these women for their joy. She did feel new, different, the mountain of shame sliding off her shoulders. But Tomman was surely back in Cenaria. Would he be so quick to forgive?

Would she ever again get to lie in his arms after lovemaking, in that time when all things were made new?

The crowd was beginning to thin, and the women who'd not found their lost loves were clumping together. They looked at each other and they knew each other, even women who'd never met. They were sisters. But even then, they were not alone. The goodwives who'd listened to the speech from the back and had known that there would be girls left over had finally pushed their way through the ranks of men and—strangers all—they embraced and wept together.

Off to one side, Kaldrosa Wyn saw Momma K, watching. There were no tears in the great woman's eyes, but though her back was as straight as a rod, she looked like she wished there had been a man who pushed through the crowd for her. Kaldrosa was starting to walk toward her, marveling at her own bravery—go to comfort Momma K!—when she saw him.

He was wearing the uniform of one of General Agon's wytch hunters: a strange short bow in one hand, a quiver on his back and boiled leather armor over a dark green tunic piped with yellow. But as he scanned the crowd, her fierce, fiery Tomman looked scared. Then their eyes met.

Like a puppet with its strings cut, Tomman dropped to his knees. The bow fell in the mud, forgotten. His face contorted. He put his arms out, eyes welling with tears. It was a more abject apology than he would ever have found in words.

Kaldrosa ran to him.

"I feel like I've been here more than some of the people who live here," Kylar said.

"Quiet," Vi said.

When he'd come to get Logan, Kylar had taken a skiff barely big enough to hold them. Though small, the vessel had been incredibly fast, and he'd been able to evade the single boat that had patrolled Vos

Island. Now three boats were on patrol, so they were going to cross to Vos Island the same way he had when he'd come to rescue Elene.

Following her lead, Kylar looped a knee over the rope and climbed hand over hand across the line as it dangled beneath the bridge. Vi's shot had been perfect, so they were able to pull the line much tighter than he had on his previous trip. When she passed the remains of his bolt stuck in the wood from his horrible shot four months ago, she stopped. "Legend, my butt," she mumbled.

Which brought Kylar's attention to her butt. Again. While the first word that popped into his mind wasn't *legendary,* Vi's butt was quite pert. Nicely round. Worthy of the stretchy-tight garb she wore. Unlike many athletic women, Vi had curves. Nice hips and awe-inspiring breasts.

Why am I thinking about Vi's breasts?

Kylar kept pulling himself hand over hand, scowling. This was a distraction he didn't need. He looked at Vi's butt again. Shook his head. Looked again. *Why am I attracted to her butt? How weird is that? Why do men like butts anyway?*

Vi reached the castle wall and let down a rope. She whispered something and shadows obscured her. It wasn't great, not nearly what Durzo had been capable of, much less Kylar. Her shadows were merely black, and obscured the recognizable humanity of her shape. Still, it was less conspicuous than a half-naked tart whose entire body shouted, "Look at me!"

Following her, Kylar slid down the rope quickly. They huddled in the shadow of a rock as the patrol boat passed.

"So, you haven't said anything about my grays."

Kylar raised an eyebrow. "What? Do you want me to tell you if your trousers make your butt look big? They do. Happy?"

"So you have been looking at my butt. What do you think of the rest?"

"Are we really talking about this? Now?" Kylar glanced at her breasts again—and got caught.

"The haughty disdain thing will work better for you if you don't blush," Vi said.

"They're great," Kylar said. He coughed. "Your grays, that is. Not that your breasts—I mean style is perfect for you. Just over the line between sexy and obscene."

She refused to take offense. "First I take their attention, then I take their life."

"It looks cold." This time, he didn't look at her breasts. Barely—despite the small attention-getters standing at attention on top of her large attention-getters.

"I'm a woman. I don't get to pick clothes for comfort."

"I can't believe I'm having a conversation this long about clothes."

"You call this a long conversation about clothes?" Vi asked. "Haven't had many lovers, have you?"

"Just one. And not for long, thanks to you," Kylar said.

That shut her up. Thank the God.

He got up and started moving. They had to hide every time the patrol boat passed, Vi so she wouldn't be seen, and Kylar so Vi wouldn't know he could go invisible. Kylar had worn fairly tight clothes himself, an old pair of grays that Momma K had had fetched for him. The more anyone knew about the extent of his powers, the more vulnerable he was.

They reached the sunken gate to the Maw an hour after midnight. There was no one guarding it.

Kylar tried the latch. It wasn't locked. He looked at Vi. Obviously, he liked that as much as she did. Still, how could the Godking know they were coming? He moved to open the door when Vi touched his arm. She pointed to the rusty hinges, motioning for him to wait.

She touched each of the hinges in turn, murmuring, then nodded to him.

He tried the rusty door. It opened silently.

"Well, I'll be damned," Vi said. "So it doesn't just work on little girls."

Kylar eased the door shut and stared at her. "Why don't you try it on yourself?" he asked.

"I already did," she said. "Anyone further than five feet away can't hear me."

"That's not what I meant. Anyway, how can you be sure it works?"

"You didn't hear what I just called you."

"Which was?"

"True, but not clever enough to repeat."

He hesitated. "Vi, before we go in, I need to ask you something."

"Shoot."

"I got into wet work because of a child named Rat. He was Garoth Ursuul's son, and it was to please Garoth that Rat cut up Elene's face and raped Jarl and tried to rape me."

"I didn't know," Vi said. "I'm sorry."

"It's not important," Kylar said gruffly. "I got away."

"I didn't," Vi said quietly. She sank into herself, into those years of nightmare. "For me it was my mother's lovers. She knew what they did, but she never stopped them. She always hated me for what I cost her. As if I was the one who fucked some stranger and got pregnant and made her run away. I don't know if she wanted me at first or if she was just too much of a coward to take ergot or tansy tea."

Vi knew it was a reasonable fear. A sufficient dose to induce an abortion was a hairsbreadth from a lethal dose. Every year, Hu claimed, thousands of girls who "took sick and died" had actually taken too much poison. Others took too little and bore maimed children.

"After she ran away, my mother had nothing to survive on but her looks. She was too proud to be a whore outright, so she attached herself to one bastard after another. She could never do what had to be done."

"And that's how you're different from her?"

"Yes," she said softly. Then she came to herself. Why had she been talking so much? She'd never told anyone about that shit. She'd never had anyone who would have cared. "Sorry, you didn't need to hear that. You had a question?"

Kylar didn't answer. He was looking at her in a way no one had ever looked at her before. It was the look a mother gave her child when she fell and bloodied her knees. It was compassion, and it went right through her, past her sarcasm and her bravado. It knifed through the ice and dead flesh that were all she thought she had inside and found something small and alive and bathed it in warm light. He was seeing all the putrefying yuck that she'd walled up, and he wasn't recoiling from her the way he should have.

"Hu Gibbet made you kill her, didn't he?"

She looked down, unable to face the open warmth any more. She didn't trust her voice.

"Second kill? One of the boyfriends first?"

She nodded.

This was ridiculous. They were having this conversation outside the Maw? "What was your question?" she asked.

"When I quit wet work, I couldn't let it go, and it's only now that I know why. When Jarl showed up at my door, part of me was relieved. I had what I'd wanted for my whole life, but I still wasn't happy. Have you ever had someone look at you and understand you and totally accept you? And for some reason, you just couldn't accept that acceptance?"

Vi swallowed. Her heart filled with longing.

"That's what Elene was for me. I mean, is for me. I promised her that I'd never kill again, but I can't be happy if I don't finish this. When I left, I left her a pair of wedding rings so that she'd know I still love her and want to be with her forever, but I'm sure she's furious with me."

The weight in Vi's pocket burned. She told her tongue to move, to tell him, but it was lead in her mouth.

"If it were any hit but this, she'd never forgive me. If I do this, the

Khalidorans will lose, Logan will be king, the Warrens will be different forever, and Jarl won't have died in vain. If there is a One God, like Elene always says there is, he made me for this kill."

Jarl? How can he talk so calmly about Jarl to me? "So what was your question?" She sounded a bit militant, even to her own ears—Jarl! Gods! Her emotions were so out of control she couldn't even identify them—but Kylar answered gently.

"I needed to know if you were in this with me. All the way to the Godking. All the way to death, if it takes that. But I think you've already answered me."

"I'm with you," Vi said. Her whole heart swore it.

"I know. I trust you." Looking in his eyes, Vi knew he was telling the truth. But the words made no sense. Trust? After what she'd done?

He turned back to the door.

"Kylar," she said. Her heart was pounding. She'd tell him about Jarl first, then the note and the earrings, everything. She'd throw herself at his feet and dare him to accept all of it. "I'm sorry. About Jarl. I never meant—"

"I know," he said. "I don't see his murder in you."

"Huh?"

"Vi..." he said softly. As he put a hand on her shoulder, tingles shot through her whole body. She looked at his lips and he was stepping close and her head was tilting of its own accord, her lips parting slightly, and he was so close she could feel his presence like a caress on her exposed skin, and her eyes closed, and his lips touched her—forehead.

Vi blinked.

Kylar dropped his hand as if her shoulder was on fire. Something black flitted across the surface of his eyes.

"What the fuck was that?" Vi demanded.

"Sorry. I almost—you mean my eyes? I was checking if you were using a glamour. I mean, I'm sorry. I was just— Uh, let's get this done, huh?"

Now she was totally confused. He'd thought she'd used her glamour? Did that mean he'd wanted to—he almost what?—no, surely not.

What were you thinking, Vi? "Sorry I killed your best friend, Kylar, wanna fuck?"

Kylar opened the door and Vi saw the gaping mouth for which the Maw was named for the first time. The Maw looked like a dragon opening its mouth to swallow her. Red glass eyes with torches behind them glowed with evil intent. Everything else was carved from black fireglass: the black tongue they walked on, the black fangs poised overhead. Once they stepped into the mouth, there was no light.

"This is wrong," Kylar said. He stopped. "This is totally different."

When Kylar had saved Elene and Uly, the ramp into the Maw had led down a short tunnel and then forked. The nobles' cells had been to the right, and the rest to the left. The ceilings had been about seven feet high everywhere, giving a claustrophobic feeling to the Maw.

"I thought you were in here a couple months ago," Vi said.

"Looks like the wytches have been busy."

They entered a vast subterranean chamber. The ramp that had once descended thirty feet now plunged more than a hundred. The nobles' cells and the cells from the first and second levels of the Maw were gone. The ramp was wide enough for four horses abreast and it spiraled around a great central pit. At the bottom, they could see a gold altar with a man tied to it and meisters around him.

"Shit," Vi breathed. "We have to go down there."

Kylar followed her eyes. She wasn't looking at the man on the gold table. She was looking at the south end of the pit, where a small tunnel led toward the castle.

The place felt wrong. It wasn't the altar or the darkness. The smell of the Hole was thick here now. Sulphuric smoke crawled along the floor. It reminded Kylar of his fight with Durzo.

Beneath the smoke, there were other smells. Old blood and the cloying stench of decaying flesh. Beneath the darkness and the queer chanting of the wytches and the reedy cries of pain from deep in the tunnel—mercifully toward the Hole, not the way he and Vi would go—there was something else.

It was a heaviness. Oppression. Kylar had made the night his home for too many years to be afraid of the dark—he thought. But here, in the very air he breathed, was something deeper, darker, more ancient and more vile than he could imagine. Just smelling the reek made him remember killing. He recalled the shameful glee he felt as the noose slipped around Rat's ankle. He remembered when he'd poisoned a saddlemaker's stew and the man hadn't been hungry and had let his son have it. He remembered the exact shade of purple the boy's face had turned as his throat had swollen shut and he'd suffocated. He remembered a hundred deeds he was ashamed of, a hundred other things he should have done and hadn't. He stood paralyzed, breathing the foul air.

"Come on," Vi said. Her eyes looked haunted, enormous, but she was moving. "Breathe through your mouth. Don't think, just do."

Kylar blinked stupidly and came back to himself and followed Vi. The presence was Khali. Just like Logan had warned.

They made their way down into the pit. Kylar walked near the edge, looking down. As he got nearer, he could see that the meisters weren't sacrificing the man, at least not in any conventional sense. Their victim was a Lodricari with tattoos covering his entire body. His skin hung thin and loose on his big, withered frame. He was bound with thick chains face down on the gold table and he was stripped to the waist.

Six meisters were seated at the points of the gold Lodricari star inlaid in the floor, cross-legged, their eyes closed, chanting. Two more stood on either side of the altar. One was holding a hammer and the other . . .

Kylar couldn't believe it until he moved to the very last spiral and the level of the floor. The first meister was holding a carpenter's hammer and gold nails while the second was holding a horse's spine in his hands, positioning it above the tattooed man's tailbone.

The meister set the spine in place and the other meister, gritting his teeth, set the six-inch-long golden nail above it. He slammed the hammer down. The tattooed man screamed and bucked. In two more heavy whacks, the nail sank all the way in. Then both meisters backed up and Kylar saw their victim well for the first time.

There was something wrong with his skin. At first, because of all the tattoos, Kylar couldn't tell what it was, but between the tattoos he could see that the man was flushed. His veins pressed against the surface of his skin as if he were lifting a great weight. That would have been understandable, given what he was enduring, but the veins weren't in the right places. Thick veins and arteries, blue and red, pushed up against his skin everywhere. And the skin itself seemed oddly dimpled, as if he had pockmarks over his entire body.

The meisters stepped back and called out an order. A prisoner was brought out of the north tunnel, where Kylar could see a holding cell with a dozen men in it. The man was shackled hand and foot and a rope was tied around his neck. A young, pretty meister took the rope and unstrung it, taking care not to let any part of her body enter the circle of magic. She stood on the far side of the circle from the prisoner, who was bleating with fear. Cold sweat poured from the man's face and urine coursed down his leg. His eyes were locked to the man on the altar.

The young meister began pulling on the rope around the man's neck, drawing him toward the circle. He took one hobbled step before he started fighting, and then it was too late. He lost his balance and came shambling forward to keep himself from falling. When he saw that his path would bring him straight to the tattooed man, he threw himself to the side.

With his hands shackled behind him, the victim had no way to catch himself. His face cracked against the fireglass floor.

The meisters who weren't seated or chanting cursed. The woman repositioned herself, flinging the rope over the altar. A meister joined her and they began pulling the semiconscious man toward the altar again.

Why don't they just use magic? But then Kylar looked through the ka'kari and thought he knew why.

This entire chamber was full of magic. It billowed from the meisters the way sulphuric smoke billowed up from the Hole. It seeped along the ground. The very air was thick with it—everywhere but around the altar. There, the air was dead. The meisters were creating something that would resist magic—even theirs. But as Kylar looked closely, he saw that the man wasn't untouched by their magic. All the meisters who were chanting were weaving something together in the air above the altar, and they were sinking it into him at two points. In the back of the man's neck, on either side of his spine, sat two diamonds, each the size of a man's thumb, nailed in. In the visible spectrum they were invisible, covered with blood and grime and the man's hair. In the magical spectrum, they blazed. Only through them could the meisters touch the man's body.

The meisters finally pulled the prisoner up, gagging and choking. Kylar felt Vi tug on his tunic, an urgent let's-get-the-hell-out-of-here, but he ignored her. The prisoner lurched forward and fell on top of the altar, across the tattooed man.

Though he landed at an angle and should have rolled off, he stuck. The meisters dropped the rope and stepped back fast, almost fleeing. The pitch of the chanting rose. The prisoner screamed, but Kylar couldn't see why. The tattooed man's muscles were bunched, his skin flushing even redder—and then blood washed over his back.

The prisoner was yanked off his feet and sucked onto the tattooed man's back. Then the prisoner's tunic was ripped away and Kylar saw the tattooed skin writhing. Each of those thousands of pockmarks was opening as a fanged little mouth. Everywhere, tattooed skin was chewing into the prisoner.

As the prisoner was consumed straight into that tattooed back, the man on the altar screamed in agony equal to his victim's. Through the ka'kari, Kylar saw whole ribs ripped from the prisoner and pulled through the undulating back and attached to the new spine. Skin swelled and grew over the spine as well. The meisters chanted and Kylar saw that they were directing the growth. Whatever this tattooed beast was, they weren't making it. It had already been made. They were just growing it into a shape fit for war.

In another ten seconds, the prisoner was gone. Sort of. Parts of him had been incorporated into the new creature. The monstrosity on the altar had gained perhaps half of the prisoner's mass. The prisoner's spine had reinforced its spine. Ribs had given the torso more length. Skin had been stretched over the new growth, though now it too was pockmarked with those little mouths. The prisoner's bones had been ground down and transported to the creature's skull, which had doubled in thickness.

The meister in charge barked something that sounded like approval, and then motioned for the next prisoner.

Vi jerked on his sleeve again. Kylar turned and looked into the shadows where her eyes would be.

"You go ahead," he whispered. "I'll catch up."

"You're about to do something stupid, aren't you?"

Kylar smiled grimly. She just shook her head.

62

$\mathcal{L}$antano Garuwashi led his bloodied, exultant men out of the caves that had let them pass through the mountains. Two hundred sleeping Khalidorans had filled the last chamber. Their four wytches had slept deepest in the cave, probably thinking it the safest place, and died before the alarm had even gone up. The rest of the Khalidorans, disoriented, managed to kill as many of themselves as Garuwashi's men had.

In the predawn light, the sa'ceurai emerged southeast of Pavvil's Grove. Two armies camped opposite each other on the plain. It surprised Garuwashi that it was the Khalidorans who'd been in the caves. Fighting on their home territory, it should have been the Cenarians who had reserves hidden there. If this cave was a sample, the Godking could easily have another five thousand men tucked out of sight, deployable within ten minutes.

It was almost enough to make Garuwashi turn back. Unless the Cenarians had better tricks up their sleeves, it looked like Khalidor was going to be Ceura's northern neighbor permanently.

Still, this would be the last battle of the season. If he could see the outcome, Garuwashi would know if the rebels would be able to regroup or if they were wiped out. He would see Khalidoran tactics firsthand, which might save him in the future.

"Have the men fan out," he told his balding captain, Otaru Tomaki. He stepped to the entrance of the cave, binding in the four forelocks of black hair he'd taken with the quick precision of long practice.

"You won't believe our luck, War Master," Tomaki said.

Garuwashi cocked an eyebrow.

"Sir, he's right there." Tomaki pointed.

Barely three hundred paces away, through the trees, Garuwashi saw the giant running up a hill toward the battlefield. He was heading for the Cenarian camp. He looked over his shoulder. For a moment, Garuwashi couldn't see why because of the trees. Then four Khalidoran cavalrymen burst from the trees up the hill.

The giant saw that he wasn't going to make the crest of the hill before they caught up with him. He stopped and drew his sword.

"The gods have delivered him into my hand," Garuwashi said. "After he kills the horsemen, we'll see if this giant's a match for Lantano Garuwashi."

"You secure the tunnel to the castle," Kylar whispered. "When they come after me, we'll need to move fast."

"What are you going to do?" Vi whispered.

They were bringing out another prisoner. This one shuffled forward like a lamb.

"Just go," Kylar whispered.

"I'm not your fucking lackey," Vi said, raising her voice to a dangerous level.

"Well, then. You do what you have to," Kylar said.

Vi glared—and went.

Kylar waited while the meisters argued briefly and then cut the prisoner's clothes off him to make him easier to digest. Kylar had an idea of what to do, but everything had to be in place. That meant waiting so Vi could secure the tunnel. It meant letting the prisoner die.

He hated it. But he waited. *Dammit, man, fight. That will give me all I need.* But the naked prisoner did nothing. He stared at the writhing mass on the gold altar with horror.

Why don't you fight? All they can do is kill you.

At the last moment, the man let out a strangled sob and tried to stand, but the rope around his neck yanked him forward. He stuck to the creature and screamed. The chanting rose again and meisters who weren't chanting from the corners of the Lodricari star watched wide-eyed as the prisoner was devoured. This time it was even faster than before.

Kylar fully cloaked himself, the ka'kari whooshing over his skin like a well-worn tunic. He ran toward the altar, right past a chanting meister.

As he stepped into the circle circumscribing the Lodricari star, his skin burned with the potency of magic in the air. Khali's voice shrieked through him, a voice of despair, of suicide, of shame, of corruption.

Another step and he jumped, flipping his body into a no-handed cartwheel over the altar and the creature chained to it. It was like jumping through lightning. Needles jabbed every surface of his skin, injecting every vein with power. As he passed over the creature's misshapen gray head, he grabbed the diamonds.

They slid out as if the creature's skin were butter. He landed on the other side of the altar and flung the diamonds away like burning coals. In another second, he was out of the star and leaping for the wall, which was inscribed with runes and designs cut deep enough that he could cling to them. Whatever happened next, he was content to get the hell out of the way and watch invisibly.

Eyes flicked open around the star. The creature was still devouring the prisoner, but the meisters' magic hung in the air like the dangling tentacles of a jellyfish. It had nowhere to go.

The chanting meisters broke off, one by one. Every one turned toward Kylar and stared, mouth agape as if seeing the impossible.

They can see me! Kylar clung to the wall like a spider, facing out, his hands and feet wedged in cracks behind him, waiting for the first attack.

The silence was broken by the sound of a snapping chain and a throaty, almost-human roar. The creature, long-backed now like an enormous caterpillar, shook itself and the rest of the chains popped like roasting corn. Kylar was forgotten.

Standing on six human arms, the creature rushed a meister and trampled him. Six arms and hands tore the meister apart and stuck his limbs to its body. The little mouths worked better than any glue. A fireball caromed off the beast's hide. It wasn't so much blocked as redirected. The fireball lost no momentum, did no damage.

Three more fireballs followed in the next moment, each flying away and bursting against the walls or the floor. The meisters shrieked. One ran up the stairs that spiraled out of the depths. The creature ran after her, but instead of following her up the stairs, it cut across the circular hall. It tried to grab her. She fell back against the wall, as far away from the grasping hand as she could get.

It was far enough. At that height, the creature's arm couldn't reach her. She started scurrying back up the stairs on her hands and feet. Kylar thought she was going to get away, but then the creature slumped. Its arm-legs sagged. Under the surface of its skin, long arm bones slid, one after another, to the arm reaching for the woman. The hand detached and slid forward, each section locking with the sickly sucking sound of a joint being dislocated and relocated. In no time, the arm had added four more arm-lengths. The creature grabbed the woman and pulled her onto itself. Her screams became muffled burbles.

The creature rounded and crushed three more meisters against the wall. It paused as all its little mouths chewed through their clothing and flesh. A fourth wytch grabbed one of the three by the hand, trying to pull her free. He put a foot on the creature's hide to get leverage. But even though the creature didn't seem to notice, it was as if its very skin was possessed of intelligence or at least insatiable hunger. The meister hadn't pulled for a second when his eyes bulged. He threw himself backward, but his foot stuck to the creature's hide. He landed on his back, screaming. For a second, it looked like he might pull free, at the cost of all the meat on his foot.

One flank tremored, the way a horse's flank twitches to rid itself of flies, and in a wave, the toothy skin lapped up over the meister's foot up to his ankle. Another twitch and it reached up to mid-calf. Another, and the creature was digesting four meisters.

It was all the break Kylar needed. He launched himself off the wall and ran up the south tunnel toward the castle. He passed four bloody meisters that Vi had dispatched on the way. He found Vi rifling through the purse of a dead guard standing in front of a formidable oak door. He smiled recklessly. She looked at him, wide-eyed.

"Shit, Kylar, you're glowing."

"I was amazing back there," he said, forgetting that he should have been invisible.

"No, I mean, shit, Kylar, you're glowing."

Kylar looked down. He looked like he was on fire, all in purples and green in the magical spectrum and in a dull, forge-fire red in the visible spectrum. No wonder the meisters had been staring. He'd jumped through the heart of all their magic and it had been too much for the ka'kari to devour. It was bleeding excess magic as light.

Without thinking, he tried to suck the ka'kari back in. It was like taking a bellyful of hot lead into his glore vyrden. "Ow! Ow!"

"Did you kill it?" Vi asked.

Kylar looked at her like she was crazy. "Didn't you see what that— that thing did?"

"No. I obeyed my orders and secured the tunnel." Vi, Kylar realized, could be a real snot. "Not that it does a whole helluvalotta good, because there's no key. They must have been afraid of that—that thing," she mimicked. "Now we're going to have to go back. I'd recommend sneaking, but you seem to be on fire."

Kylar pushed past Vi and put his hands on the near edge of the oak door, one above the other.

"What are you doing?" she asked.

Gods, the door was thick. Still, if he couldn't take the magic in, why couldn't he channel it out? He felt the whoosh of magic leaving him. He looked down and saw tunnels the exact size and shape of his hands bored through the foot-thick oak and iron hinges.

Swallowing—*how the hell did I do that?*—Kylar pushed on the door. It didn't budge until he used Talent-strength, then it yawned open, twisting on its locks, then crashing to the floor.

Kylar stepped through. When Vi didn't follow, he turned. She had an expression on her face so stunned and puzzled and eloquent, he knew exactly what she was going to say.

"What the hell are you?" Vi asked. "Hu never taught me anything like that. Hu doesn't know anything like that."

"I'm just a wetboy."

"No, Kylar. I don't know what you are, but you're not just anything."

63

"Why have you denied me my royal garments?" the girl demanded. The princess was wearing a drab dress several sizes too big and had pulled her hair back in a simple ponytail. The Godking had denied her even combs.

"Do you believe in evil, Jenine?" Garoth sat on the edge of Jenine's bed in the north tower. It was before dawn on the day that he would finally massacre the Cenarian resistance. It would be a good day. He was in high spirits.

"How could I sit in your presence and not?" she spat. "Where are my things?"

"A beautiful woman does things to a man, young lady. It would not do for you to be ravished. It would displease me to have you broken so soon."

"Do you not have control of your men? Some god you are. Some king."

"I do not speak of my men," Garoth said quietly.

She blinked.

"You stir me. You have what we call *yushai*. It is life and fire and steel and joy-of-living. I have extinguished it in my wives before; that is why you're cloistered and forbidden comely clothes. It's why I sated myself with one of your ladies-in-waiting: to protect you. You will be my queen, and you will share my bed, but not yet."

"Not ever!"

"See? *Yushai*."

"Go to hell," Jenine said.

"You are a woman cursed, aren't you? Mine is the third royal family you've belonged to—and the first two didn't fare so well, did they? Your husband lasted—what?—an hour?"

"By the One and the Hundred," she said, "may your soul be cast in the pit. May every fruit within your grasp turn to worms and rot. May your children betray you—"

He slapped her. For a moment, she worked her jaw, blinking the tears out of her eyes.

Then she continued. "May—"

He slapped her again, harder, and felt a dangerous surge of pleasure down to his loins. Damn Khali.

She was about to spit on him when he gagged her with the vir.

"Never tempt a man beyond what he can endure. Do you understand?" he asked.

She nodded, eyes wide at the black vir raking his skin.

The vir released her. Garoth Ursuul sighed with disappointment, denying the Strangers. Jenine looked terrified.

Good. Perhaps it will teach her caution. After Neph had produced the princess as a gift and apology for what a mess Cenaria had become, Garoth had been instantly smitten. He had first sent Princess Gunder to Khaliras with the baggage train carrying all the best plunder, but he hadn't been able to get her out of his mind. He'd ordered her brought back. It was a crazy risk. If the Cenarians learned she was alive and saved her, they would have a legitimate ruler. And this girl would rule, given the chance and a little luck. She was fearless.

"Back to my question, Jenine. Do you believe in evil?" the God-king asked. Best to engage his mind, if this interview weren't to end in tears for her and sated disgust for himself. "Some people call it evil when my soldiers knock on a door in the night and ask a man where his brother is and the terrified man tells them. Or when a woman sees a full purse lying in the road and takes it. I'm not asking if you believe in weakness or in ignorance that harms others. I'm asking if you believe in an evil that glories in destruction, in perversion. An evil that would look on the face of goodness and spit on it.

"You see, when I kill one of my seed, it's not an act of evil. I know when I rip the beating heart from that young boy's chest that I'm not just killing him. I'm inspiring such fear in all the others that it makes me more than a man. It makes me unquestionable, unfathomable, a god. That secures my reign and my kingdom. When I want to take a city, I herd the inhabitants of nearby villages in front of my army. If the city wants to use war engines against my men, they have to kill their friends and neighbors first. Brutal, yes. But evil? One might say it saves lives because the cities usually surrender. Or they do when I start catapulting the living into the city. You'd be amazed at what the simple sound of a scream changing in pitch and ending with a thump will do to soldiers when it's repeated every thirteen minutes. They can't help but wait, can't help but wonder—do I recognize this voice? But I digress. You see, I don't call any of that evil. Our society rests on the foundation of the Godking's power. If the Godking doesn't have absolute power, everything crumbles. Then comes chaos, war, starvation, plagues that don't discriminate between the innocent and the guilty. Everything I do staves that off. A little brutality preserves us like a surgeon's knife preserves life. My question is, do you believe in an evil possessed of its own purity? Or does every act intend some good?"

"Why are you asking me?" Jenine asked. She had gone pasty pale. It would have made her look Khalidoran if it weren't tinged with green.

"I always talk to my wives," the Godking said. "First, because only madmen regularly speak to themselves. Second, there is the off chance a woman might have an insight."

He was baiting her, and was rewarded as she recovered some of her yushai. She reminded him of Dorian's mother, and Moburu's.

"I think evil has agents," Jenine said. "I think we allow evil to use us. It doesn't care if we know what we're doing is evil or not. After we've done its will, if we feel guilty, it can use that to condemn us in our own eyes. If we feel good, it can immediately use us for its next objective."

"You are an intriguing child," Garoth said. "I've never heard such an idea." Garoth didn't like it. It made less of him: a mere tool, ignorant or knowing, but always complicit. "You know, I almost left this throne. I almost rejected everything it is to be in the lineage of gods."

"Really?"

"Yes, twice. First when I was an aetheling, and then when I was a father. Strength brought me back, both times. *Non takuulam.* 'I shall not serve.' You see, I had a son named Dorian. He reminded me of me. I saw him turning away from the path of godhood, as I almost had." He paused. "Have you ever stood on a height and thought, I could jump?"

"Yes," Jenine said.

"Everyone does," Garoth said. "Have you stood with someone else and thought, I could push him?"

She shook her head, horrified.

"I don't believe you. Regardless, that is how it was with Dorian. I thought, I could push him. So I did. Not because it helped me, just because I could. I brought him into my confidence and he almost turned me away from godhood—so I betrayed him in the most profound way I could imagine. It was the moment closest to a purity of evil I have come.

"You see, to my eyes, the world holds only two mysteries. Evil is the first, and love is the second. I have seen love used, exaggerated into a mockery of itself, perverted, faked, betrayed. Love is a fragile, corruptible thing. And yet I have seen it evince a curious strength. It is beyond my comprehension. Love is weakness that once in a great while triumphs over strength. Baffling. What do you think, Jenine?"

Her face was stony. "I know nothing of love."

He snorted. "Don't feel bad. One interesting thought is more than I get out of most of my wives. Power is a whore. Once you finally hold her, you realize that she is courting every man in sight."

"What's the purpose of all your power?" Jenine said.

He furrowed his brow. "Whatever do you mean?"

"I'd say that's your problem, right there."

"Now you speak with the insight I'd expect from a woman. Which is to say none."

"Thanks for clarifying."

Ah, so she was as smart as they said. He'd wondered when he'd heard she was requesting books. Better not to let women read. "You're welcome. Now, where was I?"

She answered, but he didn't hear her. Something had just happened to Tenser's ferali. He could feel it through the webs of magic he'd anchored throughout the castle. Whatever had just done that, it was more powerful than he'd expected.

"I can tell you're not happy here, so I'm sending you to Khaliras," he said, walking to the door. "If you send any messages or attempt escape, I'll round up all your friends and a hundred innocents and kill them." He strode across the room and kissed her fiercely. Her lips were cold and utterly unresponsive.

"Goodbye, my princess," he said.

He paused outside the door until he heard her burst into tears, the rustle of covers as she threw herself on the bed, and what he thought was Logan's name. He'd have to give orders about that. If Jenine found out Logan was alive, she'd never bend to Garoth's will. That tug on the web pulled him, but still he paused. Usually, a woman's weeping meant nothing to him, but today.... He turned the feeling over like a strangely colored stone. Was this guilt? Remorse? Why did he have the insane desire to apologize?

Curious. He'd have to think about this later. When Jenine was at a safe distance.

He ordered six huge highlanders from the Godking's Guard to take her to Khalidor immediately, and then went down the stairs.

64

Feir searched the Cenarian army in the dusk, looking for Solon or Dorian. Neither man could be found. When he asked why the garrison at Screaming Winds wasn't here, a count named Rimbold Drake told him of the massacre and shared a worry: If Khali had slaughtered veterans, what would happen if they brought her here?

Desperate, Feir rode on. He was carrying the only possible salvation for the entire ignorant army. To make matters worse, he was no seer, at least not in any useful sense. He could see weaves of magic that were close as if through a Ladeshian enlarging glass, but if you put a man even as Talented as Solon fifty paces away, Feir couldn't see so much as a flicker.

After frenzied inquiries, he'd found two mages: a husband and wife, neither very Talented, but both healers. They said they'd seen no great Talents in the entire army. But then Tevor Nile had gazed around hopelessly—and stopped.

"Drissa," he said.

She came and took his hand. Both of them fixed their attention on a foothill a few hundred paces from the army.

"Lend us your power and we'll lend you our sight," Drissa told Feir. He'd done it, feeling queasy to surrender himself while carrying Curoch, and then the foothill was ablaze in light.

The men were too far away for Feir to recognize faces, and they'd taken care not to skyline themselves, but each man's Talent blazed, as individual as the patterns of his irises. Feir knew those men, had rubbed shoulders and locked horns with them. They were six of Sho'cendi's most powerful magi. Feir knew what they'd come for.

No doubt the bastards actually believed Curoch belonged to them. But they could wield the sword; he couldn't. If he took Curoch to them and swore to surrender it conditionally, any one of those men could incinerate the entire Khalidoran army. Feir didn't have Solon's silver tongue, but with Curoch in hand, his leaden tongue might do just fine.

So he rode pell-mell for the brothers on a horse he borrowed from the Niles, praying that he could get to them before the armies closed ranks. If he reached them in time, Cenaria might win without losing a man.

The path took him into a ravine out of the sight of the magi, and there he'd promptly run into Khalidoran outriders. His horse had been killed by an archer, and then the lancers had come for him, disdaining arrows for the sport of killing a man on foot.

Now three of them were dead, and Feir had bigger problems. Beyond the Khalidorans, unbelievably, were sa'ceurai.

So as he fought the last horseman, he tried to move into the magi's line of sight. Gods! They were barely a hundred paces away. If they saw Feir, not even a thousand sa'ceurai would be able to stand between those six magi and Curoch.

The sa'ceurai wouldn't let Feir break their ranks. They were too disciplined. What they would do was judge him by how he fought, and sa'ceurai had very particular notions about how one should fight.

The Way of the Sword had peculiar notions about fighting. It entailed assuming every time you went into battle that you would die, and disdaining death so long as you died honorably. The ultimate way to strike an enemy was to strike him in the fraction of a second before he landed a killing blow.

To Feir's way of thinking, that was fine and practical when the margins were slim, as they were between the best fighters. If you cared too much about getting hurt, you'd never brave the damage you'd need to take to kill the best. That would make you flinch. If you flinched, you'd die and—worse, to the Ceuran mind—you'd lose.

Killing three horsemen was no mean feat. A veteran horseman was worth ten footmen. But a mage on foot wasn't just a footman, and Feir had had no compunction about using magic to help slay the first three. He knew he could kill the last Khalidoran bearing down on him, but the how of it eluded him. What impression did he want to leave with these sword lords? To a Ceuran, combat was communication. A man might deceive with his words, but his body spoke true.

Feir sheathed Curoch—that was another problem he'd think about later—and ran toward the horseman on the lance side. In battle, the man would be content to let his mountain pony run Feir down, but now, Feir was sure the man would try to kill personally. And...there!

The man leaned out to the side and leveled his ten-foot ash pole. Feir leapt into the air. It was no great leap, but the Khalidoran was riding a twelve-hand mountain pony rather than some hulking eighteen-hand Alitaeran destrier. Feir's flying sidekick took him over the lance and his foot caught the Khalidoran's face.

Feir realized two things at the point of impact: First, the Ceuran villagers who'd devised a kick to unseat horsemen probably didn't try it when the horse was galloping. Second, something popped, and it wasn't the Khalidoran's neck.

He crashed to the ground. When he stood, his ankle screamed and black spots swam in front of his eyes. But there was no revealing his weakness, not in front of sa'ceurai. Even as he stood, they closed the circle. One of them checked the Khalidoran, with a knife drawn to dispatch him, but he was already dead.

Feir stood in haughty silence, meat-slab arms folded, but his heart was cold. There was one more bend of solid rock between him and the magi on the hill. If he could move ten paces and draw in his Talent, they would see him despite the trees. But he couldn't move ten paces. He couldn't move five.

Outside the circle of drawn swords and nocked arrows, a man was checking each of the corpses. Everywhere through his hair were the bound forelocks of his dead opponents. Most were bound at both ends—sa'ceurai he'd killed—but others were bound only to his hair—foreigners. The circle of iron parted and Lantano Garuwashi looked up at Feir.

"You stand as tall and fight as well as a nephilim, yet you didn't even bloody your sword with these dogs. Who are you, giant?" Lantano Garuwashi asked.

A nephilim? Feir wracked his brain for everything he knew about Ceura. Thank the gods, it was a fair amount. Most sword masters learned a lot about Ceura, since not a few of their trainers were exiled Ceurans who had served on the wrong side of one or another of their incessant wars. But a nephilim? The Way of the Sword. The first men crafted from—iron? The soul of a man is his sword. . . .

I can't fight! I'm lame! Lantano Garuwashi saw me fight and now he'll want to prove he's bigger than this "giant."

That was it! "These were the heroes and the great men of old." The nephilim were the children born of mortal women to the sons of the gods. Or was it the God? Ah, hell, he couldn't remember if Ceurans were polytheists. Well, he'd just have to be religiously obscure.

"Be not afraid," Feir said.

He saw consternation ripple across those iron faces. Who told Lantano Garuwashi not to be afraid? Feir figured that if he was going to bluff, he might as well play it to the hilt.

Speaking of hilts . . . now might be the time for Curoch to do its trick. Part of Curoch's latent magic was that it would become any shape of sword its owner wished. Parts of it never changed, but enough of it could to help Feir take on his suddenly conceived role of Divine Messenger. He'd read descriptions of a Ceuran sword that ought to do nicely, so he willed Curoch to take the right shape—*is that all I have to do?*

He drew the sword slowly, and kept his eyes on Lantano Garuwashi's until the man looked down. Around the circle, eyes were widening, men were gasping, jaws were dropping—among these, Lantano
Garuwashi's elite!

Feir followed their eyes. Curoch had not only understood the type
of sword Feir wanted it to emulate, it had known the very sword itself.
Feir had imagined that a sword "with the fires of heaven along the
blade" meant either the patterns of exquisite steel or an engraving of
fire. Another translation was "with the fire of heaven in the blade."
Curoch had taken the latter approach.

Twin dragons, Feir didn't have to look to know that they would be
twins, each subtly different, were engraved on either side of the blade,
near the hilt. Each was breathing fire toward the tip of the blade. But
it wasn't an etching of fire. It was fire, inside the sword. Where the
fire burned, and for several inches past it, the sword blade became
as transparent as glass. It was as if Feir were holding a bar of flame.
The sword stayed a constant length, but fires within grew and shrank
depending on—Feir didn't know what it depended on, but right now
the dragons blazed out fire all the way to the tip of the sword, three
and a half feet from the hilt, and then the fire died down.

Feir had been looking to impress, but the looks on the sa'ceurais'
faces were closer to worship. He was barely able to wipe the amaze-
ment off his own face before eyes began turning back to him.

Lantano Garuwashi looked as if he'd just been stabbed with fear
for the first time in his life. Then it was gone, and out of all the men,
only he looked angry. "Why does a nephilim bear Ceur'caelestos?"
The Blade of Heaven. Feir had a sudden suspicion that Curoch had
become that particular blade too easily. It was like it had known what
it should look like. *What if it isn't pretending to be Ceur'caelestos,
what if it* is *it?*

*I didn't make an impressive blade. I made the most holy artifact
these people know. How do I go limping away now?* It didn't matter. It
was too late to stop.

"I am a mere servant. I bear a message for you, Lantano Garuwashi, should you be sa'ceurai enough to accept it." Feir laced his voice with magic, altered it, added resonance and depth befitting the voice of heaven. "This path lies before you. Fight Khalidor and become a great king." Not the greatest message for a god, but short enough that Feir's lack of eloquence might not shine through. With the added tones and volume, he thought it respectably awe-inspiring.

But Garuwashi didn't look awed. He drew his sword slowly. It hung from his grip, limp and dull. Feir saw his mistake too late. Why had he held out that particular prize? He'd told Garuwashi he would be a king, but to a son of a commoner, it was an impossibility. Garuwashi's sword was plain iron, a battered, sad thing he held with fierce pride because it was such a deep shame to him.

An iron sword would never rule. There was no trading swords. A sa'ceurai's soul was his sword. To Ceurans, that wasn't an abstraction. It was fact.

That sharp, sad length of iron gave stark testament of Feir's lie. Garuwashi's grip tightened on his soul and the tip of the blade lifted in defiance. Around the circle, the sa'ceurai still held their weapons, but the bows were no longer drawn, and the swords had been forgotten. The sa'ceurai looked as if this moment were being etched forever into their minds. Their War Master, the greatest sa'ceurai of all time, facing a nephilim bearing a sword out of legends—and their Lantano Garuwashi showed not a shred of fear.

"If I am sa'ceurai enough?" Lantano Garuwashi asked. "I will die before I accept mockery, even the mockery of the gods. I am sa'ceurai enough to die by the sword of heaven or I will be sa'ceurai enough to kill the gods' messenger."

Then he attacked with the speed that had made Lantano Garuwashi legend.

Feir couldn't fight. Fighting this man with only one good leg was suicide. Feir blocked Garuwashi's first attack and then reached out with magic and yanked the man toward him.

The Ceuran flew into him and the men pressed against each other, swords crossed, faces inches apart. Curoch—or Ceur'caelestos, whichever it was—flared to life. The dragons breathed fire out to the tip of the blade.

Feir's only thought was that his arms had to be stronger than Garuwashi's. If the man stood at a distance, he'd murder Feir, but in close to Feir's massive arms, Feir had a chance. But before either of the men could do anything, light began to bloom in a second bar between the two men. It must have taken only a second, but for that second, it seemed both men's martial training abandoned them. They each stood merely straining to throw the other off-balance, each trying to ignore what each wanted so desperately to look at. Feir hadn't done anything—maybe Curoch was reacting to the magic he had used to pull Garuwashi to him. Garuwashi's sword went red and then white. It burned brighter than Curoch and then, as the men pushed against each other, Garuwashi's sword exploded.

As explosions go, it was gentle but implacable. No burning fragments of sword tore through Feir's flesh, but there was no stopping the force, either. He was flipped head over heels backward and landed face down, a good fifteen feet away. He tried to stand, but the pain in his ankle stabbed through him so fiercely that he knew he would black out if he did. He stayed on his knees. He stared up the hill and took in as much power as he could hold.

Look, damn you, Lucius! Look! He was still hidden by trees, but if one of the seers just looked they would see him.

Thirty feet away, Lantano Garuwashi rose to his feet. Impossibly, he was holding his sword—no, not his sword. His sword had vanished, disappeared. There weren't even smoldering fragments of it left. With a look of absolute wonder in his eyes, he held Ceur'caelestos and it looked perfect, as if Lantano Garuwashi had been born for that sword and the sword made a thousand years ago with Lantano Garuwashi in mind.

If the sa'ceurai had been astonished before, now they were stricken dumb. They dropped to their knees even as Feir was. One of them said, "The gods have given Lantano Garuwashi a new sword." He meant that the gods had given Lantano Garuwashi a new soul, a legend's soul, a king's soul. In every eye, Feir saw that the men approved. They had known it. They had served Lantano Garuwashi before he had become The Lantano Garuwashi, King Lantano, before he had defied and humbled a nephilim.

Now Feir was on his knees, unable to stand. Lantano Garuwashi's eyes were aflame with destiny as he looked down on the giant.

"Indeed, it is as the gods foresaw. Ceur'caelestos is yours," Feir said. What else could he say?

Lantano Garuwashi touched the blade to Feir's chin. "Nephilim, messenger and servant of the gods, you have the face of an Alitaeran, but you fight and speak as only sa'ceurai can. I would have you serve me." His eyes said, *or you can die.*

Feir needed no nephilim from the gods to tell him his destiny. He glanced up the hill, and no help came. He wasn't surprised; he already was what he would forever be: The Small Man Who Served Great Men. He would forever be The Man Who Lost Curoch. He lowered his head, defeated.

"I... I will serve."

65

Four hundred paces away, Agon heard the explosion and whipped his head around, trying to locate its source. The Khalidoran army was camped to the west, but none of those distant soldiers reacted as if the explosion had come from there. He looked at his captain.

"I'll send a runner to Lord Graesin," the captain said. The queen had placed her little brother Luc in charge of the scouts, seeming to think that she had to give the young cretin some responsibility, and thinking that it was one he couldn't possibly screw up. The seventeen-year-old had decided that all scouts would report only to him. Only after the scouts reported to him, sometimes waiting for an hour or more in line behind other scouts, were they able to go to the lords who needed to know.

Combined with everything else, it made for a lot of swearing from Agon's officers. None of them voiced their fears. There was no need. Every veteran knew that they were going into battle with a raw army. Calling it an army was, in fact, a stretch. The units hadn't trained together enough to act coherently. Different lords had different signals, and in the crush and cacophony of battle, voices frequently couldn't be distinguished. One officer wouldn't be able to give a hand signal to the officer down the line to relay the general's orders or even to react to a new situation. That, with the queen's positioning of units according to politics, made every veteran grit his teeth.

Agon was lucky to get even the thousand men he had. He only had them because Duke Logan Gyre had spent all his political capital asking it—and the men who had previously served under Agon threatened mutiny if he didn't lead them.

So Agon had a tenth of the Cenarian army. The queen had given him the center of the line, though she pretended that that honor had gone to the lord stationed next to Agon.

"Forget it," he said. "The battle will be over before we hear back from a scout. How are the men?"

"Ready, Lord Gen—my lord," the captain said.

Agon looked at the lightening sky. It was going to be the kind of day a man should spend beside a fire with ootai—or brandy. Dark clouds obscured the rising sun, extending the darkness into the day and delaying the inevitable battle. The flat field, which was really a dozen farms together, was bare. The wheat harvest had been taken in and the sheep moved to winter pastures. Low stone sheep fences crisscrossed the battlefield.

It would be a messy, slippery, awkward place to fight. That was a mixed blessing. Between the fences and the mud, the Khalidoran heavy cavalry would be cautious and slow. Making a heavily armored horse carrying a heavily armored man jump over a fence onto muddy ground was a good way to kill both. On the other hand, it would slow Agon's men, too, and that meant it would give the Khalidoran wytches more time to fling fire and lightning.

Agon drew his horse up before his foot soldiers and archers. He had no horsemen except for his Sa'kagé guards and wytch hunters.

Having heard Logan speak last night, Agon knew that if he were here now, Logan would have made these men see themselves as part of something vast and good. Logan would have given each of them a hero's heart. Under Logan, these men wouldn't hesitate a second to give their lives. Those who survived, even if they lived maimed for the balance of their lives, would count themselves blessed to have shared the field with the man. Agon wasn't like that.

"I am a simple man," Agon told the group lined up to face the horrors of magic and death. "And I have only simple words to give you. Most of you have fought with me before, and it..." Gods, were those tears? He blinked them away. "It honors me that you would have me lead you again. This will be no easy fight. You know that. But we fight an evil that cannot be allowed to win. It is up to us to stop this evil, and today is our only chance.

"Men, if we win, I will be stripped of command, so if you do what I'm about to ask you, you may be punished, but I ask you regardless. Duke Gyre has been given the...honor of leading the first charge." The men rumbled at that. They knew what the queen was hoping. Agon held up a hand. "If he survives the first charge, I ask that you guard him with your lives." Agon dared say no more. If they won, the queen would doubtless hear of everything he'd said.

His men were left sober and dutiful, ready. Agon wished he were the kind of leader who left them cheering and fiery-eyed, but this, with these men, would do.

He rode toward the conferring lords to get last-minute instructions, not that he intended to obey them. Agon had thought long and hard about how to charge a force that included wytches, and he thought he'd come up with a better strategy than any of these peacocks could. But it brought him close for the last time to Logan.

"My lord," Agon said.

Logan smiled. "General," he said. He looked dashing in his family armor, though it had taken some alterations to make sure it didn't hang loose on his bony frame.

Agon struggled to find words. "Sir," he said. "You will always be my king."

Logan put his hand on the general's shoulder and looked him in the eye. He said nothing, but his face told Agon everything.

Then a Sethi woman on horseback emerged from the line. Agon didn't recognize her. She was armored, wearing a sword and carrying a lance.

"My lord," she said, addressing Logan. "Captain Kaldrosa Wyn. We've arrived."

"What are you talking about?" Logan asked.

She raised a hand and the ranks of men parted in curiosity as thirty women armored as Kaldrosa was came through the ranks, each leading a horse. Not all of them were beautiful, and not all of them were young, but all of them were members of the Order of the Garter.

"What do you think you're doing?" Logan asked.

"We're here to fight. Everyone wanted to come, but I limited it to women who have some experience fighting. We're pirates and merchant guards and pit fighters and archers, and we're yours. You have given us new lives, my lord. We won't let her throw yours away."

"Where did you get the arms?"

"The women who can't fight all helped," Captain Wyn said.

"And thirty horses?"

"Momma K," Agon guessed, scowling.

"Yes," Momma K's voice rang out behind them. Thank the gods, at least she wasn't armed. "Duke Gyre, your steward found a few fine warhorses that the queen's auditors somehow...overlooked. You'll find these ladies eager to accept any order that includes fighting."

"These women aren't—" Logan stopped. He wasn't about to insult them. He lowered his voice. "They'll be slaughtered."

"Momma K didn't ask us to do this," Kaldrosa Wyn said. "She told us we were fools. But we wouldn't be swayed. Sir, yesterday you took away our shame. You gave us honor. It's fragile yet. Please don't take it away."

"What's going on here? What are these whores doing in front of my army?" Terah Graesin shouted, reining her horse in viciously by Agon.

"They're fighting for you," Agon said. "And there's not a damn thing you can do about it."

"Oh, I can't, can I?" Terah asked.

"No, because of that." Agon pointed. In the first hazy light of dawn, the Khalidoran army was advancing.

*   *   *

As Kylar and Vi ascended from the Maw into Castle Cenaria, the hot stink in the air faded and even the taint of Khali seemed to hang less heavily. He'd walked these halls just four months ago, taken some of the same passageways on his way to kill Roth Ursuul. This time, however, he used a different strategy.

By now, Khalidorans would know all the castle's secrets: the back passages and false walls, the spy holes and hidden doors. This time, there would be no taking the tunnels right into the throne room. But this far from the throne room and the king's chambers, the tunnels were safer for Vi, who couldn't become invisible. So an hour before dawn, they entered the passages and moved silently over the heads and behind the backs of scores of soldiers.

Kylar didn't think they could have any idea he was coming, so he hoped their presence only meant that with a battle looming, Garoth Ursuul wanted more security. The sheer numbers of soldiers worried him. With a battle coming, an ordinary commander would leave a skeleton crew at the castle.

The king's chambers were in the west wing. Kylar and Vi left the tunnels in an empty servant's room at the base of the last flight of steps before the king's apartments. Kylar poked his head out into the hall.

The door to the king's bedchamber was at the end of a long, wide hallway. Two highlanders with spears stood guarding the door. Other than the numerous doors to servants' rooms that lined the halls, the hall offered no cover. Again, Kylar thought, not a problem for him, but a serious problem for Vi. Maybe he shouldn't have brought her along. Momma K thought he would need her, but it was starting to look like she'd just slow him down. He was going to have to take down both guards by himself. It was possible, but each man had a bell rope to sound an alarm. Kylar had no doubt he could kill them both, but killing both and getting them away from their ropes?

Stepping back into the room Kylar said, "Why don't you wait here until they're—"

Vi was topless, unfolding a dress she'd taken from her pack. Kylar gaped, frozen. When his eyes finally lifted, Vi's expression was perfectly casual. He turned his head, blushing. A pack hit him in the stomach. "Grab the bodice, would you?" Vi said.

He pulled the bodice out of the pack and handed it to her as she wriggled into a tight servingwoman's dress. She leaned over and pulled up the legs of her pants so they wouldn't show under the dress, again giving Kylar an eyeful. He coughed.

She grabbed the bodice from his nerveless fingers. "Seriously, Kylar, stop acting like such a virgin—" Virgin! How he absolutely loathed the word! "I'm sure it's not the first time you've seen a woman naked."

Actually, it was, but Kylar would have died—for real—before he admitted it to Vi. Elene had never let him see her breasts, though he hadn't always stopped his hands from straying into that golden territory. She'd always wanted to save everything she could for when they were really married. And if Kylar had eroded those boundaries somewhat—bastard—every step seemed huge, a precious gift. It had been vastly frustrating then, but as Vi laced the bodice rapidly and adjusted the amount of cleavage, it was different. For Vi, showing her breasts was nothing. She didn't even turn as she grabbed each breast within the bodice and pulled it this way and that to show it to best advantage. Kylar had thought that Elene's were the ultimate of all breasts, but Vi's breasts were fuller, larger. You couldn't look at her and not notice her breasts. It automatically made her sexual—and yet... and yet, to her, they were just tits. Tools.

Elene was less blatantly sexual, maybe less sexual, period. But there was something cheap about Vi's sexuality, something that told Kylar she took no joy from it. That had been taken from her, taken by her mother's lecherous lovers, by Hu Gibbet, by Momma K's clients and casual fucking. Kylar's emotions skittered from aroused to mournful.

Vi picked up a wicker laundry basket and stuffed it full of clothes, including her own tunic. Under the last tunic, she secreted a dagger.

"How do I look?"

The outfit did look oddly familiar. She'd shown substantially less cleavage that day, in keeping with the modesty of the Drake household, but they were exactly the same clothes Vi had worn when she tried to kill him. "Son of a bitch," he said.

She chuckled and turned, modeling for him. "Does it make my butt look big?"

"You get your big ass in the hall."

She laughed and put the basket on her hip. She was provocative, gorgeous, tempting, and now she had to add fun to the mix? Dammit, he'd almost kissed her outside! No doubt he'd be wearing a knife in his back if he'd done it, but for a second he'd even thought that she wanted him to. She sashayed down the hallway, and the Khalidorans' eyes locked onto her. One of them muttered an oath.

"Hello," Vi said, coming to stand in front of the guard on the left. "I'm new here and I was wondering if—" Her knife slashed so deeply across the man's neck it almost decapitated him.

Kylar broke the other man's neck with a sharp twist and a meaty crack.

Vi looked over to where he was—or wasn't, since he was invisible.

"Un-fucking-believable," she said. She cleaned the dagger and put it back in the basket. "Fine, you come in after ten seconds or as soon as you hear my voice. If the Godking wakes up, I'll distract him and you kill him. If he stays asleep, I'll take him."

She opened the door slowly and silently and stepped inside.

A few moments later, she came out. Her face was green. "He's not there," she said.

"What's wrong?" Kylar tried to step past her, but she blocked him.

"You don't want to go in there."

He pushed past her.

The room was full of women. They stood frozen, like statues in various poses. One, on all fours, naked, supported a sheet of glass on her back, forming a table. Another, a tall noblewoman Kylar recognized but couldn't name, stood on tiptoe, stretching seductively, one arm and one leg wrapped around a post of the Godking's massive four-poster bed. Chellene lo-Gyre sat, legs crossed in her shift, in a wing-backed chair. Kylar didn't know anything about her except her reputation for a fiery temper. Her expression showed it, as did her disheveled hair and the tension in her lean muscles. Most of the women were naked, the rest wore little. Two, on their knees, held a washbasin. Two others held a mirror. One was manacled to the wall, a scarf around her neck. Kylar's breath stopped.

It was Serah Drake. Like all of them, she wasn't as still as a statue; she was a statue. With a little cry, Kylar touched her face, touched the lips he'd once kissed. They were as yielding as living flesh, but cool, and there was no life in her open, shining eyes. Her flesh—all of the women's flesh—had been frozen in place with some magic, then left here. As art.

Beneath the scarf, Kylar could see the bruises circling Serah's neck. He looked away. There were two ways to die when hanged: if you fell far enough, your neck would break and you'd die quickly, otherwise you strangled slowly. Serah had died the hard way.

He stepped away, but everywhere his eyes turned, he saw gruesome detail. The women wearing bracelets concealed gashed wrists; chemises concealed pierced hearts; those wearing more clothing did so to conceal the imperfections of their taxidermy: they were the ones who'd thrown themselves from their balconies and now had bulges where no bulges belonged.

Kylar staggered like a man drunk. He needed air. He was going to throw up. He burst out onto the Godking's wide balcony.

She sat on the stone railing, feet hooked through the posts for balance, leaning far back, naked, a nightgown in her hand, fluttering in the wind like a flag. Mags.

Kylar screamed. Talent leaked through his fury and the scream reverberated over the castle, echoing back from the courtyard far below. All life in the castle stopped. Kylar didn't notice, nor did he notice the ka'kari rushing over his skin, the face of judgment covering his anguish.

He hammered a palm down on the stone railing and crushed it on one side of Mags, then again on her other side, then he lifted her and carried her back inside. The feeling of her skin, so like living skin, was obscene. But her limbs were locked in place. He laid her on the bed, then tore the bolts holding Serah Drake to the wall. He laid Serah beside her sister. As he covered them, he saw that each girl's left foot was signed in a bubbly script, as if their corpses were art: Trudana Jadwin.

Vi was staring saucer-eyed from him to the shattered six-inch stone railing. "Fucking fuck," she whispered. "Kylar, is that you?"

He nodded stiffly. He wanted to remove the mask of judgment, but he couldn't. He needed it right now.

"I checked the concubines' rooms," Vi said. "Nothing. He must already be in the throne room."

Kylar's stomach flipped. He jerked involuntarily.

"What?" Vi asked.

"Bad memories," Kylar said. "Fuck it. Let's go."

Dawn was coming. By killing the two guards, they'd tipped their own hourglass. Someone would check the men's post soon—probably at dawn. Worse, the Cenarian army's glass was already draining. The battle would begin soon and then the nasty surprises would start. If Logan were to have a chance to be king, Kylar needed to hand him a victory. Killing Garoth Ursuul would unman the Khalidorans.

They walked through the halls brazenly, Vi in her serving girl uniform, and Kylar invisible but flitting from doorway to doorway as if he weren't, in case any meisters were wandering the halls. As they came to the last hallway, they passed six of the largest highlanders Kylar had ever seen. Kylar dodged behind some statuary as he saw that the highlanders were accompanied by two Vürdmeisters. Most curious of all, the protection seemed to be for one woman—apparently one of the Godking's concubines or wives—all wrapped up in robes and veils so that not an inch of her skin showed.

When Kylar drew his knives to kill them, Vi laid a hand on his arm. He turned judgment's eye on her and she flinched, but she was right. A fight here was a distraction that might jeopardize the real mission, and there was nothing that was going to stop Kylar from killing Garoth Ursuul.

Kylar's stomach was a riot. It didn't quiet even when the group rounded a corner and disappeared. This was the same hallway he'd stood in with Elene and Uly, when he'd gone to his first death.

He calmed. Garoth Ursuul was far more powerful than Roth Ursuul, but Kylar was more powerful now, too. He was more confident. He'd been a boy trying to prove he was a man then, now he was a man making a choice, knowing what it might cost.

He smiled recklessly. "So, Vi, you ready to kill a god?"

66

The men perched on the crest of a hill south of the battlefield: six of the Sa'seurans' most powerful magi. Their clothing betrayed none of that. Each dressed in the plain clothes of a trader from his own homeland: four Alitaerans, a Waeddryner, and a Modaini. Their sturdy packhorses even bore a respectable amount of trade goods, and if their mounts were a little better than most traders would own, they weren't so fine as to attract comment. But if the men's clothes didn't betray them, their bearing did. These were men who strode the earth with the assurance of gods.

"This oughtn't be pretty," the Modaini said. Antoninus Wervel was a short butter-tub of a man with a bulbous, florid nose and a fringe of brown hair combed over his shiny pate. In the Modaini fashion, he wore kohl around his eyes and had darkened and lengthened his eyebrows. It gave him a sinister look. "How many meisters you figure they've got?" he asked one of the Alitaeran twins, Caedan.

The gangly youth twitched. Caedan was one of two Seers in the group, and he was supposed to be spotting. "Sorry, sorry. I was just—are that man's bodyguards all women?"

"Surely not."

"They are," Lord Lucius said. He was the leader of the expedition, and the other Seer. But he was more interested in the opposing side.

"The Khalidorans have at least ten meisters, probably twenty. They're standing close together."

"Lord Lucius," Caedan said timidly. "I think they've got six Vürd-meisters there, back farther, in the middle. It looks like they're gathered around something, but I can't tell what it is."

The butter-tub hmmphed. "How many of the Touched fight for Cenaria?" He said it to irritate the Alitaerans. In Modai, *touched* meant Talented, not *crazy* as it did in Alitaera.

Caedan was oblivious. "There's a man and woman in the Cenarian lines, both trained, standing together. Several others untrained."

"And among the Ceuran raiders?"

"I haven't seen the Ceurans since they went around the bend."

The other young Alitaeran, Jaedan, looked unhappy. He was the identical twin of the young Seer, with the same handsome features, same floppy black hair, and totally different gifts.

"Why are they being so stupid?" he asked. "We all saw the Lae'knaught army coming up from the south. Five thousand lancers who hate the Khalidorans more than anything. Why don't the Cenarians wait until they get here?"

"They might not know the Lae'knaught are coming," Lord Lucius said.

"Or they might not be coming. They might be waiting to pick off the victor. Or Terah Graesin might want all the glory for herself," Wervel suggested.

Jaedan couldn't believe it. "We aren't just going to sit here, are we? By the Light! The Cenarians will be destroyed. Twenty meisters. We can take them. I'm good for three or four, and I know the rest of you are as good or better."

"You forget our mission, Childe Jaedan," Lord Lucius said. "We haven't been sent to fight in anyone's war. The Khalidorans aren't a threat to us—"

"The Khalidorans are a threat to everyone!" Jaedan protested.

"*SILENCE!*"

Jaedan cut off, but the defiance on his face didn't alter a whit. The Cenarian line began moving at a slow jog, allowing the army, like an enormous beast, to gain momentum.

Caedan twitched. "Did—did any of you feel that?" he asked.

"What?" Wervel asked.

"I don't know. Just—I don't know. Like an explosion? May I go see what the Ceurans are doing, Lord Lucius?"

"We need your eyes on the battle. Watch and learn, childe. We have a rare opportunity to see how the Khalidorans fight. You, too, Jaedan."

The Khalidoran army was formed in loose ranks, with space beside every warrior for an archer. The archers readied themselves now, each putting arrows in the ground where they could be grabbed quickly. In the front of everyone, the two-man teams of meisters sat on horseback. To the Seers, they glowed.

"What will they do, Caedan?" Lord Lucius asked.

"Fire, sir? And lightning second?"

"And why?"

"Because it will scare the shit out of the Cenarians? I mean, uh, the effects on morale, sir," Caedan said.

The Cenarian line was still jogging forward. They were four hundred paces away now. The group under General Agon had advanced to the fore and split. But they didn't just split into one or two or even three groups. His few horsemen, and his foot soldiers, formed a fragmented line as long as the Cenarian front.

"What the hell is he doing?" one of the Alitaerans asked.

For a long moment, no one answered. He couldn't hope to break the Khalidoran line with such a ragged line of his own. His move also left a gap in the Cenarian center. But even as the men watched, another of the Cenarian generals, Duke Wesseros, ordered his men into the gap.

"It's genius. He's minimizing his losses," Wervel said.

For a moment no one asked. If there was one thing magi hated more than not understanding something, it was not understanding something after someone had understood it first and had given them a hint.

"What?" Jaedan asked.

"Think like a meister, childe. You'd have enough vir for what, five? ten? fireballs before you're spent. Usually, you'll kill two to five men with each fireball. With the line this thin, you'll kill one. You might even miss completely. Agon knows he's gambling. If the main line comes to support his line too late, his first line will be slaughtered, but if they hit within five or ten seconds, he'll have saved hundreds and nullified the, uh, effects on morale. It looks like we've found a general who knows how to fight meisters. There might be hope for Cenaria after all."

At two hundred paces, the line picked up speed.

The archers in the Khalidoran lines loosed their first volley, and a flock of two thousand black-feathered arrows took flight. For a long second, they darkened an already bleak sky, casting the shadow of death across the dawn. When they dove back to earth, they buried their barbed beaks in earth and armor and the flesh of men and horses.

Again, the dispersed ranks saved hundreds, but up and down the Cenarian line, men flopped over onto the stubbly fields, going from a full sprint to the rest of death in an instant. Others fell, injured, legs or arms pierced, and were trampled by their friends and countrymen a moment later. Horses lost riders and continued the charge merely because the horses to their right and left still charged. Riders lost horses and pitched to the earth at great speed, sometimes flying free of the saddle and rising to run with their earthbound comrades, sometimes getting caught in the saddle and crushed beneath their horse's body.

The Khalidoran army performed as only veterans can. The archers loosed as many arrows as they could in a few seconds, then, as a flag went up, each grabbed his remaining arrows and retreated. There were perfect lines in the ranks to allow each archer to get to the back behind the spearmen and swordsmen who would protect them from the melee. As they retreated, without even a separate order being given, the rear lines filled in the gaps the archers had left. The maneuver was nothing special, but the speed at which the army carried it out with thousands of enemies sprinting toward it was.

The meisters loosed fire. Their original plan in shambles, some of the meisters hurled balls of fire at the charging horses while others, still hoping for the effect of running into a firestorm, swept gouts of fire across the stubbly fields. What would have ordinarily broken up and disoriented an entire line in the crucial seconds before impact didn't even slow the Cenarians.

The crash of the lines was distinctly audible to the magi, even as far away as they were. Men and horses impaled themselves on spears and their momentum carried them into the Khalidoran ranks. Others crashed full force into Khalidoran shields and sent men sprawling, but the Cenarians in that first rank must have been veterans. In most armies, no matter what their commanders told them, many of the men would slow before that last impact. The idea of crashing full force into a line bristling with swords and spears was too viscerally paralyzing for most men. These had no such doubts. They burst into the Khalidoran line with all their might. It was an awesome and fearful sight.

But they were almost swallowed up before the main body of the Cenarian line hit the Khalidorans. The shock of it rippled through the entire Khalidoran line, pushing them back a good ten feet.

On their horses, the meisters laid about themselves with fire and lightning, but far behind the Cenarian front lines, archers on horseback were hunting them, riding back and forth, stopping, shooting arrows from short bows and moving on. The shots seemed impossible— a short bow killing from two or three hundred paces? Caedan checked the archers again, but they weren't Talented, he was sure of it. To Caedan, it was like watching candles being snuffed one at a time as meisters toppled from their saddles.

The lines heaved back and forth and disintegrated into a thousand clumps of individual combat. Horses wheeled and stamped and kicked and bit. Meisters burned holes in men, set fire to others, laid about themselves with cudgels or swords of pure magic, and sometimes fell dead, pierced by arrows.

In five minutes, seventeen of the twenty meisters were riddled with arrows and the Khalidoran line was stretching at the middle. The giant Cenarian who'd led the first charge seemed to be a beacon of hope. Wherever he went, the Cenarians pushed to go there, too. And now, he was pushing to cut all the way through the Khalidoran line.

Caedan muttered an oath. "Where did *they* come from?" he asked. The magi followed his eyes. Rank upon rank of Khalidoran highlanders were forming up to each side of the battlefield.

"The caves," Wervel said. "What are they doing?"

The highlanders spread out and jogged toward the flanks and back of the battle. There were at least five hundred of them, but they didn't charge into the battle. They didn't seem at all disturbed that they were losing the advantage of surprise. They spread their line thinner and thinner, as if to cup the entire rear of the battle.

"Sir," Caedan said. "I thought you only tried to surround an enemy if you outnumbered him."

Lord Lucius looked disturbed. He was looking to the back of the Khalidoran line where the Vürdmeisters were gathered. "What is that chained between the Vürdmeisters?"

"That isn't a—" one magus said.

"Surely not. They're just legend and superstition."

"May the God have mercy," Wervel said. "It is."

67

No," Vi said. "I can't."

Kylar turned the face of judgment on her.

"You—you don't know what he's like. You've never looked into his eyes. When you see yourself in his eyes, you look in the face of your own wretchedness. Please, Kylar."

Kylar gnashed his teeth. He looked away. It seemed like it took conscious effort, but slowly that terrifying mask melted away and his own face emerged—his eyes still icy cold.

"You know, my master was wrong about you. He was there when Hu Gibbet presented you to the Sa'kagé. He told me how you trashed those other wetboys. He told me that if I didn't watch out, you'd be the best wetboy of our generation. He called you a prodigy. He said that there wouldn't be five men in the kingdom who could beat you. But they don't have to. You've beaten yourself. Durzo was wrong. You aren't even in the same class as me."

"Fuck you! You don't know—"

"Vi, this is what matters. If you're not with me now, it's all horseshit."

As his eyes bored into her, she felt herself changing. She was angry at herself, and at him, and at herself again. She couldn't let Kylar down. She had never let anything be more important than herself.

And now, in the blind stupidity of infatuation, it was more important that she have this man's respect than that she live.

The infuriating thing was that it wasn't even a contest. And yet her weakness for Kylar was propelling her toward strength against the one she really should fear—Nysos! This was all too confusing.

"Fine!" she practically spat. "Turn your back!"

"Got a dagger?" Kylar asked as he turned.

"Shut up, you smug sonuvabitch." *Oh, brilliant, Vi. You realize you like him, so you insult him—for helping you find your guts.* She pulled off the dress and pulled on her wetboy tunic. She was being a real wench. AAAHHH! She'd just had eight emotions in the space of three seconds.

"Fine," she said. "You can turn back around. I'm sorry for...before. I was hoping to—" What had she been hoping? To impress him? Entice him? To see the heat of desire in those cool eyes? "—to shock you," she said.

"You, uh, succeeded."

"I know." She couldn't help but smile. "You're not like any man I've ever known, Kylar. You've got this, this, innocence about you."

He scowled.

"When you've been where I've been, it's really...cute. I mean, I didn't know guys could be like you." Why was she running off at the mouth all of the sudden?

"You barely know me," Kylar said.

"I...shit, it's not just like it's a list of facts that prove you're different, Kylar. You feel different." She was flustered. Was he being deliberately dense?

"Ah, fuck it," she said. "Do you think we could ever work out?"

"What?" Kylar asked. The tone of his voice should have shut her up.

"You know. You and me. Together."

Incredulity spread across his face, and the expression confirmed every damning thought she'd ever had about herself.

"No," Kylar said. "No, I don't think so."

No, she could tell he meant, you're damaged goods.

She shut down. "Right," she said. Once a whore, forever a whore. "Right. Well, we've got work to do. I've got a plan."

Kylar looked poised on the verge of saying something. She'd caught him totally off guard. Shit, what did she expect?

Nysos, so he looked at your tits. So he's nice to you. You're still the one who killed his best friend, kidnapped his daughter, and split up his family. Shit, Vi, what were you thinking?

"All right," she said before he could say anything. "If we go in the side here, they'll know it's an attack. We have no idea what their strength is or how many of them there are. But if I walk right in to report on your, well, your death, they won't suspect a thing. If you go in the side door, you can decide when to strike. As soon as I see palies go down—preferably starting with the king—I'll fight too, all right?"

"Sounds pretty weak," Kylar said. "But it also sounds better than anything I've got. But one thing..." He trailed off.

"What?" She was eager to go now, to stop talking, stop messing up.

"If he kills me, Vi...Get my body out of there. You can't let them have it."

"What do you care?"

"Just do it."

"Why!" Now she was taking her frustration out on him. Beautiful.

"Because I come back. I don't stay dead."

"You're mad."

He held up a black shiny ball. It melted and wrapped around his hand like a glove. His hand disappeared. A moment later, it was a ball again. "If Ursuul takes this, he takes my powers. All of them."

She scowled. "If we make it through this, you have a lot of questions to answer."

"Fair enough." Kylar paused. "Vi? It's been good working with you." Not waiting for her response, he squeezed the ball and disappeared.

Vi turned down the hall and started walking. Ironically, she ran into no patrols at all until she came to the four soldiers guarding the main doors of the throne room. The men eyed her with disbelief. They seemed to forget their weapons as their eyes lingered exactly where they were supposed to.

"Tell the Godking that Vi Sovari has come to receive her reward."

"The Godking isn't to be disturbed except in the case of—"

"This counts," Vi hissed at the man, first leaning forward until his eyes were pegged to her cleavage and then pushing his chin back up with the knife that had materialized in her hand. He swallowed. "Yes, ma'am."

The guard eased the great double doors open. "God, our God of the High Realms, Your Holiness, Vi Sovari begs admittance."

The guard stepped aside and motioned to her. "Good luck," he whispered, smiling apologetically. *The bastard. How dare he be human?*

Standing in the last hall, Kylar brought the ka'kari to his eyes. He didn't see any magical alarms. Invisible, he moved to the door. The hinges were well-oiled.

"Come in, come in, Viridiana," he heard the Godking say. "It's been too long. I was afraid I was going to have to enjoy the death of ten thousand rebels all by myself."

Kylar cracked the door open as the Godking spoke, and as the man took in the admittedly impressive sight of Vi in her version of wetboy grays, Kylar stole into the throne room. He slipped behind one of the enormous pillars supporting the ceiling. The servants' entrance he'd used opened near the base of the fourteen steps to the dais. Ursuul sat at the top of the steps in his black fireglass throne.

In the center of the vast room was a rolling plain at the base of the mountains. There were tiny figures on each side of the plain, moving in concert. Kylar realized they were miniature armies, lining up in the dawn light. It wasn't a painting or embroidery of a battle; it was a battle. Fifteen thousand tiny, tiny figures strode across the plain. Kylar could even pick out flags of the noble houses. The Cenarian lines were forming up, following...Logan? Logan was leading the charge? Madness! How could Agon let the king lead a charge?

The great doors closed behind Vi as the Godking waved her in. Kylar had seen the man only briefly when Jonus Severing tried to assassinate him. Kylar would have expected Garoth to be old and decrepit, swollen or sagging from a life of evil, but Garoth Ursuul was in excellent health. He was perhaps fifty, looked at least ten years younger, and though he had the thick body and cool skin of a Khalidoran highlander, he had a fighting man's arms, a lean face with an oiled black beard, and a head shaved bald and gleaming. He looked like the kind of man who not only would shake your hand but when he did, you'd find calluses and a firm grip.

"Don't mind the battle," the Godking said. "You can walk through it; it won't harm the magic, but be quick. The rebels are about to charge. It's my favorite part."

Through the ka'kari, however, Garoth Ursuul was a miasma. Twisted, screaming faces streamed behind him like a cloud. Murder lay so thick on him it blotted out his features. Betrayals and rapes and casual tortures wreathed his limbs. Threaded through it all, like noxious green smoke, was the vir. It somehow fed off and deepened all that darkness, and it was so powerful it seemed to fill the room.

As he stood behind the pillar, Kylar noticed a small group of the tiny men fighting three feet away from him. Off the battlefield proper, a big man was about to be ridden down by four Khalidoran lancers.

Except the man wasn't ridden down. In seconds, he killed three lancers. There was something familiar about him. *Feir Cousat!*

Kylar knew he should be trying to figure out a way to move without being seen, but he was rapt in the drama unfolding silently, inches away. The Ceurans' parted leader came forward. Feir drew a sword that looked like a bar of fire. It stunned the Ceurans. Feir and the leader fought for about half a second: the first time their swords crossed, there was a flash of light. The Ceuran came away with the sword.

"What was that?" the Godking said.

"What?" Vi asked.

"Out of the way, girl."

As Feir knelt before the Ceuran (knelt? Feir?), the image of the battle suddenly spun around, putting the Khalidoran lines at the base of the steps and the Cenarian lines close to the great doors.

Garoth hmmphed. "Just some raiders."

Kylar brought some of the ka'kari to his fingertips, sharpened it into a claw, and tested it against the pillar. His fingers sank in like it was butter. He eased back on the magic and tried again until he was able to sink his fingers in and get a grip. *This is going to be fun.*

He shook his head. It seemed the ka'kari had no limitations, and that was just making Kylar more aware of his own.

Kylar sent some of the ka'kari to his feet and climbed the pillar. There was a tiny hiss and a tinge of smoke at every step, but it was as effortless as climbing a ladder. Kylar reached the fifty-foot ceiling in seconds.

Figuring out how to adjust the claws to work on the ceiling took a few seconds, but then he was clinging to the throne room's high, vaulted ceiling like a spider. His heart was in his throat. He crept across the ceiling until he was directly above the throne, his body shielded from view by one of the arches, only his invisible head exposed.

The Godking gave a running commentary to Vi. "No," he was saying, "I don't know why the Cenarians are using that formation. Seems awfully open to me."

Kylar watched, upside down, as the Cenarian ranks slammed into the Khalidoran line. The first rank to hit them was thin—he wondered if they'd lost so many from the archers, but a few seconds later, the next line slammed into them.

The Godking cursed. "Damn them, brilliant. Brilliant."

"What is it?" Vi asked.

"Do you know why I made all this, Vi?"

Heart pounding, Kylar released the ceiling with his hands and slowly uncurled, upside down. He drew his daggers, hanging on the ceiling with his feet, bat-like. Garoth Ursuul stepped directly beneath him.

Then there was no fear, only calm certainty. Kylar dropped from the ceiling.

One of the dark faces twisting in the miasma around the Godking screamed. Green-black caltrops of vir burst in every direction from the Godking. Kylar hit one and they all exploded.

The concussion blasted Kylar off course. He sprawled sideways, missed his landing, and tumbled down the stairs. He rolled across the landing and down the second flight. When he came to rest at the bottom of the stairs, his head was ringing. He tried to stand and promptly fell.

"I made it because a god ought to have some fun. Don't you agree, Kylar?" Garoth smiled a predatory smile. He wasn't surprised. "So, Vi, you've done what you promised. You killed Jarl, and you brought Kylar to me."

Kylar had trusted her. How could he have been so foolish? It was the second time he'd walked into a trap in this room. Inexplicably, he felt calm. He felt lethal. He hadn't come this far to fail. This kill was his destiny.

"I didn't betray you, Kylar," Vi said in a small, desperate voice.

"Oh, he put a spell on you that made you do it? I gave you a chance, Vi. You could have been different."

"She didn't betray you," the Godking said. "You betrayed yourself." He pulled out two diamonds, each the size of his thumb. They were the ones that had held the monster downstairs together. "Who else would have the physical prowess to snatch these but a wetboy, and who else could survive the magic but the bearer of the black ka'kari? I've known you were here for an hour."

"So, why are you going to reward her?" Kylar asked.

"What, you want me to kill her, too?"

Kylar scowled. "I did until you said that."

The Godking laughed. "You're an orphan, aren't you, Kylar?"

"No," Kylar said. He stood. His head was slowly clearing, and he could swear he could feel his body healing his bruises.

"Oh right, the Drakes. Magdalyn told me all about that. She thought you'd save her. Sad. When you killed Hu Gibbet, you really upset me. So I killed her."

"Liar."

"Hu's dead?" Vi asked. She seemed absolutely thunderstruck.

"Do you ever wonder who your real father is, Kylar?"

"No," Kylar said. He tried to move and found thick bands of magic around his body. He examined them. They were simple, unvaried. The ka'kari would devour them easily. *Go on, keep smiling, you fiend.*

Garoth smiled. "There's a reason I knew you were coming, Kylar, a reason you're so extraordinarily talented. I'm your father."

"WHAT?"

"Ah, just joking." Garoth Ursuul laughed. "I'm not being much of a host, am I? You came in here all prepared to fight some big battle, didn't you?"

"I guess so."

Garoth was in high spirits. "I could use a bit of a warm-up myself. What do you say, Kylar? Want to fight a ferali?"

"I don't actually have a choice, do I?"

"No."

"Well, then, golly, I'd love to fight a ferali, Gare."

"Gare," the Godking said. "Haven't heard that in thirty years. Before we start..." He turned. "Vi, decision time. If you serve me willingly, I can reward you. I'd like that. But you'll serve regardless. You're chained to me. The compulsion won't allow you to hurt me. It won't allow you to let anyone else hurt me while you live, either."

"I'll never serve you!" she said.

"Fair enough, but you might want to leave the worst of the fighting to the boys."

"Fuck you," she said.

"A distinct possibility, child."

Garoth gestured and a door flew open behind him. "Tatts, why don't you come in?"

The ferali shuffled in. It now had the shape of an enormous man, tattoos still visible on its lumpy skin. Despite his height—at least nine feet—and the thickness of his limbs, Kylar saw that the ferali wasn't as big as it had been just an hour before. The monster's face was all too human, though, and it looked ashamed.

"It'll all be better in a moment. I promise," the Godking said. He slammed the diamonds into the ferali's spine. It cried out with a voice no longer human, and then was still. Garoth abruptly ignored it. "Do you know why you've never heard of a ferali? They're expensive. First, you need diamonds or you can't control the damn things. But you already figured that out, didn't you? Second, you have to take a man and torture him until there is nothing left but rage. It usually takes hundreds of tries to find the right kind of man. But even that isn't enough. The magic involved is beyond what even a Godking can do unaided. They require Khali's direct intervention. That has a cost."

"I don't understand," Kylar said. He was studying the ferali. It only had so much mass. It could only change shape so quickly. Fixing those things in mind would change everything.

"Neither did Moburu or Tenser. They do, now. This time I made them pay the price. You see, Khali feeds on suffering, so we dedicate every cruelty we can invent to her. In return, she gives us the vir. But for greater power, Khali asks more.

"When I was warring with my brothers, She offered to help me create a ferali if I would host a Stranger. You're not familiar with them? My first was named Pride. He was a small price to pay for godhood. Unfortunately, Khali didn't tell me that a ferali will devour itself if given no other meat. I didn't make another until my son Dorian betrayed me, and I've found Lust to be a more odious companion—as Vi shall discover, my appetites grow ever more exotic. Hold on, that line's not doing well, is it?" On the phantom battlefield, Logan was pushing the Khalidoran line out into a half moon.

"Hmm," the Godking said. "Much faster than I expected." He pulled out a stick. It started flashing in his hand. From the edges of the battle-field, thousands more Khalidoran troops began closing on the Cenar-ian army's flanks. Other ranks moved to reinforce the arcing section of the line.

Garoth wasn't trying to win the battle. He merely wanted to fence in the Cenarians so he could unleash Moburu's ferali on them. Kylar felt sick. What would it do with an unlimited number of victims?

"It will take a few minutes before they get in position," Garoth said. "Where was I?"

"I think we were at the fight-to-the-death part," Kylar said.

"Oh, no, no. You see," Garoth went up to the carved fireglass throne and sat. Kylar could see him erecting magical wards around himself. "Left alone, a ferali is nearly mindless, but—and this is the beautiful thing—they can be ridden. Tell me, how much fun is that?"

"It's a lot more fun if I can move," Kylar said.

"Do you know why I've gone to so much trouble to bring you here, Kylar?"

"My excellent wit?"

"Your Devourer has another name. It is also called the Sustainer. It heals everything shy of death, doesn't it?"

"It won't help you," Kylar said.

"Oh but it will. I know how to break the bonding. There's an unnat-ural growth in my brain. It's killing me, and you've brought the only thing that can save me into my hands."

"Ah. The tumor it can help," Kylar said, "but your arrogance is terminal."

The Godking's eyes flashed. "How droll. Come. This 'Night Angel' business is finished."

"Finished?" Kylar said. "I'm just warmin' up."

68

The bonds dropped away and Vi started fighting. She swore constantly under her breath to use her Talent, but she wasn't angry. She'd always thought she was a cold, heartless bitch. She'd taken hold of that identity. It had made her strong against the nightly emptiness, the soul bankruptcy she'd carried for as long as she could remember. With the declaration that she would never serve the Godking—melodramatic or not—she felt that she'd made her first deposit in that bank ever.

Now she was fighting for something. No, for someone, and it was the first selfless thing she'd ever done.

The ferali hunched and its bones sped beneath its skin. In the time it took Vi to armor herself, it had become something like a centaur, except instead of a horse's body, it had a cougar's. It was shorter, more mobile on its four legs, but it had a human torso and arms. It grabbed a spear in its human hands and launched itself after Kylar, who dashed behind a pillar.

Vi sprinted up the steps three at a time, to attack the Godking. He was about to find out how wrong he'd been about the compulsion. Let Kylar fight the beast; she'd cut it off at its source.

She was drawing back her sword when she hit the ward that extended ten feet around the Godking like a bubble. It was like sprinting into a wall. She found herself sprawled on the stairs—she must have rolled partway down them without even noticing. Her nose was bleeding and her head was ringing. She blinked at Kylar.

The man was a virtuoso. As the ferali charged with spear leveled, Kylar waited until the last moment and then launched himself forward. Knives flashed as he passed over the beast and its spear passed inches under him, harmlessly. But he wasn't done. He threw out a hand and somehow hooked the marble pillar, scoring it with a smoking gouge. As the ferali spun to catch him, Kylar emerged from the other side of the pillar and flew over the ferali's back, blades flashing again.

Kylar landed in a crouch, one hand on the ground, the other on his sheathed sword. The ferali paused, bleeding profusely, the mouthy skin cut open over the back of one hand, one shoulder and across the cougar's haunches. The blood was red, all too human, but even as Vi watched, the gouges knit together in scars. The ferali threw its spear at him. Kylar deflected it with a hand, but the ferali was already moving.

As Kylar leapt toward the wall, the ferali slashed one arm at him, and in the space of the heartbeat that it took for its arm to move forward, the arm elongated, bones snapped into place and an enormous scythe-blade of a claw swept through the air. Kylar flipped off the wall directly into the path of the claw. It slammed him to the ground.

Vi thought he was surely dead, but even as Kylar hit the ground, the claw snapped off and skipped along the floor away from the ferali. Kylar had somehow managed to draw his sword and block the slash. The ferali, its left leg hanging limp and boneless, looked stunned. It sank into itself, becoming a great cat.

Before the beast could attack again, Vi finally gathered her wits and charged it, screaming. It wheeled. She danced just outside of the range of its claws, the sides of which it had armored into bone. Kylar got back to his feet, but was swaying from side to side, dazed. The ferali dashed away from Vi and touched its belly to the ground where its dead claw lay.

In a second, that flesh was part of the ferali again. Bones shifted and it stood as a tall man with bone-swords for arms. It seemed more comfortable in this guise, thickly muscled, quicker than any man, much of its skin reinforced with bone armor plates.

Together, Vi and Kylar fought. Kylar was capable of aerial moves Vi couldn't even comprehend, flipping off walls and the pillars, always landing on his feet like a cat, always leaving bloody furrows with his steel claws. Vi had less strength, even with her Talent, but she was quick. The ferali morphed again and again. It became a slight man with a living chain that it whipped around its head and flung around the pillars, hoping those mouthy links would catch either one of them. One of the links snagged Kylar's sleeve in midflight. It flipped him off balance and he crashed into the floor. The ferali pulled the chain in until Vi's sword passed in the inch between Kylar's skin and his sleeve and freed him. Kylar didn't even pause. He was just up and fighting.

Then the ferali was a giant with a war hammer. Marble exploded as it laid about itself with the huge weapon. Kylar and Vi ranged through the illusion of battle on the throne room floor, fighting as desperately as those men and women fought.

As they fought together, Kylar and Vi began to not just fight in unison, but with unity. As Vi understood Kylar's strengths, she could move, counting on him to react appropriately. They were warriors, they were wetboys, and they understood. For Vi, who had always had trouble with words, battle was truth.

She and Kylar fought together—leaping, meeting in mid-air, pushing off to go flying a new direction before the ferali could respond. They covered each other, saved each other's lives. Kylar clipped off the end of a bone mace Vi could have never avoided. Vi said, "Graakos"— and jaws closed on Kylar's arm and then bounced off.

It was, for her, a holy moment. She had never communed with another, never trusted another so implicitly, as she communed with and trusted Kylar. In this, through this, she understood the man in ways a thousand thousand words wouldn't have revealed. They were in total harmony, and the miracle was how natural it was.

At the same time, despair rose in her. They cut the ferali a hundred times. Two hundred. They attacked its eyes, its mouth. They cut off parts of its body. It bled, and its total mass decreased by a few pounds, but that was all. They cut it and it healed. But they could never make a mistake. Once that skin touched theirs, they would die.

~I also cut.~

Kylar alighted on the side of a pillar and stopped. Runes were glowing in ka'kari black edged in blue along his arm. He stared at them. "You what?" he asked.

"I didn't say anything," Vi said. Her eyes were on an enormous spider chittering on the floor in front of her.

"Stupid! How slow am I?" Kylar said, dropping to the floor.

~Is that a rhetorical question?~

The ka'kari poured a dark liquid from his hand onto his sword. But then the liquid solidified as a thin sword. Kylar cut left and right and spider legs went flying. It wasn't like hacking through bone, he was shearing them off like butter.

He dodged back, and the spider gathered its legs to itself, but this time, the stumps kept bleeding. They smoked and wouldn't allow new limbs to be grown there. It morphed back into the man with swords for arms, but now the wounds were on the man's chest, still flowing with blood and smoking. It roared and attacked Kylar.

Kylar slashed left and right and the sword-arms tumbled across the floor. He rammed the ka'kari into the ferali's chest. With a sharp motion, he pulled it down to the creature's groin. Smoke billowed, blood gushed. Kylar yanked the sword up, making another huge cut.

He saw it too late. The ferali's skin drew back from the sword, like a pond might crater when a stone falls into it, only to burst upward. The skin rushed up the sword all at once.

It engulfed Kylar's hand.

He threw himself back, but the ferali, limp now, fell forward with him, attached to his hand. Kylar jerked the sword back and forth and smoke gushed from the ferali as he gutted it, but it didn't lose its grip.

Kylar reached for a dagger, but he'd used them all in the battle. "Vi," he shouted. "Cut it off!"

She hesitated.

"Cut off my hand!"

She couldn't do it.

The skin twitched again and it rushed up his forearm.

Kylar screamed and twisted. A blade of ka'kari formed along the ridge of his left hand and he cut off his right arm. Released from the pull of the dying ferali, he collapsed backward.

He held the gushing stump in his left hand. A moment later, black metal shimmered in every exposed vein and the bleeding stopped. A black cap sheathed his stump. Kylar looked at Vi dumbly.

Ten feet away, the ferali's corpse was oozing. It began to break apart, weaves of magic unraveling. The mouthy skin rippled and evaporated and then all that was left was stinking ropes of meat and sinew and bone.

"That," the Godking's voice said, "was impressive, Kylar. You showed me some things that I wasn't aware the ka'kari could do. Most instructive. And Vi, you'll serve admirably, and not just in my bed."

Something in Vi snapped. In the last two days, she'd changed every-thing. A new Vi was fighting to be born—and the Godking was here, saying nothing had changed. The new Vi would be a stillbirth. She'd go back to being a whore. She'd go back to being the same cold, hard bitch.

She'd thought that life was the only one open to her, so she'd borne the unbearable. But having seen a way to be a woman she didn't hate, she couldn't go back.

"Get it through your fat head, Gare," she said, even as she felt magi-cal bonds wrapping around her limbs and Kylar's again. "I won't serve you."

Garoth smiled godly benevolence. "The feisty ones always make me hard."

"Kylar," Vi said. "Snap out of it. You gotta help me kill this fucking twist."

The Godking laughed. "Compulsion doesn't hold on everyone, Vi. The Niles' magic would have freed most people. About nineteen years ago, there was some Ceuran slut that I seduced during a diplomatic trip. I sent men to collect her when I found out she was pregnant, but she ran away before they got there. When I found out she bore a girl, I dismissed the matter. I usually have my daughters drowned—it's good practice for my boys, it makes them tough—but it wasn't worth the effort. Compulsion, Vi, only works on family, and sometimes not on boys. You—"

"You're not my father," Vi said. "You're just a sick fuck who's about to die. Kylar!"

"Now Vi, let's not get all teary-eyed," Garoth Ursuul said. "You're nothing to me but five minutes of pleasure and a spoonful of seed. Well, that's not true. You see, Vi, you're a wetboy I can trust. You will never disobey me, never betray me."

Vi was gripped by terror tighter than the magic that bound her limbs. Possibilities were dying on every side.

Kylar stirred. His eyes came back into focus. He wiggled his eyebrows at her, trying to be charming. The outrageous cuteness of it cracked her paralysis. His pale blue eyes said, You with me?

Hers answered him with a fierce, desperate joy that needed no translation.

Under his breath, Kylar said, "You take his attention, I'll take his life." He smiled and the rest of Vi's fear blew away. It was a real smile, with no desperation. There was no doubt in Kylar's eyes. Any additional obstacle—whether magical bonds or the loss of an arm—would only sweeten his victory. Killing the Godking was Kylar's destiny.

"You leave me no choice," Garoth Ursuul said. He pursed his lips. "Daughter, kill Kylar."

The ka'kari opened and devoured the bonds holding Vi and Kylar. Vi was moving, beginning a flashy, eye-grabbing stunt.

Then...everything stopped.

There was a gap of volition. In her mind's eye, Vi was leaping through the air, flying toward the Godking, her blade descending, his face twisting into a rictus of fear as he saw that his shields were gone, as he realized she'd defeated his compulsion—

But that was only her imagination.

A shock of impact ran up Vi's arm. Her wrist flexed as if to complete a horizontal slash through a heart, but she saw nothing, knew nothing except that there was a blank.

The gap cleared, and Vi was aware once more. Her fingers were uncurling from the familiar grip of her favorite knife. Kylar—so slowly, so painfully slowly—was falling. He drifted toward the floor, his head arcing back in a slow whiplash from having her knife rammed into his back, his dark hair rippling from the shock. It wasn't until he hit the floor that Vi realized that Kylar was dead. She had killed him.

"That, my dear daughter," Garoth Ursuul said, "is compulsion."

69

$\mathcal{K}$ylar pushed through the fog in a rush. In a moment that seemed out of joint, as if time didn't work the same way here, he was back in the indistinct room, once again facing the lupine, gray-haired man with his hair pure white on one temple.

"Two days isn't going to cut it," Kylar said. "I need to go back now."

"Impertinence last time, demands this time," the man said.

The man cocked his head, as if listening, and Kylar was again aware of the others. They were invisible when Kylar looked directly at them, but definitely there. Could he see them a little better this time? "Yes, yes," the Wolf said to a voice Kylar couldn't hear.

"Who are they?" Kylar asked.

"Immortality is lonely, Kylar. Madness need not be."

"Madness?"

"Say hello to the grand company of my imagination, gleaned from those profound souls I have known over the years. Not ghosts, just facsimiles, I'm afraid." The lupine man nodded his head again toward one of them and chuckled.

"If they're not real, why are you talking to them and not to me?" Kylar asked. He was still angry and this time, he wasn't going to take the man's chiding or his mysteries. "I need your help. Now."

"You'll find such urgency hard to hold onto as the centuries pass—"

"It'll be real hard if Garoth Ursuul takes my immortality."

The Wolf tented his fingers. "Poor Garoth. He believes himself a god. It will be his undoing, as it was mine."

"And another thing," Kylar said. "I want my arm back."

"I noticed you managed to lose that. You actually pulled the ka'kari out of every cell of the arm you lost. Was that intentional?"

"I didn't want the ferali to have it." Cell?

"A wise thought, but a poor choice. Do you remember what they call your ka'kari?"

"The Devourer," Kylar said. "So?"

The Wolf pursed his lips. Waited.

"You're joking," Kylar said. He felt sick.

"Afraid not. You didn't have to fight. What the ka'kari did while coating your sword it could have done while coating your body. You could have just walked through the ferali."

"Just like that?"

"Just like that. Because you cut your arm off instead—and pulled the ka'kari out of it first—your arm won't grow back. Sorry. I do hope you can fight with your left."

"To hell with you! Send me back or Ursuul wins."

The man gave him a toothy grin, as if being damned amused him. "Sending you back two days early will cost me," his eyes flicked up. "Three years and twenty-seven days of my life. Sort of like the rich stealing from the poor, wouldn't you say, immortal?" He held up his burn-knotted hand before Kylar could curse him. "I'll send you back if you make an oath to me. There's a sword. It's called Curoch, and I'd be lying if I didn't tell you that it's intensely desired by any number of powerful factions. You know the town of Torra's Bend?"

"Torras Bend?"

"That's the one. Get the sword and take it there. Go into the wood, past the oak grove, stop forty or fifty paces from the edge of the old forest, and throw Curoch in."

"Is that where you live?" Kylar asked.

"Oh no," the man said. "But something else does. Something that will guard Curoch from the world of man. If you do this, I will send you back now, and when you deliver the sword, I'll make your arm grow back."

"Who are you?" Kylar asked.

"I'm one of the good guys. At least as much as I can be." His golden eyes danced. "But I want you to understand something Acaelus never did: I'm not a man," he paused, grinning, and Kylar did indeed wonder how much humanity was behind those lupine eyes, "to cross lightly."

"I figured."

"Are you in?"

"That's odd," the Godking said, coming to stand over Kylar's corpse. "Where's the ka'kari? I sense . . . it's in his body?"

"Yes," Vi said, unable to stop herself.

"Fascinating. I don't suppose you know what all it does?"

To her horror, Vi found herself answering. It hadn't been a direct question, so she veered as hard as she could. "No. I know it makes him invisible." She'd tried to say "made," but she couldn't force the past tense into the sentence. She hoped he didn't notice.

"Well, regardless, your lover will have to wait. I have a massacre to attend."

Vi screamed and grabbed Kylar's sword. Garoth watched her curiously. The sword swung in an arc—and stopped. She stopped it herself. She couldn't do it.

"Amazing, isn't it?" he said. "Funny thing is, I learned compulsion from one of your southron mating rituals—ringing—but you people completely misunderstood its true power. Anyway, feel free to watch the battle—and stop grunting, dear. It's unbecoming."

Abruptly, his eyes went vacant. Vi tried to move the sword, but it was impossible. The compulsion was undeniable.

As the wytches released the ferali, Vi sat on the steps before the throne to watch. But even that terrible spectacle couldn't hold her attention.

She should have given up long ago. All her fighting was a farce. She'd done everything the Godking had wanted her to do. She'd killed Jarl and she'd killed Kylar. In the years to come, she'd doubtless kill hundreds more. Thousands. It wouldn't matter. No one else could ever mean what Jarl and Kylar had meant to her. Jarl, her only friend, dead by her hand. Kylar, a man who had somehow stirred . . . what? Passion? Maybe just warmth, in a cold dead heart. A man who could have been . . . more.

She hated every man she'd ever known. It was man's nature to kill, to destroy, to tear down. Woman was the giver of life, the nurturer. And yet . . . Kylar.

He stood athwart her suppositions like a colossus. Kylar, the legendary wetboy who should have been the very quintessence of destruction, had saved a little girl, adopted her, saved a woman, saved nobles who didn't deserve saving, and tried to leave the bitter business. *Would have left it, too, if not for me.*

If not for Vi, Kylar would be in Caernarvon, leading some sort of daylight life that Vi couldn't even imagine. And what was it with Elene? Kylar could have had any woman he wanted, and he'd chosen a girl covered with scars. In her experience, men went for the hottest bitch they could get their cock in. If the bitch was hot, they didn't care that she was a bitch. Kylar wasn't like that.

Vi had an awful flash of intuition. She saw Elene—a woman she'd never met—as her twin and opposite. Elene had scars an inch deep, but beneath that she was all beauty and grace and love. Vi was all ugliness except for the thin veil of her skin. Kylar's love was a mystery no more. The man who could see past Jarl's murder could easily see past a few scars. Of course he loved Elene. Or had, before Vi killed him.

Kylar had said he would come back. But he wouldn't come back. The Godking had won.

Vi pulled her knife out of Kylar's back and rolled him over. His eyes were open, blank, dead. She closed those accusing eyes, pulled his head into her lap and turned to watch the Godking massacre Cenaria's last hope.

70

*A*ll pretense of scholastic detachment was gone. At first, the magi had to strain to see the ferali. It entered the battle virtually unnoticed.

Within a minute, one of the mages said, "McHalkin was right. I thought he made it up."

"We all thought he made it up. What does this mean about all those other creatures in his writings?"

"Gods, it's just like he said. It's being ridden, possessed."

On the battlefield, the beast's presence was becoming known. It had become a great bull, plowing through the lines of Cenarians. Whatever gashes the soldiers managed to inflict were quickly filled, and the creature grew.

The clamor of battle, the shouts of rage and pain and ringing steel had been drifting up to the promontory since the battle began. Now, new sounds rose: screams of terror.

The enormous bull lumbered out the side of the Khalidoran line. Half a dozen men, some still alive, were stuck to the beast. It paused as it digested them and began rearranging itself. The ferali curled into a ball and sheets of plate metal bobbed to the surface of its skin. It unfolded itself and stood.

The ferali now wore the shape of a troll. It was three times the height of a man, its skin was armor and mail and gawping little mouths. It had even taken into itself the swords and spears of its dead opponents, which now bristled from its back and sides.

The Cenarians' first reaction was surprisingly heroic. They charged the beast.

It was futile. It beat its way through the lines, never moving so fast that the Khalidoran line couldn't close behind it, and everywhere it went, killing, it was careful to lift every man it had killed or maimed in one of its four arms and stick him to its skin, or impale him on the spears on its back. One would be devoured, and then the next, and the next, and the next.

If the soldiers even wounded the beast, the magi couldn't tell. Never slowing, it tore apart line after line.

In the face of that inexorable death, General Agon charged part of the Khalidoran line with everything he had, trying to escape. By luck or leadership, hundreds of his men joined him, all attacking one place, desperate. The Khalidoran line bowed and nearly broke, but the Khalidoran prince Moburu's cavalry reinforced the line until the ferali waded through the ranks to get there. Abruptly, the charge broke off, and the Cenarian generals tried to get their men to charge another way. But the din of battle, the confusion of being ringed by the Khalidorans, and the terror at the ever-enlarging beast was too much.

The Cenarians were fighting in a desperate frenzy. They were moments away from panic.

"We have to go help them," Jaedan said.

The magi looked at him like he was insane.

"What? We're some of the most powerful magi in the world! If we don't help them, they'll die. If we don't oppose Khalidor now, it'll be too late."

"Jaedan," Wervel said quietly. "The ferali is almost impervious to magic—and that was to the ancients. It's already too late."

Lord Lucius was in no mood to placate the youth. He said, "We were sent to find, or find word of, the great sword. If Curoch is here, believe me, Jaedan, we will know of it presently. If the Cenarians have it, they will use it now. The council—"

"The council isn't here!" Jaedan said. "I think—"

"What you think is irrelevant! We will not fight. That's final. Understood?"

Jaedan's jaw clenched with the effort of holding back words he would be made to regret. He turned his eyes back to the men dying because of Lord Lucius's apathy. "Understood, sir."

One thing the stories never mentioned about battles—the stories Logan had loved so much as a boy—was the smell. He thought that after the Hole, nothing could ever shock him again, but he was wrong. He'd lost count of the men he'd seen die in the Hole, but whatever the number was—twelve? fifteen?—it was nothing compared with the number dead here in the first charge alone. The smell had been excitement and fear and rain and mud, insignificant smells next to the sights of flashing steel and proud horses, the fierce faces of the women who rode with him.

The Khalidorans had hemmed them in. Without flags or hand signals to communicate with distant commanders, the Cenarians couldn't escape. If too few joined a charge, it went nowhere. If too many, they'd be massacred from the rear. The Cenarian army was paralyzed, and more and more Khalidorans emerged—from where? Why the hell hadn't they known they were there? Had Luc Graesin blown his assignment or had he betrayed them? It didn't matter now, only avoiding slaughter mattered, and the stench filled his nostrils.

It was the men packed tightly together, their heat and their sweat and their fear commingling with the terror of the panicky horses. It was a sewer, as the dead and the fearful lost control of their bowels. It was gastric juices from stomachs cut open, intestines slashed, dying beasts kicking at the earth and bawling. It was blood so thick it gathered in pools with the rain. It was the sweeter smell of women's sweat, their numbers dwindling but still fearless so long as Logan was fearless.

Wherever he went, the Cenarian lines rallied. It wasn't only his presence. It was these magnificent women, streaked with blood and cursing like sailors. The very sight of them bewildered the Khalidorans.

If it weren't for the Order, Logan would have died in the first charge. They fought with nearly suicidal frenzy to be at his side, and they'd paid the price for it. Of the thirty women who'd ridden with him, only ten remained. With such a small bodyguard, Logan surely would have been overwhelmed had not more than a hundred men joined them in the minutes after the first charge—Agon's Dogs. He'd given them words, and now they gave him their lives.

Logan couldn't have said how long it was into the battle when a new smell cut through the ranks. It was something rancid, which made no sense. Tonight, the armies would leave plenty of meat on the field to rot, but nothing should be rotten yet. He heard and felt the Cenarians reacting long before he saw the source of their newest fear. Then, from the back of his horse, he saw what looked like a bull, a bull the height of a destrier, blasting through the lines and out of the battle, dragging men with it.

A different creature returned. It was a troll with four arms, four eyes, lumpy grayish skin, and blades sticking out of its back. Logan knew that he should have been afraid, and part of him marveled that he wasn't. Fear simply wasn't there.

Battle became simple, one understanding that led to one fact: that creature was killing his people. He had to stop it.

General Agon led another charge. His men smashed into the cavalry like a balsa hammer on an anvil. It was all Agon could do to break away from that damned cavalry officer with Ladeshian skin and Alitaeran clothes and horses.

Logan charged at the beast. It seemed to be even bigger now. One entire arm now was a scythe blade and the troll swept it across the field about three feet above the ground, reaping a full harvest. There was no way to dodge. Some men jumped, and others dove to the ground, but most were cut in half. The troll moved forward, arms lifting the dead and impaling them on the lances and swords that studded its body.

Logan rode into the space created as the Cenarians pushed back as far back from the troll as they could. His white charger danced nervously.

The troll stopped and regarded Logan. It made an indistinct roar that nearly took Logan's horse out of his control, then shook itself. A human head pushed out of the troll's belly.

"Logan," the head said in a perfectly human voice with only a touch of Khalidoran accent. The head pushed further out of the troll's stomach toward Logan.

"Ursuul," Logan snarled.

"There's something you should know about Jenine."

Logan hadn't been strong when the battle began. Months of privation had left him emaciated and weak. He'd survived today on luck and the ferocity of the Order of the Garter and Agon's Dogs, not his own strength or skill, but at the passage of Jenine's name across this beast's foul tongue, Logan felt the power of righteous rage.

"Your lovely, lovely wife is ali—"

Logan's sword flashed and he struck the head off. It burst apart on the ground into clumps of rotting flesh.

For a moment, the beast froze. It didn't move a muscle, and as the moment stretched, the Cenarians suddenly cheered, thinking that Logan had somehow killed it.

Then the troll raised its arms to the skies and bellowed a roar that shook that very ground. Two of its eyes fixed on Logan, and the enormous bone scythe drew back.

71

$\mathcal{V}$i brushed back Kylar's hair with gentle fingers. Before them, the ferali had transformed into a troll and was wading through the Cenarian lines. She barely saw it. She was staring at Kylar's dead face. For the first time, she realized how young he looked. Kylar was serene, beatific. Vi had murdered him. She'd delivered immortality to the Godking.

Something splashed on his cheek. Vi blinked. *What the hell?* The drop slid down his cheek to his ear. She blinked again, more rapidly, refusing to believe she was crying. What had Sister Ariel said? Something about being an emotional cripple? Vi looked at her tear, glimmering on Kylar's ear, and wiped it away. *That bitch called me stupid.*

And so she was. Her finger froze.

It hit Vi like a warhorse at a full gallop. She hadn't escaped Sister Ariel at all.

Suddenly, Vi couldn't breathe. She saw the Sister's trap now, laid out for her in every word Ariel had spoken. She saw the bait and the consequences. It wasn't escape, but it was escape from the Godking.

It only required Vi to do something worse to Kylar than anything Hu Gibbet had ever done to her. She put an unsteady hand into a pouch and found the box right where she'd put it. She opened the box and looked at the Waeddryner wedding rings tucked inside.

If she did this, it would be like rape, and Vi knew rape.

Yet it was the only way. Sister Ariel had the Niles plant all the information Vi would need. They'd told her she needed to show "an outward sign of an inward change" to break the compulsion, a transfer of loyalties. They talked of the powerful magic in some of the old rings, how they held a type of compulsion spell. And the Bitch Wytch had dangled the carrot herself: quick advancement, private tutoring, being important.

Vi didn't care. She wouldn't do this for herself. She'd do it because if she didn't, the Godking would become immortal. Vi would become his pet assassin, a one-woman plague slaying any who dared defy him. She'd do this for those poor bastards getting eaten alive on the battlefield. She'd do this because if she didn't, Kylar would die, truly die.

But he would never forgive her.

She ran her fingers through Kylar's hair. His face looked cold and still, judgmental. She would escape; she would change, but Kylar and Elene would pay the price.

The earring pierced her left ear, and the hoop melded together seamlessly. The pain made her eyes water. Tears streaming down her face, she pierced the other ring through Kylar's ear.

A rush of warmth lit her from head to toe. She felt the compulsion shrivel and burst apart. That was nothing compared to the sudden longing she felt. She gasped. In her very skin, her stomach, her spine, she felt Kylar. He was healing, but he was hurt so badly it made her ache. Her fingers tingled where she was touching his face. He was more handsome than ever. She wanted him to know her. She wanted to confess the truth and be forgiven and have him love her back. She wanted him to hold her, to touch her cheek, to run his fingers through her hair and—

That thought exploded against everything she'd ever known. Vi pushed Kylar roughly out of her lap and staggered to her feet. The rush of emotion was too much, too intense, too vast to read, yet it didn't feel alien. It didn't feel counterfeit. It felt like her love was being purified, the coal blown on so that it flared up into fire. It left Vi gasping. She could hardly bear to look at Kylar. But she was free. The compulsion was gone.

Free! Free of the Godking. On the floor, a lone horseman stood in front of the massive troll. Vi took her dagger and staggered toward her father. She grabbed his body and made him stand. She shook him.

"Father! *Father!*" someone was screaming. Who the hell was screaming that on the battlefield? A moment later, Garoth realized what it must be and brought his consciousness back to the throne room. Logan could wait a few seconds. To hell with him if he didn't want to know Jenine was alive.

"Father," Vi said, "can you tell me one thing?" She had obviously come to terms with her compulsion, because she was touching him.

" 'Father'? I'm right in the middle of something, do you mind?"

"Did you make me kill Jarl? Was it compulsion?"

He smiled. The lie came easy to his lips. "No, *moulina*. You did that yourself."

"Oh." The single syllable popped like a little bubble from her lips.

Garoth grinned and slid back into the ferali. Garoth roared toward the heavens and brought his scythe-arm back. Logan rode straight at him until his horse shied. Logan kicked and sawed at the reins, but the horse refused to obey. It turned around in a desperate circle and stumbled on a body. As Garoth swung the enormous scythe at a level to cut Logan in half, one of the mounted wytch hunters burst into the clearing and leapt out of his saddle, tackling Logan. The scythe swept through both horses' necks and the beasts went crashing to the earth in twin sprays of blood.

Logan rolled away and got to his feet. Beside him, the archer was already drawing an arrow. He shot one of Garoth's eyes and then another. Garoth blinked and new eyes pushed out the old. It didn't matter. Logan was standing, defiant but defenseless. Garoth's next slash would tear the little man in half—

Something hot went into his back. Once, twice, three times. Again and again. He lifted the ferali's hands to its back, wondering what could pierce his thick hide, wondering why his other eyes hadn't seen the attack, but there were no arrows or spears in his back.

The ferali was fading, and as Logan charged at him to stick his sword in his belly, Garoth realized it wasn't the ferali that was bleeding.

He was.

He heard the sound of weeping and he was back in the throne room.

Vi was hugging him against her breast, and stabbing him, again and again, against herself, as if she wished the dagger would go all the way through him into her own heart.

Garoth told his limbs to move, but they were empty slabs of meat. His body was dying, dying! and his vision was going black, black—

He triggered the death spell. It was a terrible risk, trying to hurl his consciousness into another body. If Khali granted this, her price would be grievous, but he had nothing to lose.

The vir ripped from his arms and engulfed Vi in a forest of black fingers. They pulled her closer.

He was close! It was working! He could feel it!

And then every finger of vir was sheared off by an iridescent blade passing between Garoth and Vi. The vir, cut off from their source, froze, cracked, and evaporated into black smoke. Garoth turned and saw the impossible.

Kylar was alive. He stood with judgment writ on every feature and a blade of black ka'kari in his fist. Realization swept through Garoth like a tidal wave.

The Devourer devoured life itself. The Sustainer sustained life itself. It was not just extended life or healing. It was true immortality.

Garoth had had a chance for real godhood, and he'd let it slip right through his fingers. Impotent rage washed through him.

Then Kylar's ka'kari-blade descended once more toward his head.

Logan rammed his sword into the troll's belly and the creature rocked back. It dropped to its knees as if it had suddenly lost all coordination. Logan jumped backward and narrowly avoided being crushed. He wasn't sure what had just happened, but it didn't seem that the troll's reaction was right. Logan had seen it take worse wounds and not even flinch.

Both armies' eyes were fixed on Logan and the beast. Logan stabbed it again, and a third time, but the wounds sealed as soon as the sword pulled out.

As it was still on its knees, the plates covering most of the beast's stomach slid out to its sides—gurgling and grinding like a breaking nose, but repeated a hundred times. From the gap between the plates, something pressed out against the skin, bulging and glooping. In another second, the form resolved itself. Pushed out from the troll's stomach, like a living bas-relief, was a woman. Her face worked and a mouth appeared.

"I can't fight it, King. So hungry. Just like in the Hole. I can't stop, King. Look at what they made me. It won't let me kill me, King. So hungry. Like the bread. So hungry."

"Lilly? I thought it was Garoth," Logan said.

"He's gone. Dead. Tell me what to do, King. I can't stop me. I'm so hungry it's eating myself."

Logan realized that even in the time since Garoth Ursuul's face had protruded from it, the troll had shrunk. It was devouring itself. He had to do something fast. They couldn't kill it. The beast healed its wounds without even conscious thought, and now the form of Lilly was becoming indistinct.

"Lilly," Logan said. "Lilly, listen to me."

She rallied, and her form protruded once more, though this time without a mouth.

"Lilly, eat the Khalidorans. Eat them all, and run up into the mountains. All right?"

But she was gone. The plates snapped back into place and the troll lumbered to its feet. It fixed its eyes on Logan and raised its scythe, all trace of Lilly gone.

Logan walked straight toward it. "You wanted to make things right, Lilly? You remember, Lilly?" Logan asked, hoping that he could draw her back with the sound of her name. "You want to earn your pardon, Lilly? Am I your king or not?" The ferali blinked, paused. Logan's voice pitched with an authority he'd never known he had, and pointing at the Khalidorans he shouted, "GO! KILL THEM! I COMMAND IT!"

The ferali blinked, blinked. Then in a movement faster than any Garoth had ever made in it, it slashed an arm through the Khalidorans behind it. Logan turned and saw thousands of pairs of eyes locked on him in disbelief.

Logan Gyre, the man who commanded a ferali to stop, and it did.

The battle had come to a standstill. Khalidorans and Cenarians stood within easy reach of each other and didn't fight. The ferali, easily thirty feet tall now, commanded all attention. It didn't turn. It merely went gelatinous for a moment, and then what had been its front was its back, and it was facing the Khalidorans.

A fireball arced up from a meister and ricocheted off its skin harmlessly. Ten more followed and did nothing. Lightning hit an instant later and barely left a black mark on its skin. The ferali crouched and flexed every muscle in its body. All the arms and armor that Garoth had incorporated in the beast exploded from its body in all directions, breastplates and mail shirts and spears and swords and war hammers and daggers and hundreds of arrows rattling to the ground in a great circle.

A glowing white homunculus streaked out of the Khalidoran lines and stuck to the ferali. In a line between the Vürdmeister and the homunculus, the air seemed to distort as if anything viewed through it were being seen in a bent mirror. The air bubbled in a streak toward the ferali.

Ten paces from the ferali, the distortion in the air ripped open with red fire. The pit wyrm struck. But its lamprey mouth closed on nothing. The ferali was unbelievably fast. The pit wyrm twisted, black and red fiery skin lurching further into reality, forty feet, sixty, with no sign of its body tapering.

Logan heard weapons rattle to the ground, dropped from nerveless fingers as the titans warred.

But the battle lasted only one strike more. The pit wyrm missed again, and the ferali didn't. An enormous fist crushed the wyrm's head and snapped its body like a whip onto the Khalidoran lines beneath it. It broke apart in bloodless black and red clumps that sizzled on the ground like water drops on a hot skillet, hissing into green smoke and disappearing.

The ferali turned to the Khalidoran lines and a dozen arms sprang from its body. It began snatching up soldiers like a greedy child snatching sweetmeats.

Then the men on both sides remembered the battle. The Cenarians remembered their weapons and the Khalidorans remembered their heels. They cast away weapons and shields to run faster.

A shout went up as the Khalidorans around the ferali broke. Logan couldn't believe it. The impossibility of it was too much to accept.

"Who do you want to go after them?" General Agon asked. He and a bloodied Duke Wesseros had appeared out of nowhere.

"No one," Logan said. "She can't tell friend from foe. Our fighting's done."

"She?" Duke Wesseros asked.

"Don't ask."

Agon rode off shouting orders, and Logan turned to the man who'd tackled him from his horse. He didn't recognize him. "You saved my life. Who are you?" Logan asked.

The Sethi woman who'd been stuck to his side for the entire battle, Kaldrosa Wyn, stepped up. "My lord, this is my husband Tomman," she said, fiercely proud.

"You're a brave man, Tomman, and no mean shot. What boon would you ask?"

Tomman looked up, and inexplicably, his eyes shone. "You already gave me back more than I deserve. You gave me back my love, my lord. What's more precious than that?" He extended his hand, and his wife took it.

The Cenarian ranks reformed in the tightest square the generals could manage and just watched as the Khalidorans were massacred. There was no retreat. It was a rout. The rest of the circle broke, men running in every direction. The ferali tore through them. It became a snake and rolled over whole sections of the line, men sticking to its body, screaming. Then it was a dragon. Always it had dozens of hands. Always it was quick and terrible. Piteous screams rose on every side and men tore at each other in their panic. Some crouched behind the sheep fences, some huddled in the lee of boulders, some climbed trees at the edges of the field, but the creature was meticulous in its savagery. It picked up men everywhere—whether alive or dead or wounded or feigning death or hiding or fighting—and devoured them.

Not all the Khalidorans fled. Some turned and fought. Some rallied their fellows and attacked with more courage than the Cenarians would have believed possible, perhaps more courage than they would have shown themselves. But in the face of that horror, courage was irrelevant. The brave and the cowardly, the high and the low, the good and the bad died alike. And the Cenarians watched open-mouthed, not one forgetting that the massacre should have been their own. The few times that a Cenarian here or there cheered, no one took up the cry. The ferali tore this way and that, not catching every group of Khalidorans, but getting most of them, and always, always veering far from the Cenarian ranks, as if it feared the temptation of going too near them.

Finally, having devoured the last group large enough to be worth its time, the ferali fled toward the mountains. Cenaria was either blessed or lucky or Lilly was in better control than Logan had hoped, because it headed in a direction where there were no villages for a hundred miles.

In the silence, someone let out a whoop. For a moment, it hung alone in the air. Logan had been given a new horse and, mounted, he turned and was again aware of thousands of eyes on him. Why were they all looking at him?

Then someone cheered again and the thought wormed its way into Logan's consciousness: They had won. Somehow, against everything, they had won.

For the first time in months, Logan felt his mouth curl into a grin. That let loose a flood and suddenly, no one could stop smiling, or stop yelling, or stop pounding each other on the back. Which noble's flag they had fought under no longer mattered. Agon's Dogs embraced Cenaria City levies: former thieves and former guards standing together as friends. Nobles stood arm in arm with peasants, shouting together. The shattered links binding the country together seemed to be reforming even as Logan looked over the tight-packed army. They had won. The costs had been grievous, but they had stood against the might of a monster and the magic of a god, and they had won.

A cry began to emerge over the sound of swords and spears pounding rhythmically against shields.

"What are they saying?" Logan shouted to Agon, but even as he asked, Logan made out the words, shouted in time with each crash of sword on shield: "KING GYRE! KING GYRE! KING GYRE!" It was audacious; it was treasonous; it was beautiful. Logan looked through the throng for Terah Graesin. She was nowhere to be found. And then he did smile.

72

The dead god fell like a sack of wheat. Vi was trembling, but she didn't seem to have been harmed by the vir that had wrapped around her. Kylar stared at Garoth Ursuul's corpse, disbelieving.

Kylar's destiny was dead on the floor and Kylar hadn't killed him.

The Wolf had kept his part of the deal: Kylar was alive. But something felt different. Vi was staring at him, still shaking with emotion, tears still wet and hot on her cheeks. He glanced up and read shock and fear in every line of her body—along with a tinge of hope?

What the hell? Since when can I see what a woman feels?

Vi was spattered with the Godking's blood. It was invisible against the background of her dark wetboy grays, but there was something terrible about seeing flecks of red wetness splattered in her cleavage.

As Kylar looked at her, she was so distraught he wanted to take her in his arms. She needed him to love her, to lead her out of the valley of death that was the way of shadows. He knew the way out, now. It was love. They'd go find Uly, and he and Vi would walk that path together—

Me and Vi?

Her eyes went wide with fear and remorse. She was weeping. For a split second he wanted to understand, but then his fingers went slowly up to his ear. There was an earring there, a perfect hoop with no opening, and it was swimming with magic so potent he could feel it in his fingertips.

"I'm so sorry," she said, backing away. "I'm so sorry. It was the only way." She turned and he saw his last gift to Elene—his pledge of love that he had sold his birthright for—sparkling in Vi's ear.

"What have you done?!" he bellowed, and he could see that his rage was amplified through the earring. As it buffeted her, he could feel her remorse and terror and confusion and desperation and self-loathing and... hells, her love? Love! How dare she love him?

Vi fled.

He didn't follow. What would he do if he caught her?

She burst through the main door of the throne room, and the guards looked after her, stunned.

They turned and saw Kylar standing over the body of the Godking.

Then it was whistles and alarms and charging highlanders and chanting meisters. Kylar was glad for the nepenthe of battle. It blotted out a future that would never hold Elene. It took all his attention. With only one hand, killing was actually a challenge.

Lantano Garuwashi couldn't stop touching the Blade of Heaven, though of course he kept it sheathed. Once a sa'ceurai drew his sword, he did not sheathe it without first letting it taste blood. As night descended, his men covered the mouth of the cave so their campfires wouldn't be seen by the celebrating Cenarians. After conferring with the spy who'd returned from the Cenarian camp, Garuwashi stood up on a ledge.

In the firelight, his men's eyes glowed with destiny. They had seen wonders denied to their fathers and grandfathers before them. The Blade of Heaven had returned.

Garuwashi began without preliminaries, as was his way. "The Cenarians did not win this battle. That creature won it for them. Tonight, they drink. Tomorrow, they will begin hunting down the scattered Khalidorans. Do you want to know what we will be doing while these buffoons swat at flies?" Men nodded. They held the Blade of Heaven. They followed the Garuwashi. They were invincible.

"Tonight, we will gather the uniforms of the Khalidoran dead. At dawn, we will attack and inflict enough losses to infuriate the Cenarians. We will draw their army east, always just slipping through their fingers. In three days, the rest of our army will arrive here. In five, they will take the undefended Cenaria City. In a month, this country will be ours. In the spring, we will return to Ceura and give them their new king. What do you say?"

Every man cheered but one. Feir Cousat sat silent, stoic. His face might as well have been carved of marble.

Epilogue

$\mathcal{H}$orses' hooves clattered behind Dorian as he came over the last rise in the foothills and saw Khaliras. He stepped aside and waited patiently, enrapt by the view. The city was still two days distant, but between the Faltier Mountains and Mount Thrall the plains spread broad and flat. The city and the castle rose with the mountain, one lonely spike in an ocean of grazing land. It had once been his home.

The party began passing Dorian, riding on magnificent horses. Dorian got down on his knees and gave a peasant's obeisance. It wasn't a normal scouting party. Nor were they regular soldiers, though their armor said they were. Their weapons and horses gave them away. The six huge soldiers were members of the Godking's Guard. And from their smell, despite the half-cloaks, the meisters accompanying them were actually Vürdmeisters. They could only be coming from Cenaria, probably bearing great riches in the few chests they carried.

Dorian was stealing brief glimpses when he saw the real treasure. A woman rode with the meisters, wearing thick robes, her face veiled. Something seemed oddly familiar about the way she carried herself, and then he saw her eyes.

It was the woman he'd foreseen. His future wife. A shiver passed through his whole body and he remembered bits and pieces of his old prophecies—something about the process of searing his gift had blocked his memories of them.

When he came to himself, he was still kneeling. His muscles were cramped and the sun hung low in the sky. The party was miles ahead of him out on the grasslands. He'd been unconscious for half the day.

Solon, where are you? I need you here. But Dorian knew the answer. If Solon had survived Screaming Winds, he was probably already sailing home to Seth to face his lost love. That woman, now Empress Kaede Wariyamo, would be furious. Because of Dorian's prophecies, Solon had abandoned his homeland in its hour of need. Dorian could only hope that Solon's path wasn't as lonely as his own.

Because even without prophecy, Dorian knew that whichever way he went, he would walk a path in darkness, alone, suffering so much that giving up his visions had seemed a good idea.

With fear and trembling, Dorian stood. He looked at the path before him and the path behind, the road to Khaliras and his future wife—Jenine, that was her name!—or the road back to his friends. Death and love, or life and loneliness. The God felt as distant as a summer in the Freeze.

Face set, back straight, Dorian continued his long walk to Khaliras.

Ghorran was always watching Elene, his gaze dark, intense. The first day, that hadn't been a problem, because she hadn't needed to relieve herself. The second day, it had. Elene had followed him a short distance into the woods, then stepped behind a bush for some privacy. He waited until she was squatting and lifting her skirts, and then followed her just to shame her. Of course, then she couldn't go.

That night, as they did each night and each morning, the Khalidorans prayed, *"Khali vas, Khalivos ras en me, Khali mevirtu rapt, recu virtum defite."* Ghorran threw Elene to the ground and straddled her. As he prayed, he ground his fingers into the pressure points behind her ears. She screamed and felt warm wetness soak her dress as she lost control of her bladder.

When the prayer was finished, Ghorran got up, clouted her ear, and said, "You stink, filthy bitch."

They didn't let her wash when they crossed a small mountain stream. When Ghorran took her aside that evening, Elene hiked up her skirts and relieved herself as he watched. He took no special delight in watching until she blushed and looked away. "Tomorrow," he said, "I make you wear shit on your face. Yours or someone else's. Your choice."

"Why do you do this?" Elene asked. "Isn't there anything decent in you?"

The next morning, however, they were awakened early. They set out immediately. The captives traveled in a line, tied together, walking behind the Khalidorans. Elene was sixth in line out of six captives with the young boy, Herrald, right in front of her. It took her a while to figure out why the Khalidorans were anxious because they beat the captives if they talked.

There were only five Khalidoran soldiers this morning.

That night, Ghorran seemed to have forgotten his threat. When he took Elene aside to let her relieve herself, he kept the camp in easy sight. Elene squatted among the tamaracks, which were dropping their golden needles with the onset of autumn, and pretended his presence didn't bother her. "The meisters might meet up with us tomorrow," Ghorran said, keeping his eyes on the camp. "We'll hand all of you over then. That bastard Haavin probably run off, the coward."

Elene stood, and not ten paces from the oblivious Ghorran, she saw a man leaning against a tree. The stranger wore a multitude of cloaks, vests, pocketed shirts, and pouches of all sizes, all of them horsehide, all tanned the same deep brown and worn soft from long use. Twin, forward-curving gurkas were tucked into the back of his belt, an elaborately scrimshawed bow case was slung over his back, and hilts of various sizes hung among the garments. He had an affable face; wry, almond-shaped brown eyes; and loose straight black hair: a Ymmuri stalker. He touched a finger to his lips.

"You finished?" Ghorran asked, glancing toward her.

"Yes," Elene said. She glanced back to the stalker, but he was gone.

There were only four soldiers when they camped that night at the edge of the woods to take advantage of the shelter of the trees. The Khalidorans quarreled about whether they should press on in the darkness or if Haavin and the other missing man had really run away. The night was short, and Ghorran woke Elene in the dark of the morning.

He took her silently into the woods. She hiked up her skirts like it didn't bother her. "How did your chest get hurt?" Elene asked.

"That wild bitch stabbed me with a pitchfork after I killed her husband and gutted her brats." He shrugged, like letting her stab him was a moment of carelessness, embarrassing but not serious.

To Ghorran, eviscerating children held no special significance. He had hurt Elene and shamed her; she could forgive those. But that dismissive shrug blew on the small spark of fury in her heart. For the first time in her life since Rat, Elene hated.

Ghorran had brought a bow with him and now he strung it. "This day, we get to camp," he said, "Neph Dada will do terrible things to you." Ghorran licked his dry lips. "I can save you."

"Save me?"

"What he does should not be done. It is Lodricari foulness. If you run now, I will put an arrow in your back and spare you."

His mercy was so bizarre that Elene's hatred dissolved.

A flash of light burst from the camp fifty paces behind them, throwing shadows against the trees. A scream followed it. Then the sound of galloping horses.

Elene turned and saw a dozen unfamiliar Khalidoran horsemen charging into the camp from the north. They had come early to collect their slaves.

"Run!" a shout rang out, louder than a man should have been able to yell.

Through the trees, Elene saw the Ymmuri stalker fighting the Khalidorans. He cut through two of them in a single move. Fire leapt from one of the horsemen's hands, but he dodged it.

Ghorran nocked an arrow and drew it, but there were too many trees and Khalidorans between him and the Ymmuri. Then, only paces away, the young boy Herrald burst from the woods, running away.

Ghorran turned and aimed, leading his new target.

All Elene thought was *no.*

She grabbed Ghorran's dagger from his belt, brought it over his arm, and buried it in his throat. He spasmed and the arrow leapt from the bow, whistling harmlessly over Herrald's head.

The bow dropped from Ghorran's fingers, and he and Elene regarded each other, shock widening his eyes. The dagger was lodged squarely in the center of his throat, its wide blade blocking his windpipe. He exhaled, his chest straining, and air whistled. He put a hand to his throat and felt the blade, still unbelieving.

Then he tried to inhale. His diaphragm pumped like a bellows, but he couldn't get air. He fell to his knees. Elene couldn't move.

Ghorran ripped the dagger out of his throat and gasped, but the gasp turned to a gurgle. He coughed and blood sprayed over Elene.

He kept trying to breathe as his lungs filled with blood. In moments, he dropped to the forest floor.

Despite the blood on her face, her dress, and her hands, despite the piteous look on Ghorran's face and the horror of watching a man die, Elene didn't feel sorry. She had hated Ghorran only a minute before, but she hadn't killed him out of hatred. He simply had to be stopped. If she could have the moment back, she'd do the same thing. And just like that, she understood.

"My God, what a fool I've been," she said aloud. "Forgive me, Kylar."

With magic bursting in the woods behind her, setting the trees alight, Elene ran.

On the north side of Vos Island in the gloom of the rainy autumn day, Kylar stood staring at the unmarked cairn he'd built. Durzo's grave.

Kylar was spattered with blood, his wetboy grays scored and singed with magic. In a rage he'd fought for hours, killing every Khalidoran soldier and meister he laid eyes on. From the slowly diminishing magic on the throne room's floor, he'd seen Logan's stand, seen the ferali turn, and witnessed the destruction of the Khalidoran army. He'd seen how the men had looked at Logan. Though the figures were tiny, it was written in every line of their bodies.

Logan would march his army home, and in two days when they arrived, he would find his castle swept out and cleansed of the Khalidoran presence—except for Khali, but that was one creature Kylar was going to steer clear of. Let King Gyre invite some mages to take care of that.

"We won, I guess," he told Durzo's grave. Kylar knew there was no use railing against his life. He was the Night Angel, and he didn't get celebrations. As Durzo had told him long ago, he would always be separate, alone.

~It is just so hard to be immortal,~ the ka'kari said.

Kylar was too exhausted to be surprised or offended. The ka'kari had spoken before, he remembered now, trying to save his life. "So you can talk," he said.

The ka'kari puddled into his hand and formed a stylized face. It smiled and winked at him. Kylar sighed and sucked it back into his skin.

Kylar stared at his stump. He'd lost his arm for nothing. He'd made an oath to the Wolf for nothing. Everything Kylar had ever learned, everything he'd ever suffered, had been for one thing: killing Garoth Ursuul was Kylar's destiny. Garoth was the vile fount from which Kylar's and Jarl's and Elene's misery flowed. It was only fitting that the man who'd led Kylar to become a wetboy would be Kylar's last deader. Without Garoth, there would be no Roth. Without Roth, Elene would be unscarred, Jarl would be alive and whole, and Kylar would be—what?—well, not a wetboy.

Count Drake had once told Kylar, "There's a divinity that shapes beauty from our rough-hewn lives." It was a lie, as Kylar's destiny was a lie. Perhaps that was why this was so hard: he'd begun to believe in Elene's divine economy. So now he hadn't just lost Elene, who'd been part of him from the beginning, who'd made Kylar believe good things about himself; he'd also lost his destiny. If he had a destiny, he had a purpose: some pearl being built around the evil he'd suffered and inflicted. If he'd been shaped for a purpose, maybe there was a Shaper. If there was a Shaper, perhaps its name was the One God. And perhaps that One God was a bridge over the chasm between killer and saint that separated Kylar from Elene. But there was no bridge, no God, no Shaper, no purpose, no destiny, no beauty. There was no going back. He'd been cheated of justice and vengeance and love and purpose at once.

He'd thought he could change, that he could buy peace for the price of an old sword. But Retribution was only an instrument of justice. It was Kylar who thirsted to mete it out. He'd killed many men today, and he couldn't make himself feel sorry for it. This was what it was to be the Night Angel. Perhaps a better man could lay down the sword. Kylar could not, not even though it had cost him Elene.

Every time he thought of Elene, her face morphed into Vi's. Every time he thought of Vi, his fantasies morphed from meting out punishment to fantasies of another kind.

"Master," he said to the cairn. "I don't know what to do."

Finish the job. He knew exactly the intonation Durzo would have given the words, exasperated but firm.

It was true. The Wolf had fulfilled his part of the deal: Kylar had come back from death immediately. It turned out to be a lousy trade, but a deal was a deal, so Kylar would go steal Curoch and ride to Torras Bend and get his arm back. It sounded simple enough. After all, stealing wasn't hard when you could make yourself invisible. It wouldn't be a second too soon to get his arm back, either. His stump was aching, and he wouldn't have thought it, but losing a hand threw off his balance.

You're not here because you don't know what to do, boy. You always knew what to do.

That was true, too. Kylar would do this job and then go find Vi and kill her.

~*You won't kill her,*~ the ka'kari said.

"Chatty all of a sudden, aren't you?" Kylar asked.

The ka'kari didn't answer. It was right, though. Kylar wasn't here for direction. Not really. He just missed his master. It was the first time he'd been to the grave since Durzo had died.

Tears started flowing, and Kylar knew only that they were tears of loss. He'd lost his master; he'd lost the girl he betrayed his master to save; he'd lost his master's daughter. He'd lost his one chance at a peaceful life. Mild-mannered herbalist! It had been a sweet delusion, maybe, but it had been sweet. Kylar was lonely, and he was tired of being lonely.

A gopher had dug a hole near the foot of Durzo's cairn. Durzo would be pissed if he had to spend eternity with gophers pawing his corpse. Kylar looked at the hole, irritated. It was deep enough that to normal eyes, the hole would just appear black, but Kylar saw a distinct metallic glimmer at the bottom.

He got on his knees and his stump—oww—and shifted to his elbow—better—and reached in. He stood with a small, sealed metal box in hand. One word was etched on it: "Azoth." It sent a shiver through him. How many people knew that name? Kylar cracked it open awkwardly between his stump and one hand. There was a note inside.

"Hey," it said in Durzo's tight handwriting, "I thought it was my last one, too. He said I got one more for old time's sake..." Kylar's eyes blurred. He couldn't believe it. The letter went on, but his eyes were drawn to the final words: "MAKE NO DEALS WITH THE WOLF." The letter was dated a month after Kylar had killed his master. Durzo was alive.

The story continues in …

BEYOND THE SHADOWS

Book Three of the Night Angel trilogy

by

Brent Weeks

Logan Gyre is king of Cenaria, a country under siege, with a threadbare army and little hope. He has one chance – a desperate gamble, but one that could destroy his kingdom.

In the north, the new Godking has a plan. If it comes to fruition, no one will have the power to stop him.

Kylar Stern has no choice. To save his friends – and perhaps his Enemies – he must accomplish the impossible: assassinate a goddess.

orbitbooks.net

extras

orbitbooks.net

about the author

Brent Weeks was born and raised in Montana. He wrote on bar napkins and lesson plans before landing his dream job years and thousands of pages later. Brent lives in Oregon with his wife, Kristi, and their daughters. Find out more about the author at brentweeks.com or on Twitter @brentweeks.

Find out more about Brent Weeks and other Orbit authors by registering for the free monthly newsletter at orbitbooks.net.

about the author

if you enjoyed
SHADOW'S EDGE

look out for

THE COMBAT CODES

The Combat Codes: Book One

by

Alexander Darwin

Hundreds of years ago on a planet once ravaged by war, the nations swore an armistice never to use weapons of mass destruction again. Today, battle-hardened warriors known as Grievar Knights train to represent their nations' interests in brutal hand-to-hand combat.

Murray Pearson was once a famed Knight until he suffered a loss that crippled his nation – but now he's on the hunt to find and train the next champion.

In ruthless underground combat rings, an orphaned boy called Cego is making a name for himself. Murray believes Cego has what it takes to make it in the world's most prestigious combat academy – but Cego has to fight his way out of the underground first.

CHAPTER I

Into the Deep

We fight neither to inflict pain nor to prolong suffering. We fight neither to mollify anger nor to satisfy vendetta. We fight neither to accumulate wealth nor to promote social standing. We fight so the rest shall not have to.

First Precept of the Combat Codes

Murray wasn't fond of the crowd at Thaloo's. Mostly scum with no respect for combat who liked to think themselves experts in the craft.

His boots clung to the sticky floor as he shouldered his way to the bar. Patrons lined the counter, drinking, smoking, and shouting at the overhead lightboards broadcasting SystemView feeds.

Murray grabbed a head-sized draught of ale before making his way toward the center of the den, where the crowd grew thicker. Beams of light cut through clouds of pipe smoke and penetrated the gaps between cluttered, sweaty bodies.

His heart fluttered and the hairs on the back of his neck bristled as he approached. He wiped a trickle of sweat from his brow. Even after all these years, even in a pitiful place like this, the light still got to him.

He pushed past the inner throng of spectators and emerged at the edge of the action.

Thaloo's Circle was eight meters in diameter, made of auralite-compound steel fused into the dirt. Standard Underground dimensions. On the Surface, Circles tended to be wider, usually ten meters in diameter, which Murray preferred. More room to maneuver.

Glowing blue streaks veined the steel Circle, and a central cluster of lights pulsed above the ring like a heartbeat, shining down on two boys grappling in the dirt.

"Aha! The big Scout's back. You runnin' out of kids already?" A man at the edge of the Circle clapped Murray on the shoulder. "Name's Calsans."

Murray ignored the greeting and focused on the two boys fighting. One of them looked to be barely ten years old and had the gaunt build of a lacklight street urchin. His rib cage heaved in and out from beneath the bulk of a boy who outweighed him by at least sixty pounds.

Many of the onlookers flicked their eyes between the action and a large lightboard that hung from the ceiling. Biometric benchmarks of each boy in the Circle flashed across the screen: heart rate, brainwave speed, oxygen saturation, blood pressure, hydration levels. The bottom of the board displayed an image of each boy's skeletal and muscular frame, down to their chipped teeth.

As the large boy lifted his elbow and drove it into the smaller boy's chin, a red fracture lit up on the board. The little boy's heart rate shot up.

The large boy threw knees into his opponent's rib cage as he continued to hold him down in the dirt. The little boy writhed, turning his back to his opponent and curling into a ball.

"Shouldn't give your back like that," Murray muttered, as if trying to communicate with the battered boy.

The large boy dropped another vicious elbow on his downed prey. Murray winced as he heard the sharp crack of bone on skull. Two more elbows found their target before the little one stiffened, his eyes rolling into his head as he fell limp.

The ball of light floating above the Circle flickered before it dissipated into a swarm of smoldering wisps that fanned out into the crowd.

"They call the big one there N'jal; he's been cleaning up like that all week. One of Thaloo's newest in-housers," Calsans said as the boy raised his arms in victory.

Beyond a few clapping drunks, there was little fanfare. N'jal walked to the side of his Tasker at the sidelines, a bearded man who patted the boy on the head like a dog. The loser's crew entered the Circle and dragged the fallen fighter out by his feet.

"Thaloo's been buyin' up some hard Grievar this cycle," Calsans continued, trying to strike up conversation with Murray again. "Bet he's tryin' to work a bulk sale to the Citadel, y'know? Even though they all won't pan out with that level of competition, there's bound to be a gem in the lot of 'em."

Murray barely acknowledged the man, but Calsans kept speaking.

"It's not like it used to be, y'know? Everything kept under strict Citadel regulations. All the organized breeding, the training camps," Calsans said. "I mean, course you know all about that. But now that the Kirothians are breathin' down our necks, Deep Circles are hoppin' again, and folks like Thaloo and you are making the best of it."

"I'm nothing like Thaloo," Murray growled, his shoulders tensing.

Calsans shrank back, as if suddenly aware of how large Murray was beside him. "No, no, of course not, friend. You two are completely different. Thaloo's like every other Circle slaver trying to make a bit, and you're a…or used to be…a Grievar Knight…" His voice trailed off.

The glowing spectral wisps returned to the Circle like flies gathering on a fresh kill. They landed on the cold auralite steel ring and balled up again in a floating cluster above. As more of the wisps arrived, the light shining on the Circle grew brighter. Fresh biometrics flashed onto the feed above.

It was time for the next fight, and Murray needed another ale.

*　　*　　*

Murray drew the cowl of his cloak over his head as he exited Thaloo's den, stepping directly into the clamor of Markspar Row.

Stores, bars, and inns lined the street, with smaller carts selling a variety of acrid-scented foods on the cobbles out front. Gaudily dressed hawkers peddled their wares, yapping like bayhounds in a variety of tongues. Buyers jostled past him as ragged, soot-faced children darted underfoot.

Much had changed since Murray had first returned to the Underground.

Two decades ago, he'd proudly walked Markspar Row with an entourage of trainers in tow. He'd been met with cheers, claps on the back, the awed eyes of Deep brood looking up at him. He'd been proud to represent the Grievar from below.

Now Murray made the habit of staying off the main thoroughfares. He came to the Deep alone and quietly. He doubted anyone would recognize him after all these years with his overgrown beard and sagging stomach.

A man in a nearby stall shrieked at Murray, "Top-shelf protein! Tested for the Cimmerian Shade! Vat-grown in Ezo's central plant! Certified for real taste by the Growers Guild!" The small, bald hawker held up a case with a variety of labels stamped across it.

Compared to the wiry hawker, Murray was large. Though his gut had expanded over the past decade and his ruffled beard was now grey-streaked, he posed a formidable presence. From beneath the cut-off sleeves of his cloak, his knotted forearms and callused hands hung like twin cudgels. Flux tattoos crisscrossed the length of Murray's arms from elbows to fingertips, shifting their pig-mented curves as he clenched his fists. His sharp nose twisted at the center, many times broken, and his ears swelled like fat toads. His face was overcast, with two alarmingly bright yellow eyes penetrating from beneath his brow.

Murray turned in to a narrow stone passageway sheltered from the central clamor of the row. He passed another hawker, a white-haired lady hidden behind her stand of fruit.

"The best heartbeat grapes. Clerics say eat just a few per day and you'll outlive an archivist." She smiled at him and gestured to her selection of fruit, each swollen and pulsing with ripeness. Halfway down the alley, as the sounds of the market continued to fade, Murray stopped in front of a beat-up oaken door. A picture of a bat with its teeth bared was barely visible on the faded awning overhead.

The Bat always smelled of spilled ale and sweat. An assortment of Grievar and Grunt patrons crowded the floor. Mercs keeping an ear to the ground for contract jobs, harvesters taking a break from planting on the steppe, or diggers dressed in dirt from a nearby excavation project.

SystemView was live and blaring from several old boards hanging from the far wall.

And now...broadcasting from Ezo's Capital, in magnificent Albright Stadium...

The one thing that brought together the different breeds was a good SystemView fight. Though most of the folk living in the Underground were Ezonian citizens, their allegiances often were more aligned with the wagers they placed in the Circles.

Most of the Bat's patrons were tuned in to the screens, some swaying and nearly falling out of their chairs, with empty bottles surrounding them. Two dirt-encrusted Grunts slurred their words as Murray pushed past them toward the bar.

"Fegar's got the darkin' reach! No way 'e'll be able to take my boy down!"

"You tappin' those neuros too hard, man? He took Samson down an' he's ten times the wrestler!"

Grunts weren't known for their smarts. They were bred for hard labor like mining, hauling, harvesting, or clearing, though Murray often wondered if drinking might be their real talent. He didn't mind the Grunts, though—they did their jobs and didn't bother anyone. They didn't meddle with Grievar lives. They didn't govern from the shadows. They weren't Daimyo.

The man behind the bar was tall and corded, with near-obsidian skin. The left side of his face drooped, and his bald head gleamed with sweat as he wiped down the counter.

Murray approached the bar and caught the man's good eye. "Your finest Deep ale."

The man poured a stein of the only ale on tap, then broke into a wide half grin. "Old Grievar, what brings you to my fine establishment on such a sunny day in the Deep?"

Murray took a swig of the ale, wiping the foam off his lips. "Same thing every year, Anderson. I'm here to lay back and sweat out my worries at the hot springs. Then I figure I'll stop by the Courtesan Houses for a week or so 'fore returning to my Adar Hills mansion back Upworld."

Anderson chuckled, giving Murray a firm wrist-to-wrist grasp from across the bar. "Good to see you, old friend. Though you're uglier than I remember."

"Same to you." Murray feigned a grimace. "That face of yours reminds me of how you always forgot to cover up the right high kick."

Anderson grinned as he wiped down the bar. Both men were quiet as they watched the SystemView broadcast on the lightboard above.

The feed panned across Albright Stadium, showing thousands of cheering spectators in the stands before swooping toward the gleaming Circle at the heart of the arena. Two Grievar squared off in the Circle—one standing for Ezo and the other for the empire of Kiroth.

Murray downed his ale and set it on the bar for Anderson to refill.

A list of grievances popped up in one corner of the screen to remind viewers of what was at stake in the bout: Rubellium reserves in one of the long-disputed border regions between Ezo and Kiroth, worth millions of bits, thousands of jobs, and the servitude of the pastoral harvesters that lived out there.

The fate of nations held in the sway of our fists.

The fight began, and Murray watched quietly, respectfully, as a Grievar should. Not like crowds modernday—booing and clapping, hissing and spitting. No respect for combat.

Anderson sighed as Ezo's Grievar Knight attacked the Kirothian with a flurry of punches. "Do you remember it? Even taking those hits, those were good days."

"Prefer not to remember it." Murray took another gulp of his ale.

"I know you don't, friend. But I hold on to my memories. Blood, sweat, and broken bones. Locking on a choke or putting a guy down with a solid cross. That feeling after, lying awake and knowing you'd done something—made a difference."

"What's the darkin' difference? I don't see any. Same lofty bat shit going on up above." Murray sniffed the air. "Still got that same dank smell down here."

"You know what I mean," Anderson said. "Fighting for the good of the nation. Making sure Ezo stays on top."

"I know what you mean, and that's what just what those Daimyo politiks up there say all the time. *For the good of the nation.* That's why I'm down here. Every year, the same thing for a decade now. Sent Deep to find fresh Grievar meat."

"You don't think the Scout program is working?" Anderson asked.

Murray took another long swig. "We'll discover the next Artemis Halberd. That's what that smug bastard Callen always says. The man doesn't know how to piss straight in a Circle, yet he's got command of an entire wing of Citadel."

"You never saw eye to eye with Commander Albright—"

"The man's a coward! How can he lead? The Daimyo might as well have installed one of their own to Command. Either way, doesn't make a difference. Scouts—the whole division is deepshit. Grievar-kin are born to fight. Thousands of years of breeding says so. We're not made to creep around corners, dealing out bits like hawkers."

"Times are different, old friend," Anderson said. "Things are more complicated. Citadel has got to keep up; otherwise, Ezo falls behind. Kiroth's had a scout program for two decades now. They say even the Desovians are on their way to developing one."

"They know it's just the scraps down here, Anderson," Murray said. "Kids that don't fare a chance. And even if one of them did make it? What have we got to show for it? Me and you. For all those years we put in together in service. The sacrifices—"

Their conversation was interrupted as the door to the bar swung open with a thud. Three men walked in. Grievar.

Anderson sighed and put his hand on Murray's shoulder. "Take it easy."

The first to enter had piercings running along his jawline, glinting beside a series of dark flux tattoos stamped on his cheekbones. The other two were as thick as Murray and looked to be twins, with matching grizzled faces and cauliflowered ears.

The fluxed man immediately caught Murray's stare from the bar. "Ah! If it isn't the mighty one himself!"

Murray left his seat with alarming speed and moved toward the man.

Anderson shouted a warning from behind the bar. The man threw a wide haymaker at Murray, who casually tucked his shoulder, deflecting the blow, before dropping levels and exploding from a crouch into the man's midline. Murray wrapped his arms around the man's knees, hoisted him into the air, then drove him straight through a nearby table, which splintered in every direction.

Murray blinked. He was still in his seat by the bar, the pierced Grievar hovering over him with a derisive smirk on his face.

"Nothing to say anymore, huh, old man? I can't imagine what it's like. Getting sent down here to do the dirty work. Digging through the trash every year."

Murray ignored the man and took another swig of his ale. "Think any of your trash will even make it through the Trials this year?" the man taunted. "Didn't one of your kids make it once? What ever happened to him? Oh, I remember now…"

Anderson pushed three ales across the bar. "Cydek, these are on the house. Why don't you and your boys find a place over in that corner there so we don't have any trouble?"

Cydek smirked as he took the drinks. He turned to Murray as he was walking away. "I'm scouting Lampai tomorrow. Why don't you tail me and I can show you how it's done? You can see some real Grievar in action. Nice change of pace from watching kids fighting in the dirt."

Murray kept his eyes fixed on the lightboard above the bar. SystemView was now replaying the fight's finish in slow motion. The broadcaster's voice cut through the quieted Ezonian crowd at Albright Stadium.

What an upset! And with the simple justice of a swift knee, Kiroth takes the Adarian Reserves!

Anderson leaned against the bar in front of Murray and poured himself an ale as he watched the knockout on replay. "The way things are going, I hope the Scout program starts working…or anything, for that matter. Otherwise, we'll be drinking that Kirothian swill they call mead next time I see you."

Murray let a smile crease his face, though he felt the tension racking his muscles. He downed his ale.

*   *   *

Murray realized he'd had a few too many, even for a man of his size, as he stumbled down Markspar Row. The duskshift was at its end and the arrays that lined the cavern ceiling bathed the Underground in a dying red glow. Murray had stayed at the Bat chatting about old times with Anderson for the entire evening.

Though he often denied it, he did miss the light. He wished he was back in fighting form, as he was during his service.

That's the thing with us Grievar. We rot.

He cracked his knuckles as he walked in no particular direction.

Murray felt his body decaying like the old foundations of this crumbling Underground city. His back always hurt. Nerve pain shot up his sides whether sitting, standing, sleeping—it didn't matter. His neck was always stiff as a board. His wrists, elbows, and ankles had been broken multiple times and seemed like they could give way at any moment. Even his face was numb, a leathery exterior that didn't feel like his own anymore. He remembered a time when his body was fluid. His arms and legs had moved as if there were a slick layer of oil between every joint, seamlessly connecting takedowns into punches into submissions.

He'd seen his fair share of trips to medwards to sew up gashes and mend broken bones, but he'd always felt smooth, hydraulic. Now Murray's joints and bones scraped together with dry friction as he walked.

It was his own fault, though. Murray had his chance to stay young and he'd missed it. The first generation of neurostimulants had debuted when he was at the top of his fight game. Most of his team had started popping the stims under the *recommendation* of then–Deputy Commander Memnon. "We need the edge over the enemy," Memnon had urged the team of Grievar Knights.

Coach hadn't agreed with Memnon—the two had been at each

other's throats for those last few years. Coach believed taking stims was sacrilege, against the Combat Codes. The simplest precept of them all: *No tools, no tech.*

The man would often mutter to Murray, "Live and die like we're born—screaming, with two clenched, bloody fists."

It wasn't long after the stims started circulating that Coach left his post. The bridge in Command had grown too wide. Memnon would do anything to give Ezo the edge, even if that meant harnessing Daimyo tech. Coach would rather die than forsake the Codes.

Even after Coach left, Murray kept with his master's teachings. He'd refused to take stims. A few of his teammates had stayed clean too—Anderson, Leyna, Hanrin, old Two-Tooth. At first, they'd kept up with the rest of the team. Murray had even held on to the captain's belt. It wasn't until a few years later that he'd felt it.

It had been barely perceptible: a takedown getting stuffed, a jab snapping in front of his face before he realized it was coming. Those moments started adding up, though. Murray aged. He got slower and weaker while the rest of Ezo's Grievar Knights maintained their strength under the neurostimulants.

And then came the end. That fight in Kiroth. His whole team, his whole nation depending on Murray. Everything riding on his back. And he'd failed.

Wherever Coach was right now, he'd be spitting in the dirt if he could see what Murray had become. Skulking in the shadows, stuck with a lowly Grievar Scout job, to be forgotten. Another cog in the Daimyo machine.

Before Murray realized it, the light had nearly faded. The streets were quiet as most Deep folk returned to their homes for the blackshift.

Murray was walking on autopilot toward Lampai Stadium, now only a stone's throw away, looming above him like a hibernating beast. Shadows clung to him here, deep pockets of darkness filling the folds of his cloak as he made his way to the base of the stadium.

Murray stopped abruptly, standing in front of Lampai's entrance. He stared at the old concrete wall and the black wrought-iron gates. He craned his head at the stadium's rafters towering above him.

Murray placed his hand against a gold plaque on the gate.

It was cold to the touch. It read:

LAMPAI STADIUM, CONSTRUCTION DATE: 121 P.A.
LET THIS BE THE FIRST OF MANY ARENAS, TO SERVE AS A SYMBOL OF OUR SWORN ARMISTICE AND A CONSTANT REMINDER OF THE DESTRUCTION WE ARE CAPABLE OF. HERE SHALL GRIEVAR GIVE THEIR BLOOD, IN HONOR AND PRIVILEGE. THEY FIGHT SO THE REST SHALL NOT HAVE TO.

"We fight so the rest shall not have to," Murray whispered. He had once believed those words. The first precept of the Codes. He would repeat the mantra over and over before his fights, shouting it as he made entrances into stadiums around the world.

The Mighty Murray Pearson. He'd been a force of nature, a terror in the Circle. Now he was just another shadow under these rafters.

Murray inhaled deeply, his chest filling with air. He pushed it all out again.

* * *

Murray returned to Thaloo's every day that week and saw more of the same. Just like it had been every year before. The well-nourished, stronger Grievar brood beating down the weaker lacklights. There was little skill involved; the brutal process pitted the weak against the strong. The strong always won.

Eventually, the weaker brood wore down. Patrons didn't want to buy the broken ones, which meant that Thaloo's team of Taskers was wasting their time training them. Thaloo was wasting bits on their upkeep. So, like rotten fruit, the slave Circle owner would throw the kids back to the streets where he found them. Their chance of survival was slim.

Murray's head throbbed as he stepped back to the edge of the Circle. Spectral wisps gathered above as the light intensified on the dirt fighting floor.

The first Grievar emerged from the side entrance, stopping by his Tasker's corner. He looked to be about fifteen, tall for his age, with all the hallmarks of purelight Grievar blood—cauliflowered ears, a thick brow, bulging forearms, bright eyes.

The boy's head was shaved like all the brood at Thaloo's to show off the brand fluxed on his scalp. Like any other product in the Deep, patrons needed to see his bit-price. This kid looked to be of some value—several of the vultures were eyeing him like a slab of meat.

The Tasker slapped the boy in the face several times, gripping his shoulders and shaking him before prodding him into the Circle. The boy responded to the aggression with his own, gnashing his teeth and slamming his fist against his chest as he stalked the perimeter. The crowd clapped and hooted with anticipation.

The second boy did not look like he belonged in the Circle. He was younger than his opponent and gaunt, his thin arms dangling at his side. A mop of black hair hung over the boy's brow. Murray shook his head. They'd just taken the kid off the streets, not even putting in the effort to brand him yet.

The boy walked into the Circle without expression, avoiding eye contact with his opponent and the crowd around him. He found his designated start position and stood completely still as the glowing spectrals rose from the Circle's frame and began to cluster above.

"The taller, dark one—name's Marcus. Saw 'im yesterday." Calsans pulled up to Murray's side, just as he'd done every day this week. Murray expected the parasite to ask him for a favor any moment now. Or perhaps he was one of Callen's spies, sent to ensure Murray didn't go rogue.

"Nearly kicked right through some lacklight." Calsans smirked. "This little sot is gonna get thrashed."

The skinny boy stood motionless, his arms straight by his side. At first, Murray thought the boy's eyes were cast at the dirt floor, but at second glance, Murray saw his eyes were closed. Clamped shut.

"Thaloo's putting blind kids in the Circle now…" Murray growled.

"Sometimes, he likes to give the patrons a show," Calsans said. "Bet he's workin' on building Marcus's bit-price. Fattening him up for sale."

The fight began as Marcus assumed a fighting stance and began to bob forward, feinting jabs and bouncing on the balls of his feet.

"It's like one of them Ezonian eels about to eat a guppy," Calsans remarked.

Murray looked curiously at the blind boy as his opponent stalked toward him. The boy still wasn't moving. Though his posture wasn't aggressive, he didn't look afraid. He almost looked…relaxed.

"Wouldn't be so sure," Murray replied.

Marcus approached striking distance and feigned a punch at the blind boy before whipping a high round kick toward his head. A split second before the shin connected, the boy dropped below the kick and shot forward like a coiled spring, wrapping around one of the kicker's legs. The boy clung to the leg as his opponent tried to shake him off vigorously, but he stayed attached. He drove his shoulder into Marcus's knee, throwing him off balance into the dirt.

The boy began to climb his opponent's body, immobilizing his legs and crawling onto his torso.

"Now this is getting good," Murray said as he watched the blind boy go to work.

Marcus heaved forward with his full strength, pushing the boy off him while reversing to top position. Hungry for a finish again, Marcus straddled the younger boy's torso, reared up, and hurled a punch downward. The boy slipped the punch, angling his chin at just the right moment, his opponent's fist glancing off his jaw.

Marcus howled in pain as his hand crunched against the hard dirt. Biometrics flashed red on the lightboard above.

Capitalizing on bottom position, the blind boy grasped Marcus's elbow and dragged the limp arm across his body, using the leverage to pull himself up and around onto his opponent's back.

Murray raised an eyebrow. "Well, look at that. Darkin' smooth back take."

The crowd suddenly was paying close attention to the turn of events. Several spectators hooted in approval of the upset while others jeered at a potential bit-loss on their bets.

Murray saw the shock in Marcus's eyes. This was supposed to be an easy win for the Grievar, a fight to pad his record. His Tasker probably told him to finish the blind boy in a brutal fashion. Instead, Marcus was the one fighting for survival, looking like he was treading water in a tank of razor sharks. Marcus grunted as he pushed himself off the ground. He stood and tried to shuck the boy off his back, bucking wildly, but the climber wrapped around him even tighter.

The blind boy began to snake his hands across Marcus's neck, shooting his forearm beneath the chin to apply a choke. Either as a last resort or out of pure helplessness, Marcus dropped backward like a felled tree, slamming the boy on his back into the dirt with a thud. A cloud of dust billowed into the air on impact. The crowd hushed as the little boy was crushed beneath his larger opponent's bulk.

Murray held his breath as the dust settled.

The blind boy was still clinging to his opponent, his two bony arms latched around his neck, constricting, ratcheting tighter. The boy squeezed until Marcus's eyes rolled back into his head and his arms went limp.

The light flared and died out, the spectrals breaking from their cluster and dissipating into the den.

The boy rolled out from beneath his unconscious opponent, his face covered in dirt and blood, his eyes clamped shut.